Tracy & Colin
& the 'babies'
Thanks for all your
support. 🙂

BOOK OF TRINITY

A.J. RYDER

FIRST EDITION

Dedicated to:

Canon Mark Fitzwilliams

for showing me the way

and also

Rev. Angela Butler

&

Rev. Peter Lawrence

for upholding the true Christian Spirit.

CONTENTS

	Acknowledgments	i
1	26TH MARCH 1988	1
2	14TH JUNE 1988	7
3	17TH JUNE, 1988	10
4	11TH DECEMBER 1988	15
5	5TH OCTOBER 1989	20
6	18TH DECEMBER 1989	28
7	23RD DECEMBER 1989	34
8	12TH JULY 1990	41
9	6TH MARCH, 1993	51
10	10TH APRIL, 1993	58
11	12TH APRIL 1993	68
12	3RD JUNE 1993	71
13	15TH JUNE 1993	79
14	27TH JULY 1993	87
15	30TH JULY, 1993	99
16	31ST JULY, 1993	104
17	4TH AUGUST 1993	107
18	11TH AUGUST 1993	119
19	14TH AUGUST 1993	128

20	15TH AUGUST 1993	141
21	27TH AUGUST, 1993	146
22	28TH AUGUST 1993	154
23	29TH AUGUST, 1993	158
24	30TH AUGUST, 1993	172
25	30TH AUGUST, 1993	177
26	31ST AUGUST, 1993	203
	POSTSCRIPT	221

ACKNOWLEDGMENTS

To all my family and friends, for helping me through those dark days.

CHAPTER ONE
26TH MARCH 1988

10.30am Hemel Hempstead

That particular Saturday Paul Hitt, a professional psychic, wandered aimlessly around the market, just as he had done many times before.

Keeping with the flow of the crowd he ambled from stall to stall, despite not knowing the reason why he had been drawn there. It was only when he reached the far side that, curiously, he found his eye fall upon the New-Age stall tucked away behind the fruit and vegetables. So, fighting against the tide of punters, he made his way to the array of crystals, Tarot cards and incense sticks.

As the twenty-two year old man approached it, he noticed the two traders sitting behind their stall playing with some rune stones. Neither acknowledged him so, feeling uninhibited, he started to browse through the crystals glittering in the sunshine.

As Paul started examining them in more detail, he suddenly found his attention being drawn to a large lump of rough rose quartz. This was an unusual occurrence, for he had never felt an affinity with this particular stone before. However, this crystal seemed to be calling him, willing him to buy it. Unable to resist a closer inspection, he picked up the quartz to examine it in more detail.

At this, the woman trader focused her attention on him. "Can I help you?" She asked, coldly.

Paul promptly placed the crystal back on the stall. "No." He smartly replied. Then, with a wry smile he continued, "It's strange, but I've never really been attracted to Rose Quartz before, but somehow this one seems to be different."

"Some crystals just seem to get you like that." The woman grinned. "Maybe you should have it?"

"Can't really afford paying £4.50 for a crystal I don't even like. It seems such a waste of money."

At this point, the male trader cut in. "Won't be a waste if you are drawn to it. You more than likely will need its properties at some point in time to help you. If you do not have the money to pay today; we could always set it aside for you until next week."

"No, don't worry. I can't think of any reason why I would need it, now or in the future."

Paul's attention then turned to the runes that the two traders were using and, changing the subject, he said, "They're unusual runes. Amethyst aren't they?"

"Yes." The woman replied. "Do you read runes? "

"Not runes, no. I'm a Tarot reader." Paul then fumbled around in his shirt pocket and pulled out a card. "Here you are." he smiled as he handed it to them. "Paul Hitt."

"Pleased to meet you Paul." the woman welcomed him. Then, as a frown crept on her face, she continued, "There are quite a few Tarot readers in Hemel, aren't there. I bet there is quite a lot of competition for business, yes?"

"Most of my business comes from recommendations."

"Then why not learn to read the runes, then you could advertise as a rune reader instead." the man advised. "That might prove a good way of gaining new business."

"Maybe." Paul sighed. Then, looking at his watch, he announced "Well, best be off. See you both again, maybe. Be lucky." and with that he made a hasty retreat, to look around the other shops in the town centre.

11.00am Slapton

Jon Waller swung his Ford Escort onto the parking space outside the run down end-terrace and turned off his engine. Looking forlornly at the For Sale sign nailed precariously on the rickety fence post, he turned to his wife Joanna and groaned "What a dump. Let's just drive off."

"We can't do that." His wife replied. "The Estate Agent is due any minute to show us around. We could at least humour him for half an hour or so, then go on our way."

Jon sighed in despair. "Well, I suppose." he mumbled, as he stared in disbelief at the 1908 cottage. "Can't hurt." So with that flat statement, they both climbed out of the car and gazed up at the building with gaped mouths.

At that moment, the Estate Agents car screeched around the blind bend and skid to a halt next to theirs, making the stones fly in every direction. A smartly dressed young man then jumped energetically out of his BMW and approached the couple, with a grin on his face and a bounce in his stride.

"Morning." he beamed, as he stretched out his hand to shake theirs. "Mr and Mrs Waller?"

Jon tiresomely smiled back at the little man, "Yes." he confirmed, flatly.

"My name is Vito Iannelli, the Agent from G.A. You found the property alright?"

"Yes, thank you." Joanna replied. "I know Slapton quite well."

"Yes?" Vito gave her a grin and wink. "Did you used to live here?"

"No, no. nothing like that. I was on a canal holiday some years ago and we moored up at Slapton lock one night, to go to the pub for a meal."

"The Carpenters? I've heard that they do excellent meals there. Did you enjoy yours?"

"It was wonderful." She replied with a shy smile.

"Excellent, excellent."

Vito then abruptly cut the idle chatter short and changed the conversation back to business. "Well, lets look at the house." With that, he clasped his hands together and bounded up the overgrown garden towards the front door.

The key was in the lock and, Vito inside the house, before Joanna and Jon got half way up the path. The Italian then poked his head around the doorframe, to see where his two prospective clients had disappeared too.

"Come in, come in." he invited them and, as Jon stepped over the threshold, his eyes widened in delight at what he saw.

"Hey Jo." his voice was now full of wonderment. "Come and have a look. This place is like the TARDIS from Doctor Who. Its massive inside, Just take a look at this kitchen."

Joanna slipped into the house behind her husband but, although also surprised at the size of the room, she did not get good vibes off of the place.

3

As Vito eagerly showed them around, Jon became more and more enchanted with the cottage. The kitchen was approximately thirteen foot square, with a blocked in fireplace on the opposite wall to the front door. There were not many cupboards, despite the size of the room, and the North-East facing window let in little light.

Admittedly there was plenty of room for improvement and, with Jon being the sort of person who enjoyed DIY, it certainly captured his imagination. But Joanna was not so convinced. As it stood, this room did not lend itself to any form of culinary skills.

The sitting room was slightly more relaxing, for the brick built fireplace, with its beam and Parkray, proved to be the major focal point. It was also bigger than the Kitchen, being sixteen foot by eleven, with a large South-Westerly window which allowed the sun to stream into the room.

Vito then led the two back through the kitchen and up the stairs to view the first floor. It was at this point that Joanna started to feel the atmosphere in the building grow heavier.

The first room that they entered was the main bedroom, directly above the kitchen, and was of the same dimensions. Although this room was also a wonderful size, she felt decidedly uneasy in it.

Then through to the second bedroom, which was long and thin. This was eleven-foot by eight but, as it also housed the immersion heater, it's actual usage size was about three foot less than that. Although considerably smaller than the main bedroom, the atmosphere in this room was far lighter. There did not appear to be any heaviness in it, unlike the other bedroom. Maybe, Joanna thought, this might be because it had a South-Westerly window which allowed the light to enter its perimeters, just as the sitting room window did.

Finally, Vito escorted them to the bathroom. This was the room that the impresario was interested in showing his clients most of all, for it boasted a corner bath, bidet and 'his and hers' wash basins. He adored the flashiness of the room and was anxious to experience the Waller's reaction to the wonders within its walls. Jon was the first to enter and was duly impressed by what he saw. However, Joanna began to feel uneasy as she approached the doorway, and as she stepped over the threshold into the bright, ostentatious room, a feeling of darkness washed over her.

She lent against the wall to steady herself.

"I know it's an amazing room," Vito joked as he watched the young woman lose her balance, "but it's never affected anyone quite like that before." But Joanna had not heard his remark, for it had taken her all her time to focus on the negative energies that engulfed her. She did not have a clue as to who, or what, was there in that room with her and her husband, only that something did not welcome their presence and showed its feelings by intimidation. This was not a good sign.

"You alright?" Jon's voice broke through her barrier of thought.

She stared back at him vaguely. "Sorry?"

"You look pale. You ok?"

Joanna composed herself and, after a second's thought, replied with a shaky voice "Yes. Yes, I think so. Thought I was going to pass out there for a second though."

Vito smiled nervously, as he tried to make light of the situation. "Best we go back downstairs then, if you have both seen enough of the house that is? "

"Yes, thank you." Jon replied as he and his wife joined Vito on the landing, before following the bouncy little Italian down the stairs and back into the kitchen.

"Well, what do you both think?" the Estate Agent pumped them. "Not a bad size for a two-bed cottage, eh?"

"We think it's great." Jon informed the agent on behalf of himself and his wife. "I can just see myself sitting in front of the fire on a cold winter's night. Can't you Jo?"

Joanna opened her mouth to object, but was cut short by Jon's overwhelming enthusiasm as he continued, "You say the owners are buying a new house in Luton?"

"Yes. There is no chain from their side. What about yourselves, have you got a house to sell?"

"We have a house in Houghton Regis. A couple of first time buyers have put an offer in, so looks like there will not be any worries on that score either."

"Great, great." Vito rang his hands together, "So you are definitely interested?"

Joanna cut in, "Well, we'll have to talk about it ... " but Jon interrupted, "We will contact you about making an offer later this afternoon, if that is alright?"

"Fine, fine." Vito's grin was full of satisfaction at the certainty of his commission. "Tell you what, here is my card. Give me a ring once you have discussed your offer and then I will put it to the owners. Hopefully, then we can do business."

"Wonderful." Jon beamed as he gazed dreamily about the kitchen. "Yes, I think I could be very happy here. Couldn't you Jo?" But before Joanna could reply, Vito was shaking Jon's hand before ushering them both out of the house and into the sunlight.

Joanna took one final look over her shoulder before walking back to the Escort, but her feelings about the house were unchanged. She was completely drained by the visit and the cliquey atmosphere of the place made her feel decidedly uneasy. She certainly was not over enamoured with the place, unlike her husband, and felt she needed more time to think about whether or not she was prepared to live there, especially after what she had experienced in the bathroom. The biggest obstacle though, would be for her to try and dissuade Jon. Unfortunately for her the place had already sold itself to him, which would undoubtedly mean that they would end up living there.

11.30am Hemel Hempstead

Having wondered aimlessly around the shopping centre, Paul found himself standing at the New Age stall in the market place for the second time that day.

"Hello again." the woman greeted him. "Couldn't keep away?"

"Hi." he nervously replied. "You probably think I am nuts, but I just could not get that lump of rose quartz out of my mind."

"Thought that would happen." the other trader replied. "Stones are like an itch that you can not scratch. Once one has got under your skin, you just have to have it."

"I know." Paul smiled, "Guess, no matter what you think at the time, there are certain things that you just have to have." And, with that, he pulled out a five-pound note from his pocket and bought the crystal.

CHAPTER TWO
14TH JUNE 1988

10.30pm Houghton Regis

Joanna climbed into bed and snuggled up to her husband. Jon placed his arm around her, whilst sighing with contentment, and stated, "Well, just a couple more days and we will be in our new home."

Jon could not wait to move from Houghton Regis. His Escort had been broken into, three times in the last two months, which gave concern that the house might be next.

Joanna remained silent, allowing her thoughts to consume her. However, despite the rising crime in the area, she could not help but think that other problems would replace the ones that they were experiencing in the present. As she lay there, Jon's arms around her, she could not help but think that the tenderness that her husband was presently showing would not last, once they had moved. She did not know why she thought that, just that she did. She hoped she would be wrong, but something inside told her differently.

There were also a number of physical discrepancies about the house in Slapton that concerned her. Firstly, although it was a two-bedroomed cottage, there was only one door into the premises, for it had no back garden. Rather, there was only an alleyway for access to the rear, for maintenance purposes, which made an escape route dangerously limiting.

The place they currently lived at also had quite a lot of land. Joanna adored her garden, but the new house did not offer any inspiration to create a horticultural paradise. The front garden was like a miniature field of meadow grass. There were no flower borders, no bushes to obscure it from the road and poor fencing on each side, which were in urgent need of replacing.

The interior was not much better. The kitchen, which the current owners had started to redecorate, had been left so that the first job would be to gut the room and start again from scratch. The carpets in the sitting room, as well as on the stairs, were threadbare and stained from many parties over the last few years. To cap it all, the back boiler on the solid fuel fire leaked. But despite all this, there was something else bothering her, something far beyond reason. She could not put into words how she felt about number 14, but her gut told her that she was not welcomed within its walls. It was as if the whole house oozed with negative energies, and it was definitely not sending out a welcoming party for her.

Although she had experienced similar feelings in other places before, she had never stayed long enough for it to be of effect. One such place, she recalled, was at Little Dean Hall, which she and Jon once visited. The place was supposed to be the most haunted house in England. Now that place was full of negativity, even Jon refused to go into the 'Blue' room, despite not being able to explain why. She had put it down to the fact that they were ghost-hunting at the time and his imagination had run away with him, but her feelings now were different. This time it was esoteric; it was real, and she was scared. There was at least one undesirable presence in the house, which had made itself known to her. Joanna lay there pondering until, eventually, she was able to push all her fears to the back of her mind and, falling into a slumber, she began to dream.

She found her imagination taking her to a far off place. The sun was shining brightly, the land was abundant with fruit-bearing trees, vibrant coloured flowers and clear streams teaming with life. Standing in the shade of a fruit-laden tree was a young girl of about nine years of age. She was not of Joanna's time, rather a child from the turn of the century. She wore a blue dress with underskirts and a frilly white apron. Her long light brown hair was in plaits, and she held a tatty old teddy bear in one hand whilst sucking the thumb of the other. But instead of laughing, as Joanna would have expected a child of that age to be doing, tears were rolling down the little girl's cheeks.

Joanna approached her. "Why are you crying?" she asked, but the child just turned and ran down to the stream, then stood there gazing at the water.

Joanna began to wander down towards the little girl, but as she approached she caught sight of a middle-aged man with grey hair and glasses trampling across the flowers towards them.

The man wore brown trousers, a tweed jacket and brown shoes. He was stern-faced, with a menacing stare, and was heavily built for his five foot ten inch frame.

She froze and watched him intently, until he stood between her and the child. He stared, first at Joanna, and then at the little girl. "Emma." he called fearsomely and the child immediately responded by turning and walking up to him. Joanna could tell by the expression on Emma's face that the man was not kind to her.

Another presence then appeared. This was a tall, slim woman of about thirty-seven. She had long straight hair, almost black in colour, with the darkest eyes Joanna had ever seen. Both the man and the child started stepping backwards away from the woman, as if afraid of her, but she stretched out her hand beckoning them to her. They tried to resist, but the dark woman's gesticulation was wilful and eventually the grey-haired man left the child's side and walked, trance-like, towards her.

As soon as the man reached the woman's side he stepped into her, and the two became one. Joanna then watched, helpless, as the clouds collected in the sky, rolling across it with anger until they had covered the sun, leaving the earth in darkness. The man and woman then disappeared from view as, they too, became engulfed by the choleric veil until only Emma could be seen.

Without thinking, Joanna ran to the little girl and crouched down. She wrapped her arms around the child to comfort her, as she proclaimed. "Don't worry Emma. I'm here to protect you."

But the child's eyes were filled with inconsolable sadness as they both became concealed by the darkness and the dream faded into obscurity.

CHAPTER THREE
17TH JUNE, 1988

2.00pm Slapton

The Mercedes van pulled up onto the parking space outside number 14. Pete Lowe swung open the van door and jumped down from the cab. "Come on kids." he joked. "I want to see this new abode of yours."

Pete was an old friend of Joanna's. She first met him when she worked for a company in Watford, with him being a self-employed delivery driver for the business. Ironically, her father was also Pete's Accountant and had been so for a number of years.

Pete was a bit of a cheeky chap. He was the sort of person that was always joking around, did not have a quiet manner and enjoyed nothing more than teasing people; especially young ladies. He never seemed to take anything seriously, which was the best sort of person to have around at such a stressful time.

Jon jangled his new set of keys in his hand. "Well, what do you think, Pete?"

The jolly middle-aged man beamed as he gazed at the overgrown garden. "I know a good gardener mate." he giggled.

"We thought you were going to offer." Joanna replied wittily.

"Na. Do my poor old back in, that would." He joked, "would ruin my love life. I'll leave it to you young'uns."

Joanna laughed at Pete's cheek, "Thank you very much - most kind." she retorted.

Ignoring the banter, Jon placed the key in the lock and turned. With a click, the door swung open to reveal the kitchen beyond. He then stepped back to allow the cheeky driver to enter first.

Pete stepped over the threshold. "Wow." he gasped. "It's amazing in here."

"Wait 'til you see the rest of it." Jon said conceitedly, and with that promptly gave Pete the grand tour.

Having completed the excursion Pete and Jon returned to the kitchen. "Well?" Jo asked. "Approve?"

"Lovely isn't it. I could quite easily live here. That fire in the sitting room would be just right for Christmas day. Toasting the ol' tootsies and all that." his broad grin filling his face but, after a moment or two of contemplation, his face changed to a serious expression as he continued "Best start moving things in then kids." and with that he marched out of the house and up the path towards the van.

As the afternoon went by the Waller's contents gradually moved from the back of the van to the house, until finally they had officially moved in.

"Well, put the kettle on then Josephine ." Pete ordered with a giggle as he lifted the kettle out of one of the tea chests.

"There's the tap." she replied, pointing at the sink.

Pete raised his eyebrows in defiance so, huffing loudly, she snatched the kettle from the clown and marched over to the tap.

Pete wandered through to the sitting room. "See Jon, treat women the right way and they always do exactly what you want." he winked as his dulcet tones carried over into the kitchen.

"Oi. I heard that." Jo shouted through from the other room as she switched on the kettle, "Carry on with comments like that and I'll go on strike."

"Oh come on Josephine, you know you would not like to see a grown man cry." Pete chuckled as Joanna jointed them in the sitting room. "Try me." She retorted with a grin.

A few minutes later and the kettle was at boiling point. Having poured out the beverages, Joanna returned to the sitting room once more. Pete was sitting on one of the tea chests, whilst Jon stood to one side of the fireplace. Joanna handed Pete his well-earned cup of tea.

"Thanks love." he acknowledged gratefully. Then, his face lifted and a twinkle came to his eye. "Shame it's not a pint though."

"Well, you know where the pub is." Joanna chuckled. "Jon and I wouldn't object to you treating us."

"I bet." he giggled. "But, unfortunately I came without my wallet."

"Poor excuse, eh Jo." Jon smirked and with that they started to relax after their labour.

10.00pm Hemel Hempstead

Paul lay on his bed, listening to Jon and Vangelis' 'I'll Find My Way Home' on his CD player, whilst dreamily staring up at the ceiling. He felt restless, almost uneasy, although he knew not why.

He broke his stargazing briefly to look at his watch then returned to his meditation for a few minutes more.

After a fashion, he lazily swung his legs over the side of the bed and sat up. Combing his fingers through his dark hair, he rose to his feet and stretched. Then, as he turned off the music, his car keys caught his eye. He stared at them momentarily, pondering over the decision of whether or not to turn in for the night, or to go for a drive.

"Oh, why not." he muttered under his breath as he gave in to temptation, and so, snatching the keys, he quickly made his way down the stairs and out of the front door to his Mark-One Astra.

Paul did not have a destination in mind when he started the engine and pulled away from the curb. To him, that was half of the fun of it - not knowing where he was going to end up.

The night was so humid that even the air rushing in through the open window was not enough to cool him. Paul drew the lighter out of his pocket, pulled out a cigarette from its packet and placing it between his lips, he lit the Superking.

Taking a long slow drag, he began to drive in the direction of Leighton Buzzard along the A1416. He pushed his foot hard on the accelerator, causing the Vauxhall Astra to judder violently as it increased speed. The road was dark and deserted, twisting its course between open farmland like a winding river.

As Paul reached Northall, he found himself indicating right as soon as he noticed the signpost to Whipsnade. This road was narrower than the other, but never the less it was just as difficult to negotiate with the constant bends, as it climbed the hillside. One more right turn and he found himself driving alongside the Zoo, then through the gated road past Whipsnade common, until he reached the crossroads on the other side of the village.

He turned left at the junction and proceeded to make his way towards Dunstable Downs. It was at this point that he decided to park at the peak of the Downs for a while to look across the valley below at the night-lights of Leighton Buzzard.

Reaching the car park he swung the car off the road and rolled to a halt at the far side. He turned off his engine then, retrieving his keys from the ignition, he placed them in his pocket, picked up the packet of cigarettes and got out of the car.

He ambled around to the front of the Astra and leant on the bonnet. Paul gazed across the expanse of the brightly-lit countryside below. The orange of the lamp lights, the white of the windows of houses, the moving red of car taillights. The night was alive although, from his vantage-point, Paul felt as if he were the only person on the earth at that moment in time.

His attention then left the Leighton lights and moved to a small cluster of brightness that had broken away from the main life force. The evidence of life was Slapton itself, with only approximately one hundred houses huddled together for security amongst the wilderness that surrounded it.

He lit another cigarette and stared at the array of lights. He felt drawn to the village below. It was as if he were compelled to protect those who resided in it from that which was far beyond, lurking in the darkness. And so there he stayed, watching.

10.30pm Slapton

Having provisionally tided up the house, Joanna and Jon decided it was time to turn in for the night and so, they made their weary way to the bedroom.

Joanna climbed into bed and snuggled down under the duvet. The softness of the pillow was welcoming to her weary head and she sighed deeply, allowing her body to relax after the heavy day's work.

Jon wandered into the bedroom, got undressed and joined her. She turned towards her husband and placed her arm around him.

He sharply turned to face her. "Don't." he growled.

"What?" she enquired, confused by his order.

"I want to go to sleep."

"I was only going to cuddle you." She justified her actions. Then trying to make light of the situation she continued, "Wasn't going to jump your bones or anything."

"Oh, piss off." and with that he abruptly turned his back on her and, within moments, he was snoring.

Joanna lay there for quite some time after that, just staring into the blackness of the room. She was confused at Jon's reaction, although to some extent it had not come as a surprise to her, for she knew inside that this was what was going to happen. But gradually she allowed herself to relax and slowly drifted off to sleep to dream of angels keeping watch over her.

CHAPTER FOUR
11TH DECEMBER 1988

11.00am Slapton

Having not long woken up, Joanna and Jon sat in front of the coal fire sipping their first coffee of the day. It was dull outside, with persistent drizzle and gusty wind. Certainly not a morning to go Christmas shopping. The prospect of Jon playing football that afternoon was not an event to look forward to either, for the pitch was sodden and the air had an icy feel to it.

Joanna's attention left the depths of her mug for an instant. "Fancy putting up the Christmas decorations this morning?" She yawned.

Jon glared back at her, with an icy expression. "Why?"

"Because it is just over a week away from Christmas, that's why. Might even get you into the Christmas spirit."

Jon's response was to mumble into his mug as he sipped at his coffee.

"Oh come on." she continued, "What's up with you? Aren't you looking forward to our first Christmas here?"

"Can't afford it." he grumbled.

"We're no worse off now than we were last year," she reminded him, "and you got excited about last Christmas for ages before it arrived."

"That was last year."

"Why are you so grumpy?"

"Need your permission now do I?"

"Don't be silly Jon. I'm just concerned, that's all." her voice full of worry. "It's just that you seem to be really unhappy at the moment, I don't know why. Please talk to me Jon, that way I can help."

"Oh. So you are the Fairy Godmother now are you?"

"Don't be like that." she felt the tears start to well in her eyes. "What have I done, Jon?"

He rose to his feet and with an awesome growl he said, "Nothing. Why, got a guilty conscience?" And with that, he strode out into the kitchen and up the stairs.

Joanna sat there, shell-shocked for a moment, not knowing what had sparked off the confrontation. Jon had never been moody like this before they moved into the house, but these days he seemed to be constantly shrouded by a black cloud.

A few minutes dragged by, then Jon returned from upstairs, his face beaming as he ambled into the sitting room. "You alright?" he grinned as he returned to her side on the settee.

"Fine." Joanna replied, perplexed at his change in attitude. "You?"

"Couldn't be better. So, I'll get the ladder from the shed, while you decide where the best place for the tree is. Yes?" he chirped as he stood up again.

"Jon?"

"Yes?"

Joanna went to ask him what the scene earlier was all about, but decided it was probably best to leave it, so just replied "Oh. Nothing."

Jon flashed a dashing smile at her, "Right, I'll get the ladder then." And with that he wandered out of the room.

Half an hour or so later and the Christmas tree and boxes of decorations were down from the loft and scatters all about the sitting room floor. Jon's attitude was not unlike one of a small child, over excited at the prospect of Christmas just around the corner. His face radiant, as he sifted through the boxes.

The decorations of varying size and shape scattered about the floor, his attention fell upon the two red and two yellow ceiling streamers. "Put this across the kitchen ceiling?" he grinned as he handed them to Joanna.

She took the plastic streamers from him and smiled. "Good idea." and, with that, she carried them out into the other room.

She placed the four streamers on top of the tumble drier before wondering back to her husband's side. "Tell you what, I'll help with the tree, then we can do the kitchen together afterwards."

"Right you are." Jon beamed as he dragged the tree over to the corner. Then he and Joanna started to retrieve the fairy lights from their protective box.

In no time at all the tree was complete and so, briefly standing back to admire their work, they then both wandered back into the kitchen.

Jon was the first to the tumble dryer. There was a pause, then he said, "Where did you put the other two?"

"Other two what?" Joanna queried, as she wandered through behind him.

"The two yellow streamers. What did you do with the two yellow streamers?"

"I put them on the drier with the other two." she replied.

"Well, they're not here now." His voice had a touch of agitation about it.

"What do you mean?"

"Just what I said. There are only two streamers here."

Joanna started to look around on the floor to see if they had fallen off, but found nothing. "Well, you definitely gave me four. What could I have done with them?" she scratched her head.

"Can't trust you women with anything." Jon jested sarcastically. "Never mind, they'll turn up. Maybe you just thought I had given you four. Go and look in the box and see if they are still there."

So with that Joanna obediently wandered back into the sitting room and started sifting through the box of decorations. After a few moments, Jon was kneeling at her side, but despite an extensive search by the pair of them, the yellow streamers were nowhere to be seen.

"Well, that's that then." Jon groaned and marching back into the kitchen, he picked up the other two from the tumble dryer, strutted back into the sitting room and threw them both into the box. "What else do you suggest we do for the kitchen?" he snapped.

"Tell you what, let's leave it for now, have a cuppa, then think about it later."

"What's the point." he snapped.

"I could always pop into town later and buy some more, Jon."

Jon shrugged his shoulders. "Why not." then stormed off into the kitchen, mumbling to himself as he went.

2.00pm Slapton

With Jon departed for his football match, Joanna finally had the house to herself. She breathed a sigh of relief as she sank back on the settee with her mug of coffee, for Jon had been decidedly craggy that morning. Nothing she did or said seemed to appease him. His mood swings were totally irrational.

She then found her thoughts turning from Jon to the mysterious disappearance of the streamers. The more she thought about it, the more she was convinced that Jon had given her all four. So what had happened to the yellow ones?

A knock at the front door interrupted her thoughts. Placing her mug on the floor, she wandered out through the kitchen to answer it. Swinging the door open, she found herself confronted with the beaming face of their next door neighbour, Jenny.

"Hi. Jen."

"Hello Jo. Sorry to trouble you, but John has got to do some work on that lorry there," she pointed behind her to the nine ton as she spoke. "Alright if it is parked across your drive? Only there isn't really anywhere else to work on it, and they've called round on spec."

"That's fine. Jon won't be back for a few hours yet. Fancy coming in for a coffee?"

Delighted at the offer Jenny waltzed into the kitchen, her face beaming. Joanna invited her neighbour into the sitting room. Jenny sat on the chair in front of the fire and looked about her. "See you've organised yourself and got the decorations up." she smiled.

"Not without its mysteries though."

Jenny raised her eyebrows in an enquiring manner. Joanna then proceeded to tell her all about the four streamers, whilst Jenny just sat there, open mouthed, as she listened to the story.

Upon completion of her tale, Joanna asked her neighbour if the previous owners, Ollie and Paula, had ever experienced any poltergeist activity.

"Well, Paula never said anything," Jenny enlightened her, "But funnily enough she could never stand being in the house on her own. If Ollie wasn't there, Paula would always be, either around my house, or at Bob and Alison's."

"But she never said anything about the atmosphere in the house?"

"How do you mean?"

"Well ..." Joanna paused for a moment, not knowing quite how to explain. "... like an oppressiveness in certain rooms I guess; the bathroom, for example. Or the feeling of someone, or something watching her. Did she ever mention anything along those lines?"

"No." Jenny frowned as she turned her mind back to the many chats that she and Paula participated in. "Sorry, can't say she mentioned anything. Only that she could not stay here alone, as I mentioned earlier."

"Oh well. Thought I'd moved into a haunted house there for a second." Joanna made light of the conversation. "Never mind, maybe next time."

"Don't think you'd really enjoy that." Jenny giggled. "I knew someone once who had a problem spirit. It got so bad in the end that they had to get the Church in to do an exorcism. Very nasty experience, from all accounts."

"Really? Do tell." Joanna prompted her, with a twinkle in her eye.

"Well, I don't know all the gory details, but apparently that was a poltergeist. Used to throw ornaments about and things."

"You're right." Joanna laughed. "I would be scared shitless if that happened here." And with that the conversation of hauntings was cut short, turning to lighter, more mundane subjects instead.

Jenny was an hour, or so, into her visit when there was a second knock at the door. Making her apologies, Joanna ambled out, through the kitchen, to the front door. Answering it, she found herself confronted with Jenny's husband, his face and hands black with motor grease.

"Jenny hiding in there?" he smirked, as he wiped his hands down his overalls.

"Yes. One mo, John, I'll get her for you." and with that Joanna turned and shouted, "Jen. It's your hubby come looking for you."

"Ok." Jenny shouted back and, within seconds, she was standing at Joanna's side.

"Your mother's on the phone." John informed her flatly, with his broad Hertfordshire accent.

"Wonder what she wants?" Jenny responded in a flat voice. She then turned to Joanna. "Thanks for the coffee and the chat, Jo."

Stepping over the threshold to follow her husband up the garden path, Jenny turned momentarily. "I'll have a good think about what we talked about earlier ... reference Paula. See if I can remember anything. Or even anything from the owners before them." A frown crept across her face as she paused in deep thought. "Come to think of it, this house does have a history of a quick turnover of occupants. New people seem to be moving in here every couple of years - might have some relevance. Oh well, I promise to look into it. Thanks again. Bye for now." and with that, she marched up the path with a determined stride and was gone.

CHAPTER FIVE
5TH OCTOBER 1989

6.00pm Slapton

It was Joanna's birthday and so she had decided to take the day off work to celebrate.

Jon had refused to have time off with her. In fact he had been in a peculiar mood for a few days, reluctant to speak. Despite not knowing exactly what was wrong, she felt she must have done something terrible for him to behave like that. So she decided to cook a lasagna not only for a birthday treat but, as lasagne was Jon's favourite Italian dish, it would act as a peace offering.

Another idea that she had was to put on some slinky underwear and that particular dress that Jon found so arousing. This was sure to bring him round if nothing else would.

She was upstairs putting the final touches to her make-up when she heard his Escort pull up outside. Quickly tidying up, she rushed out of the bedroom and down the stairs, just in time to welcome her husband home.

The key clicked in the lock and the door flung open. Jon's face was as black as thunder as he entered. He sullenly looked at his wife as she stood there, radiant and embellished, then marched straight past her and into the sitting room. His angry eyes then fell upon the dining table as he entered, which was set out with the best crockery, cutlery, candles and flowers. Throwing his case to the ground, he turned and marched back to his wife in the kitchen. "What's all that for?" he growled, as he pointed behind him at the dressed table.

"Thought I'd give you a treat." She replied timidly, trying to justify her actions.

"What for, guilty conscience?" and with that, he marched up the stairs to get changed out of his work clothes.

Joanna remained in the kitchen, unsure of what to do next. She had tried to make an effort for her husband, not only to show him that she cared, but also to try and get him to like her again. However, it was now clear to her that whatever she had done was not reconcilable at this time. And so she just sat there on the kitchen stool, her head resting on her hand, trying to find a solution.

A short while later Jon returned from upstairs, wearing his jogging bottoms and T-shirt. He crashed through the stair door and into the kitchen. Joanna looked across to him but, looking straight through her, he stomped into the sitting room and threw himself onto the settee.

Joanna rose from the stool and stood in the doorway looking at her husband as he sat there, seething. "Fancy a coffee?" She timidly enquired.

"Why not." he mumbled in reply.

So she turned and dragged herself over to the kettle and proceeded to make her husband a drink.

When she returned to him, with piping hot coffee in hand, she handed him the mug before crouching down on the floor. He took the coffee but did not make eye contact, instead he just stared into space, his eyes angry and foreboding.

"Lasagna all right?" she tried to break the deadly silence, as she played with her neckline.

Jon turned and stared at her intently. "If that's what you've done for tea, that'll do."

"What's wrong?" She tried to reason with her husband. "What have I done? Whatever it is, I am truly sorry Jon." However, apologies were beginning to become a bit of a bore.

"What makes you think you've done anything?" he sneered.

"I've tried to make amends, Jon. I've cooked your favourite dinner and done the table up nice. I've even dressed up in an effort to try to make things better between us. What more can I do? I don't know what I've done to deserve such a cold response from you. If only you would tell me I could do something about it. But if you won't tell me, I can't even start to put things right. Come on Jon, it's my birthday, at least you could make an effort, just for me, eh?"

21

Jon abruptly rose to his feet. "Why should I? If you don't know what's wrong, then I I'm not wasting my breath on explaining." and with that, he stormed off out of the room.

Joanna slowly rose to her feet and walked back into the kitchen. Grabbing the oven gloves, she retrieved the lasagna dish out of the oven and placed it on the work top. She was determined to get some enjoyment out of the hours of hard work that she had put into this meal, even if Jon refused.

She proceeded to dish up the dinner and, with two steaming plates piled high with melted cheese, mince and pasta, she returned to the dining table and placed them on the mats. "Jon, your dinner is ready." she called out from the doorway of the sitting-room, before taking her place at the table to commence satisfying her hunger with the tasty offering.

She was half way through her dinner when Jon finally emerged from upstairs and took his place at the elaborately decorated table. Then, without a word, he made a start at devouring his meal.

Joanna gazed up at her husband from time to time, checking his response. Then, as she took her final mouthful, she placed the cutlery neatly on her place and asked, "Is it alright?"

Jon's attention changed momentarily from his food to her and stated coldly "Alright I suppose." before diverting his glare back to the remains of his lasagna.

Disheartened, Joanna rose from the table and, taking her plate, she returned to the kitchen and started to organise herself for the mammoth task of washing up.

Having devoured all his dinner, Jon entered the kitchen and placed his empty plate on the work surface next to the rest of the dirty crockery. But, without uttering a word, he just turned and sauntered back to the sitting room, put on the television, then flopped onto the settee to settle down for an evening of idle viewing.

11.40pm

That night Joanna had the strangest dream. At first she was convinced that she was still awake when she saw the figure standing at the bottom of her bed, but what happened after that was so obscure that she reasoned it could not have been anything else but a delusion.

The figure slowly walked around the bed until it was standing at her side. At first she did not recognise the silhouette, until it held out its hand and said softly in a childlike voice, "Don't' be afraid Joanna, it is only me. Come, let us play, I've got a friend I'd like you to meet."

Joanna lifted her head from the pillow and supported her upper torso with her elbows. "Emma? Emma is that you?"

"Take my hand. Come on, we haven't much time."

Joanna hesitantly extended her hand and caught Emma's but, as soon as they touched, they found themselves rushing through the air, bright colours surrounding them both. Within seconds they both arrived at that far off place where she had first met Emma, some eighteen months earlier.

Joanna looked about her to re-familiarise herself with the strange lands before her. It was much as she had left it; dark formidable clouds hung in the sky which blocked out the sun; the earth was barren; the once clear streams were dry and lifeless and it had an overwhelming feeling of depravity.

Emma did not allow her to absorb the sensations for long, however, and tugging at Joanna's hand, she whispered excitedly, "Come on. Come on. He's waiting."

As Joanna allowed the little girl to escort her across the desolation, she noticed a single figure standing in the distance, patiently waiting for their arrival. As she drew nearer, she began to observe the person in more detail; he was tall, dressed in black robes, flapping in the breeze, with a cloth of the same colour wrapped about his head, and a bright, pure white aura completely surrounding him.

A few feet away from this imposing figure and Joanna froze. She was not sure whether she was afraid or joyful to meet this stranger. She looked at him intently, studying his features in great detail.

The man was six foot one tall, about thirty-five years of age and of athletic build. His complexion was dark although a neat black beard hid much of his face. Although he wore a stern expression, his eyes were extremely kind and forgiving. In fact, with such perfect bone structure and those wondrous, long eyelashes that curled up at the ends, he proved to be an extremely handsome figure of a man.

The stranger held out his left hand towards her, braking her adoration of him and, smiling softly, invited her to move closer. Instinctively she knew that there was no need to feel threatened by the man so, conceding to his bidding, she stepped forward until she was at his side.

"Bet you know him?" Emma giggled as she tugged at Joanna's hand. "Bet you do?"

Joanna broke her gaze from the stranger for a moment and focused on the little girl as Emma continued, "Tell me, then. What's his name?"

Joanna shook her head, before returning her attention to the man.

"You do know who he is. You do." She spiritedly tormented the woman.

"Sorry, I don't." Joanna cut the little girl of short. She then looked directly into the sparkling brown eyes of the stranger and, with a softer tone to her voice, she declared, "Forgive me, but I don't know you."

"I know." Emma piped in, precociously swinging her shoulders from side to side, determined not to be ignored, "I can tell you." But the man placed his finger to his lips, to signify that he wished the child to be silent.

"But I want to tell her." Emma protested, stamping her foot hard on the ground. "Oh go on. Let me, pleeeease?" But the stranger shook his head. "A clue then." the child insisted.

At this, the man smiled down at the little girl and without any further encouragement she continued, "Can't tell you his name, you have to work that out for yourself. But I'll tell you this much Joanna," Emma giggled as she spoke, "the Sire before you is the Ravenous Wolf; in the morning he devours the prey, in the evening he divides the plunder."

Horrified, Joanna immediately withdrew from the man's side. A ravenous wolf? Was this the entity that had attacked her in the bathroom eighteen months ago? She was perplexed at how someone so pleasing to the eye could be so vindictive.

But the man did not seem in the least concerned at her reaction and just stood there quietly, his eyes sparkling. Emma's reaction was also strange, for she just tittered excitedly and said, "Don't worry. He won't bite you."

"I've been tricked." Joanna shouted hysterically, as she focused her attention on Emma. "You've lead me into a false sense of security. I thought I could trust you, Emma, but you've tried to trick me." She then backed away from the pair of them; "I don't like this. I want nothing more to do with either of you. Leave me alone."

Joanna turned and ran, but Emma called to her across the arid land. "Joanna, we mean you no harm. We are your friends. You need help. Please … let us help you."

The woman stopped in her tracks and turned to face them once more. "Help with what?" she shouted angrily.

"Come back to us Joanna, for we, your true friends, only wish to help you." Emma cried out.

Joanna was uncertain whether or not she should retrace her steps, for she no longer felt confident of her safety. This place was nightmare enough without unbecoming riddles about ravenous wolves enticing her into their presence.

But the stranger spoke with a soft, reassuring, far ancient accent, "You want to know who we are, then I will tell you. We are of the light, not the dark as you might suppose. Emma is your guardian; your helper. Listen to her, for she speaks the truth."

Joanna found herself approaching them both once more, although she kept her steps slow and deliberate. "Then who are you?" her voice gravely as she spoke the words, "No riddles; no nicknames; no beating about the bush - just tell me straight; who are you?"

He smiled at her as he held out his left hand a second time, welcoming her back to his presence, "I am the twelfth number. I am the Israelite whose descendants are the first of the numbers at thirty-six and thirty-seven. The numbers from the tribe of my descendants are 35,400. My tribe is lead by Abidan. I am Holy in the eyes of the Lord; I am of God's light."

Joanna instinctively moved towards him confidently and took his hand. Curiously she accepted his words, without question, now knowing that there was now nothing to fear. It did not matter that she did not know his name, for names were not important. As she placed her hand in his, she noticed a ring on his third finger. She studied it closely. It was silver, with a black stone set into its ornate borders. The black inset had silver engraving of a coiled snake upon it. The ring was beautiful. But the Israelite broke her admiration of the ring, as he turned her to face the horizon, to the north, without uttering a word.

As she squinted her eyes, Joanna could just make out movement through the sullen clouds that donned the land. There were a number of objects moving swiftly towards them, but she was unable to visualise properly, for they were too far in the distance.

The Israelite turned his gaze towards her momentarily and whispered, "Now watch carefully and learn. Nothing will hurt you, for I am with you. Do not be afraid." But although she heard his words, Joanna's attention was drawn to the horizon with such intensity that she could not break her concentration to acknowledge him.

The entities moved ever close, with the swiftest of speed and with them came the sound of thundering hooves, the heavy drone filling the air until it drowned out every other resonance. As they approached, she began to visualise them until they could be identified. There were four of them. Four riders on jet black horses. Each rider was cloaked in the darkness of the mist, and each looked fearsome. She could almost smell the evil emanating from these beings. They were not of God's light.

The noise of the hooves echoed all around, ever louder as they approached. The riders were heading straight for the group of three, their speed unwaning, and their motive deliberate.

The lead horseman was a scar-faced man, with long tatty grey hair that wrapped itself about his face. One eye was drooped, whilst the other was of the steeliest blue. He wore upon his forehead the sign of the pentagon, but there was something untoward about the ancient Christian symbol. The five-sided polygon was reversed.

Joanna immediately recognised the second and third riders, for she had encountered them before. The first of these was the tall, slim woman, her dark eyes flashing fury as she drew closer. This was the woman who had tried to entice Emma to join her. The second horseman had the menacing stare of the middle-aged man, also of that dream.

The fourth rider was a little behind the others and it took Joanna a further few seconds to distinguish him from the frenzy of the others. However, as he drew nearer she recognised him, with horror, for this horseman was her husband.

She tried to cry out, but not a sound passed her lips. She then attempted to break free from the Israelite's grasp, but he held her firm, in the knowledge that so long as she was at his side, she would be safe.

The riders were now upon them - only feet away. The hooves of the black horses beat the ground with as much anger as the riders expressed on their faces. They showed no mercy. They were out to destroy.

Suddenly, to the East, the brightest light shone through a crack in the clouds, emitting the darkened land with gold, pink and white. At the moment the illumination struck, the four riders pulled their horses to a halt, sending the equines into violent outbursts of squeals, as they rolled their eyes. The lead rider's horse repeatedly reared up and twisted round at the vehemence of its wondrous supremacy being harnessed.

All four turned their attention from their victims, to the horizon, as the light spread across the land, filling every orifice with warmth and love. As the light drew nearer, another rider could be seen, galloping at speed, from the heart of the light, towards them. But this rider's mount was not a horse, but Pegasus, his greatness showing in every stride, his wings outstretched in flight and his nostrils flared with intent.

The rider on the white stallion gained ground with such swiftness, that he was soon upon them. He separated the two groups as he halted Pegasus between the four horsemen and the others, then drew a golden sword from its sheath and held it high above him, so that it reflected the light from the East into the harrowed eyes of the riders.

The horsemen turned to flee. Only the leader turned his mount, momentarily, to show his rebellion at his defeat, then galloped off after the rest of the group to the North, until they had all disappeared into the black mist.

The rider from the light then faced the three as he placed his sword back in its sheath. He looked down upon them triumphantly from his magnificent mount, as it poured at the ground with jubilance.

He then approached them, turning Pegasus side on to the group, and smiled as he threw a small object to the ground at Joanna's feet. But before she could respond, the rider gave a gentle nudge in Pegasus's ribs, sending it off at a collected canter to return to the light.

Joanna looked at the object lying on the ground before her. Stooping down, she picked it up and stared at it intently as it rested in her palm. The object was a quartz crystal, approximately three inches across, and of the purest pink she had ever seen. It seems alive with light, and she could feel the power of its properties vibrating in her hand, as she slowly closed her fingers around it.

Joanna suddenly found herself sitting bolt upright in bed. The bedclothes were sodden from her sweat; her heart was beating loudly and her breath, quick and full of hysteria.

In the gloominess of the room she could just make out her husband, sleeping like a baby next to her. She looked across at her clock radio. It read 5.30 am. Slowly, she sank back down onto her pillow, staring quietly into space. She did not fully understand what had happened to her. Despite trying to retrace her steps, nothing seemed to make any sense.

Taking a deep deliberate breath, she decided to concentrate on calming herself down, so pushed her nightmare to the back of her mind until another time.

CHAPTER SIX
18TH DECEMBER 1989

9.30am Chipperfield

Joanna sat at her desk; her head buried deep in Pete Law's books as the bright winter sun shone through the frosted window to warm her.

Pat sat opposite, occasionally cussing over her client's lack of book-keeping skills, but apart from the odd profanity, the atmosphere was full of deep concentration. Pat was a quiet character in her late thirties, with long tassels of curly dark brown hair. She was normally a very cheerful woman, so her temper over her work was unusual.

The telephone intruded into the peace as it began to ring. Pat broke her concentration and, reaching out her hand, she picked up the receiver, with a certain lack of enthusiasm. "Anthony Racen Accountants. How may I help you?" She said softly.

"Hello." a Welsh accent came through from the other end. "Joanna?"

"No, it's not. Would you like to speak to her?"

"Well actually," he continued, "I would like to speak with either Tony or Margaret."

"Who shall I say is calling?"

"Eric." He replied flatly. "Eric Salusbury."

"May I ask what it's in connection with?"

"It's personal."

"One moment please." And with that she placed the receiver on her working papers, stood up, then wandered through the office door and shouted up the stairs, "Tony, its Eric Salusbury for you."

Joanna's father acknowledged her, before taking the phone call upstairs. Pat quietly ambled back to her desk, placed the receiver back on its hook and, sighing deeply, returned to her laborious work.

A few minutes later and Tony's footsteps could be heard coming down the stairs, before wandering through to the sitting room where Joanna's mother, Margaret, was sitting reading the paper.

Muffled voices could be heard, as the Accountant and his wife had a discussion about their conversation with the Welsh relative. Then, moments later, both Tony and Margaret came into the office, with an air of seriousness about their faces.

Joanna looked up from Pete Lowe's books, "What's up?" she asked.

"That was Eric on the phone." Her fathers voice sounded shaky, "Some bad news about Stephanie. He phoned to tell us that she died in the early hours of this morning."

"Oh no." Joanna said as she placed her pen softly on the desk.

Margaret then proceeded to inform Pat that Stephanie, Eric's wife, had suffered from Multiple Sclerosis for the past sixteen years and that for the last two, she had been in the Denbigh Infirmary.

"When's the funeral?" Joanna asked.

Tony ran his hand across his balding head, as he sat down at his desk. "They're not sure yet. The vicar at Henllan Church want's to do the funeral before Christmas, so they are frantically making arrangements. Eric seems to think that it will be Thursday."

"Do you mind if I ring Jon, to let him know what's happened?" Joanna requested and at the nod of authorisation from her father, she dialled the number.

The phone at the other end seemed to ring endlessly before the secretary answered it.

"Tay Homes, Leighton Buzzard." she sang from the other end, "To whom to you wish to speak?"

"Jon Waller, please." Joanna requested.

"One moment." and a few clicks later, Joanna was through to her husband.

"Hi Jon, it's Jo." she greeted him.

"Hello." he flatly replied, for he detested private phone calls when he was at work.

"Sorry to trouble you, Jon, " She apologised, "but we've just received some sad news from Eric."

"What?" he snapped back.

"Stephanie died last night."

"Oh." his reply had a slightly softer tone. Then after a pause he continued, "When's the funeral?"

"Eric's not sure yet; thinks it might be on Thursday." She informed him.

"Do you want to go?"

"Certainly."

"Well, let me know when its definite so that I can book the time off work." he then abruptly cut the conversation short, "Look, I've got to go now - got tons of work to get through before I break up for Christmas. We'll talk about it tonight, alright?"

The day seemed to drag by, as the family waited patiently for Eric's phone call, until eventually, at four thirty that afternoon, he contacted them again. The Welshman confirmed that although it was not possible to arrange for the funeral during the week, the vicar had agreed that he would lay her to rest that Saturday, as he did not feel it appropriate to leave it until after Christmas. And so it was all arranged; two thirty Saturday 23rd December.

6.15pm Slapton

Joanna had already gotten the dinner organised, had changed and was in the middle of getting the fire started by the time Jon returned home from work. At the sound of the key in the lock, she raced through to the kitchen to greet her husband.

Jon wandered in, his face sullen and his eyes hard and foreboding. He then threw his case on the floor next to the breakfast bar before slumping onto the stool. "What's for dinner?" he mumbled.

"Cod ..." she then smartly changed the subject, "Eric phoned back at mums. The funerals on Saturday."

Jon completely ignored the latter half of his wife's sentence, "Cod." he shouted in outrage, "What possessed you to cook that? You know I hate fish." and with that, he marched off into the sitting room, threw himself onto the settee, and began to sulk.

Joanna followed him into the other room, "Cod was all we had in the freezer." she justified her actions. "Besides, it won't kill you." She then continued with the important issue of Stephanie's funeral, "The funeral's on Saturday, two thirty, at Henllan Church."

"It doesn't matter when or where it is, " he growled spitefully, "We're not going."

"Well why not?" she gave a sharp reply.

"Because I didn't know her very well, that's why."

"You were quite happy to go when I spoke to you this afternoon."

"I've changed my mind. Alright?" He then got up to leave the room, but as he departed, Joanna's passing shot was, "Because you can't possibly forego your football match, 'suppose." But he did not retaliate, for her comments were beyond contempt.

8.00pm

Turning off the tap, Joanna sank into the hot bath water, until her body was completely engulfed by the soothing liquid. She ducked her head under the bubbles, soaking her long golden locks. This place was now her sanctuary, far away from all the worries of the day.

As she surfaced, she suddenly became aware of another presence in the room. Rubbing the suds from her eyes, she looked about her through the steam, until she spotted the culprit. In the far corner, standing just in front of the wash basin was a dark shadow, about five foot ten inches and of stocky build. She froze, rubbed her eyes a second time and squinted, as she tried to identify the entity. But the manifestation just remained there, watching.

Joanna suddenly found herself overwrought with fear. Whatever it was in the room with her, it was certainly not there for reassurance. Quickly grabbing the bath towel, she scrabbled out of the bath and bolted for the door. Reaching for the handle, she glanced over her shoulder in the hope that this had all been her imagination, but the spectre was still visible amongst the steam.

She pulled the handle down, but the catch caught causing the door to rattle furiously in its frame. She tried a second time, but again found her escape route obstructed. Fear flowing through every vein, she let go of the handle and begun to bang violently on the door. "Jon. Jon." she cried out, "Come quick."

With no obvious movement from her husband downstairs, she turned to face the intruder but the dark shadow remained motionless. It just stood there, defiantly, enjoying the intimidation.

She leant against the door. "What do you want?" she whispered as she stared at the entity. But it did not reply.

Composing herself, she concentrated on the shadow, trying to visualise its features. It started to materialise before her in the form of a grey haired, middle-aged man with glasses, wearing a tweed jacket. As he transfigured before her Joanna realised, to her horror, that this was the man who had been in her dreams. "Shit." she muttered under her breath and quickly turned back to the door, trying the handle a second time as she did so. This time the door swung open with ease, giving her the escape route she so desperately required.

Hot-footing it down the stairs, she dashed through the kitchen to the sitting room, where Jon sat watching the television.

"Didn't you hear me calling you?" Joanna panted as she stood in the doorway, water dripping from her body.

"Yes." he growled back.

"Why didn't you come?"

"Why? Something wrong then?"

"Of course there's something wrong. There was something in the bathroom with me."

"Like what?" he mocked.

"Well I don't know." she squealed. "A ghost I suppose."

"A ghost." Jon scoffed. "How ridiculous. Next, you'll be saying it was your Auntie Stephanie."

"No. It was a man."

Her husband stared at her with the coldest of eyes. "A man? Well, I must see this for myself." and with that, he got up and marched out of the sitting room, grabbing her hand as he went.

As they reached the landing, Jon paused as he stared intently at the closed door of the bathroom. Joanna stood behind her husband, fidgeting nervously. Jon then turned back to her, "Well? Show me your ghost then?" he smirked, as he invited her to enter the bathroom first.

"Why don't you go in first?"

"If there is a spook in there," he jested "then I'd rather it possessed you, not me."

She stared up at him, feeling her fear turn to anger. "You don't believe me, do you?" She snapped.

"What do you think? A ghost in the bog - I ask you."

"Right." she proclaimed and with that she pushed her husband to one side and firmly gripping the door handle, she entered the bathroom.

The air inside was consumed with moistness by the steam rising from the bath. She looked over to the basin, then turned and checked every corner of the room, but could see nothing untoward.

Jon stepped over the threshold after her. "Where is this man of yours then?" he ridiculed her.

"Gone." she replied flatly.

"Thought as much. You'll do anything to get your own way, won't you."

"What do you mean by that?" she questioned his statement, as she stared back at him intently.

It was at this point that she noticed the overall change in her husband. As she stared back at him, she realised for the first time how scruffy he had become. Jon had always taken a pride in his appearance. His hair always had to be just so, he never could abide stubble on his chin and he loved wearing the best clothing that money could buy. But looking at him now, the change in his appearance seemed so clear. He had long since given up going to the barbers and his once neat, wavy, dark auburn hair, was now falling about his nape in an unruly fashion. His chin showed a week's worth of growth and his hazel eyes, that once seemed so soft and gentle, had now sunk deep in their sockets creating a hardness that she had never witnessed before. The overall shape of his face had also changed from a fullness about the cheeks, to having drawn and haggard contours with heavy bags under the eyes.

Jon frowned back at her. "Well, I'm not wasting any more time over your little game. See you down stairs." and with that he turned and marched out of the room, slamming the door shut in her face as he departed.

CHAPTER SEVEN
23RD DECEMBER 1989

6.00pm Slapton

With Joanna in Wales and safely out of the way, Jon found that he could finally relax in his own home. He had endured a dreadful day's football, losing four-nil, but despite that disappointment, he knew that he could now spend the best part of the evening doing exactly what he wanted, without any irritating interruptions from his wife.

Switching on the television, he snuggled into the settee with piping hot coffee in hand, and began switching from channel to channel. However, nothing the broadcasting companies offered seemed to catch his imagination so, placing his mug on the wooden arm of the settee, he wandered over to the cupboard and pulled out a film recorded from the television a few weeks earlier. Roughly snatching it from its casing, he pushed it into the player and hit the play button.

He snuggled back down into the cushions of the settee as the credits appeared on the screen. Then jumped up and dashed out to the fridge to grab a beer, before running back into his seat and getting himself comfortable.

It was an hour or so into the horror movie before Jon started to notice a strange thumping sound coming from upstairs. At first he tried to ignore it, but the persistent noise distracted him from the film. Sighing with annoyance, he pulled himself out of his comfortable seat and wandered through towards the stairs to investigate.

As Jon opened the stair door, the landing light turned itself on, to reveal the stair-well and landing beyond. Although alarmed, Jon saw no real reason to panic at this stage of the game. So he boldly ascended the stairs, two steps at a time, in search of the source from which the banging came.

Upon reaching the landing he paused, for he found his nerve starting to dwindle away. Momentarily running his square-shaped hand through his wavy hair, he listened intently, but it was a second or two before he could pinpoint its whereabouts. He finally realised that the rhythmical thump-thump-thump was coming from behind the closed door of the bathroom so, nervously stepping forward, he reached out and grabbed at the handle. The catch clicked, and the door swung ajar. Letting go of the handle, he pushed the door until it was fully open, before gingerly peering inside.

The room was pitch black, hiding all within from view. He took one deliberate step forward and reached for the light switch. He pulled on the string until the light clicked on, filling the room with brightness. He then took a second, more hesitant step forward over the threshold, before stopping just inside the bathroom to look about him for whatever it was that was creating such a din. Never the less, despite straining his ears, the noise was no more and all he was left with was a feeling of unease.

Suddenly, he heard the main bedroom door open behind him, the break in the eerie silence making him jump. He turned to face the door on the far side of the landing, and watched, agog, as the door creaked open to reveal the gloominess of the bedroom beyond.

Turning off the bathroom light, he cockily strode across to the bedroom, for he was determined not so show any fear, but as he entered the room, the bathroom door swung shut, slamming violently in its frame as it did so. Jon froze. A cold shiver ran down his spine as he focused his attention, firstly at the bathroom door and then, the bedroom. Should he go into the bedroom, as he had been invited, or back to the bathroom? Or should he get the hell out of there? He was certainly in a conundrum.

He hovered on the spot, trying to rationalise what he had just experienced but, as he pondered on the best course of action, the landing light began to flicker as it threatened to explode and die.

Instinctively, he reached out and turned on the bedroom light for security, for his logic stated that nothing could harm him provided there was light. Feeling safer, now the bedroom was void of darkness, he stumbled inside. He did not know what he should expect to see there, but he still gave the room a thorough inspection before deciding that it must have been his overactive imagination. Then, brushing all negative thoughts from his mind, he turned and swiftly made his way back down stairs, to the sanctuary of the sitting room. "This'll teach me to watch horrors when I'm here on my own." he muttered to himself, as he returned to his seat and settled down to continue watching the film.

He had just got back into the plot, when the Christmas tree lights suddenly started to flicker. Then seconds later, the video decided to stop playing. He went to get up to find out what had happened when the machine, with a mind of its own, proceeded to rewind the tape. Reaching the machine Jon crouched down in front of the video and scratched his head, perplexed as to what was going wrong. But as he stared at it, the player stopped rewinding and switched itself to record. Then it stopped, rewound itself again, before switching back to play, enabling him to watch something from Channel Four that it had just recorded. Then turning itself off once more, it fast forwarded, and returned to the exact place in the film that he had been watching prior to this paranormal event.

Jon slowly rose from his haunches, unable to take his eyes off the machine. Maybe his wife had had reason to be afraid in this house after all, for no amount of reasoning could justify the amount of things that he had witnessed that evening. He felt decidedly uneasy, so returned to his seat, although he perched precariously on the edge of the cushion, nervously watching for any further events.

7.45pm

Jon was totally unaware of how long he had been perched there, just waiting. It was the key in the lock that brought him back to reality, as Joanna returned from her trip to Wales.

"Is that you, Jo?" he shouted, the tension prominent in his voice. She acknowledged him flatly as she threw her bags on the floor and wandered over to the kettle.

With his wife's return, the fear within him suddenly lifted and he found himself confident once more. He could now get his own back on his wife, for what her spooks had put him through earlier, so getting up, he cockily strutted out into the kitchen and leant on the breakfast bar. "Coffee would be nice." he informed her, with a persuasive grin.

"Really." she stated coldly, but despite her inner most feelings to tell that husband of hers to 'go to Hell' she found herself putting a second mug next to the kettle and placing coffee granules in it for him.

Jon's face then took on a harsher expression. "Good day?" he enquired sarcastically, finding himself able to return to his old ways as if nothing untoward had happened to him that day.

"What do you think?" she snapped.

Ignoring her reply, he continued, "Lost four-nil today." Selfishly disregarding his wife's obvious distress. "Dave scored an own goal, which didn't help. Wanker."

Joanna then mumbled, "Like you then." under her breath, before handing him a mug of steaming hot coffee. Then picking up her own drink, she flatly stated, "I'm going upstairs for a bath, then I'm off to bed. Goodnight." and with that, she retired.

11.30pm

Joanna was rudely awoken by Jon stomping around upstairs, as he got ready for bed. He crashed around the bedroom like a hurricane, still totally insensitive to her needs after the stresses of the day. His attitude was totally selfish. He cared for nobody but himself.

Turning off the light, he clambered into bed and fidgeted indiscreetly, with the sole intention of disturbing her. With sleepy eyes, Joanna blinked at her clock, before pulling the duvet closer to her, to stop the draft, allowing herself to return to her slumber.

Jon lay quietly for a few seconds, before starting to huff and puff loudly, as if in annoyance at something. Then he sat up abruptly, causing the top half of the duvet to drag away from Joanna's shoulders. "Did you lock the front door?" he shouted at the top of his voice.

Startled, Joanna lifted her head off the pillow and grunted.

"Well?" he growled. "Did you lock the door?"

"Jon, I've been in bed since nine. I'd hardly set the alarm for eleven thirty just to go down stairs and lock the door. Idiot." and with that, she grabbed the corner of the duvet and pulled it back over her, before settling down for a second attempt at sleep.

"Well, you're not asleep now, "he growled, as he placed his hands on her back and pushed her out of bed, "So you might just as well do it now."

Joanna landed on the floor with a loud thump. She lethargically grovelled about on the carpet for a moment, then clambered back onto the bed and under the warm duvet.

He went to push her out of bed again, but she was ready for him. Bracing every muscle in her body, she managed to prevent him from hurling her out a second time. Then, with anger rushing through her, she turned to face him and shouted, "Fuck the door, and fuck you."

Furious at her disobedience, he grabbed at the duvet, pulled it from her and rolled himself inside it, so its edges were underneath him. He then turned his back on her and snuggled down, ready for a peaceful night.

"Let me have some duvet." she pleaded, "It's cold."

"Tough luck." he snarled. "Night."

Joanna tugged at the quilt, but failed to recover her half. Sighing to herself, she lay on the bed, the cold enveloping itself about her. After a fashion she wearily got up from her rest place and wandered over to the cupboard above the stairs to retrieve a sleeping bag, for she no longer had the fight in her to bother with Jon's childish behaviour.

The sleeping bag placed neatly on the bed, she clambered inside. The nylon felt cold and unwelcoming, but at least she could rest assured that once her body heat had warmed it up, she could sleep cosily for the rest of the night without fear of Jon trying to take that from her, as well.

As she snuggled down inside the bag, Jon lifted his head and turned to face her. "What are you doing now, you ugly bitch?"

"Trying to get some sleep." She softly replied whilst trying, in vain, to relax.

"Well, you're not sleeping on my bed in that." and unwrapping himself from his cocoon, he placed his feet on her side and pushed, sending the sleeping bag sliding, effortlessly, across the bed and back onto the floor. He then continued, "You either sleep in that on the floor, or without that on the bed."

"Fine." she replied, her tone still soft and undeterred by his outrageous behaviour.

"Well, just remember that." he snarled. There was a moment's pause before he broke the silence. Suddenly, he leapt out of bed and, before she knew what was happening, Joanna found the bag being pulled from the far end, until he was holding it in his arms, whilst she lay on the floor, in nothing but her night shirt. "By the way," he informed her aggressively, "as this is my sleeping bag and, as you didn't ask permission, you can't use that to sleep in either."

Incensed, Joanna jumped to her feet, now completely alert. "Oh. Go to Hell." she screamed, before storming off to the spare room.

The single bed was unmade, but this inconvenience did not deter her, for she soon had it ready for a good night's sleep. Finally, away from all that tormented her, she wearily clambered under the welcoming covers and soon found herself drifting once more.

A quarter of an hour later or so, she abruptly came too, as she heard movement in the main bedroom. Burying her head under the covers, she tried to ignore the sound, but moments later Jon had invaded her sanctuary and was sitting on the bed next to her.

He gently pulled the covers back from her face and tenderly stroked her face. "I'm sorry." he whispered.

Joanna lifted her head and asked, "Why were you in such a bad mood?"

"I just felt like you had abandoned me today."

"What?" she snapped, surprise prominent in her voice, "Me abandoned you? More like you abandoning me, Jon."

He then lifted the bedclothes, clambered into bed next to her and snuggled up. "Life just has no meaning, Jo." he stated, "Why don't we have children. Everything will be alright, once we are a proper family." He then began to caress her, in the hope of starting the ball rolling.

Joanna grabbed at his hand, putting an abrupt end to his intentions. "You have got to be joking Jon. I've had a bad day, and all you can think about is sex. There is no way that I would even consider starting a family with you, until we have sorted out our problems."

"The problems will go away. Children will help us get closer. That's the problem, there is nothing to pull us together at the moment. Children will change that."

"I'm sorry Jon." she found herself apologising for his preposterous remark. "I won't. Not until I feel more settled."

Incensed, he knelt up and pulled the pillow from under Joanna's head. As she tried to get up, he placed the pillow over her face and pushed down hard, forcing the back of her head into the mattress.

Instinctively she struggled, as she tried to catch her breath beneath the tort pillow, which had just enough leeway to enable her to move her head to one side, in search of air.

Jon bore down on top of her, allowing his full weight to pin her to the bed, as she lashed out her arms in an attempt to fight him off. Then, one at a time, he grabbed at her wrists and, using brute force, he pinned both her arms and the pillow firmly down.

Joanna thought she was going to die there and then. Her breathing shallowing slightly as the underside of the pillow forced itself into the side of her face. She stopped struggling and remained perfectly still.

Jon lay on top of her, laughing like a madman. He had become aroused by the torment that he was inflicting upon his wife. Oh yes, the pleasure of domination certainly was intoxicating to him. He had the power to do anything he liked and there was nothing his wife could do about it. This was, indeed, a good game to play.

Moments passed like hours. All Joanna could do was accept her fate and remain passive until it was over. Then, as quickly as it had begun, Jon angrily jumped out from under the covers and, with his parting shot of, "If that's how you want to play it, you will get exactly what you deserve." echoing around the room, he stormed off, leaving his wife sobbing quietly to herself into the pillow.

CHAPTER EIGHT
12TH JULY 1990

7.00pm Slapton

The last six months had proved to be anything but stable between Jon and his wife. Jon's moods had increased over that period making him more withdrawn and intense.

After the experiences of Christmas 1989, Joanna had noted every development between her and her husband and, with a catalogue of information now at her finger tips, she decided it was time to confront her husband with the facts as she saw them, in order that their marriage might still be salvageable despite all that had been said and done.

The atmosphere in the house was oppressive that evening as Jon sat in the armchair, staring into space. His body seemed to be engulfed by a black cloud and there was no reaching him.

Reaching for her handbag, Joanna retrieved her notes and thrust them at her sulky husband. He broke his stare and looked down at the note pad with an air of disinterest. "What's this?" he groaned.

"Notes about your behaviour." she informed him.

"How pathetic." and with that he threw the note pad across the room until it bounced off the Parkray and landed in an unruly heap on the hearth.

Joanna wandered over to the fireplace and, picking up her crumpled notes, she said, "I don't think they are. Look Jon, I don't know why you treat me like you do, but maybe if you could find it in your heart to read these then maybe, we could sort something out."

"Like what? There's nothing wrong with me - it's all in your head. I'm perfectly happy." He scoffed.

"Really? Sorry, but I don't agree. You treat me like shit and here is the proof." She replied, as she waved the notes in front of his face. "Admit it Jon, you've got a problem. We've got a problem. If we don't sort it out then it'll end up destroying what we have got."

She then placed the note pad on the arm of his chair. "Look, I'm going out for a while. Promise me that you will read them, then when I return we can talk about it."

"You've got all the answers haven't you Joanna." he snarled.

"Just promise me you'll read them." and with that she snatched up her car keys and marched out of the house to leave Jon to ponder at his predicament.

Jon sat there, motionless, until he had heard the front door slam shut and was confident that his pathetic wife had left him in peace. He then slowly reached out and picked up the notes left by his side.

He flicked from page to page; casually skimming over the dates and alleged emotional and physical cruelty he had afflicted on his wife over the last six and a half months. He even found himself chuckling from time to time at the incidents as he browsed through the pages and was impressed at some of the antics that he was supposed to have executed, for even he could not believe that he was capable of such brutality.

Finally ending the perusal of Joanna's journal, Jon lazily rose from his seat, wandered over to the Parkray and promptly placed the notebook, with its detrimental contents, into the flames. He got a buzz from watching the paper curl up and burst into flames, as the evidence against him destroyed itself in front of his eyes. Surely, he could really have fun at his wife's expense now that her fabrications had been eradicated. All he had to do now was to wait patiently for her return.

10.00pm

The sound of the key in the lock gave Jon a wonderful sense of self-enlightenment causing an evil, sadistic smile to creep across his face, as Joanna returned home.

He did not move from his seat, as he heard her fumbling about in the kitchen, just waited patiently for his prey to wonder into his trap, in order that he could finally completely destroy her.

Having made herself a coffee, Joanna entered the sitting room and sat down on the settee. "Well?" She questioned him, "Read my notes?"

Jon turned and scowled. "Quite amusing actually." He snarled. "Shame it's all lies."

"You really believe that?" she questioned him further.

"A load of crap." he stated coldly.

"Maybe we should go to Relate or something then, because I feel that there is a problem with our relationship."

"Oh and because you think there is, then there must be. Yes?" he snarled, sarcastically.

"What do you suggest we do then?"

"About what?"

"Our marriage Jon. Come on, there must be something wrong, or else I would not have written those notes."

"Oh yes, those notes." he swiftly turned from the subject away from counselling. "Very amusing. I laughed all the way through reading them." A heinous smirk crept across his cruel face as his words came forth with smug satisfaction. "However, as they were not worthy of any literary awards, I saved you the embarrassment of keeping them, just in case anyone should accidentally stumble across them in the future. Could make you a laughing stock you see, so I thought I'd dispose of them accordingly. I only did it for your own good."

"Really?" Joanna remained undisturbed by his sarcasm.

"Really. You should be grateful to me you know."

"So, purely out of curiosity, what have you done with my notes?"

"I did with them what you do with all rubbish - I burnt them in the fire." His barbarous voice echoed about the room as he spoke the words, for he relished putting the woman back in to her place. But his plan backfired, for Joanna was not as gullible as he had suspected, and with an angelic face and innocent smile she replied, "Just as well that they were only copied from the original notes then, and that the original ones are safely tucked away at work."

Jon may have lost the battle, but he was determined not to lose the war. He quickly backtracked to the subject of counselling and promptly started to attack again, "So you think that you need counselling then."

"We need it, yes."

"Well I don't."

"So what makes you think that you don't need any then."

"I don't want to be married to you anymore." The words cut through Joanna like a knife. This announcement was like a bolt out of the blue and knocked her for six.

"What?" she shakily replied, her whole body trembling at the shock, "Why?"

"Well, I can't settle to married life. It's not been as I would have expected."

"How do you mean?"

"I feel restricted. I can't do all the things that I want to do."

"Like what? You play for two football teams, you go training twice a week as well, you regularly play squash with Tom from your office, oh and let's not forget about the office cricket team as well. What more freedom do you want? Most partners would not have put up with that, because they would have felt deserted."

"Oh come on, its me that has felt deserted, by you." he retorted as he tried to turn the guilt back on his wife, "You go out riding on Ryan and you do that stupid course for the Assistant Instructors exam at the riding stables. No wonder I've had to find other amusement."

"Hold on a minute." She retaliated. "The only reason I started riding Mrs Browns horse, and the only reason I started doing the A.I. course is because otherwise I would have been left at home on my own, because you were already doing all these other things and have been since before we met. So don't try to put all the blame on me. Besides, I only ride when you are out playing football, and the riding course is on a night when you do training so, you see, I have not left you sitting here on your own, 'feeling deserted', as you put it."

Jon, now two-nil down on the argument, changed the direction of his attack. "Well, let's face it Jo, you've never been a very good wife to me have you?"

"What do you mean by that?"

"The place is a mess, you never cook me my favourite dinners, you deliberately disobeyed me with regard to working for your parents and you do not bring home the same amount of money as me - something that I think you should do as my equal."

"As your equal." Joanna repeated his final words slowly and deliberately. "Funny that because, surely as an equal I was entitled to share the duvet covers and not have to sleep on the floor. Surely as an equal, I'm entitled to have an equal share from you with the housework. Surely as an equal I can pursue my hobbies with the same enthusiasm as you pursue yours. Surely as an equal I have as much rights as you. So don't talk to me about equal when you do not practise what you preach." She then rose from the settee. "I'm going upstairs to move my things into the spare room. I will then start proceedings with regard to divorcing you on the grounds of mental and physical cruelty. Life's too short for having to put up with the crap that you dish out at me. I've put as much into this marriage as I can, but you've put nothing into it. You are pathetic Jon and the sooner you are out of my life, the better." and with that she stormed off out of the room.

11.30pm

No sooner had Joanna fallen off to sleep than she found herself being drawn from her body and flying off towards the astral planes. Golden light completely surrounded her as she travelled, creating a tunnel of warmth that soothed her spirit, and of brightness that calmed her. She was at peace in this state as she allowed the healing process on her soul to commence. Nothing on earth could measure to the ecstasy of this experience and she wished that she could stay in this state forever.

The reality of the experience, however, was merely to prepare her for transportation to that far off land that she had visited on two previous occasions, where the Israelite was waiting patiently for her arrival. And she shortly found herself leaving the tunnel of golden light and standing next to her guardian.

There was no one else around, not even little Emma. Just her and the Israelite solemnly standing amongst the vast and barren foreboding land.

Joanna was uncertain on how best to greet the man, for despite being pleased to see a familiar face, she found his stance daunting. But, sensing her uncertainty, he merely held out his left hand and with a gentle smile he softly said, "Don't be afraid of me, for I am of Gods light and bring you good tidings."

Joanna stepped forward and without uttering a word, tenderly placed her hand in his. With the connection she felt his strength rushing through her as though her whole spirit was being energised. The white light around him expanded and, as she stood there totally perplexed at the experience, the white light engulfed her also, until the wasteland vanished and the only things that seemed to exist in the universe were herself and the Israelite.

The power of the light was strong. It encompassed them, contracting as it whizzed around and around, until it penetrated into her heart centre causing her aura to explode into streams of white light.

The Israelite then spoke, his voice full of knowledge and sincerity, "You are now filled with the Holy Spirit, child. Nothing can touch you. Nothing can hurt you. You have been energised with the power of God. Do not be afraid to stare your enemies in the eye, for the Lord is your rock, your fortress and your deliverer. When the cords of death entangle you, when the torrents of destruction overwhelm you, or when the snares of death confront you, call to the Lord for He is your shield and the strength of your salvation. He will reward you according to your righteousness; to the faithful He shows himself faithful, to the blameless He shows himself blameless, to the pure He shows himself pure. But to the crooked He shows himself shrewd. Remember my words for this wisdom is yours for the taking."

Joanna looked up at him blankly; "I don't understand what you are saying. Why all this talk of God? I do not go to Church. I don't believe in religion. I am an atheist."

But to her surprise, the Israelite just smiled serenely at her, with an inner wisdom. "Do you believe in God?" he questioned her.

"Yes."

"Do you believe in Jesus Christ?" he continued.

"I've been baptised into the Christian religion, but I am no Christian."

The Israelites face took on a sterner expression, "That is not what I asked you." he pointed out sternly. "Listen to me. Do you believe in Jesus Christ?"

"Yes."

"Thank you. Now, what is atheism?"

"The belief that there is no God."

"Then you are not an atheist. You have an inner faith. A faith that is stronger than any religion. Religion is man-made and is of no consequence unless faith accompanies it. Faith is a spiritual gift given to the common good by the Holy Spirit, as are the gifts of wisdom, knowledge, healing, miraculous powers, prophesy, distinguishing between spirits, speaking in tongues, and interpretation of tongues."

"But God will surely punish me, for I have broken a promise made in His house."

"How so?"

"I made a vow to God when I married Jon, that I would remain with him until 'death us do part', but today I find that I have told him that I want a divorce."

"Does Jon love you with all his heart?"

"The only person that he loves is himself."

"Then he broke the promise to love and cherish you, that he made to God in His House. Without love he is nothing. Love is patient, love is kind. It does not envy, is does not boast, it is not proud. It is not rude, nor is it self-seeking. It is not easily angered, nor does it delight in evil but rather it rejoices with the truth. It always protects, always trusts, always hopes and always perseveres. If you can say from your heart that Jon possessed these qualities and that you did not, then wonder and perish, for you are not worthy in Gods eyes. However, it is God who judges and the law of the Lord is perfect. It is He who keeps his servants from wilful sins. If His law had not been your delight, then you would have perished in your affliction. The wicked were waiting to destroy you, but His commands are boundless. You need not fret at your dilemma for you have defeated your enemy."

Joanna frowned as she mulled over the Israelites words. What he had spoken justified her actions, but never the less she still felt in the wrong for turning her back on her husband and her marriage.

"You are still uncertain?" the Israelite questioned her. "Then let me show you what Jon is." and with that the white mist evaporated from around them to reveal the barren land once more.

The atmosphere was oppressive; the darkened clouds swept across the sky like a veil of darkness, with only a hint of purply-pink breaking through just over the Eastern horizon, as if there was a dawning upon the land.

The barren land was scorched and seared with not a blade of grass to be seen. The bark had crumbled from the trees that donned the land and the air lacked the chorus of bird song.

The Israelite pointed in the direction of the Northern Hemisphere, making Joanna's attention turn to the horizon to the North instead of taking in her surroundings. In the distance she could see four faint figures approaching on horseback out of the black mist that engulfed them, the dust of the land sweeping out behind them like smoke from a chimney. Immediately she knew who they were, for she had encountered them on her previous visit.

Her guardian then redirected her attention to the East, as a lone figure rode swiftly towards them, his mount in full flight. But she did not retain her gaze on the lone rider, for she knew that he was of no threat to her. The danger lay in the laps of the four from the North and so, she helplessly returned her observations to the darker elements.

The four riders approached with deliberation, just as they had done some nine months earlier. The nostrils of the horses were flared with intent and their hooves pounded the ground with a fury that Joanna had never experienced in an equine before.

The riders' eyes were filled with anger and destruction, for they had a score to settle. They were not going to be so easily put off this time and were prepared for battle.

As they drew closer Joanna noticed that the leader, with his long grey locks floating out behind him, was carrying a steel sword in his right hand which he held high above his head. He also wore a shield that was hooked over his left arm, to protect him from his enemy. It was black in colour with a silver symbol engraved upon its face, but she did not recognise the emblem, nor make reason of its significance.

The tall, slim woman and the middle-aged man with the menacing stare rode side by side, just behind the scar-faced man. The two also held swords, which they repeatedly sliced through the air to show their great strength against the enemy.

Her husband rode to the rear of the group. He did not hold any weapon, for he no longer knew the strength of the dark side to be of any significance. His presence was only for intimidation of numbers, and nothing more.

The vibration of the hooves shook the ground as both the group of four and the lone rider approached the spot where Joanna and the Israelite stood. The sound echoed around the barren land, filling the deadly silence, sending it into an orchestra of frenzied Pandemonium.

The lone rider was the first to reach them both, pulling his winged mount up just in front of Joanna and her guardian, for he was their protection against the invading evil. But it was not long before the four black riders were also at the scene, their sweating horses squealing excitedly as they were halted only feet away from the lone rider and his steed, Pegasus.

The leader of the four violently dug his mount in the ribs with his ankles, sending the animal shooting forward a couple of feet in startlement. "Get thee out of my way, for I now knowest who thou art - Taliesim." The scar-faced man growled at the rider of the winged mount, "And I know that thou art powerless against my might, for I am the Archangel of Despair, " he announced as he waved his weapon about his head, "thoust can not touch me now. Get thee out of my way, so that I may destroy the spirit of ye woman and her envoy, for I have been sent as their assailant."

"I fear you not, sorcerer." Taliesim replied, with a calmness in his voice, "You can not touch me, nor my people." and with that he drew his golden sword from its sheath, held it high above him for a moment, the sliced it downwards, through the air, towards the earth. Then, as the tip of the sword touched the ground, there was a great explosion as the brightest of white light came from within the centre of the blade and out through its point and into the earth.

The earth rumbled beneath them, causing the crust to form hairline cracks as the energy from the light penetrated into the soil. But Taliesim did not withdraw the sword, instead he continued, causing the ground beneath their feet to shake violently, like an earthquake, causing the hairline cracks to expand making a furrow between Taliesim and the four dark riders.

The wall of the furrow continued to break down as the earth shook, growing in width and depth until a vast abyss appeared with white light shining forth from its core, cutting off the Sorcerer and his followers from the others.

Once Taliesim was content with his work, he withdrew the golden sword from the ground and stood triumphant at the edge of the abyss.

Thwarted, the Sorcerer cried out, "Thou hast not won yet. I must not return empty handed. So who wouldst thou sacrifice, Taliesim?"

"I murder no one. Take one of your own kind." and with that, he turned Pegasus to face Joanna and the Israelite as he placed the sword back in its sheath.

"Thou hast angered me a second time." the scar-faced man growled from the far side of the abyss, "Thou wilst pay for thy crimes." and with that, in his infinite temper, he turned to Jon and continued, "Thou hast failed me, slave. Thy spirit wilst burn in ye flames of ye eternal pit for an eternity", and with that he pointed his sword at the ground under the hooves of Jon's mount and, with a rumble from beneath the earth, the soil gave way under the animal causing both it, and its rider to vanished into the bottomless pit of despair.

Joanna watched in horror as the animal and her husband were swallowed, squealing and screaming, into the void. She covered her ears so that she could not hear the tormented cries from the depths of the abyss, for the sound of suffering was too much for her to bear.

The Sorcerer then turned his attention back to his prey, "For thy fate, Joanna, I curse thee with unmentionable misfortune from this day forth.

Thou wilst be forever looking over thy shoulder, for I wilst be just a step behind. Thou wilst never rest until I hast taken thy soul. Thou is cursed."

With a boldness of stride, Joanna instinctively stepped forward and replied to his curse with a fearlessness that even surprised her, "Your black magic and your black sorcery are powerless to injure me, I send thy curses back to thee, return, return by three times three, return I say, so mote it be."

As soon as her words were spoken, a black shroud started to engulf the three evil entities. Their mounts became restless at the phenomenon and proceeded to flatten their ears and roll their eyes. As the cloud thickened the horses started to rear up, with flared nostrils and fearsome squeals. But just before the remaining three were completely submerged by the darkness, the Sorcerer could be heard shouting angrily, "Thou art a Pharisee. Remember to keep watching over thy shoulder, for my guises are many and my cunning great." then with an explosion of black mist, they were gone, lost in time and space.

CHAPTER NINE
6TH MARCH, 1993

1.30pm Leighton Buzzard

Joanna and Jon finally parted company later in 1990 and divorced the following year. Joanna remained at Slapton, having bought Jon's share of the house, whilst he moved back to his mothers home in Croxley Green. Time moved on, and Jon was no longer affected by the negativity of their marital home; rather he reverted back to his old self, just as he was before moving to the cottage in Slapton.

Joanna was now with her new partner, Lewis, as they stood in the queue at the checkout counter of the supermarket, patiently waiting for their turn to be served by the assistant at the till. Joanna leant on the bars of the trolley staring dreamily into space, whilst Lewis chattered on about a job that he might be acquiring shortly in Jersey, fitting milking parlours.

Lewis was a large man; six foot four inches, stockily built and of an earthy character. He wore thin, silver rimmed glasses, which hid a round, chubby cheeked face, and his mousy hair was thinning slightly on top.

He and Joanna first met ten years ago, when they both used to attend the South West Herts. Young Farmers Club. She had known him long before she met Jon, although there had never been any romantic involvement between the two prior to her marriage.

Ironically, almost as soon as Jon walked out of her life, Lewis walked in, finally moving in with her in June 1991. This was a partnership totally opposite to that of her's and Jon's for, whereas her attraction to Jon had been based on the physical aspect, she saw Lewis as a friend first and foremost. He was safe, reliable and even-tempered, with no ego for her to contend with.

When Lewis first entered her life the second time, he took on the role of emotional prop, so it only seemed natural that this would progress further and that a partnership would evolve. However, although she always knew where she stood with him, she did not really feel complete with Lewis. She felt that there was something missing within the partnership, for although she loved him in her own way, she was not in-love with him.

The check-out girl started running their goods over the bar code machine and shortly afterwards, the items were packed in the plastic bags and Lewis was parting with his money. He and Joanna then ambled down the isle towards the cigarette counter with another weeks groceries in tow, grinding the vehicle to a halt as they reached the paper and magazine rack at the side of the kiosk.

Lewis turned to her. "You stay here while I get some cigars." his gruff voice echoed around the store as he began to slouch off in the direction of the cigarette counter.

Bored, Joanna started to browse through the magazines, then ambled over to a pile of books stacked up just in front of the counter. Although she had no intention of buying anything, she wearily began sifting through the variety of literature.

The books on display were all non-fiction, ranging from dream analysis to horoscopes and the subjects surprised her somewhat, for never before had she been so overwhelmed by such a variety of new age subjects in one place, and soon became engrossed in the assortment of topics on the subject.

Lewis, having been served, was standing at her side before she had had time to investigate the whole pile. Grinning down at his girlfriend, he chuckled, "What's all this rubbish then?"

"Books on psychic stuff." she proclaimed in awe, "There's loads of them."

"And you were just saying the other day that it was about time you had a another reading." he smiled, and with that he eagerly wandered around to the far side of the pile to begin browsing through the books himself.

His gaze immediately fell upon a thick paperback, entitled The Giant Book Of Fortune, and promptly picked it up and started to flick through its contents.

"What you got there?" Joanna questioned him, as she pushed the trolley around the far side of the mound of books, to reach his side.

"Tells you different ways of telling fortunes." he explained, "Here, take a look." and with that, Joanna took the book from him and began scanning through it with interest.

"What do you think?" he prompted her.

"Looks very interesting. Especially the chapter on divination with cards."

"Want it?"

"You don't want to wait around while I queue." she replied.

He took the book back from her, "Do you want it?" he asked again.

"How much is it?"

Lewis turned it over, looking for the price. "One pound, ninety-nine."

She gave him a broad grin, "Well, I've always wanted to learn how to read the cards."

"That's all I wanted to know." and with that he sifted through his trouser pockets for some change and shuffled his way back to the counter, with book in hand.

5.00pm

Joanna had not managed to avert her attention from the book, from the moment they had returned from the supermarket. Although she had originally planned to go out riding on her pony, Zephyr, she found herself so fascinated by its contents that she could not draw herself away from the book, and had even found a deck of playing cards to practise layouts, suggested from it.

"Do us a reading then." Lewis said in a jocular fashion, as he sat on the floor opposite her.

"Alright .. But don't expect anything spectacular." She grinned, and with that she picked up the cards and handed the pack to Lewis, who shuffled and cut them with his left hand, before placing them back on the floor in front of him. She then picked up the pack and proceeded to lay them out using a method called the Temple of Fortune.

She started by laying out the first six cards on her right hand side, the first being closest to her and the sixth being furthest away. The seventh to twelfth cards were placed to the left-hand side, again the seventh closest to her, whilst the twelfth nearest Lewis.

She then proceeded to place the thirteenth to sixteenth to the left of the first six cards, the seventeenth to twenty-first across the top working from right to left, and the twenty-second to twenty-fifth just to the right of the seventh to twelfth cards, making what looked like a doorway.

Finally, she placed the twenty-sixth to the thirty-second cards across the top above the sixth, seventeenth to twenty-first and seventh cards, completing the Temple of Fortune layout. Ready to begin, she returned to the book for the next step.

"Right." she stated as she pointed to the first six and the thirteenth to sixteenth set of cards laid out. to the right of the Temple. "These ten cards represent your past. Let's have a look."

The first card laid was the king of clubs. "This I see as you." she said with an air of confidence, as she scanned over the other cards around it, whilst referring to the book at the same time. "There has been disappointment or annoyance to do with the heart," she continued as she pointed to the reversed eight of hearts. Then noticing the reversed seven of the same suit next to it, she continued, "which to be honest with you was a worthless infatuation on your part." She looked up at him for confirmation, but his expression gave nothing away.

The trend of the reading then took a sudden change to business, for the thirteenth card laid was the ten of diamonds. Flicking through the book, she read out loud, "A ten of diamonds next to an enquirers card and the eight of hearts, signifies a journey, which was a sea voyage. Ever worked overseas, Lewis?"

"Went to Jersey a couple of years ago, if you can count that."

"By plane, or ferry?"

"Ferry. I had to take the car and tools with me."

"Well, there you go then." She then continued to scan the cards. "Oh, dear. Did you suffer losses to do with this job?" she asked as she played with the reversed eight of clubs.

"Yep. The job was a pig, from start to finish. Lost quite heavily on that one."

Joanna then noticed two reversed sevens together, "Blimey." she stated, with a hint of a giggle to her voice. "According to the book, these two together mean that you will have a lover that will deceive you."

"Oh I see." he teased, "Going to run off with the milk man, are we?"

Ignoring his flippant remark, she continued "You've got a lot of reversed cards in your past."

Lewis then pointed to the final three cards, which were all aces. "Well, these aren't upside-down. What do these mean?"

"Umm." Joanna stalled for time, as she consulted the book. "Ah. This is better, these three mean that you show too much kindness."

"That's Me." he joked, as he threw his hands up in the air. "Too wonderful for my own good."

"Get away with you." she retorted and playfully pushed him over, sending him into a fit of giggles.

Joanna, composing herself, pointed to the cards laid out along the top of the Temple. "Right then, these are the cards that represent your present situation."

"Get on with it then, gi'l." he jested.

The first card, the seven of clubs, confused Joanna with its meaning, leaving her scratching her head in bewilderment.

"What is it?" Lewis broke her concentration.

"Well, according to this book, that card means a dark-haired child." She then looked up at him and, with a cheeky smile and a twinkle in her eye, she asked, "Is there something in your sordid past, that you haven't told me about. Enquiring minds need to know."

Lewis chuckled, "Not that I know of."

"Just as well." she continued to tease, before returning to the book, "Well, I don't understand that."

"Just skip over it then." Lewis suggested.

So she went to the two cards, which were both kings. "Ah. Well, these two mean that your good fortune will vary according the efforts that you put in." an audacious smile then crept across her face a second time, "Probably something to do with the dark-haired child." and promptly found a cushion being thrown at her from across the room.

Looking back at the cards, she found three tens together. "Guess what?" she stated, as she read from the book, "Yet more money worries."

"Oh what a surprise."

"Moving swiftly on, I think." she brushed over the last comment, "The queen of hearts, well, that must represent me." She then looked for the meaning of the following card, "And the nine of clubs reversed ... ah. An unexpected present."

"Hope that's got nothing to do with that dark-haired child." Lewis turned the tables to tease her.

"On your bike, buster." and with that she threw the cushion back at him. Joanna then moved on, looking for the meaning of the following two cards, which were both nines. "Now, these mean that impediments are on the way. So watch your comments, or another cushion will be heading in your direction."

Finally, she gazed upon the last two cards that represented his present situation. These were two knaves. "These two donate disagreements. What could this mean?"

"Probably with the old man. We're always arguing over something or other."

"Quite possibly." she confirmed, before turning her attention to his future, which were the ten cards to the left of the Temple. The first two cards were the reversed eight of spaces, followed by the knave of clubs. "According to the book, the eight represents temptation, " she then picked up the knave of clubs, "and this represents a dark, ardent young man."

"So you are going to run off with the milkman. Or ol' Tifty, the farrier. Well, I can quite see how Tifty would be such a temptation. All that earthy charm and subtle flirtation in Zephyr's stable. Don't think I haven't noticed?" he ribbed.

"Oh very funny. Chorkle. Chorkle. Besides, I said young man and Mr Tift is old enough to be my father. Mind you he is prone to being a tad ardent, I must confess; I have to wear my running shoes every time he comes to shoe Zephyr. That's apart from having you come with me, as my body guard - not that that's ever stopped him yet." she giggled. "Keeps me fit though - all that running around the yard." She then returned to the cards, "But seriously now, I see trouble concerning another man." She then noticed the queen of spades, "And this I think must be me, because it represents a divorced woman. Oh dear. Doesn't sound too good, does it? And look," she continued as she noticed the king of hearts next to the queen of diamonds, "Dangerous intrigues."

She quickly skipped over the meanings just divulged and moved on to the final five cards. The first two were the nine of hearts reversed and the eight of diamonds. "These two mean that there will be worries and obstacles concerning a social gathering in the country."

"A what?" he queried her.

"That's all it says here. Sorry, I do not know what else it could mean?" She then continued with the next two cards, which were the ace and queen of clubs. "These mean that there will be success in business dealings concerning a dark woman."

Finally, she turned to the last card, the knave of spades. "However, "she warned Lewis again, "The young man mentioned earlier is very prominent in your future. Beware of him, for he brings with him treachery and envy."

Having finished, Joanna gathered up the deck, with an air of regret for reading the cards. There had been no intent for upsetting her boyfriend, but she felt he was uneasy at what she had said the future held.

In desperation at lightening things up, she commented, "All a load of rubbish really."

"Hope so." Lewis replied flatly, "Maybe I had better go and see a professional reader myself."

"Tell you what, Pat often goes to clairvoyants. When I go to work on Monday, I'll ask her. I think she knows one in High Wycombe that is pretty good. Geraldine, I think her name is. Maybe Pat could give me her details, then we could both go together."

"Ok." His face then lifted into a boyish grin, "Fancy a cup of coffee then, Gypsy Joanna-lea?" and with that he jumped up and ambled out into the kitchen, leaving Joanna watching after him with sad eyes, and a feeling of regret for unduly upsetting her dearest friend.

CHAPTER TEN
10TH APRIL, 1993

1.50pm High Wycombe

Upon reaching Flackwell Heath, Lewis swung his Peugeot 405 into Treadway Hill and ground the car to a halt. They were lucky to have made an appointment to see Geraldine at such short notice, especially on a Saturday, for it was only due to a cancellation that the clairvoyant was able to see them both so quickly.

Clambering out of the red saloon, Lewis and Joanna wandered up to the wrought iron gate, with its peeling blue paint, which was partially obscured by an overgrown hedge.

"Well, this must be the place," Lewis pronounced as he pointed at the weathered house name nailed to the gate post, "Courtnell. Yes, this is it." And with that he boldly swung open the rusty old gate and, with rounded shoulders, he wandered up the overgrown garden path to the front door.

The detached house was remarkably larger than either of them had imagined, and despite the unkempt appearance of the boundary hedge, the building had been recently whitewashed. Hanging baskets, with winter pansies hung either side of the porch, wonderfully complementing the stained glass motif on the glazed front door, and polyanthus, with vibrant colours, were scattered haphazardly around the garden borders.

Joanna hesitantly reached out and rang the bell and, a few moments later, they heard footsteps on the wooden floorboards inside. The glazed door swung open and they were greeted by a small, ordinary looking woman, who invited them inside and led them through a corridor, to a tiny office at the rear of the property.

Then, in a business like fashion, she invited them to make themselves comfortable, whilst she dashed off momentarily to prepare herself for the consultation.

Lewis and Joanna sat quietly on a couch, gazing about them. The office had a small desk in the bay window, with a computer and answer phone sat upon it. There were pictures of the Madonna everywhere, along with various bible quotes and other religious artefacts. Only a framed certificate from the British Astrologers and Psychics Association broke the Catholic feel to the office.

Geraldine returned moments later. "Right. Who's first then?" her West Country accent prominent, as she beckoned one of her two clients to follow her.

"Do you want to go first, Lewis?" Joanna smiled nervously at her partner.

"It's alright, you go." So with that, Joanna tentatively trailed behind the woman into the sitting room, which overlooked and large and peaceful garden.

"Please sit." Geraldine invited the young woman to make herself comfortable on a two-seater settee. Obediently Joanna gingerly sank down into the plump, flowery cushions, perching herself precariously on the edge of the seat, in anticipation of the forthcoming events.

"Have you been to a clairvoyant before?" Geraldine enquired.

"Yes. Once. The woman gazed into a crystal ball."

"Right. Well I don't use a crystal ball, nor tarot cards or any other form of divination aid. I work as a medium, which means that I will just tell you what I am being given by spirit. You happy with that?"

"Yes." Joanna felt her guard start to come up, for the woman's abruptness made her feel slightly uncomfortable.

"Right then, we shall begin." and with that the clairvoyant placed a tape in the recorder and switched it on.

"Let me see." Geraldine started gazing about the room as if she was checking for something. "Let me see."

A moments pause, then the woman started rubbing hers hands together in an anxious fashion. "Why are you and your boyfriend not married, dear?" she asked, as she stared straight past Joanna's shoulder and out into the garden.

"Don't feel the need for it." Joanna found her reply sharp with annoyance at such a question.

"I've got a child around you. A little girl. Do you plan to have children?"

"No." Came the abrupt reply.

"Shame. I've got a little girl around you. I would like to see you with children." Geraldine then veered off onto another track.

"You like everything labelled and neat. Videos and things like that. Perfection coming out in you, you see? You love it. It's like a hobby, in a way. It's quite nice for you - doesn't harm any one does it? I like that actually, I like that a lot. Everything labelled; dates, times. Do you like photography also?"

"My boyfriend does, yes."

"Yes, I see that. Cameras. And videos, he likes watching videos also?"

"Yes."

"Yes. You're both a lot alike, aren't you? Everything labelled, in order. He is quite an interesting man. Bit of a wanderer at times, if you know what I mean? He's not always there, head in the clouds. He keeps himself to himself, no trouble to anybody, dear. He's one of them chaps that the more I see of him, the more I feel your suited to each other. Take your time. Get finances sorted out. People should wait to get their house in order, but they don't do they dear?" Geraldine tutted. "Well, there we are. Are you an animal lover, dear?"

"Yes."

"I see you surrounded by animals; dogs, cats. Array of animals. Suit you to have a farm or something. I feel that would be rather nice for you. This make any sense to you?"

"I have four cats, and my boyfriend has a dog."

"Gracious. What a menagerie." the woman gave a quick smile, before changing direction a second time.

"A lot of your problems stem from back in time. Looking back, I felt wealth around you, dear. Were your parents wealthy?"

"Comfortable I suppose."

"I think so, I would say yes. You could always have what you wanted. Then there was this row with your parents, either you and them, or a row between themselves. Then there was this resentment in you - no body will give you anything. You've had to do it on your own. There had always been someone to bale you out, but now there isn't. You are responsible for your own debts, dear. You must work for what you want. Grow up, dear, if you went out and got extra work, then you would be too busy to worry about how hard done by you think you are. Why should your family, or boyfriend support you financially? You brought your worries on yourself, so you must pay for them yourself. You understand me, dear?"

Geraldine then began to twitch her nose. "Oh." she commented with surprise "I've got horses with you. You got a horse?"

"Yes."

"Know what I just got then? The smell of horse muck." the clairvoyant's face then dropped, and she glared at Joanna furiously, "Why do you keep it? You can't afford to give it what it needs, dear. The place you keep it is not satisfactory, now is it. You haven't the time, or the resources, or the knowledge. Never mind about what you love in life, or what you want, it's a wise person who knows what they can cope with, and what they can not. Understand me dear? Loan the horse out, or get rid of it. You feel you are doing the horse some good by keeping it, but you're not. Let it go to a better home and live a better life with someone who can look after it better. Wake up, be practical. Stop living in a dream world. Prevents you from doing a lot in your life, dear. It stands in the way of holidays, the mountains, the this the that; it gets in the way of everything, understand? Now why that doesn't bother you, that's all right, but I feel your boyfriend has a choice, don't you? If he wants to go to Europe or something like that then he should have the opportunity to do it, not be told by you 'we can't because of this horse, or that animal', it's not fair. You've got to learn how to share. You've got to learn also that you can't have every thing you want. You are terribly selfish, dear. You always want your own way and, if you can't get it, then you will create such a din; shouting and screaming, until you get what you want. Please don't think I am being unkind to you for the sake of it - I am just trying to help you by getting you to realise what you are like, as a person. You're very difficult to live with, dear. Your nagging is enough to drive a man to distraction, yes it is."

The woman's face then lifted, taking on a completely different expression. "Twenty six it quite a good age. Are you twenty six now?" She enquired, in a much softer voice.

"Yes" Joanna flatly replied.

"Oh good. When were you twenty-six?"

"5th October."

Ignoring the reply, Geraldine continued, "I liked March, when you're twenty-six. Did you move in with your boyfriend in March?"

"No. He moved in with me a year last June."

Geraldine looked puzzled. "Why do I feel commitment? Was that just a particularly good month for you?"

"No." Joanna gave a nervous laugh.

"It was not? How strange, I quite like March. So perhaps something happened in March that was not agreeable to you; a bit of trouble, but it turns out for the better, because it brings a change, see? Whatever happened in March brings a change in your life, which I quite like. A new beginning. Perhaps we haven't seen the good side of this yet, but we'll look for that, OK?"

"I do feel that you can see into the future, yourself. Are you aware of that?"

"I've started to learn how to read the playing cards."

"I've got someone holding a crystal ball to you, you see, which is symbolic of the ability of looking into the future. I feel that you can do that, so if you want to do this, I would recommend that for you, I don't see that as a problem. I think you would rather enjoy it. Also, I feel that you will also begin to hear a voice in your ear. Do you get that yet?"

"No."

"Oh." the disappointment was prominent in Geraldine's voice, "Well, don't be surprised one day, if you do. Like someone telling you to say something else; telling you what to say, you see?"

"I do get vivid dreams." Joanna found herself begin to open up to the clairvoyant. "Some recurring; some prophetic ..."

Geraldine cut her off, "That come true? That's right. Same thing, but watch for the voice."

She then stared back out into the garden, smiling serenely. "Watch also for a young man coming into your life, to do with work. He will help you a lot, so take notice of him. Also a change of job. I'd like to see you travelling around - not stuck in one office all day. Drives you bananas, that does. Also I get study. Are you studying at the moment?"

"Yes. I am doing a home study course for writing; articles, short stories - that type of thing."

"Really? Well, I feel this is good for you." Her face then dropped once more, "Who is Mark please, dear?"

Joanna looked puzzled, as she wracked her brains trying to think of a Mark.

"An older man," Geraldine tried to help her, "I'm getting told to beware of a Mark; don't take him too seriously. As with the younger chap, I also feel he is to do with work. That new job I mentioned. This Mark's alright, but don't take him too seriously, dear."

Her gaze then returned to the room. "I will say by the time October comes, life will be richer for you. Much better. A new beginning. Everything will be much more settled for you, from September, October time onwards. You will begin to start looking forward, instead of behind you, you see?"

Geraldine then began to sum up the reading, as she drew their meeting to a close, "I'd love a daughter for you - the name Emma springs to mind, how strange." she giggled, "Just, no more showing off though. There is a little girl in you, in a way it's kind of nice about you. I wouldn't like you to change too much, but it does get you into trouble at times, you know? Finances will come better, it just needs time and effort, and then you can have your horses and your animals. Is there anything you wish to ask me please?"

Joanna thought for a moment, then replied, "I don't think so?"

"Have I answered what you wanted to know then?"

"Yes, I think you've about covered everything."

"Good." Geraldine stated, as she turned the tape off and ejected it from the recorder. "Well then," and rising to her feet, "That's you done." and promptly ushered the bewildered young woman out of the sitting room, and back into the office.

"Lewis, isn't it?" Geraldine smiled sweetly at the six-foot-four man."

"Yep." he gruffly replied.

"Follow me, please." and with that, Lewis found himself being lead into the sitting room.

Throwing himself into the plump, fluffy cushions of the two-seater, Lewis made himself at home before Geraldine had had chance to invite him to take a seat. Undeterred, Geraldine took her place on the seat opposite and, smiling at the thirty-two year old man, she enquired, "Have you been to a clairvoyant before?"

"No." came the abrupt reply, followed by a deep, hearty laugh.

"Well, Lewis, I don't use Tarot cards, or crystal balls, or any other form of aid. What I do is allow spirit to tell me what they want to tell you. In other words, I just sit here talking to you." she then placed another tape in the recorder. "Are you ready?"

"Yep."

"Right then." and with that she turned the tape onto record and commenced. "I am getting told that you work very hard, with little reward. Does that make sense to you?"

"Overworked and underpaid - that's me." he giggled, as he crossed his legs and reclined deeper into the settee.

"With little, or no support. Yes?"

Lewis shrugged his shoulders.

"Things will settle for you after September. Are you living on your own? I am getting that you are very much on your own?"

"No, I live with my girlfriend."

"Then maybe she does not support you as much as she should. Seems to me she is quite happy to spend your money, but not to give you support when you need it, understand? I keep getting two rings with you. One is whole, but the other broken. Are you divorced?"

"No."

"Were you in a previous relationship where you lived as man and wife, that failed?"

"Nope."

"Strange. I am definitely getting the two rings. Are you happy with your present relationship?"

"Yes. Couldn't be happier."

"Is she happy with the relationship?"

"Yes, as far as I know."

"I feel that there are problems here, you mark my words. Someone is telling me that you are not suited and that there is unhappiness around you."

Geraldine then swiftly moved on to another subject, leaving that one truly up in the air, "I see you sitting by a river, drinking wine. You seem very contented. This I feel is in the future; ten years time or so. You're reflecting on the past. You are very successful by this time. I feel you have got two businesses; one is to do with food and drink. A restaurant, or a pub, or something. This is where you are, by the river. Oh yes. Life is good. The other business is more in the mechanical line. Does any of this make sense to you?"

"The mechanical bit does, yes. I'm a dairy engineer."

"Self-employed, yes?"

Lewis nodded.

"Well, I feel that you will be balancing the two up, although I don't feel you will be doing engineering, as such. More of a shop type thing. You know, buying and selling machinery."

"Possible, I suppose. Don't know about the restaurant bit though."

"Well, I can see you sipping wine, and surrounded by food. Watch out for that waistline though. And take care over how much you drink. I know you are rather partial to the vino, but too much is not a good thing, understand? Just keep an eye on it."

She then changed direction; "The present is not as settled as you would like. I feel there are many problems now. Who are you infatuated with, please?"

Lewis shrugged his shoulders.

"I am getting worthless passion for someone. This I feel stems from way back in your past, but you are still carrying this around with you, even now, you understand me?"

"Not really, no."

"Think on my words, yes? Spirit are very concerned." Geraldine then turned to his current relationship, as she turned her gaze to the garden. "Your girlfriend. Do you plan to get married?"

"One day maybe, yes."

"Yes, I think that would be good for you, dear; give you more security. Children also?"

"If I could persuade her, yes. She doesn't want kids though."

"I see a boy around you, in the near future. She will come round to your way of thinking. It would be good for you both. Your girlfriend likes her own way, doesn't she? Gives you a hard time, if she don't get it either, yes? Children would stop that." her attention then returned to him, and looking him straight in the eye she stated confidently, "There are a lot of money worries around you at the moment. It's as if there is more going out than coming in."

"My work is slack at the moment."

"Yes, I can see that. Does your partner work?"

"Yes."

"Well, let her take on the responsibility of paying some of the bills, dear. Blimey, how can you be expected to do it, if you've not got it? After all, she has created half the debts, so let her deal with them, understand? Look after yourself more. Your health needs attention. I feel you get hot very quickly. More exercise would help, yes?"

"I agree I am rather podgy," Lewis grinned as he patted his tummy.

"No, I didn't mean that you were overweight, just a little unfit." Geraldine paused for a moment, frowned, then stated coldly; "I feel there is going to be some jealously around you in July, August time concerning a third party. This will cause disagreements between you and your partner, but I am being told that the effort that you put in will be the rewards that you reap, understand? I am also getting the name Mandy, dear. Does this mean anything to you?"

"No."

This Mandy is in some way connected to the problem, and also work. But don't worry, it will all sort itself out, about September time. Do you have a dog, or puppy?"

"Yes."

"I am being told, by your grandfather, to pay attention to its feet. He seems concerned that the claws should be cut or something. Funny thing to come out with, that. Still, take note, as he is quite worried about it. Also, I feel that you do not have enough space around you at the moment. By that I mean that the place where you live seems too small for what you want to do. Your granddad is telling me that you should consider moving to somewhere bigger, with more land or something. Somewhere where you don't feel so hemmed in, you see? I've got America, and I get a lot of travelling with you. Do you like travelling, or travel around with your job?"

"Yes, I work all around Britain. Not aboard though."

"Well, America seems to be prominent, in connection with work. Maybe even emigrating to America? Watch out for an opportunity to work there, for it will make you very happy. Oh. Someone has just told me that you like to invent things. Anything mechanical. You love to tinker with machinery. There is something mulling around in your head at the moment, which I am being told that you should start putting in practice. What is this, please?"

"I am thinking of making a machine that picks up horse droppings from the field, which can be either towed on the back of a tractor or four wheel drive, or something that is light enough to push around the field. There doesn't seem to be anything on the market at the moment that can do that and I know that my girlfriend gets fed up of wondering around the field for hours, shit shovelling."

"Is there a call for that type of thing then?" Geraldine asked, intrigued by the idea of anyone even wanting to pick up horse dung from a field.

"Yes, because a horse, or a cow will not eat grass grown where their droppings have fallen, so the ground has to be managed accordingly. At the moment, the shit has to either be picked up using a shovel and wheel barrow, or the grazing has to be rotated with cows, or sheep, to refertilize the land."

"Really, how interesting. Learn something new every day. Sounds viable, you should do something about it. I feel it would prove successful. If you have a talent, you should use it, in my opinion. Would it cost much to develop a crude prototype?"

"Not really no. My dad's got loads of scrap iron lying around at his yard that I could use."

"Then maybe, while work is slack, you should concentrate on developing it. Putting your ideas into practise, so to speak. I like that idea, I like that a lot. Funny, I got this invention thing come through so strongly. It's unusual to get something like that on a reading." She seemed to have amazed herself at picking up on something so extraordinary, and the delight showed in her face.

She then began to summarise the reading, as it drew to an end, "So money seems to be the prominent thing in your life at the moment, although this will prove a temporary predicament. After September, as I said, I see things starting to get better for you, although I would like to see you moving residence. Watch your health and tell that girlfriend of yours to contribute more. Have you any questions for me, Lewis?" she smiled.

"Yes. Umm, is my granddad always around me?"

"Yes he is. He is what I call a guide, which means that he keeps watch over you and protects you. We all have them around us. Its lovely to know that someone you love, who has passed over to the other side can still be in contact with you, isn't it? Are there any other questions?"

"No, I don't think so."

"Good." and with that she retrieved the tape from the recorder and handed it to him. She then got up and ushered him out of the sitting room and back to the office, where Joanna was sitting quietly on the couch.

"Ready then?" Lewis bellowed, as he waved his tape about. Joanna jumped to her feet, relieved that it was finally time to go and paid the woman her dues.

Geraldine ushered them both back through the corridor, to the front door. "Take care and God bless you. " Geraldine's West Country accent filled the hallway, as she touched Joanna on the shoulder. Then, moments later, the couple found themselves back outside in the sunshine, as the door swung shut behind them.

CHAPTER ELEVEN
12TH APRIL 1993

9.30 am Chipperfield

Pat dragged herself into the office, after another hectic weekend. She had a harassed air about her, for the journey to work that day had proved exasperating, on top of everything else. "That flipping daughter of mine wouldn't get up this morning, and the traffic was terrible on the roads. I think there must have been some trouble on the M25 or something, because Croxley Green was just at a stand still." she moaned.

"Good morning to you too, Pat." Joanna teased her with sarcasm.

"Oh. Yes. Good morning Jo." she giggled, as she placed her bag on the desk. "Well? How did the reading go?"

Joanna gave her half a smile. "I got well and truly told off." she proclaimed.

Sinking into her seat, Pat continued, "But why? What did she say?"

"Basically, I am a spoilt little rich bitch, who should give up Zephyr so that Lewis and I have more money for holidays. Also, Lewis should not be expected to contribute towards costs like food, telephone, electric bills etcetera."

"You're kidding." Pat's voice was full of disgust. "But Lewis should help out. After all, he is helping to create them - especially the phone bill, he is never off the bloody thing."

"Well, that's what she told me.   According to Geraldine, I created the debts, therefore I should not expect anyone else to help me pay for them."

"Was she aware that you and Lewis lived together?" Pat questioned her further.

"I said that my boyfriend lived with me, but I did not let it be known that the boyfriend was Lewis."

"What about Lewis' reading. Did she say anything about this to him?"

"According to his reading, he might as well be living on his own, because I do not give him any support. Also, I like to spend all his money."

"What money? He's never got any."

"Exactly. And Geraldine picked up on that as well. She told him that I should take care of the bills, whilst he took time out to work on his 'horse shit picker-upperer' invention."

"Well, that is all very well, provided you can both afford to eat. Surely it would be more sensible for him to find other work - not art-fart around. After all, he could always work on his invention in his spare time. Everyone else has to follow up their dreams that way, don't they?" Pat was overwrought at the prospect of such an impractical statement even being suggested, let alone from someone who was supposed to use their gift for projective guidance. She sighed, and shook her head in disgust. "I don't know." she stated flatly, "That is unbelievable. Totally irresponsible."

"Mind you, she did say the invention would be a success, though." Joanna found herself excusing Geraldine's statement.

"Oh please." Pat tutted, "Don't try and justify her actions. Yes, it would most probably be a success, if Lewis would get off his arse and do something about it, but how long has he being talking about building a prototype? I can remember you saying about this ever since you first got Zephyr, a year last June. "She shook her head. "No. If Lewis couldn't be bothered when he had the money to do it, then he certainly won't now. Not without the finances to support it." Pat was certainly incensed at such a suggestion. "So what else did this woman tell you ?"

Joanna pondered, as she recalled other things told to her by the clairvoyant. "She said that I was going to change my job, and that two men were coming into my life in connection with this. The first is a younger man who will help me, and the second an older man called Mark, who I should be aware of."

Pat pulled a face. "What did Lewis say about that?"

"He brushed it off, as he does. But ironically, he was warned about a woman called Mandy. Again to do with work. Apparently, she would be responsible for some sort of jealousy that will cause disagreements between us." Joanna raised her eyebrows as she spoke the words.

"How much did you pay for these readings?"

"Twenty pounds each."

"Well, I am speechless." she growled. "Talk about causing trouble. Did she say anything positive during either reading?"

"She likes the idea of my writing course. She told me that she felt it was good for me. She also feels that I should look for a job that gets me out and about more. A rep for example. She feels that I am not happy cooped up in an office all day."

Pat smiled softly, "Well, you're not really, are you." she confirmed, "I tend to agree with Geraldine on that one. But how do you feel about the overall reading?"

"I don't know. To be honest, I felt more unsettled when I came out, than I did when I went in."

Pat then began to rummage through her bag and, pulling out a folded piece of newspaper, she handed it to the deflated young woman facing her. "Don't know if you are interested, but I saw this article in the Watford Observer about a shop in the Lower High Street. Maybe you could see someone there, who will be able to give you some proper guidance?"

Joanna took the thin, crinkled paper from her colleges hand and, unfolding it, she began to read the feature intently.

The article was about a new age shop called the Oracle, run by a woman called Faye Cullen, who offered psychic readings from resident readers, as well as the normal occult paraphernalia.

One such consultant was specifically mentioned; 26 year old Paul Hitt. He was described as being 'exactly what a seer should look like; tall and thin, with dark eyes and long, tapering fingers. He would not be out of place in a mediaeval portrait.'

The article certainly made interesting reading and Joanna found herself intrigued with the idea of such a shop. "Have you been there yet, Pat?" she asked excitedly.

"No. But I know where it is. It is opposite Tesco's." Pat beamed. "I'm going to try to get down there next Saturday, if I've got time. If you're interested, why don't we both go together?"

Joanna thought about it for a minute, then replied, "I've got a better idea. You know I'm on this creative writing course? Well, the assignment that I have got to do next is interviewing someone who is involved in an unusual trade. What do you think to the idea of me writing to this Faye Cullen, informing her that I am doing this home study course and that I would like to interview her, with the view to having the article published with a women's magazine. Do you think she'd mind?"

Pat smiled, "Well, can't help to ask can it? The worst she could say is no."

Joanna pondered over her idea, then flatly stated, "Bit of a cheek though."

"Don't ask, don't get. I would go for it, if I were you."

Joanna scratched her head; "Maybe I'll mull it over for a couple of days." A cheeky smile then crept across the young woman's face; "I could even consult the cards about it."

"Why not?" Pat grinned back at her, "Your readings have proved accurate enough with me, so why not ask them about contacting the Oracle." and with that the two women settled down to a hard days work.

CHAPTER TWELVE
3RD JUNE 1993

10.00 am Watford

Joanna sat in Tesco's coffee shop sipping at her steaming black coffee, whilst preparing herself for the interview at the Oracle.

Her 'couple of days' to mull over the idea of contacting Faye Cullen had proved considerably more than that. In fact, she finally plucked up the courage to write the letter on the 21st May, six weeks after reading the original article, and even then she found herself carrying it around for a week or so, before Lewis finally lost patience with her and posted the letter himself.

The reason for her hesitance was not so much the thought of the proprietor telling her that she was not interested, it was more a case of what the cards had shown her. A mixed bunch foretold excellent financial opportunities, which was pleasing, and success to do with the venture. However, it also showed her that there would be a lot of trouble ahead, should she decide to contact Faye. The main concern seemed to be in connection with a young, dark haired man that had danger surrounding him.

However, there was also reference to health problems and difficulties in her current relationship, which she feared might be what Geraldine had picked up on, back in April.

Never-the-less, Lewis seemed far less deterred by the outcome each time the cards were consulted, stating that visiting the shop in a professional capacity was a one off, and that nothing further would ever come of it, either in connection with business, or otherwise. And so, she found herself sipping nervously at her coffee, whilst reading over the twenty-nine prepared questions to Faye and her consultants.

In no time at all, her appointment with Faye had arrived and so, grabbing her black bag in on one hand and the prepared notes in the other, she marched out of the cafeteria and off towards the Oracle.

Joanna apprehensively opened the shop door and crept inside. The place seemed deserted, except for the mellow sounds of a meditation tape playing in the background, accompanied by the scent of sandalwood, which allowed relaxing vibrations to ooze out from every wall, giving the shop a lifting ambience.

It was at this point that Joanna began to realise just how out of her depth she was. She had never interviewed anyone before, let alone entered a shop of this calibre. The place seemed more befitting to Glastonbury, with the hippies, than it did in central Watford. She had not had the faintest idea quite what she might find in a new age shop, but what surrounded her was a far cry from what she had imagined.

A friendly face then popped out from behind the doorframe of the back room and, gazing upon the black jeaned and leather jacketed young woman, she grinned, "Can I help you, love?"

"Are you Faye?" Joanna found it difficult to hide her nerves, as she uttered the words.

"Yes. Are you Joanna?" Joanna nodded. "Well, come on through to the back then, Jo." and with that, Faye beckoned the young woman to follow her through to the consulting room.

As she entered the back room, Joanna noticed a second person leaning against the wall. He was tall, slim and about the same age as herself. The man then turned to face her; "Would you like a tea, or coffee?" he enquired with a soft, soothing voice.

"Coffee please. Black, without." and so, he disappeared out into the kitchen area and was gone.

"That was Paul, my resident reader." Faye informed her, as she showed Joanna to one of the reading tables. "I thought we'd sit here, to do the interview."

"Thank you for agreeing to see me, Faye." Joanna smiled softly, as she made herself comfortable on the chair.

"My pleasure." The plump, middle-aged woman replied. "So where were you thinking of getting this published then?"

"There are no promises that I will get anyone interested in the article," Joanna covered herself, "but I thought I'd try some of the women's magazines to start with."

"Oh right." Faye gave a broad smile, "Well, I hope you succeed. Could prove profitable for both of us. I guess you'd get paid for the article, if they accept it, yes?"

"Hopefully." Joanna gave the motherly woman a flash of a cheeky grin, before taking on a more serious expression. "Right then, "she stated, as she shuffled the papers to find her notes, "Would you like me to start?"

"Yes. Whenever you're ready." Faye replied.

"Firstly, you will have to excuse me, but I wrote down the type of questions that I would like to ask - so that I don't forget, you know. Head like a sieve, me."

"Oh don't worry, Jo. I'm the worst one for remembering anything." the woman chuckled.

"Ok. then, Faye." Joanna said, as she smoothed a rogue curly lock from her face, "When did you first become interested in the occult?"

"I've been interested ever since I was a child. There has always been a fascination there for me. However, I didn't do anything about it until after opening up the shop."

"You said, 'after'. What do you mean by that?"

"Well, I originally got this place to open a craft shop, but decided to change it to a new age one, later."

"Really? Why the decision to change?" Joanna asked, as she began to scrawl some notes.

"Well, there is nothing else like the Oracle in this area, so I thought to myself, 'what a good idea - something different to brighten Watford up' so, here I am."

"Are you psychic yourself, then?"

"Everyone is psychic; it's a case of whether you chose to follow it up or not. However, to have a shop like the Oracle, you have to be spiritually aware. There is no point jumping onto the new age bandwagon just to make a fast buck, because most of the people who come into the shop are also of a spiritual mind and, therefore, will pick up whether you are genuine or not."

At that point, Paul returned with Joanna's coffee, momentarily interrupting the proceedings. He then sat on a chair by another reading table, to the far side of the consulting room and lit a cigarette.

"So why do people come into a shop like this?" Joanna asked, as she lifted her mug to her lips.

"Some need help or advise, either through readings, alternative medicines, or books and tapes. Others are experienced psychics who want to purchase crystal balls, Tarot decks or the like. Then there are those professional people who come in, such as astrologers, who offer their services via the shop, and also people who just want to burn incense sticks and oils, or like pot-pourri or candles in the home. Basically, my customers are people from all walks of life."

"Do you read the Tarot yourself, or do you leave that to the likes of Paul here?" she jokingly enquired, as she pointed over her shoulder at the consultant.

"I started to divine using Tarot in February of this year, and tend to read them clairvoyantly, although I usually let the resident reader deal with most of the clients."

"What exactly does clairvoyant mean?"

Sensing that Faye might have trouble answering Joanna's question, Paul cut into the interview, "Clairvoyance is using Spirit, whilst a tarot reader using psyche works with their sixth sense, or third eye."

"By Spirit, you mean your guides, yes?" Joanna tried to clarify what he meant. Paul nodded. "So if clairvoyance is using your guides, what is a medium?"

"A medium hears what Spirit is saying, whereas a clairvoyant only gets 'a feel' as to what spirit is saying. In other words, a medium can hold a conversation with Spirit, whereas a clairvoyant will just say something to the inquirer, then wonder where they got the information from."

Joanna was a little confused. "But I thought a feel for something was using psyche?"

"Yes, it is all using psyche, no matter what you do, but a psychic, using their sixth sense is merely gathering their information from the inquirer; not spirit."

"Like reading someone's mind then?" Joanna gave him a flash of a smile.

"Yes."

"Oh I see, so it works on the same lines as a psychic being, let's say, the office junior and the medium being the director. Yes?"

"Something like that." Paul tried to hold back the laughter. "However, the best of the best are the physical mediums and there are not many around, due to the psychic energy that is required."

"What's a physical medium, then?" The young woman frowned.

"You've heard of a trance medium?" Joanna nodded, although all she really knew about them was that she imagined all trance mediums' to resemble those weird, floaty-dressed, old hags portrayed in films. She certainly did not understand the concept of the way a trance medium worked. However, sensing her lack of understanding, Paul continued, "Well, as you know, a trance-medium allows Spirit to temporarily take them over, so that the spirit becomes in charge of the living body.

This enables the soul of the deceased to tell the inquirer exactly what they want to, without misinterpretation." he shrugged his shoulders. "Now, a physical medium goes one step further and, using their own ectoplasm, the spirit of the deceased person builds up into a physical form next to the medium, until it is as solid as the living body."

Joanna pulled a face, "Sounds disgusting."

At this point, Faye piped in. "It is an extremely dangerous practice, and takes years of training."

Ignoring Faye, Joanna's attention remained firmly fixed on the consultant. "So what would you class yourself as then, Paul?"

"I'm a trance medium, although as a healer I tend to work psychically."

"Which means?"

"Instead of using Spirit to assist me with healing, I tend to use my own energy," He explained, "whereas you, I feel, would heal spiritually."

"Oh. I can't heal anyone." Joanna dismissed his assumption. Then, with a glint in her eye, she continued, "Tried on my rabbit once, but it still died."

With a broad grin, Paul jumped up and crossed the room, "Hold your hands out, face up." he requested. Intrigued, Joanna immediately responded.

"Yep. As I thought. Healing hands." He confirmed his theory.

"How can you tell? Or are you just buttering me up, so that I write lots of wonderful things about you, in my article?"

Smiling softly down at her, he pointed to her palm with one of his tapered fingers, "See those white blotches? They are a sign of healing hands." He then held out his own left hand. "Look at mine. See all the white pigment on the palm there. Now hold one arm out in front of you." Completely yielding to his assertiveness, she extended an arm as requested. Placing one hand about two inches above her wrist, and the other two inches below it, he asked, enthusiastically; "Feel anything?"

"No." she replied, perplexed as to what she was supposed to experience. But within seconds of uttering her answer, she began to feel a warm glow surrounding the area, along with a tingling sensation spreading down towards her fingers. "Yes, I can feel something now. My whole arm is warming up."

He then withdrew his hands and shook them, before returning to his seat at the far side of the consulting room. "All you have to do is place your hands about two to three inches away from the patient and ask your guides to help you to heal them. Then, after a couple of minutes, remove your hands and shake the negatives from them."

"Is that it?"

Paul frowned, seemingly listening to someone else, then told her, "But don't try to heal anyone just after you've eaten, never overdo the healing - better little and often than all at once, and always thank your guides after administering healing, or they will get annoyed with you and take your gift away." His expression then relaxed once more, and leaning back in his chair, he lit another cigarette.

The shop door then opened and Faye, making her excuses, left the table and wandered through to the front, leaving Joanna alone with the consultant.

To break the silence, the young woman decided to question the psychic further, "So are your guides the same as ghosts, then?"

"No. Guides, work to help you. They are of Gods light. The Holy Spirit, if you like. Whereas ghosts are generally earthbound, which mean that they have not gone upstairs to be judged for one reason or another."

"So what about, let's say for example, I went to a medium and they told me that my granddad was saying this, or saying that. He would be earthbound would he?"

"Not necessarily. If he has gone to judgement, then he is effectively of the Holy Spirit and will therefore be a 'clean' spirit - by that I mean that he will be pure from earth bound feelings, such as greed, temptation or violence.

However, if he has not been judged, then effectively he still carries with him all that we do, as living beings."

"So let me get this straight. What you are saying is, if a rapist dies and goes to heaven to be judged, then he might return as someone's guide, without the tendency to rape. Whereas, if he has not been judged, he could still act out rape, even as a spirit?"

Paul nodded knowledgeably. "I've got something that must be earthbound in my house then, instead of a guide, because it's presence makes me feel uneasy - especially in the bathroom, for some reason."

"Only one ghost?" he raised his eyebrows.

"Well, I think there are three, actually. There is definitely a little girl around, because she often comes to me when I am about to drop off to sleep. The second spook is the dead brother of Mrs Sayles who lives up the other end of my road. Apparently, as the story goes, Mrs Sayles lived with her brother, Jesse, in my house until he died. Jesse, apparently, was a real miserable old sod, who never married, and who gave her a hell of a life while he was alive. I think that the second one is him, although I have referred to that particular spook as 'M.O.G. in the bog', for ages."

"M.O.G. in the bog?" Paul looked puzzled. "Why M.O.G.?"

"It stands for Miserable Old Git. Quite apt really, if it is him. Anyway, he doesn't bother me much, so I don't bother him."

"And the third ghost?"

"Well, I don't know much about that one. My sister once said she felt it was a little old lady dressed in black, but I don't know. I've never really been able to pick up on that spook, to be honest."

"Probably the best way." he flatly stated.

"Why do you say that?" Joanna questioned his statement, but the consultant just replied, "No reason.", then swiftly changed the subject. "You talk to spirit don't you? Claire, one of my guides, has been driving me nuts, because she wants to say hello to you."

"You're the second person to tell me that I can talk to spirit, but I've never heard any dulcet tones from beyond the grave." A hint of parody passed her lips, as she spoke the words. Then, smiling sweetly, Joanna continued, "However, not wishing to upset anyone - hello Claire."

Paul smiled softly, as his dark, almond shaped eyes danced with delight, "Claire says 'hello' back. Besides, you can communicate with spirit, so stop doubting yourself. After all, you talk with the little girl at your house, don't you?" Joanna nodded. "Well then, what makes you think that you can't now."

"Yes, but that is when I am drifting off to sleep. To be honest, I don't know whether I am dreaming it or not. She generally appears just before I have this recurring dream..."

"About what?" Paul abruptly interrupted her. And so Joanna found herself telling him about that desolate land where she first met Emma and the

Israelite. The place where Pegasus came, ridden by Taliesim, who protected her from the Archangel of Despair and his followers on their black chargers. She gave her account of how her husband was sent into the eternal pit, and the death and destruction that hung over, and engulfed, the entire land as if life itself was of no worth.

Paul sat there, motionless, listening to her words. Then, once she had finished her tale, he asked, "Were you aware that you astral project? By that I mean your spirit leaving your body during sleep and going off to other places or dimensions?"

"I haven't really given it much thought." Joanna shrugged.

"Those weren't dreams at all." Paul informed her. "You were taken to another time and place to be shown something of great importance, by your guides. Were you aware that the Israelite is one of your guides?"

"I've never really given that much thought either, to be honest."

"Well he is, and I suspect he has also told you who he is. Can you remember anything that he has told you?"

"Not really. The dreams are so weird, you see. And the Israelite seems to talk in riddles." She then frowned, as she desperately tried to recall some of what he had told her, but the only thing that came to mind was when the Israelite had once referred to himself as, 'The Ravenous Wolf.'"

"Ravenous wolf, eh?" Paul smiled, knowingly. "Have you got a Bible at home?"

Surprised that the Bible should suddenly come into the conversation, Joanna sighed with despair. "No, I don't think so." she replied as she solemnly shook her head.

Then, remembering a tatty old one in the loft, that Lewis brought with him when he moved in, she corrected herself, "Oh. Wait a minute, I think I do, yes."

"Well, get it and ask Mr Ravenous Wolf to quote a passage from it, for you. Then you will know who he really is. Or, why not ask him outright? It is obviously time for you to know who your guides are."

Paul then went onto another surprising subject, "Do you have faith?"

"Oh. I'm not religious. I think that Christians and the like are far too hypocritical.

To be honest with you, I haven't the time for all that."

Paul's face took a stern expression, as he glared back at her. "That is not what I asked. Do you believe in God?"

Joanna suddenly remembered having this type of conversation before. She also recalled being given a dressing down for confusing Faith and religion. For the fear of a second grilling, she wisely replied, "Yes. I believe in God, so yes, I have Faith."

"Good. That is all I need to know. Now, when you get home, dig out that Bible and read whatever your guide tells you to read. In fact, there are some really good stories in the Bible."

Joanna nodded submissively, although she really did not have any desire to start becoming a Bible basher. However, she had to confess that she was impressed by Paul's authority and knowledge on the spiritual aspects, as well as being pleasantly surprised that he accepted God. For some reason, she had never associated Tarot readers with being God fearing people before - thinking that religions were for God and that psychics were for atheists. The idea of a psychic acknowledging his God centre confused her somewhat, for she knew that Christians actively condemned such gifts, with hundreds of books on the market attacking the new age concept. However, here before her was a man that was actively pro-God, just as Geraldine was pro-Catholic; with her effigies of the Madonna scattered about her office. Maybe talking to, and working with spirit, gave them a greater understanding of God than someone with a dog collar, who just read scriptures from a book - who knows? But it was definitely food for thought, and Joanna began to see the whole subject in a new light.

"Do you just do readings here, or do you also do party bookings?" she found herself blurting out the words, before she had chance to think what she was saying.

"I do party bookings, yes." he replied, with his soft, soothing voice.

"Great." she smiled. "I've got quite a few friends who would be interested in having readings. Would it be possible for me to arrange for you to come to my house one evening?"

"Fine, yes. I do a maximum of six people; the readings are taped and cost twelve pounds per head, and each consultation lasts about thirty, to forty-five minutes." his eyes danced, as he spoke the words. "Just ring me here at the shop, once you've arranged with your friends what night would be best for you."

"Well, what nights are best for you?" Joanna enquired, thoughtfully.

"Probably Tuesday's, because I have a day off Wednesdays, but it really doesn't matter to me."

At that point Faye returned from the shop, having had a long chat with a regular customer. She resumed her post opposite Joanna at the reading table and, making herself comfortable, she giggled, "Sorry about that, Jo. Right then, where were we?" And with that Joanna turned her attention back to the interview and commenced with her questions with renewed enthusiasm and passion for the subject.

CHAPTER THIRTEEN
15TH JUNE 1993

1.20pm Chipperfield

Standing in the telephone box, Joanna placed a coin in the slot and dialled the Oracles number, just as the first few drops of rain began to fall from the Heavens.

The phone at the other end rang about three times, before it was answered. "Good afternoon, Oracle." a woman's voice could be heard from the other end of the line.

"How may I help you?"

"Is that Faye?" Joanna asked, apprehensively.

"Yes." came a surprised reply.

"Hello Faye. This is Joanna Waller. I came to interview you the other Thursday."

"Hi Jo. How are you?" Faye's voice raised to a joyous pitch at the realisation of the caller.

"Fine thank you. You?"

"Very well. How is the article going?"

"That is one reason for my call." Joanna began to explain. "I've now finished it and would like to send you a copy for your approval before I start forwarding it to any magazines. Is that alright?"

"Fine, yes. I look forward to reading it." The motherly woman replied.

"Right then, I'll get a copy in the post tonight." Joanna then changed the subject. "Is
Paul around?"

"He is. Shall I pass you over to him?"

"Yes please."

"Right then, one moment - and thanks for letting me know how you are getting on with the article."

"My pleasure." Joanna replied, and with that she heard the receiver thud on the counter and Faye's footsteps wandering across the shop floor, to find her consultant.

Moments later the receiver was picked up again and a soft deep voice was heard from the other end, saying. "Hello Jo."

"Hi Paul. How are you?"

"Very well. I apologise now for talking with my mouth full, but we're in the middle of eating some cream cakes at the moment. I got conned into buying some, as it's my birthday today."

"Is it really? Happy birthday."

"Thanks. To be honest I'd rather forget it, as it is one year nearer to thirty."

Joanna giggled. "Oh. You poor old thing. Hey listen, I've got six people interested in a party at my house. However, due to everyone having such busy lives, the nearest available date that we can all make is 27th July, which is a Tuesday. Would that be alright for you?"

"One moment, I'll check my diary." and with that the receiver was placed on the counter a second time, as Paul scurried off to check. Footsteps could then be heard approaching the phone, as Paul returned, "Hello Jo. Yes, the 27th would be fine, but there is a problem. I haven't any transport at the moment and you live out in the sticks, don't you? If it's all right with you, I can catch a train to Leighton Buzzard and a taxi from there. The only problem is getting home again, if the party finishes late."

"Where do you live?"

"Adeyfield, Hemel."

Joanna thought for a moment. "My sister also lives in Hemel and she is one of the party. If you like, I'll ask if she'd mind picking you up and dropping you off afterwards. If she is agreeable, it could save you quite a bit of money on taxis, otherwise your earnings are all going to go on fares."

"If she doesn't mind, tell her that I will give her a reading for nothing, as payment for her inconvenience."

"That's very kind of you, Paul. I'll let you know in a day or two what the arrangements are. Besides, if she doesn't want to do it, I could always pick you up on the way home from work, although obviously that would be about five-thirty, which might be too early for you. Anyway, we'll worry about that, if it comes to that. So, what time do you want to start the readings?"

Paul hesitated, as he worked out the length of time each consultation would take, before replying, "Oh. About seven to seven thirty should be alright."

"That's great. Well, I'll let you know who is going to be giving you a lift then. Suppose I'd better let you get back to your cream cakes, before everyone else eats them."

Paul began laughing at the other end of the line, before replying in a light-hearted fashion. "Thank for phoning Jo. I'll see you on the 27th July then."

"Right then, Paul. Take care, and say 'hello' to Claire for me." and with that she put the receiver back on the hook and made her way back to work, through the drizzle.

11.55 pm Slapton

Joanna found it difficult to settle to sleep that night, but eventually the tossing ceased and she found herself gently drifting into unconsciousness to commence her night-time travels.

Standing alone amongst the barren wasteland she timorously glanced about her, for any other signs of life. In the distance, she could hear thunder rolling through the clouds, with the occasional flash of brightness illuminating the horizon, as lightning escaped the clutches of the nebula and rushed to earth, before its energy could be harnessed.

The air was overwhelmingly torrid, making every intake of breath seem like the last. There was not an ounce of moisture in the atmosphere, nor the presence of a cool and pleasant breeze to comfort her. She felt as if she was being suffocated. She was as weak as a kitten. All her energy was being slowly drained from her, like water through a sieve. She was trapped, and alone, in this terrifying dream and she was afraid.

In the distance the silhouette of a traveller could be seen, slowing walking through the gloom, towards her. She strained her eyes to identify the nomad, but to no avail.

"If only the Israelite was here." she muttered to herself, "Then I would feel safe."

Immediately she uttered the words, her guardian arrived, dressed in his black linen robes, clinched at the waist and a kerchief covering his hair. He brought with him a zephyr to cool her brow and a sense of security that, up until that point, had abandoned her.

Joanna pointed to the silhouette in the distance, "Who is that?"

The Israelites dark eyes sparkled as he smiled down at her. "Look and you shall see, child."

She attentively studied the approaching traveller, not taking her eyes off the silhouette for a moment. "Friend or foe?" she questioned the Israelite further.

"Look into your heart for the answer to that question." came his evasive reply.

The traveller continued to advance, until he was upon them. Then stopping, he stood quietly a few feet from Joanna and the Israelite, waiting patiently for an invitation to join them.

As soon as Joanna set eyes upon the traveller she recognised him, for she had spoken to the man on the telephone earlier that day.

"Paul." she exclaimed, in surprise, "What are you doing here?"

"We need to talk." he replied. "Claire thinks that I should not go to your house. She keeps saying, 'Don't go, evil. Don't go, evil.' Can you please explain to me what she means by this?"

Joanna looked about him for a sign of his guardian, but was unable to see any sign of Claire. "So where is Claire?"

Paul frowned. "Do you want me to summons her?"

"Might be the best idea, as she is the one who is so adamant that I am evil." Joanna replied, indignant about the accusation.

Paul immediately raised his head and called her name. In a flash, a young lady of about fourteen years of age obediently stood next to her charge. She was tall, with long bunches of dark blond hair and big blue eyes. But, despite her appearance, her aura filled the air with a powerful, positive energy that oozed with protectiveness towards the man that she had been sent to defend.

Joanna softly smiled at the teenager. "Hello Claire."

Claire responded by marching forward, in an ungainly fashion, until she was standing between Joanna and the consultant. "So you are finally taking me seriously, then." she smartly replied, as she folded her arms obnoxiously.

"Claire." Paul firmly called her name, bringing the girl back into line. "Joanna wants to know why you have been telling me to cancel the readings at her house."

Claire turned and stomped back to her charge, her arms still crossed. "Hasn't her protector told her yet?"

Joanna attracted the Israelite's attention. "Told me what? What's going on?" But her guardian just placed his finger to his lips, requesting her silence.

Not satisfied, Joanna approached the teenager. "What is it that I am supposed to know, Claire?"

Claire turned to face the perplexed woman and stated, in a matter-of-fact fashion, "You are surrounded by the unclean."

Joanna looked over her shoulder at the Israelite. "Are you referring to him?" she asked, as she pointed at the bearded man.

"No, silly."

"Then who? Emma maybe?"

Claire frowned. "No. Not that little squirt, who cuddles her teddy on one hand, whilst sucking the thumb of the other. I am talking about the unclean that are out to destroy, not the clean that are sent to protect."

Joanna turned her attention to Paul. "Please, will you tell me what she's on about."

"I am afraid she won't. All I know is that she is unhappy about my going there. I will have to cancel."

The Israelite then entered into the conversation. "No." He roared. "You can't. I need you to come. Please, reconsider, souls are at stake here. You are the only one who can put a stop to all this. Look about you and tell me what you see. Could you have this on your conscience? Should this desolate land become your Jerusalem? Would you stand aside and watch the Whore of Babylon return and declare war? I think not. You have sworn an oath with God that must be fulfilled. Let go of your earthly fears, for you carry with you faith and wisdom, that outshines all that is evil." he then mellowed his tone slightly. "Your guide is concerned for your welfare and credit to her for that. But you have many powerful guardians of light that walk with you. Listen to them also, and then decide, once you have been in their counsel. But I implore you, reconsider before it is too late."

Claire was incensed by the Israelites words. "His going to that house, would be like a lamb to slaughter - you know that."

The Israelite smiled serenely down at the young girl. "You may be powerful in spirit, Claire - with the strength of a thousand, but you still think and act like a teenager."

He then looked straight into Paul's eyes. "Please call all your guides to join us." And with that, Paul did as the Israelite requested.

Four men suddenly appeared from nowhere and stood around the young psychic.

Each had a bright glow about them, just as Claire and the Israelite did, and all brought with them the spiritual gifts given by God.

The first, was extremely tall, and looked like he was over one hundred years of age. He wore a tall hat, rather like that worn by a bishop, which had brightly coloured material attached to its base that streamed down his back and across his shoulders. He was dressed in robes of fine linen, wore a gold chain around his neck and was dripping with riches. Stepping forward he took Joanna's hand and kissed it. "I am Zaphenath-Paneah." he introduced himself.

Joanna looked a little puzzled. "You are dressed very finely Zaphenath. Why is that?"

Zaphenath-Paneah smiled, for the opportunity of being able to tell of his achievements in that lifetime, gave him a sense of great satisfaction. "When I was about thirty, I entered the service of Pharaoh, King of Egypt. I was given charge of his palace and charge to the whole land of Egypt."

"Well, good for you." Joanna remarked, with admiration.

Zaphenath-Paneah then turned to face the Israelite. "Good to see you again, brother." he greeted the man, as they embraced.

Wishing to know how they knew each other, Joanna went to interrupt them, but her attention was taken by the second of the four men. "Hello. I am Peter." a wiry haired, eccentric looking man introduced himself. "I am Paul's head guide."

Joanna studied the second gentleman, who was in his mid-fifties. He had long tasselly pepper-grey hair and an unruly beard. His face drooped down, giving him a look of immense sadness, with heavy eyelids that almost hung completely over his blue-grey eyes. He was quite tall, about five-foot ten, stockily built, and wore a double breasted dark grey jacket that was far less psychedelic than Zaphenath-Paneah's attire.

Peter then beckoned a tiny Chinese gentleman to approach whom, like the Egyptian, was also dressed far more elaborately than the head guide. Responding, the petite China-man trotted forward in minute shuffled steps, stopped just before the woman, clasped his hands together and bowed. "Chi-Lau." he introduced himself, before retreating, back to his post, at Paul's side.

Peter then pointed to the fourth in line. This man was not much taller than the China-man and would not have looked out of place taking the part of Merlin in a film about King Arthur. He had an extremely long, snow-white beard, which came to a curly point at its end. His long hair, tied neatly back, was also of the same pure colour. He wore a long, dark blue coat that almost touched the ground, which seemed to swamp his delicate frame, and leant on a staff, made from beach wood to support his weight. "I am also called Peter." The magician-like man introduced himself, as he creased up his face and gave her a crooked smile. "But I also answer to either Pete, or Peter Two."

Joanna looked about her at Paul's collection of guides, and giggling, she stated, "And what a rare bunch you all are."

"Never be fooled by looks alone." Peter growled. "Together we are all-powerful." He pointed first to the Egyptian, who was now standing at Paul's side. "Zaphenath-Paneah grants Paul the gifts of prophecy, and the speaking in, and interpretation of, different kinds of tongues." He then drew her attention to the delicate China-man. "Chi-Lau grants him the gifts of wisdom, knowledge and healing ..."

Joanna scratched her head. "Healing? But Paul said he healed people using his own energy."

"Is that what he told you? The dear, innocent lamb." The head guide then turned to the China-man. "Haven't you been talking to Paul again, Chi-Lau? How can you expect gratitude, when you don't let him know you are assisting him?" The China-man grinned and nodded at Peter, before dropping his head down to proceed muttering away to himself, in his own tongue.

Peter turned his attention to Peter Two. "Peter is responsible for granting Paul the gifts of miraculous powers, and distinguishing between spirits, whilst Claire," he said, as he pointed at the teenager, "has the responsibility of protecting her charge." He then placed his hand on his own chest, "As for me, I am responsible for granting him the gift of faith, and am administrator to the attending angels. These are our main duties, however, we are each capable of doing another's job, should the occasion arise."

"So." Joanna proceeded to ask him about Claire's reluctance to let Paul visit her house, "In your opinion, should Paul cancel the party booking?"

Peter smiled down at her, with that sad, worry-worn face of his, and stated, "He is well protected."

"So there's not a problem, then?"

"Oh. There is a problem with your house, yes. But neither the other guardians, nor I would risk any harm coming to either him, or you. Ask the guides yourself." and with that, he moved away from her, inviting the young woman to question each man individually.

Joanna turned to Peter Two. "What do you think, Peter? Do you think Paul should cancel?"

"I give him the gift of distinguishing between spirits. Through me, he will know the moment he steps inside your home that all is not well. He will be prepared and therefore, able to protect himself."

Joanna then asked Chi-Lau the same question, but he just shook his head and continued mumbling to himself.

Finally, she turned to the Egyptian. "Zaphenath-Paneah, what do you think Paul should do?"

The flamboyant, aged man stepped forward and took her hand. "I am with God." he pronounced with an air of confidence, "And if by Paul's going to your house teaches him much and places him on the right path, then so be it. It is as much his destiny to go there, as it is your destiny to invite him there."

Joanna frowned, as she withdrew from the Egyptians grasp, before wondering over to Paul. "Peter, Peter Two and Zaphenath all think you should not cancel; Claire thinks that you should and I'm not sure what opinions the Chinese gentleman has on the subject. As for my guides, I only have the Israelite here, but he thinks it is imperative that you go. So then, Paul, do you want to risk it? I've been assured that you will be well protected."

Paul sighed deeply. "I am probably going to regret this, but yes, I will go."

But Claire refused to give up, despite his decision. "Don't go, evil. Don't go, Evil." she shouted at him. "You are not strong enough. You haven't the power to fight it. Don't go."

Peter grabbed at the girl's arm. "Claire. Enough. The decision has been made." but she was not going to be stopped from airing her views so, stamping on Peter's foot whilst pulling away from his grasp, she continued, "Don't go, evil. Don't go, evil."

Incensed, Peter held out his hand and, allowing a beam of bright light come from the palm, he cocooned the girl in a white sphere. "You will not be told, will you Claire." he growled, as the teenager fought to get out of her trap. "Now I command you to go from this place." and with that, Claire and her bubble disappeared into thin air.

Peter then turned to Paul. "We must leave now. Come, let us take you back home." and with that Paul and his guides became engulfed by a white mist and were gone, leaving Joanna alone with the Israelite once more.

Joanna slowly ambled over to her guardian's side. He placed a comforting hand on her shoulder, as she reached him. Looking up into his dark, shining eyes, she asked, "What exactly is in my house?"

"Have I not shown you enough, on previous visits here?" came his soft, but stern reply. "Think about what you have seen and heard. Ponder upon the words that passed Geraldine's lips. Remember what the cards said, when you gave Lewis a reading. All these things amount to one thing and one thing only. You have seen what is to come; you have prophesied the events yourself. Don't keep asking what you already know, child."

Joanna's gaze dropped to the floor for a second, as she gave a deep sigh. Then, looking back at the Israelite, she asked, "So you know Zaphenath-Paneah well, do you?"

"We are brothers."

"But you don't look like brothers. Besides, you've told me that you are an Israelite, whilst he said that he was Pharaoh's right hand man. That makes him an Egyptian, surely?"

"In his heart he is as much an Israelite as I." came the stern reply. "We were born in Canaan by the same ageing father. Through jealously, he was sent away to a life of slavery. But God smiled down on him, and eventually he resided in Egypt, as Pharaohs confidant."

"So who are you really, then? What is your proper name?" she jumped on the moment, to try and to find the true identity of her guardian.

The Israelite smiled down at her. "I have already told you, child."

"Come off it. Have I got 'gullible' stamped on my forehead or something?" her tone showed impatience, "I know as well as you that Ravenous Wolf is just a pseudonym."

The Israelite became angered. "Do I have to give you all the answers? Have you no eyes in your head to seek them out yourself? You have been told where to look to find what you are needing to know, so why have you not done it?" Then, a little roughly, he took her hand in his, "Come, I will take you back to your own time and place now." and with that, Joanna and her Guide left the dismal lands. Moments later, she was back in her own time, sitting bolt upright in bed, staring into the gloominess of her bedroom once more.

CHAPTER FOURTEEN
27TH JULY 1993

6.25 pm Hemel Hempstead

Paul waited for his lift to arrive at his nan's flat, anxiously looking at his watch, as he took a drag from his cigarette. He was beginning to get nervous about doing the party that evening, although he did not really know why. He was jittery because a single thought kept going through his mind, that he could not erase, for all day he had come to the same conclusion - don't go, evil.

The chime of the doorbell broke his contemplation. Grabbing his coat in one hand and a plastic bag in the other, he wandered through the hall to the flat door and opened it. Outside stood a petite woman in her early thirties, with long curly bronze hair and a broad smile. "Paul?" she grinned. "Hi. I'm Debbie, Jo's sister. You fit then?" and with that, the psychic followed the bouncy woman down the stairs and towards her Metro.

A second woman clambered out of the car as they approached. "Paul, this is Karen." Debbie introduced the strangers to one another. "Karen; Paul."

With introductions over, Paul squeezed into the back of the vehicle, amongst an array of sandwiches, whilst Karen and Debbie settled themselves into the front seats.

"Please excuse the food in the back." Debbie began to explain, as she started the engine, "Jo and I have done a spread between us for this evening."

Karen then held up a large bottle of wine. "And I brought the booze." She grinned from ear to ear.

"You're all well organised, aren't you." Paul gave them half a smile.

"So Paul," Debbie called over her shoulder, as she kept one eye on the road ahead, whilst catching a glimpse of the psychic in the rear-view mirror, with the other. "Are you looking forward to this evening? I mean, a gaggle of women can be a daunting prospect for any man."

"I enjoy what I do." he replied, as he stared out of the side window at the passing traffic.

Karen half turned in the passenger seat, "Do you do a lot of parties then?" she asked.

"A few, yes. But I mainly work at the Oracle, in Watford." He gave her a shy smile.

Karen pondered for a moment, then the curiosity got the better of her and so she enquired, "The Oracle, what's that?"

"A new age shop." He replied.

Debbie then piped in. "You know I told you about my little skin and blister doing an interview, for a Magazine? Well, that was at that shop."

"Oh." came the slightly disinterested reply. Then, to be polite, Karen continued, "So what sort of things can you get at a new age shop then, Paul?"

"Incense, oils, crystals, tarot cards - all that sort of thing."

"Right." came another disinterested reply from the passenger seat.

The atmosphere remained slightly strained for the entire trip from Hemel to Slapton. Karen was quite a sceptic on the quiet and, although she was pleasant enough, Paul did feel that she was mocking him slightly. Debbie tried to keep things light by talking about her kids, and about Karen's kids, and about the weather, and all sorts of safe subjects, but somehow by the time Debbie pulled the car up outside her sister's house, the strain was beginning to show.

Realising that they had arrived, Joanna skipped out into the front garden to greet her guests, and help bring some of the food inside. "Blimey." she joked, as she took one of the large oval plates, pilled high with sandwiches, "Feeding the five-thousand are we, Deb?"

"Watch it madame, or you'll be wearing them." came the tough-talking reply.

Inviting the new arrivals into her humble home, Joanna beckoned them to follow her into the sitting room to introduce the three to the rest of the party.

"Are we the last to arrive then?" Debbie giggled, as she said her hello's to group of people dotted around the room.

"Only Dawn to come, with her friend Rosie." The host then turned to Karen and Paul who were both hovering on the threshold of the room. "Come in, you two." and with that, she began introductions in a clockwise fashion around the room. "Over there, sitting in the corner by the cheese dips is Hazel," she gave a broad grin, as she pointed to a flamboyant ginger-headed woman. "Shampa." Joanna continued, as she moved on to a petite Indonesian woman sandwiched in the middle of the settee, followed by drawing their attention to her work-mate, "And Pat, who I have the misfortune of working with ..."

"Oh thanks very much, friend." came Pat's retort, who followed it up by hurling a twiglet across the room in Joanna's direction.

Giggling, Joanna caught the offending nibble whilst continuing with the introductions, "And finally, sitting over there - with the legs - is Lewis. Everybody, this is Karen and Paul. Paul is kindly doing the readings this evening."

A knock on the front door caught Joanna's attention so, leaving everyone to socialise amongst themselves, she wandered out into the kitchen to answer it.

Dawn, with a bottle of wine in hand, and her friend Rosie beamed in at her, as she opened the door. "Hi both." Joanna greeted them as she invited them inside. "Glad you could make it."

"Sorry if we are a little late." Dawn apologised with her plummy accent. "But you know me, time keeping is not my strong point."

"I'm just glad you remembered to come, Dawn." Joanna jested, before turning to her friend. "You won't believe the amount of times I have waited for this woman to arrive at the farm to give me a riding lesson, and she's totally forgotten about it. I've even seen her write it down in her diary ..."

Rosie giggled. "Don't tell me, she forgot to look at her diary."

"How did you guess?"

"Oh shut up, you two." Dawn tried to sound indignant. "Don't start picking on me, until I've had chance to attack some of that wine."

Rosie leant towards her host. "Just be grateful that you don't have to live with her, Jo." she raised her eyebrows as she spoke the words. "Totally infuriating."

"Bitch." Dawn jested, as she wandered through to the sitting room with her bottle of wine, to announce her presence to the rest of the group.

Joanna was ushering Rosie through to the other room, when she was met by Paul in the doorway. "May I have a quiet word?" he asked in a soft, gentle voice.

"Sure." Joanna replied, "Tell you what, I'll show you where your going to do the readings at the same time." and at that, she showed Paul upstairs to the main bedroom, where a table had been laid out especially for the occasion, with a table lamp placed to one side for extra light.

Retrieving his cards from the plastic bag, Paul gently placed them on the table and sat on the chair.

"What's troubling you?" Joanna sensed his agitation.

"I'm not quite sure," he tried to explain, "It is just that all day I have had this nagging sensation to cancel this evening."

"Funny you should say that, but I was half expecting you to call it off. You see, a few months ago I arranged for another clairvoyant to do a party here. It was all arranged and everything. Then, at the last minute she cancelled for no apparent reason and refused to make another appointment. Believe me, I would not have been in the least surprised if you had done the same."

"You know what I've been getting all day? Don't go, evil. Don't go, evil. But I didn't understand why I was getting that, because I certainly don't see you as evil."

"Thanks. I think." Joanna smiled, attentively.

"It was only when I got here that I realised why I was thinking, what I was thinking." he paused momentarily, before continuing, "You have a big problem in this house and I think you should contact the church as soon as possible, to get something done about it."

"Are we talking exorcisms, here?" Joanna placed her hand on the table and brushed the cloth with her fingertips, as she asked for clarification.

"Yes. And the sooner the better."

"But whatever is in this house, has never bothered me before. Why should I suddenly feel the need to do anything about it now?"

"Hasn't it? Don't you think that maybe your marriage failing and your husbands attitude towards you, might just have had something to do with whatever it is in this house?"

"How did you know I was divorced?" Joanna was taken aback by his knowledge of her past.

"I listen to your guides, even if you don't." He scolded her.

"So you won't be able to work here, then?" she felt her spirits flatten.

"Of cause I can, I know how to protect myself. I may not be all that old, but I have learned a lot in my life. Just thought I'd better bring it to your attention, that's all."

Joanna then looked at her watch. "Well, do you want something to eat before you start?"

"No. I'm fine. I'd rather get going as soon as possible, if it is alright with you."

Joanna gave him a broad grin. "I'll send the first victim up then." and with that, she got up to leave.

"Oh Jo." he called after her as she reached the bedroom door, "There are only six having readings tonight, aren't there. Only there seems to be a lot of people downstairs."

"Only six, Yes. Hazel and Pat have only come along to party and Lewis isn't bothered about having a reading."

"Good." he replied, then proceeded to retrieve his recorder and tapes from the plastic bag.

Debbie was the first to have a reading, which went to her satisfaction, despite a couple of hiccups, due to interference from the M.O.G. in the bog.

Karen was second, but she proved a much more difficult client to please, taking up an hour and a half of Paul's time, asking questions about this and questions about that. Even at the end of it all, she was still as sceptical as she was as the start of the evening, so both her time and Paul's were wasted.

Shampa was the third to see Paul and, although he told her what she needed to know, it was not what she wanted to hear, so she also returned deflated after about forty minutes with the consultant.

With the time now about ten at night, Rosie was getting anxious to go, for she had left her children with her mother. This meant that only one of them could have a reading, so Dawn got volunteered.

She arrived downstairs about half an hour later, full of her reading and overjoyed at what she had been told. However, immediately she returned, Rosie jumped up and they were rushing to the door, so Joanna did not have chance to find out all the details before their departure.

Shortly after that, Hazel, Shampa and Pat also decided that it was time to make tracks home and so, the party ended, before Joanna had a chance to have her consultation.

"I suppose you two want to make your weary way home, as well." Joanna directed the question at her older sister.

Debbie looked at her watch. "Blimey. The night is young, yet. Besides you haven't had your reading. I don't mind waiting, do you Karen?"

Karen smiled. "No not at all. Actually, I'm enjoying munching my way through all this grub."

"Are you sure? I don't won't to keep you waiting."

"Quite sure. Besides," Karen continued, "The kids are staying round my mothers tonight, so I've got nothing to rush home for."

"Well, if you are positive?"

"Oh for goodness sake, Jo." Debbie snapped at her sister in irritation, "Just go, get your cards read." And so, Joanna wandered off, to find Paul.

Reaching the top of the stairs, Joanna crept into the bedroom and quietly swung the door shut behind her. "How are you doing, Paul?" she asked softly, as she took as seat. "Feeling tired?"

"Put it this way, I am glad you're the last one."

"Look, I don't mind if you'd rather call it a night. After all, it is getting late."

Paul thought for a moment. "Actually, I know what we could do instead. I'll get you talking to some of my guides, if you like?" he wearily beamed.

"I'm game." she smiled back at the consultant. "Don't tell me, we are going to start with Claire."

Paul laughed. "Claire's happy with that. Now, just relax and clear your mind. In a moment I am going to ask Claire a question in my head, that will require either a yes or a no answer. What I want you to do, is listen for her answer and tell me what she has said, all right? The first thing that pops into your head." Joanna nodded. "Right then, here goes ..." and with that he closed his eyes for a few seconds, before opening them again and looked across at Joanna to reveal the answer.

Joanna stared at him, a touch perplexed. "Was I supposed to have already got something?"

"Yes." he sharply replied. "I'll ask again and when I look at you, I want you to say the first thing that comes into your head." and with that he went through the whole procedure again.

This time, as soon as he opened his eyes, she got a very distinctive high pitched 'yes' come through, following by deeper, 'how many times do you need this confirming'.

"Well?" he asked. "Tell me what you got?"

"I got a definite yes." she smiled at him.

"They are getting fed up of me asking that question, aren't they?" he raised his eyebrows at her.

"I would say definitely, because more than one answered your question."

"I asked Claire if a certain guide of mine was who I have been told he is. You are the forth person to confirm this."

"Well, please don't try and get confirmation from anyone else, because I would hate to be in your shoes if you do, going on the reaction I just got. Who is this mysterious guide, anyway?"

"He doesn't want anyone else to know who he is at the moment, but he has just told me that he would be happy to let you feel his vibrations, if you wish him to."

Joanna shrugged her shoulders and smiled. "Could be interesting?"

"Then just sit back in the chair and relax." and as soon as she reclined on the dining chair, she felt a warm glow come over her, followed by the sensation of one invisible hand on her upper chest, whilst the other on her forehead.

She suddenly felt uneasy with her new-found awareness. "What is he doing?" But before Paul had chance to reply, she heard a deep voice reply, "Blessing you, that's all. Do not be afraid."

"Please ask him to stop, Paul." But feeling Joanna's agitation, Paul's guide ceased immediately.

After a few moments to calm down, Joanna started to stare at something, just behind Paul's left shoulder. "Your guide?" she enquired in a slow and deliberate fashion. "He doesn't wear a tall hat, by any chance, does he?"

"Can you see him, Jo?"

"Yes, just behind you, on your left. He is very tall and slim and he is wearing a tall hat that is tapered to the top, with material flowing out from the bottom of it. He has also got something heavy around his neck, like a chain or something. Is this the same guide that you just asked confirmation for?"

"Yes. Yes, it is."

Then, with the distinct sound of recognition in her voice, she smiled, "I've seen this chap before ..." before averting her attention to the door of the built in cupboard, over the stairs.

"Who is there, Jo?" Paul suddenly felt uneasy, for he sensed trouble.

"I don't like the look of that one. Not one of your guides as well, is it?"

"Describe it to me?" Paul requested.

She stared at the cupboard door. "Well, he is standing half in, and half out of the door so it is hard to see him properly." she paused, squinted her eyes, then proceeded, "A middle-aged man. Wearing glasses. Got a tweed jacket on. Heavily built. A menacing stare - oh. What a menacing stare." But before she had chance to go into any further details, Paul's guide moved forward and, grabbing the other entity, he forced it out of the room.

"That was Jesse, wasn't it?" Paul asked, with a hint of sternness to his voice.

"Yes. Yes, it must have been." Joanna then thought for a moment, "You know, I have seen him somewhere before, as well. Not here though, not in this house, but somewhere else." she rattled her brains to try and remember, "But where?"

"Maybe another time, in another place." Paul interrupted her thoughts.

"What do you mean by that?"

"Sometimes, we see things before we actually see them." he then swiftly changed the subject, "But he won't bother us again, Joe has taken care of that." and he smiled, as he felt the presence of his triumphant guide return to his side.

"Joe? Who is Joe? Is that what you call your guide with the hat?"

"That's what I refer to him as, yes. Kind of a nickname, you see. Have you found out who the Israelite is yet?"

Joanna scratched her head. "Well, there's another story. The night after I had phoned you, to arrange for you to come here this evening, I had the weirdest dream. I can't remember the in's and out's of it, but there is one thing that I can recall; my Israelite is brother to your Joe. However, in my dream Joe was called something completely different; Zaphe-something, or something Zaphe - I can't remember. Anyway, after that dream I hunted out Lewis's old Bible and, as you suggested, I sat down quietly and asked one of my guides to give me a quote from it."

"What did you get?"

"Chronicles One. Well, that was the first hurdle to cross because there are two Chronicles, but the number comes before the name. So, was I to read 1 Chronicles, or 2 Chronicles chapter one, or any other viable combination? Anyway, I decided to ask outright whom I was speaking to and I got the name Edward. So, despite thinking that I have never come across the name Edward in the Old Testament before - not that I am very o'fey with the Bible anyway, I thought I would give it a go. So, I read the whole of 1 Chronicles and the whole of 2 Chronicles looking for this blasted Edward."

"So, I take it you are still none the wiser then?" he smiled in a boyish fashion.

"Only that I know that my guide is a brother to your guide, and if only I could remember your guides real name, then I might be half way to finding out my guides real name."

"But he refuses to tell you outright." Paul confirmed.

"Not unless it is Edward? But somehow, I don't think that it goes with his image. Personally, I reckon it was all just a ploy to get me to read the Bible."

Paul laughed at her remark, before changing the subject slightly. "Well, talking of finding out about guides and that, I've got a run-down on the other spook that resides in this house."

"What? The one that I have never been able to pick up on?"

"Yep. She is called Mandy, she is in her mid-thirties; tall and slim; long, dark hair and apparently she died in a car crash about six years ago."

"So, what is she doing here?" Joanna was puzzled as to why this entity was floating around her house. "The people who owned this house before me were living here six years ago and they're both still very much alive."

"Sorry, can't answer that, I can only tell you what I have been given." Paul then changed the subject, "How many guides have I around me at the moment?"

Without hesitation, Joanna replied, "Five.", although, once the number had passed her lips, she was surprised as to why she said it.

"Five?" Paul queried her. "Could you ask them to give you their names, please?"

Obligingly, Joanna took in a deep breath and proceeded to ask each spirit's name in turn, repeating each name as it was given. "Claire ... Joe ... Peter ... a tiny, little Chinese chappie, that I can't catch the name of ... Peter ..."

"You said the name Peter, twice." He corrected her.

"Alright then, I'll ask them again." and with that the whole process was repeated, "Claire ... Joe ... Peter ... the Chinese chappie ... Peter - sorry, still got two Peters."

"Confirmation from Claire, please. Give the answer to Jo, Claire." and with that, he asked a second question in his head.

"Yes you have. Two, that's right." Joanna repeated what she was told. She then continued to describe the two Peters, before Paul had a chance to argue. "One is tall, whilst the other is small. The tall one is your head guide, although both are powerful.

The small one has a long, white beard and equally long hair, which he wears tied back, away from his face. He wears a long coat and carries a staff. The larger Peter, is more conventionally dressed, although he has shoulder length hair and a dark grey beard."

"Oh. So the little one, that looks like Merlin, is also called Peter is he? I kept getting told that, but I thought they were just winding me up." he laughed at his own stupidity. "Oh well, can't always be right."

Joanna then looked at her watch. "I suppose we had better go back downstairs and join the others, or your lift will be going without you." She then mocked, "Have you any further questions that you would like to ask me?"

"Don't be facetious." Paul responded, as he proceeded to pack his equipment away.

"O.K, I'll see you downstairs in a mo, then." and with that Joanna wandered off, out of the room and back to the others, in the sitting room.

Moments later and Paul's footsteps could be heard running down the stairs and into the kitchen. He was then striding into the sitting room to join the others, his tired looking face, full of relief that the evening was finally over.

Debbie rose to her feet. "Right then, folks. I'll just pop up to the loo, then I suppose I had better take you two back home." and with that, she was making way towards the bathroom.

"You look all done in, mate." Lewis bellowed at the psychic.

"Yes. Quite a heavy night."

Suddenly, Debbie could be heard screaming above them and, moments later, she was thundering back down the stairs in a blind panic.

Joanna was the first to meet the terrified woman, in the kitchen. "What on earth is the matter, Deb?" she asked, as she tried to comfort her sister.

"There's something horrible in the bathroom." came the shaky reply.

Paul was through the kitchen and up the stairs, like a lightning flash, with Joanna at his heals. They both reached the bathroom door at the same time, but before entering, Paul stopped and turned to face her. "I want you to stay out here, where it's safe." and as Debbie reached the landing and stood beside her sister, Paul flashed his eyes across to her, "And you too, Deb. Stay out of the bathroom."

He then turned to enter the room, but Deb caught his arm. "Well, what's to say that it won't come out here, once your inside, eh?"

"Because one of my guides confined him to this room."

Lewis then piped in. "Well, you could have warned us, before Deb here experienced fright-night."

"My guide wasn't to know that the thing in there would go for anyone else." He stuck up for Joe's actions. "After all, how many times have you used this room this evening – all of you? No, the thing in there is only after me. You were just a pawn, Deb. I'm sorry that you've had a fright, but you were only the bait to get me up here. That is why I am going in alone."

"Not if I have anything to do with it." Joanna cut in. "This is my house and I am used to that spook being in there. I will not let you go in alone."

Paul glared at her in disapproval. "Well, do what you must, but it will be at your own risk." He then pushed open the door and confidently strided over the threshold, with Joanna close behind.

The negative energy whizzed around the room, like a hurricane. And there, in the corner by the sink, stood one infuriated manifestation.

"Close the door." Paul ordered, but as Joanna went to shut it behind her, Deb pushed past, and entered the room.

"What are you doing, Deb?" Joanna's agitated tone caused Debbie to freeze.

"I want to see what is going on, that's all." came her reply.

"What?" Joanna shouted at her sister. "Are you mad?" but before Debbie could answer the spirit flew at the woman, wrappings itself around her, trying to lock himself inside. She fell to the ground, unable to fight off the spirit, leaving Joanna watching on helplessly as the thing started taking over her sister.

Paul instinctively flew at the crumpled body on the floor and, placing his hands on her head, he proceeded to say the Lords Prayer.

The M.O.G.'s grip on the woman began to weaken as Paul roared out the words, eventually having to let go of his victim. However, he knew that Paul's aura was now weakened, from administering the healing, and so started working on him instead, trying to find a weak spot that could easily be cracked.

Paul turned to Joanna. "Get her out of this room, now." and, with the aid of Lewis, Joanna immediately assisted her sister onto the landing. Then she rejoined the psychic, despite Lewis' pleading not to go back inside, and slammed the door shut.

Paul was lying on the floor by the time she returned. The M.O.G. was on top of him, trying to get inside, whilst his Egyptian guide was inside him, fighting to keep it out. "Send me healing, Jo. Prop yourself up against the wall and ask your guides to help you to send me healing."

Doing exactly as he instructed, Joanna raised her hands and, taking a deep breath, concentrated on sending him white light. In what seemed like an eternity, Joanna started to see Paul's aura brighten and expand. The same time, she also noticed the entity get up and stand over the psychic.

It then turned and marched over to the woman, but she just turned her hands to face him, now blasting him with the same white light. He staggered backwards as the positive energy struck him, covering his eyes as he did so.

She suddenly found her energy begin to flounder. She knew that she must continue, but it was becoming difficult. Then the deep, soft voice of the Israelite spoke to her, saying, "Stop now, child. If you make yourself too weak, you too will become vulnerable." And so she ceased the healing.

Paul started to get up onto his feet. But as he got onto his haunches, the M.O.G. struck out at him, sending the psychic falling back to the floor. It then began to laugh an evil, vicious laugh. "I'll have your blood, if it's the last thing I ever do." The spirit taunted the young man, as he lay, dazed, from the blow.

"Not if I have anything to do with it." Paul retorted, and went to get up a second time. The entity then proceeded to kick and punch the psychic. His clothing could physically be seen crumpling with each blow.

"Is that the best you can do?" Paul proceeded to taunt the negative spirit back, using psychologically as a temporary weapon.

"You little cunt." the M.O.G. growled back with venom, as he put another boot in Paul's side. "You are dead meat, boy."

The Israelite then spoke to Joanna a second time. "We've nearly got him. Start to say the Lords Prayer. Say it out loud for all to hear. Say it with meaning. Say it with conviction. Say it with love."

"But I don't know the Lords Prayer - I can't remember it." Joanna informed her guardian, but his only retort was to order her to, "Just do it."

And so she started saying the first few lines, which was enough to divert the M.O.G.'s attention from Paul to her. Marching over to her, and placing his face right up to hers, he bellowed, "Shut up, slag. Or I'll have your blood as well."

"Ignore him and just continue with the Lords Prayer." the Israelite ordered, and so she continued to stumble over the words, whilst Paul slowly rose to his feet and regained his balance.

Once standing firmly, Paul joined Joanna in prayer. Infuriated, the M.O.G. marched back to the consultant and, pushing him at the shoulder, the spirit hollered, "You're nothing but a trouble maker, you little shit. Everything was fine here until you decided to come along." He then turned back to the young woman, "And as for you? You deserve all you are going to get, for this." and with that, the manifestation evanesced into obscurity.

Joanna slowly slid down the wall, until she was sitting on the floor. Paul staggered over to her, whilst nursing his bruises. "Are you alright?" he asked softly, as he reached out a hand and placed it on her arm.

"Fine." she whispered, as she smoothed her golden locks away from her face. "A tad shaken, maybe."

"Come on, let me help you up." and with that, he supported her with his arm and raised her to her feet.

"How about you Paul. You ok.?"

"Couldn't be better." he smiled, as he gave her a wink. "An everyday occurrence."

As the bathroom door was opened, the landing beyond revealed three very concerned faces. Upon seeing the state of his girlfriend, Lewis stepped forward and took her from Paul's arms. "You both alright? What happened in there?"

"Well," Joanna started to explain, "I think Paul got rid of the M.O.G in the bog."

Lewis gaze then fell upon the psychic, "You alright, mate? You look like you've been through the mill, a bit."

"I'm fine. Just a few bruises as momento's for this evenings entertainment."

Debbie then asked, "You've got rid of it for good then? What was it? Was it Satanic? I've always said that there was something evil in this house."

"When?" Joanna queried her sister's final remark, but Debbie ignored her.

Paul then pushed passed the others and proceeded to make his way back downstairs.

"I've sent it backing for now, but it will be back . My advice is to get the Church in to exorcise it, before it does some real damage ."

The rest of them then followed the psychic down the stairs with Joanna to the rear of the group. But as she reached the bottom step, the young woman paused and looked over her shoulder to see little Emma, standing there sucking her thumb and shaking her head. In a way, Joanna felt sad at the thought of losing little Emma as well, but she knew that it would probably the only sensible thing to do, after the events of that evening.

CHAPTER FIFTEEN
30TH JULY, 1993

3.30 pm Felden

As soon as Joanna's parents had heard the accounts of the evening of the 27th July, her mother contacted her good friend, and local deaconess, in the hope that the Church might be able to help her daughter. Despite Joanna not living in Reverend Butler's parish, nor the diocese for that matter, the deaconess was still more than willing to meet with Joanna, to discuss the matter in more detail. And so, Joanna found herself slowly driving down Flaunden Lane, dodging the potholes as she went, until finally reaching the Reverend Angela Butlers bungalow.

Clambering out of the car, she wandered up the gravel driveway to the front door. Joanna felt uneasy about meeting Angela, not because the woman wore a dog collar, rather because she felt the deaconess might ridicule her, for the tale sounded quite fanciful when voiced out loud. However, the time had now come for something to be done, so she had no choice. Taking a deep breath, to steady her nerves, Joanna lifted a finger to the doorbell, and rang.

A round-faced, crop-haired woman answered the door, with a smile. "You must be Joanna, Margaret's daughter." she said, with a soft and elegant accent.

"Yes." Joanna apprehensively confirmed.

"Please, do come in." The corners of the deaconess' mouth turned upwards, as she invited the young woman inside.

The Reverend beckoned Joanna to follow her through the hall way, warning her guest to mind the piles of Church magazines stacked up high along its walls, before leading the young woman into a comfortably furnished sitting-room to the rear of her home. A large patio door boasted a beautifully bright and summery garden beyond, which seemed to travel on forever, with wild birds fluttering from tree branch to lawn, oblivious that they could be seen.

The deaconess then invited the daughter of her parish member to make herself comfortable on a John Lewis couch, whilst she sat to one side in an armchair adorned with cushions.

"Right then, Joanna." The Reverend Butler opened the conversation, as she reached for her Bible, "Firstly, I am a deaconess rather than a fully fledged vicar, which means that my duties in the laity are to assist the minister. However, as you are probably already aware, Chipperfield has not got a resident vicar at the moment, therefore I have been given charge of the parish, as acting vicar, until I can be confirmed - which will be as soon as it becomes law for me to do so." she gave a nervous laugh, before continuing, "Now then, Margaret has told me, in brief, what has been going on in your house. Firstly, I have not had much dealing with this type of problem so - and I hope you have no objections to my doing this - but, I contacted my good friend and diocese exorcist, the Reverend Carl Garner. I quickly ran through what Margaret told me and he said that I should also get as much information from you as possible, before deciding what the best possible action should be. Secondly, technically speaking, I should not really be having this chat to you, because Leighton Buzzard is out of my jurisdiction. However, both Carl and myself think that, as Christians, we are in a position to advise and therefore, we are going to bend the rules a little - as your mother is a regular member of my church. So, provided what you tell me is sufficient, Carl would like for us both to see you at a later date, so that he can recommend your case to the exorcist in your diocese."

"Fine." Joanna gave the deaconess half a smile.

"Now then, Margaret told me that a tarot reader came to your house on Tuesday, and that he is responsible for stirring things up. Is that true?"

"He livened things up a bit, yes, but there has always been poltergeist activity in the house."

"Never-the-less, the Bible states that anyone who dabbles with the occult are playing with the devil and therefore, you were very silly to encourage such behaviour." the deaconess stated, as she waved the Bible about.

"How do you make that out? Paul has a great deal of faith in God."

Reverend Angela Butler gave an expression of surprise. "Really? How unusual. We are taught that people, who do that type of thing, work against God. I don't even read the astrology page in the paper, because I feel it is of no worth. I think maybe he is leading you into a false sense of security."

"I don't think so. You see, he is not the only reader I have been in contact with, who is religious."

"Well, it does state in quite a few places in the Bible, that witchcraft and sorcery are works of the devil." she started flicking through the book, "One is in Deuteronomy somewhere. Bare with me a moment, and I'll find it for you."

As the deaconess began flicking through the pages, Joanna continued to defend the psychic. "But Paul does not belong to a coven, nor does he do spells. In fact, I remember him telling me once that he feels as strongly against that type of practice, as the Church do against psychics."

Ignoring her retort, the Reverend continued to scan through the pages, until she finally found what she was looking for. "Ah. Here we are." she stated with an air of satisfaction, "Deuteronomy 18:10-12 - 'Let no-one be found among you who sacrifices his son or daughter in the fire, who practices divination or sorcery, interprets omens, engages in witchcraft, or casts spells, or who is a medium or spiritist or who consults the dead. Anyone who does these things is detestable to the LORD, and because of these detestable practices the LORD your God will drive out those nations before you'." The deaconess then stared up at Joanna, with a hint of a smirk.

Joanna frowned, "Was it Moses who said that?" The deaconess nodded. "He consulted with the dead when he spoke to God on the mount, did he not? He also disclosed future events when he told the oppressed Israelites that he was going to lead them out of Egypt."

"He prophesied - that is different." came the Reverends sharp reply.

"Alright then, what about Joseph; the one with the technicoloured coat? He was able to interpret dreams. Are dreams not the same as omens?"

"Totally different." came a slightly flatter reply.

"Let's take Jesus as another example then. Didn't he cast a spell to turn water into wine? And what about Aaron? Didn't his staff turn into a snake, when Pharaoh wanted him to perform a miracle? Sorcery approved by God, I might add."

Joanna then returned to the first of the detestable practices mentioned. "As for not sacrificing a son or daughter, God told Abraham to take his son Isaac and sacrifice him as a burnt offering, because ..."

"This debate is getting us no where." The deaconess cut Joanna short. "This meeting should be to discuss the problem in your house and not about our different views on Tarot readers. Also, as Christians, our teachings are from the New Testament and therefore, a stream of quotations from the Old Testament are irrelevant, at this time."

"Then why did you use Deuteronomy to try and prove to me that Paul is working against God, then?"

"Just to show you that the type of thing that Paul does is evil, and that you would be wise not to have anything further to do with either him, or any other Tarot reader."

"Alright." Joanna smiled sweetly, changing the subject. "I'll tell you about the things that I have experienced in my house. When I first moved in, there were just the occasional poltergeist activity - things going missing; lights turning themselves on and off; that kind of stuff. But then a figure started to occasionally appear in the bathroom. It wouldn't do anything much - just stand there, staring. I believe this entity was also responsible for possessing my ex-husband, making him do unspeakable things to me. Things which contributed to my divorcing him for 'unreasonable behaviour' in the end. Anyway, moving on; last Tuesday things took a turn for the worst again, when this thing tried to possess my sister. Paul was able to distract it long enough to get her out of danger, but it turned on him; kicking and punching - he's still got the bruises to prove it."

"What is it like now? Have things calmed down?" she asked, a sympathetic tone prominent in her voice.

"Yes they have. I had the Wednesday off, to tidy up and that, and the atmosphere in the house, especially the bathroom, was quite heavy. But that could just have been my imagination, because of the fright I'd had the night before. But it is certainly back to normal now, yes."

"Good." the Reverend smiled at her. "Now, I've been told to ask a few questions, to ascertain why this presence is in your home. Do you know why it is there?"

Joanna shook her head.

"Have you used an Ouija board?" The Reverend continued.

"No. Using those things is asking for trouble, in my opinion." Joanna replied.

"What about a seance?" Joanna shook her head once more. "And you are certain that this spirit that attacked Paul and your sister, is the same one that has always been in your house?"

"Positive." Joanna confirmed with confidence.

"So you don't think that Paul brought it into the house with him, then?" the Reverend

Angela Butler wanted to be certain that Paul was not to blame.

"Definitely not." Joanna sharply replied.

"Then why do you think it got dramatically worse when Paul was present?" the deaconess fired a further question about the psychic.

Joanna pondered at the question for a moment, before replying, "I think it must have been scared of him."

The deaconess was puzzled by Joanna's reply. "What makes you think it was scared?"

"Because, it's best form of defence was to attack."

"To destroy Paul, before he destroyed it, you mean?" the Reverend tried to clarify Joanna's theories. "So why did it attack your sister first, then?"

"Because, it knew that by using my sister, it could get Paul right where it wanted him."

"So, how did Paul manage to survive this assault on him?"

"He said the Lords Prayer."

Reverend Angela Butler's face lifted into a broad smile. "Well, at least Paul has the right idea, then." she paid him a backhanded complement.

"I am sorry that I can not be of more help, but I really don't know why this entity is in my house." Joanna found herself apologising, "To be honest, up until the events earlier this week, I was able to live with it quite happily. However, something must be done before things get out of hand, and someone gets hurt."

"I quite agree." Reverend Angela Butler approved with Joanna's conclusion. "Well, I will telephone the Reverend Carl Garner later this evening and tell him all that you've said to me. If you telephone me - say, tomorrow morning, we can then arrange for you to meet Carl to talk about how best to tackle this problem."

"That will be great, thank you. You know, I don't mean so sound rude, but I thought

you'd just think I was mad or something, and tell me to stop being so over imaginative."

The reverend gave her a kind, gentle smile. "The Church never takes this kind of thing lightly - I am sorry that I personally don't know enough about the subject to be of more help to you. However, Carl is extremely knowledgeable about these things, so hopefully it will soon be sorted out."

"Well, I'd better not take up any more of your valuable time." Joanna drew the meeting to an end and rose to her feet.

The Reverend Angela Butler pulled herself out of those plump, comfortable cushions and, without further a do, she showed the young woman to the front door.

As Joanna stepped over the threshold, she turned and held out her hand. The deaconess, responding to the young woman's gesture, took Joanna's hand with hers and shook.

"Thank you for seeing me, at such short notice." Joanna expressed her gratitude. "Goodbye."

"Goodbye." the deaconess replied. "And God bless." and with that, the Reverend Angela Butler retreated into her house and closed the door. Joanna clambered back into her car and started the engine. Moments later, she was driving along the open road and heading for home, as the meeting whirred around in her head.

There was one thing that perplexed her, as she recalled the conversation between herself and the deaconess - where did she get all that stuff in the Bible, from? What she said must have been correct, or the Reverend Angela Butler would have jumped on her immediately, but where did it all come from? She certainly did not remember a lot of what she had said being taught from her school days, and that was the only time that she was forced to sit and listen to a preacher telling stories from the Good Book. Was it Divine intervention? Who knows. But, overall she was quite pleased with how the meeting had gone with the deaconess, and was now rest assured that help was at hand.

CHAPTER SIXTEEN
31ST JULY, 1993

10.00 am Felden

The Reverend Angela Butler was busy carrying some Church magazines from the hall way to the boot of her car, when the telephone interrupted her activities.

Mumbling furiously to herself, the deaconess placed the pile back on the floor, marched over to the electrical device and snatched up the hand set. But she hid her annoyance at the interruption as she spoke down the receiver and, with a soft and elegant tone, she answered its beckoning, stating "Reverend Angela Butler speaking."

"Hello Angela. It's Joanna here; Tony and Margaret Racen's daughter. I haven't interrupted you, or anything, have I?" a young woman's voice came travelling down the wires.

"Oh . Hello Joanna ." the deaconess' voice moved up a pitch, upon identification of her caller. "No, no . I wasn't doing anything special. How are you?"

"Fine, thank you." came the young woman's reply. "I am ringing to see if you have contacted that gentleman yet ... umm ... Reverend Garner? About the problem at my house."

"Yes. Yes I have." the deaconess' voice to on a distinctly flatter tone. "I rang Carl yesterday evening and told him all about your predicament ..."

"And?" Joanna interrupted the clergywoman.

"I don't know how to put this, Joanna," the deaconess started to explain, "but Carl seems to feel that, although you obviously have a serious problem in you house, he is unable to help you further, as it is out of his jurisdiction." The Reverend Angela Butler's tone overflowed with sympathy for the poor woman. "He feels that if he get's involved with this case, he could get severely reprimanded by the doctrine. His hands are tied. He suggests that you contact your local vicar and take the matter up from there." she paused in anticipation of a comment from the caller, but Joanna remained silent. "I can not apologise enough, Joanna. My heart goes out to you."

"Thank you, Angela. You are very kind." Joanna sighed. "I am so sorry that I have wasted your time."

"Wasted my time? Not at all. I am just penitent that I have been of no help to you." The deaconess replied. "Please keep me in touch with the developments and, if you ever need a sympathetic ear at any time, do not hesitate to come and talk to me."

"Thank you." the disappointment was prominent in Joanna's voice. "Take care of yourself."

"God bless you." came the soft reply and with that, the conversation was closed.

Joanna slowly placed the hand set back on its hook and stared, in disbelief, at the telephone. Despite the deaconess having warned her that, technically, it was out of her authority, Joanna felt that the Church had firmly slammed to door shut in her face.

Suddenly, she felt as if she was not alone in the room. She spun round and looked about her. There, in the corner of the sitting room, directly below the bathroom, stood the apparition. It stared at her with those menacing eyes, as it shook its head in a slow, sarcastic fashion.

Joanna found herself squaring up to its intimidation. "Don't think I've given up yet, M.O.G.." she growled at the spirit. "Up until last Tuesday I could have lived here, quite happily, with your presence. But you stepped out of line, my friend, and so you have given me no other choice." Then, with new found strength, she marched out into the kitchen and, retrieving the local directory from a cupboard, she returned to the telephone and proceeded to flick through the pages, looking for the telephone number of her local vicar.

The manifestation moved towards her and, with a deep minatory voice, it said. "I am not afraid of you; you are nothing. You think you can cleanse this house of me? Think again, hag. I have a far greater power that walks with me, than any of those weak, cassock clad gaggle of entrails that mumble their way through the words of a book. You will not find an exorcist amongst them that will be strong enough to rid this house of my presence. Go ahead; ring up your clergy 'friends'. Invite them into my house and see just how powerful I am. I have advocates; mighty advocates, that will see you destroyed before they see me fall."

"We'll see." came Joanna's smart reply, as she stumbled across the telephone number of the vicarage and, without any further hesitation, she began to dial.

The phone on the other end seemed to ring forever, before it was answered by the quiet, gentle voice of a woman.

"Hello." Joanna proceeded with the conversation. "Is that the vicarage?"

"It is." came the gentle reply.

"May I speak with the Reverend Lawrence, please?"

"I am afraid my husband is not here at the moment. Can I help you?"

"I would like to make an appointment to see him, if that is possible, concerning an exorcism."

"Oh." Came the rather surprised reply. "Yes ... well ... umm ... one moment please, while I get his diary." and with that, the receiver was dropped onto the table at the other end and the vicars wife scurried off, to find his diary.

The M.O.G. stood there, laughing viciously at her, as she waited for the woman to return. "Mention ghosts and they all run back into those little holes in ground, that they have crawled out off." The spirit taunted. "Tell them about your dabbling with the occult and they will do not more than say that you brought it all on yourself and, that you deserve all that you get."

Ignoring his provocations, she waited patiently until the vicar's wife returned with the diary. "Sorry to keep you waiting." the woman's gentle voice flowed through the earpiece, "The Reverend Lawrence can see you on Wednesday evening, at seven-thirty, if that's alright."

"Fine, yes."

The woman then enquired, "Will anyone else be accompanying you?"

"Yes. My partner definitely. And possibly a third person."

"Can I take you name then, please?" and with that Joanna gave the vicars wife all the relevant details.

"Right then, Mrs Waller. We look forward to seeing you on Wednesday, then." and with that, the telephone conversation came to an abrupt end.

Placing the hand set back on its hook, Joanna turned to the spirit, with an air of satisfaction. "Happy now, M.O.G.?"

But the spirit just laughed; an evil, menacing laugh, as it proceeded to evaporate into thin air before her eyes.

CHAPTER SEVENTEEN
4TH AUGUST 1993

5.25 pm Hemel Hempstead

Joanna pulled up outside Paul's house, just as he swung open the front door and stepped out, into the sunlight. She had not even had time to get out of the Peugeot, before Paul was standing at the passenger door, patiently waiting for her to let him inside the car.

Leaning across the seat, she unlocked the door, enabling him to get inside. "Hello Jo." he greeted her, gently. "How are things with you?"

"Better, now the days work is done." she informed him with half a smile. "You?"

"To be honest, I will be glad when this meeting with the vicar is over." he pronounced. "I am afraid that the clergy don't tend to see eye-to-eye with me."

Joanna gave him a sympathetic smile. "Don't worry. I got the lecture about how evil psychics were from the Reverend Angela, when I first saw her last Friday but, never the less, she was still genuine about trying to help me, despite our different view on that subject."

"What did she say?" he enquired, as Joanna started up the engine and pulled away from the curb.

"Well, reading between the lines, if she had known what to do, I am certain she would have found a way around all the red tape that the Church tie themselves in knots with. But it wasn't to be. Her friend, and exorcist, the Reverend Garner was not willing to follow my case up, so that put an end to that avenue."

"What about the house? Anything eventful happened there over the last week, or so?" his soothing voice was full of concern.

"Nothing to write home about, no." She glanced at him quickly, before returning her gaze to the road. "There has only been one insistent since the evening you came, and that was when I phoned the Vicarage on Saturday morning, to make this evenings appointment."

"What happened?" Paul's voice showed apprehension.

"The M.O.G. just started saying that it was more powerful than the Church and that I could never have it exorcised."

Paul gave a wry smile, for the M.O.G.'s intimidation showed its weakness. "Don't take any notice of it."

"Oh. I don't." came Joanna's cocky reply, despite a voice inside telling her that the ride was going to get a lot rougher, yet.

The rest of the journey was done in relative silence, with just the occasional outburst of idle chatter. About half an hour later, or so, Joanna finally reached her destination and, parking the Peugeot on the wasteland outside her home, she clambered out of the car and proceeded to wonder up the path towards the front door, with Paul in tow.

As they reached the house, they were ambushed from every side, by four hungry cats.

The first to the door was Skimble, a tall, lanky black and white tom. Mungie, a cheeky little ginger cat with a white bib and paws, followed him. Chloe, a squat and dainty Tortoiseshell queen, was next with the moth-eared old granddad, Fred, limping along at the rear.

"Are you lot hungry?" Joanna grinned at her pets, as they meowed insistently, demanding to be fed.

Unlocking the door they all entered the house, with the exception of Fred, and as the troop clambered inside, their nostrils were filled with the smell of beef stew. Joanna wandered over to the slow cooker and, lifting the lid, she peeked inside to check on the dinner, whilst a hoard of hungry felines swarmed around her feet. She then glanced at her watch and pronounced. "Lewis will be home in about half an hour. I'll put the kettle on, then I'm afraid you'll have to excuse me while I feed the cats and peel some potatoes." and with that, she began organising both the beverage and the dinners, while Paul made himself comfortable on a kitchen stall.

Fred was the only animal to remain outside, and Paul watched curiously from his stool, as the cat stood on the threshold, anxiously peering inside the house.

"Come on, puss." he called to the aged animal. "Its feed time."

Dishing up the cat's food, Joanna stated, "Oh. Fred never comes inside the house. I always have to feed him outside."

Paul looked perplexed. "Why's that?" he asked.

"I don't really know." She replied. "He is a stray, you see. He lives around the farm, where I keep my pony. He just kind of adopted me one day, and followed me home. I think he must feel claustrophobic inside, or something. Anyway, he refuses to come in, so I feed him in the garden." She then proceeded to place three bowls on the floor for Skimble, Chloe and Mungie, before wondering outside with a forth bowl, for Fred.

With the cats busy gulping down their food, Joanna turned her attention to the spuds and began preparing food for herself, Lewis and their guest. Once the spuds were happily settled on the hob, she then wandered back to the kettle and proceeded with the beverages.

Finishing her chores, she picked up two piping hot mugs and, with an invitation for him to join her in the sitting room, they both ambled through into the other room and made themselves comfortable.

Paul took a couple of delicate sips of his tea, before announcing flatly, "They don't like me here, do they?" before proceeding to nervously light a cigarette.

"Who?" Came Joanna's naive reply.

"Your friends that live here with you." he gave her a quick glance from his dark eyes, before proceeding to look about him, agitatedly. "I feel him, he is walking down the stairs .. now his is in the kitchen ..." at that point Paul spun round and stared at the doorway.

"Spooks don't walk, they float about." she tried to humour him.

"He walks." came an abrupt correction to Joanna's comment, before the young psychic continued, "... he is now in the doorway." Paul's voice then angered, "What do you want? Why are you here? Why don't you just go back from whence you came, and leave us alone." But the entity just stood there, its arms folded in an arrogant fashion.

Joanna sat motionless, on the settee; her eyes firmly fixed on the doorway. She began to feel decidedly uneasy. What if it tried the same trick as before with her sister, only using her as the bait this time? But Paul, sensing her agitation, merely stated, "It won't harm you, Jo. It is me, he is afraid of."

The spirit laughed at the psychic's comment. An evil, mocking laughter that filled every corner of the room. Then, with an expression of contempt for Paul's words, the apparition proceeded to envelope itself in a shroud of black mist before disappearing into insignificance, and was gone.

The sound of a key in the lock broke the silence, as Lewis crashed his way into the house with his Collie, Nell, trotting along behind. Joanna immediately jumped up and was out in the kitchen, as her partner threw both his van keys, and mobile phone, on the worktop.

"Hi, Lewis." she greeted him, with an air of relief. "Cup of tea?" and at a nod from the tired, grease covered dairy engineer, she was busy making him a welcoming cuppa.

"Dinner smells good." he commented, as he beamed at his girlfriend, "I'm starving."

Joanna handed Lewis his tea, as she informed him, "Paul is in the other room."

Taking the mug in his grimy hand, Lewis left his girlfriend to feed the dog, whilst he ambled into the sitting room. "Alright mate?" he greeted his guest, as he threw himself onto the settee, then proceeding to tell the psychic about the life and times of a dairy engineer.

7.15 pm

The three of them clambered into the Peugeot, with Lewis at the wheel, then set off in the direction of Ivinghoe. Despite Lewis trying to keep a conversation going, neither
of the other two were particularly responsive.

Paul sat in the back, worrying about the vicar ridiculing him, whilst Joanna slouched
in the passenger seat, anxious as to whether the Reverend Lawrence would believe them, or not.

Five minutes later, they found themselves outside the vicarage, the evening sun lighting the building up, like a jewel.

The three abandoned the car and wandered up the path, towards the porch. Lewis took the lead, and then Joanna and finally, Paul brought up the rear. They were met by the kind faced, white-haired vicar, who promptly invited them into a square, bare-
boarded hall way, with an open staircase leading up to the first floor.

With a humble smile and melancholy eyes, he showed them into his sun-lit study,
with a picture of the Egyptian Sun God, Ra, on the chimney-breast and a Chinese rug
on the floor.

"Please sit." he invited his guests to make themselves at home. They all promptly sat. He then slowly wandered over to his desk chair and eased himself into it, pausing only for a moment to catch his breath, before informing them in a quiet manner. "I apologise if I seem a little vague, "he announced, "I am due to go into hospital for an operation, which is why I am trying to take things a little easy at the moment." He then turned to Joanna, "I don't know if my wife told you, but I don't generally see anyone in the evenings. However, because of the serious nature of your predicament, she felt that we should meet as soon as possible, which is why I made an exception in this case."

"I am sorry to hear you are not well." Joanna sympathised with the vicar, "Your wife said nothing about you being ill, or I wouldn't have bothered you."

The vicar smiled serenely, "Don't be silly. You have a problem with a ghost, I understand, and you would like the Church to get rid of it for you?"

"Well, yes. If the Church feels it is appropriate."

The vicar reached over the desk for his note pad, as he continued to his audience, "Before telling me what has been going on, I would appreciate each of you giving me your names and telling me a little bit about yourselves, in turn, so that I can get a better understanding of you all, as people. I do think it is so important that I get to know who I am dealing with, as individuals." He then retrieved some spectacles from their case and, placing the pair of half moon glasses on his nose, his gaze then fell upon Joanna. "Would you like to start then?" he smiled a soft, warm smile.

"My name is Joanna Waller and I am twenty-six years old. I am a bookkeeper by trade. I have lived in Slapton for approximately five years and am divorced."

The vicar nodded, in a slow deliberate fashion, as he took down the notes. Once he had completed jotting down the details, he looked up over his half moon glasses at Lewis.

Leaning back in his chair and crossing his legs, Lewis began to bellow, in that hearty fashion of his, "Lewis Chetfler; thirty-two. Self-employed Dairy Engineer. I live with Jo, and have done since 1991."

"And you have experienced strange phenomena in the house also?" the vicar paused from his scribbling, to ask the question.

Lewis pondered for a moment, then replied, "I've not actually seen a ghost, no. But I have been in the house when it has played up, yes."

"Right." the vicar evasively replied, as he returned to the note pad, to complete Lewis' particulars.

Finishing his report on Lewis, the vicar turned to Paul. "And who are you?" he smiled at the psychic.

"My name is Paul Hitt." Paul replied, his voice full of nervousness at the anticipation of the vicar's reaction once he disclosed himself fully. "I am twenty-seven and am a professional Tarot reader."

The vicar immediately stopped jotting his notes and looked up, over his half-moon glasses, at the dark haired young man. "Do you live at the house, as well?" came an unexpected question from the vicar.

"No." Paul replied, surprise showing in his face. "No, I don't. I live in Hemel."

"Then why are you here?" the vicar smiled at him from behind his glasses.

Paul looked across at the other two momentarily, then turned his gaze back to the white-haired clergyman. "Because I am a witness to the activities in the house." came his reply.

The vicar returned to his note pad and, slowly repeating Paul's words, he wrote down the details. He then paused for a moment and dreamily staring at the picture of Ra on the chimney breast, before turning his attention to Joanna and smiled, softly. "Please tell me as much as you can remember about the things that you have experienced in you house, Joanna." he coaxed the woman into revealing her plight.

Joanna proceeded to tell the Reverend Lawrence about the poltergeist activity, the possession of her ex-husband, what took place on that fateful Tuesday and of the couple of visitations since then. As she disclosed the facts to the vicar, he smiled upon her with an air of sympathy and warmth that filled her heart with hope. He would only break the eye contact briefly, to make a few scrawny notes, before turning his attention back to her various accounts.

When she finally finished, he turned to Paul, "Do you feel that the spirit in the house should be exorcised, Paul?" he enquired, as he slide his glasses down his nose to focus better on the young psychic.

Paul smiled. "Yes. Yes, I do. It has proved that it is a danger."

The vicar nodded at Paul's reply, before turning to Lewis. "And how do you feel about all this?" he questioned the dairy engineer. "Do you feel threatened by the presence?"

"Well, personally no." Lewis gave a macho reply. "But, I've seen how it has affected both Jo and Paul and it can't be allowed to get away with that, now can it? So, I think that the best thing all round, would be for it to be exorcised."

The vicar nodded, as he listened to Lewis' thoughts on the matter, before finally turning his attention to the young woman. "And how do you feel about an exorcism?"

"As Paul said, it has become a danger. I agree with both him, and Lewis that it should be sorted out. What do you think, Reverend Lawrence?"

The vicar leant back in his chair, as he took his glasses away from his face. "Having heard your account of paranormal activity in your house, I recommend that I contact the diocese exorcist and relay this information to him, for his consideration.

However, I feel it is only fair to warn you all that, from past experiences on this matter, the offending spirit will become a little more restless than usual, as soon as it catches wind of an impending exorcism. This being the case, I would suggest that the less you talk about the subject in your home, the better. Also," he smiled at Joanna, "You have given me you home number, haven't you?" Joanna nodded. "Well, I think that it would be wise if you could give me another number to contact you on - a work number, or Paul's maybe, so that we do not alarm the offending spirit with talk of this nature at your home." He then averted his gaze to the psychic, "Does that seem like the best idea to you?" he respectfully asked for Paul's opinion and duly received a confirming nod.

The vicar then handed Joanna his note pad. She jotted down her parent's number, as well as Lewis' mobile telephone number as a second option, then handed the pad back to the reverend.

Rising from his seat, the vicar stated, "Well, I think we have done all we can at this stage. I will notify the exorcist as soon as possible and will contact you, when I have spoken to him." The vicar gave each and every one of his audience a serene smile. "Then, we can all discuss the next stage." and with that, the three found themselves being ushered back out, into the square hall.

As they reached the front door, Joanna turned and, shaking the vicar's hand, she smiled, "Thank you very much for seeing us. I hope you are feeling better, soon."

"Oh. I'm sure I will be." he replied, with an exuberant air about him. "Take care, all of you." and with that, the three were back outside, in the evening sunshine and wondering down the path towards the car.

"Fancy coming back for a cuppa, before we take you home?" Lewis invited Paul back to the house.

"Thanks." Paul smiled, glad that the meeting with the Reverend Lawrence was finally over.

"Wasn't too bad, was it Paul?" Joanna gave the psychic a flash of a smile.

"No. He's quite a nice chap, really."

"Well at least he believes us." Lewis bellowed, "Now, maybe something can be done about that bloody M.O.G.." and with that, he started up the engine and headed for home.

The house was uncannily quiet as the party wandered into the kitchen. Even Nell lay quietly on the Keshan wool runner, just nervously wagging her tail as she set eyes upon them.

"What's up with you, dog?" Lewis' bellowing voice echoed around the kitchen, but Nell just made a grunting sound as she placed her head on the carpet. Unconcerned about the dog's neurotic behaviour, he gave her a rough stroke on the head, before striding over to the kettle.

After the teas and coffees were made, the three wandered through to the sitting room, followed by the dog, and made themselves comfortable.

Paul sat in a pine-framed rocking chair, whilst Lewis and Joanna both sat on the settee opposite him. They just stared at one another, each waiting for someone else to open a conversation.

Paul was the first to break the silence. "Found out anything more about your guides, Jo?" he enquired, with a soft, soothing voice.

"Not really, no." Her face gave an expression of disappointment. "Although I have
been talking to a number of them, just as you showed me the other Tuesday, Edward seems to be the one who comes through the most."

"May I speak with Edward?" Paul asked.

"Sure, if he wants to talk to you." came her reply.

"No, it is if you want me to talk to him." Paul corrected her, firmly.

"Fine by me." she beamed at him.

The psychic placed his mug of tea on the carpet and clasped his hands together. "Edward." he called, and the spirit duly appeared before him.

"Please identify yourself." Paul requested, in a serious tone.

"Cei. Edwardo." came a bubbly reply.

"Edwardo?" Paul scratched his head. "Estu Espaniol?"

"Cei ." the spirit confirmed, though his voice had an air of detachement about it.

Paul then continued the conversation, in Spanish. "Youi cares tu ablah sombre tu ."

"Oui soi Mexicano . Mei anui este beinto-neubo. Oui soi temata en me penultamat vivo ."

Joanna and Lewis just stared at each other, perplexed as to what was going on.

Paul frowned. "Oui soi cares tu ablaha en Englietre?"

Edwardo's voice took on an uncommited tone. "Cei . Un poko ." he replied.

The psychic then smiled at the spirit, pompously. "Bien." he stated, "Ablaha Englientre ahora, por favour."

But Edwardo, not happy about the request, asked, "Pourque?"

Paul's voice rose, authoritively. "Because I said so." came his abrupt reply to Edwardo's question.

Lewis interrupted the psychic's conversation with the spirit. "What is going on?

What are you babbling on about?"

Paul turned his attention to the dairy engineer. "I was just asking Edwardo some questions, that's all."

"Like what?" Lewis demanded to be told what had been said.

"Well, I asked Edwardo if he was Spanish. He replied that he was Mexican, twenty-

nine years of age and was murdered in his last life. I then asked him if he spoke English. He replied that he spoke a little, so I told him to speak in English from now on. He asked me why, so I told him that it was because I wanted him too."

"So this Edwardo," Lewis continued, "what does he look like?"

"He is short; about five foot four inches, he has long, black curly hair, a stubbly beard and wears a poncho and a sombrero." Paul answered Lewis' question.

Edwardo then piped in, with a distinct sing to his voice, " También monto a una mula." He stated, with pride.

"Oh . And he also rides a mule ." Paul repeated the Mexican's words.

"That's nice ." Lewis replied sarcastically, then gave a hearty giggle.

Joanna, bored with hearing about Edwardo, turned to Paul and asked, "What about any of my other guides? Can you find out more about them?"

Paul paused for a moment, closed his eyes, then opening them again, he stated. "They are all here. What would you like to know."

Joanna thought for a moment, then tentatively asked, "Is the Israelite here?"

"Yes." came Paul's reply. "He has just told me that his name is Benjamin. Please refer to him as that, in future." The psychic then turned his attention to another guide, "You also have a young girl around you called Emma. She is not earthbound, as you suspected, although she is responsible for some of the poltergeist activity in this house, to get your attention."

He then pondered for a moment, before turning to Lewis. "Has you granddad passed over?" Lewis nodded. "And he is very knowledgeable about dogs, yes?"

"Yes. When I went to see that Geraldine person in High Wycombe, he was the one who said about the dog's feet. The strange thing is, when we got home, I had a look at her feet and discovered one of her claws was so long that, if it was left much longer, it would have pierced the paw, because it was growing in a circular fashion."

"He is your head guide," Paul informed him, "and he is always at your side. He has just told me that, if you ever feel threatened in this house, just call him and he will protect you."

Lewis leant forward in his chair and arrogantly stated, "Come off it, Paul. Once you're dead, you're dead - six foot under, pushing up daisies. What both you, and Geraldine, picked up on was memories from me about my granddad - that's all. All this nonsense about spooks and guides, it's all in your head."

"If that is what you believe ." Paul was undeterred by Lewis' opinion.

But Joanna was not so laid back about Lewis' comment. "So how do you explain what happen the other week, when both my sister and Paul were attacked, eh?"

"Over active imagination." came his abrupt reply.

"Well, you didn't think so at the time." she reminded him, with indignance.

Paul began to feel uncomfortable as the other two discussed the activities in the use. It was not because of Lewis' dismissal of his way of thinking, nor the couple indulging in a heated discussion, rather because he felt another presence enter the room.

Nell, also sensing something untoward going on, got up from the spot she was laying and stared at the doorway, her hackles raised.

Upon the dogs unrest, Lewis and Joanna stopped arguing and focused their attention on the collie, as Nell's eyes followed something, as it slowly moved from the doorway, to just behind Paul's chair. She then started to whine, before screwing her mouth up to bark.

Paul looked across at Joanna. "He's behind me, isn't he?" he asked, as he saw the expression of horror creep across the young woman's face.

"It's M.O.G., yes ." Joanna confirmed.

The entity then lifted up a hand and began to manipulate Paul's aura, trying to find the weakest spot at the point of his psychic gate.

Paul grabbed the back of his neck. "He is getting to be a real pain." he tried to make light of the situation, as he got off the rocking chair and turned to face the spirit. "Trying to sneak up on me now, eh? You'll have to do better than that, if you want to possess me." he informed the M.O.G., in a sharp manner.

Laughing callously, it stepped forward into the rocking chair, then dematerialised before their eyes.

10.00 pm Hemel Hempstead

Shortly after that, Lewis and Joanna drove Paul back to Hemel, having mutually decided that the psychic's departure would be the most sensible thing to do.

They remain at Paul's house for quite a while, chatting about their meeting with the vicar until, at ten o'clock, Lewis looked at his watch and declared that it was time to make a move home.

Within seconds, they had said their goodbyes and were outside the front door, with Lewis marching off towards the car. "Wait, Jo ." Paul caught Joanna's arm, as she went to follow her partner.

"What's up?" Joanna frowned at the psychic.

"Peter Two is coming with you." he informed her in a quiet tone.

Joanna was puzzled by his statement. "Why?"

"For extra protection. Both he and Benjamin think it is for the best."

"Do I have a say in the matter?" she questioned their motive.

Paul shook his head. "Not really, no." he replied, flatly.

"What about you? Surely you need protecting too?"

Paul looked down at her seriously, "Not half as much as you do." he replied.

So, with that, she turned and jogged up the path, to join Lewis in the Peugeot. She clambered inside the vehicle and had hardly had time to put her seat belt on, before Lewis was roaring up the road.

As they reached Edlesborough, she heard a soft voice in her ear. "I am Pete, Paul's guide, and I represent God's light ." She then felt two hands touching the back of her head, as Peter Two continued, "Can you feel my presence?"

Joanna turned to Lewis, "Did you hear that?"

Lewis fleetingly turned to face his girlfriend, and asked, "Heard what?", before returning his gaze to the road.

"You didn't hear someone else talking in the car then?"

"Na. Must be one of your spooks ." he ribbed.

Peter Two then continued, "Now listen to me, Joanna, and take heed," the magician-like guide informed her, "When you reach the house, an unclean spirit will attack you.

When this happens you must acknowledge my presence by saying 'The Holy Ghost is with me; your evil will not prevail.' This will give you extra protection."

"The Holy Ghost is with me; your evil will not prevail ." she repeated his words.

"What?" Lewis broke her concentration. "What did you say?"

"It is something that has just come through my mind." she informed her boyfriend. "If I get attacked by M.O.G. I must say, 'The Holy Ghost is with me; your evil will not prevail.'"

"Good idea ." Lewis smiled, as he turned off the A4146 towards Slapton.

In no time at all, Lewis was swinging the Peugeot onto the wasteland, outside the row of cottages. As soon, as the wheels left the road, Joanna suddenly became aware of another presence in the vehicle with them. She went to unlock the seat belt as Lewis ground the car to a halt, but as she moved her hand towards the button, something grabbed her from behind with such force, that she was immobilised.

Peter Two rushed inside her body, like a warm summer breeze, to protect her but, as she tried to open her mouth, the force of the negative energy in the car was so strong, that every ounce of strength that she had, was sapped from her.

Despite Benjamin and Peter Two's efforts, the entity began breaking through her defences and she could feel it slowly seeping into her body. She was helpless, like a baby, and completely out of control. Her head began spinning uncontrollably and everything around her began to distance itself, as if she were about to faint.

"Are you alright?" came a far off voice, which she hardly recognised as Lewis'.

She tried to grab for the seat belt clasp, but there was no energy left in her to move.

"Jo. Jo. What's wrong?" she heard the faint voice of her boyfriend again.

Without trying to answer him, she mustered all the strength she could find and, slowly opening her mouth, she mistakenly whispered the phrase, "The Holy Ghost is with me; your evil will prevail.".

She then heard Lewis' voice again, as the realisation of what was going on, dawned on him. "Will NOT prevail . Will NOT Prevail . Say it again, Jo - for God's sake."

Joanna opened her mouth a second time, but as she went to utter the words, she felt a hand clasp itself around her neck and squeezed so tightly, that it choked the life from her.

Lewis grabbed her hand. "The Holy Ghost is with us; your evil will not prevail." he bellowed out, and as the words past his lips, Joanna felt the grip around her neck slacken. Taking advantage of the entities weakened state, she took a deep breath, opened her mouth again, and uttered in a hoarse, weak voice, "The Holy Ghost is with me; your evil will not prevail. The Holy Ghost is with me; your evil will not prevail."

Suddenly she felt the entity slip off her and slump in the back of the car. Sensing that it was still there with them, she clasped her hands together and began to stumble her way through the Lords Prayer, as best she could. Lewis followed her lead and the two of them sat there, preying for their lives.

Half way through, the atmosphere of the car lifted and she felt Peter Two leave her body and move back, behind her. He then placed his hands on the back of her head, sending a warm, comforting sensation through her.

As she regained her strength, she unclasped the belt and slowly fell out of the car.

Lewis jumped out of his side and was round at the passenger door, just as she righted her stance. He grabbed her arm to steady her. "You alright? What was all that about?"

Joanna stared up at her boyfriend, in bewilderment. "Something horrible, something evil was trying to take me over. I could taste it; smell it; feel it caressing me. It was disgusting."

"That M.O.G. is getting out of hand. Look, let's go and book a room in the motel up the road. It's too dangerous for you to stay here ." he pointed at the house. "I'll get hold of the Reverend Lawrence first thing in the morning to tell him what has happened."

"I don't think that it was the M.O.G. this time. Besides, I'm not letting some dead-beat run me out of my own home ." she informed him with vigour. "I'll sleep on your bible, tonight . At lease that'll ensure that I can have a good nights sleep ." And with that, she boldly marched off towards the front door.

The house had an eerie feel to it, as the two of them entered the kitchen, with an oppressiveness that oozed from every part of the room. However, despite what had just happened, Joanna was stubbornly determined not to be driven out by the entity so, striding into the sitting room, she grabbed the Bible before making her way upstairs to bed.

CHAPTER EIGHTEEN
11TH AUGUST 1993

6.30 pm Slapton

Despite contacting the Reverend Lawrence the day after Joanna was attacked in the car, neither she nor Lewis had received any further communication from the vicar of
the Holy Cross Church.

As Lewis looked upon his girlfriend, his heart was filled with grief, for she was beginning to show the strain from living in the house. The weight had fallen from her five foot four inch frame at a rapid rate, and the once healthy looking nine and a half stone woman had reduced to a frailer eight and three quarter.

Staring at her through his thin, silver rimmed glasses, he stated firmly, "I can't sit around any longer, watching you slowly disappear before my eyes, Jo. Come on, let's go for a drive and make a phone call." and with that, the two of them threw on their coats and dragged themselves outside, into the drizzle.

It was not long before the Peugeot was winding its way along the lanes, towards Ivinghoe Aston. Passing the entrance to Horton Wharf Farm, Lewis turned to his pale-faced partner and, stating in a gruff voice, he pronounced "This should be far enough from the house .", before swinging his car off the road and onto a grass lay-by.

Turning off the engine, he reached for his mobile and dialled the Reverend Lawrence's telephone number. He listened to it ring a few times then, with a click, his call was answered.

"Hello?" he bellowed down the phone. "Is the Reverend Lawrence there, please? ... Lewis Chetfler." He then waited patiently a few seconds more, before continuing the conversation. "Reverend Lawrence? Lewis Chetfler here ... hello. Have you managed to contact anyone yet? ... Yes? ... Right. ... Well, what do you want to know? ... Right. I'll pass you over." Covering the mouthpiece, Lewis turned to Joanna and stated, "The Reverend wants to ask you some further questions ." and with that, he handed the mobile to his girlfriend.

Joanna took the phone from him and tentatively placed it to her ear. "Hello Reverend Lawrence, Joanna here ."

"Hello Joanna ." came the vicar's non-offensive voice from the other end of the line. "As I just explained to Lewis; the Exorcist in Milton Keynes, that I have been trying to get hold of for you, is apparently on holiday at the moment, and won't be returning until around the 21st August. I am sorry that I have not contacted you, but I only managed to get hold of someone at his vicarage this morning. Anyway, as soon as I learnt of his absence, I contacted another Exorcist in Beaconsfield and told him of your predicament, stressing that I felt this matter could not wait until the local Exorcist's return."

"Thank you." Joanna replied.

"However," the Reverend's voice took on a sorrowful tone, "the Canon Fitzwilliams felt that more information must be obtained before he looked into the matter further, and so it is my duty to ask you some questions, if you don't mind?"

"Not at all." she frowned.

"Firstly, have you ever used an Ouija board, or partaken in a seance in the house?"

"No." came her forthright reply.

"Have you partaken in any other occult activities?" the Reverend continued.

"Paul, the chap who came with us to see you last Wednesday, did some readings at our house, and I have also seen other readers, in the past ." she explained.

"Have you got any Tarot cards, or any other occult material in your house?"

"Yes."

The vicars voice then took an abrupt turn, "Taking your replies to the questions into consideration, it is the Canon Fitzwilliams' belief that, should you throw away all the occult material that is in your home, and not invite any other psychics into your house, then the spirit will settle down again and everything will return to normal."

"What?" Joanna rose her voice, "That hardly eradicates the problem, does it? For whatever reason, I have a spook in my house. I sleep on the Bible, wear a cross and constantly say the Lords Prayer to try and protect myself from it, but it is still there, tormenting me . Throwing away books or cards, will hardly stop the attacks ."

"It might. You see, if you open yourself up to the occult, then you attract trouble of this kind. The Canon Fitzwilliams is concerned that by indulging in such activities as Paul's, you are asking for trouble."

Joanna scoffed. "What you mean is, the Canon thinks that I deserve all I get." The young woman then took on a softer tone. "I have known about this spook, ever since I moved into the house. It has always been there. I don't know why things have suddenly taken a turn for the worst, I am no expert on this subject but, never the less, they have - and to be honest with you, it is beginning to effect my health. I can't go through the rest of my life having to think twice about whom I can and can not invite to my house, for whatever reason. It can not be allowed to rule over me, like that."

"I DO sympathise with you." the Reverend commiserated, "But I have to convince the Canon that you have a genuine case, here. I mean, going on your answers to some of the questions, he will automatically assume that you have called the demon yourself, with the use of Tarot cards ..."

"But reading the Tarot is nothing like using an Ouija board. The origin of the Tarot goes back to the ancient Egypt, and that an ordinary pack of playing cards is merely a sixteenth century spin-off from the Tarot deck. Divination with cards, is no different from dice, or astrology, or tealeaves. There is absolutely no need to call upon an unknown entity for divination of this kind, it works merely on the recognition of symbols or numbers, to their meanings. However, I would agree with the Cannon that Ouija boards are extremely dangerous, for any old spook can be called in; good or evil. Therefore, this practice acts as an easy gateway for any spirit of ill intent to come through, for there is no control on who the user is going to get. For that reason, I personally would not touch an Ouija board with a barge-pole."

"I would be the first to admit that I know nothing of Tarot cards and Ouija boards, or how they work," the vicar admitted, in a non-patronising way, "Rightly or wrongly, Church ministers are taught that psychics are in league with the devil and therefore, work against God and the teachings of the doctrine. This is why the Canon asked me to clarify the situation. However, I agree that action should be taken on your house and will endeavour to contact the Canon Fitzwilliams again, asking for his assistance."

"Why is he so unwilling to help? Do you mean to tell me that if I had have used an Ouija board, even out of naivety, he would refuse to do an exorcism?" Joanna pumped the vicar for an explanation as to the Canons reluctance to do the job required of him.

"I am afraid I can not answer that. You must understand that I am merely the intermediary. I must act on what I am told to do. Unfortunately, I can only request his visiting your house - I can not order him to do so." the vicar softly explained.

"Yes, I understand that, but I am scared that the spook will soon get so strong, that either myself, or some other poor, innocent person is going to get badly hurt.."

"Please don't concern yourself .." the Reverend tried to comfort the distraught woman on the other end of the phone, "I will contact the Canon Fitzwilliams again, as soon as I am able, and endeavour to persuade him that action must be taken. Leave it with me." and with that the vicar closed their conversation and was gone.

12.45 am

The atmosphere in the house was more turbulent than of late, from the moment they returned from talking to the Reverend Lawrence. The thick and airless ambience hung in each room, like a darkened cloud, and although it never came to anything the couple got the feeling that the spirits in the house were uneasy.

At ten o'clock both Joanna and Lewis retired to bed, and although he was out like a light, Joanna found it hard to settle in such a cliquey atmosphere.

Eventually she was able to doze and soon after that she began to dream.

She found herself standing in a dark, damp alley. The walls of the buildings rose high above her on either side, blocking out the light, with only a single escape route ahead of her, in the distance.

Pausing, she looked back over her shoulder and saw her dimly lit bedroom. The covers of the bed rhythmically rose and fell again, as Lewis slept soundly, oblivious to her absence. Suddenly, the room was obscured by a figure, as it stepped from the house, into the narrow walkway, behind her. The figure then approached and, as Joanna strained her eyes in the murkiness of the alley, the silhouette slowly emerged from the shadows, until she found herself gazing upon a tall, slim woman in her mid thirties, with long, black hair and dark, cold eyes.

The woman then proceeded to walk straight past Joanna and continued to travel along the alleyway towards the other end, without acknowledging the perplexed young woman.

Instinctively, Joanna followed the tall, straight-haired woman, a respectful few feet behind, until they both came to the end of the alleyway.

Half-turning, the woman stretched out her hand and beckoned Joanna to follow, before turning the corner and disappeared from view. Joanna froze on the spot, gazing about her apprehensively. She felt threatened in this claustrophobic place and there was something familiar about that woman, which she did not like. She decided to retrace her steps back to the comfort of her bed, but upon turning to regress, she realised that the gateway to her reality had closed and the journey back home was now inaccessible.

There was nothing for it, she would have to step out of the damp, grey-bricked alley and face whatever was beyond. So, taking a deep breath and preparing herself for her fate, she nervously crept forward.

As soon as she turned the corner, the bleak buildings vanished and she found herself standing in a summer meadow, the grasses in full flower, with their long stems waving gracefully in the breeze.

The sun-bleached meadow was surrounded by glorious woodland in full foliage, with the land rolling away before her eyes, elegantly gliding down a slight incline, until it met with a brook of crystal-bright water. This place seemed like a hazy delusion of that desolate land she had visited so often in her past. Its beauty was both captivating and inspirational.

As she familiarised herself with the meadow before her, her eyes suddenly fell upon the tall, dark woman standing on the far bank of the stream, just in front of a building, which she immediately recognised as a house of worship. From her viewpoint, Joanna took note of the building that, to her surprise was in a dilapidated state. She pondered on how such a glorious place could be spoilt by such an eye-sore, but the tall woman distracted her from her contemplation's, by beckoning Joanna to join her.

Responding to the dark woman's gesticulations, Joanna began the stroll down the hillside, through the flowering meadow grass, until she reached a rickety wooden bridge, that precariously stretched across the brook.

Then, delicately treading the boards, she crossed the bridge and joined the dark-eyed woman on the far side. The woman gave Joanna a hard stare and, with a deep voice, she ordered, "Follow me ." to the young woman, before striding towards the Chapel door.

Obediently following the tall woman inside, Joanna found herself standing amongst the grime and dirt of neglect, which adorned the place. Before her stood an altar, heavily laden with dust, with gold candleholders covered with streams of blackened cobwebs. A cross stood in the centre of the altar, but its magisterial qualities had long since left the Christian symbol.

Joanna shivered from the dampness inside the building, as the smell of must insulted her nostrils, the coarseness of the air rasping the back of her nose and throat. The tall woman stood to one side, smiling smugly, as she watched the expression on Joanna's face. "Do you like what you see, dear?" her deep voice echoed around the chapel. "I know what you think about the Church. That's why I brought you here."

Joanna, recognising the way that the woman spoke, tried to recall where she had heard those tones before. But, unable to place the woman, she asked, "Who are you?"

"Mandy ." came the woman's reply.

Feeling uncertain of Mandy's role, Joanna asked, "Do you represent God's light?"

Mandy, annoyed that the young woman could ask such a question, snapped, "Of cause I do, dear ." she then turned to face the altar. "I have some 'friends' that you must meet ." and with that she stretched out her arm, summonsing her guests to come forth and reveal themselves.

As soon as she administered her demand, the room began to fill with a thick, grey mist, which completely obscured the altar. Then, from the mist, came six figures, each representing a member of the Clergy, and took their places in front of the communion table.

Joanna stood before them, her eyes flitting from one to the other, observing all six in turn. The first, to her right, took on the appearance of a deacon, the second a vicar, the third a cannon, the fourth an archdeacon, the fifth a bishop and finally the sixth, to her left, an archbishop. Each were dressed in robes befitting to their title and all had a solemn air about them.

Mandy turned back to the young woman and, with an air of supremacy about her, she stated, "These are the representatives from whom you seek your salvation. Go to each envoy in turn and ask two questions. The first being, 'are you willing to help me?' The second, 'are you able to help me?' And remember, dear, only the one who can answer 'yes' to both questions, will be able to deliver you from evil."

Responding to Mandy's words, Joanna stepped forward towards the deacon, who was the smallest member of the group. As she gazed upon the lay official, she observed a purple cloth wrapped around his face, making him incapable of verbal communication. Undeterred by this restriction, she proceeded to ask, "Are you willing to help me?" The deacon nodded, in a slow and deliberate fashion. She then continued with the second question, "Are you able to help me?" But as the words were uttered from her mouth, the deacon lifted his hands towards her and, to her horror, she found them tightly bound with purple rope. The deacon then hung his head low, and turned away from her, ending their association.

Joanna moved to the vicar who, to her delight, was neither gagged nor bound. The vicar gave her a humble smile as she stepped before him. Smiling back, she asked him the first question, just as she had done with the deacon. With a natural smile, he nodded, confirming that he was willing to assist her. Joanna then proceeded, "Are you able to help me " But the vicar shook his head, as he showed her a contract of his employ, which was entwined with red tape. Deflated, Joanna turned her attention back to the tall woman, "What are you trying to prove here, Mandy?" she growled at her escort, "This is a waste of my time."

"If that is what you think dear, then go." came Mandy's throaty reply. "But if I am to teach you anything, then continue with the task in hand."

As she returned her attention to back the vicar, she observed him facing the canon and hand him the contract before, the vicar too, turned his back on the young woman ending their association.

The canon was a fierce looking man, with eyes full of resentment and a stance rigid, from wrathfulness. Before she had chance to ask the first question, the canon thrust the Bible at her and, as she reached out to take it, the book spontaneously combusted into a fury of flames. She backed away from the flames, as he let it drop to the floor and burn until it was nothing more than a smouldering heap of ash. He then turned his back on her, as he folded his arms tight to his chest, and roared, "Able to help you, I am - Willing to help you, I am not." And with that, he cut her dead.

Mandy's face lifted into a sadistic smirk as she watched on, aware that Joanna was slowly being dismantled. But the young woman did not observe Mandy's pleasure, instead she continued down the line to the archdeacon.

The plump, rounded figure stood there, a smug expression on his chubby little face, as he watched Joanna approach. Not giving the archdeacon the chance to jump in first, she blurted out, "Are you able and willing to help me?"

"Certainly, provided you turn to God first." came his complacent reply.

"But I already have." came her sharp retort.

"But you dance with the devil. Did the canon's Bible not ablaze, as soon as you laid your hand upon its cover?"

"I never touched it." she informed him indignantly, "It was engulfed in flames, before I had the chance."

He smirked at her complacently, as he opened out a scroll and held it up to his face. "These are the rules that you must abide by, in order to turn to God." He then proceeded to read them to her, "One - Observe, and live by, the rules of Moses ..."

"I do." Joanna interrupted him, as the sound of throat clearing from the two remaining ministers echoed around the room.

The archdeacon raised his eyebrows, "If I may be permitted to proceed." He stated sarcastically, as he rattled the parchment. "Two - You must regularly attend a place of worship in order to show God that you have devoted your life to Him ..."

Joanna opened her mouth, to object to the second rule, but the commencement of a second bout of throat clearing, caused her to remain silent.

"Three." the archdeacon continued, "You must recognise Jesus Christ as Lord, and be willing to suffer, just as he did, when he was nailed on the cross. Four - you must love your fellow man; no matter what creed or colour, race or religion. Five - Always judge others as you would wish to be judged. Six - you must observe the twelve forbidden practices being, enchantment; witchcraft; sorcery; divination; wizardry; necromancy; charm; astrology; soothsaying; prognostication; observing times and magic. And that you must make an oath with God that you will never be tempted into indulging, thereof." The archdeacon paused, momentarily, to mop his brow with a dainty handkerchief, before continuing, "Seven - You must not make money your God. We Christians do not allow greed to creep into our hearts, for money is the route of all that is evil. Eight - Always give generously to the Church, for this is pleasing in God's sight . Nine - Never look down upon the lowly, or the afflicted. And finally, Ten - Welcome the Father, the Son and the Holy Spirit into your heart. Let them dwell there and carry them with you, always." He then rolled up the scroll and held it firmly in his right hand, whilst banging the roll of parchment, in a deliberate fashion, upon his left palm.

"So," Joanna stated coldly, "You think that anyone that is not a practising Christian, is against God then, do you?"

"There is only one way to God, and that is through Jesus Christ." he smugly replied, "Come. Join us. Let us teach you all that you need to know, so that your soul will be redeemed from the wicked life that you live."

"Why am I wicked, just because I have a different viewpoint to God, than you?" she questioned the archdeacon further.

"Because there is only one road to God. Follow us. Let us show you the way to Heaven. Save your soul now, whilst there is still time."

Joanna looked up at the round faced, round figured archdeacon and, with a serene smile, she slowly shook her head. "I can not practice, what I will not preach." she informed him gently, "There is much about your religion that I can not adhere to, or uphold, because I do not agree with it ."

"Then let your principles be the death of you." The archdeacon growled before, he also turned his back on the young woman denying her existence.

Joanna looked across at the bishop, with pleading eyes, for she desperately required help from some source, but the minister just scowled at her, before walking away to join the others.

With only the archbishop left, she approached the elegantly robed figure and knelt down before him.

Bowing her head, she muttered, "Please help me, for I am in desperate need. Do not hold contempt in your heart, despite the reproach the others have hurled at me, I implore you. Take pity on me and pour out your wrath upon the evil that reside in my house, for the wicked are only content with destruction. I beg of you, show the unclean the strength of your arm; disclose to them that you avenge my outpoured blood, for I am condemned to die. I am not in league with the Devil; my heart is with the Lord God Almighty."

With his fingers tightly gripping a golden cross in one hand, the archbishop stepped forward and lifted Joanna to her feet. "I may be the Head of the Church," he informed her softly, "But I can not do every job myself. I have deputies who are specially trained to administer the type of service that you seek and, therefore, I have to leave it to their judgement as to whether or not you are worthy of such assistance. I can not help you on this matter." and with that he rejected her plea and joined the other ministers, leaving her feeling dejected and alone.

Wiping a tear from her cheek, Joanna looked around the Chapel, firstly at the backs of the ministers, then to Mandy, standing a few feet away, with half a smile on her face. Finally, her gaze fell upon the dust covered alter, with the grimy ornamentation's that adorned it. Suddenly, a bright light flooded in from above and landed, like a spotlight, on the cobweb covered cross. The light illuminated the metal symbol, rejuvenating it to its former glory. The stream of light began to broaden, until it covered the whole altar, with its radiance.

She watched, in ore, at the spectacle before her, as the light grew ever stronger and thicker, until its emanation almost blinded her. Then, through the brilliance of the light, a man dressed in white, came through into the room. His aura was as strong and bright as the light from which he had come, and he brought with him the love and strength of a thousand men.

The man walked straight past the cluster of ministers and up to Joanna. When he had reached her side, he smiled a warm, loving smile and stated, "I am willing to help you and, I am also able to help you." and with that he held out his left hand, to reveal a crystal, of the most vibrant pink colour she had ever saw.

He then continued, "I will place this on my alter and, if you wish to allow me in your heart, take this quartz as a token of my love for you." and with that, he turned and walked back to the communion table. Then, having placed the crystal on the altar, he passed back through the light and disappeared from view.

Feeling her spirits rise, she turned to Mandy, but the tall woman had departed from the Chapel. She then averted her gaze to the six ministers, but they too had gone.

Overjoyed that her prayer had been answered, Joanna rushed towards the alter to pick up the stone, but as she approached it, the scene dimmed into blackness before her eyes and suddenly she found herself regaining consciousness, standing on the landing, feeling the surface of a table, in search for a stone that existed only in her dreams.

CHAPTER NINETEEN
14TH AUGUST 1993

11.30 am Slapton

Lewis sat on the settee, his nose buried deep in Jack Higgins' 'The Eagle Has Landed', when the telephone interrupted him, at a most inconvenient moment.

Mumbling to himself, Lewis threw the book on the cushions, rolled off his seat, and marched over to the contraption. Snatching up the receiver, he bellowed, "Hello?" down the mouthpiece, with a gruff, agitated voice.

"Lewis?" came soft, soothing tones from the other end of the line. "It's Paul."

"Hello, mate." Lewis lightened his tonality at recognition of the caller. "So, what do I owe this pleasure?"

Paul paused, on the other end of the line, before blurting out, "Faye has asked me to leave the Oracle."

"Leave? Why?"

"There is a problem in her cellar and she is blaming you and Jo for it." Paul explained.

"Problem? With what?"

Paul continued, "I've been telling her there is something evil down there, ever since I started working at the shop. I've always refused to venture into the cellar. But she pooh-poohed it. Anyway, her son, Ashley, and a friend went down there today and it attacked them."

So why are we getting the blame?" Lewis growled down the phone.

"Because Faye is convinced that whatever it is down the cellar, has followed me from your house."

"What utter rubbish." Lewis aggressively proclaimed. "Whatever was in our house the day you came to do the readings, is definitely still here."

"I know that. You know that. But try telling Faye." Paul agreed.

"Look, where are you now?"

"I'm at the bus stop, in Hemel. The one by the market."

"Look. Jo's not here right now, she is at her parents doing a charity coffee morning for Lupus. Her mum is a sufferer of S.L.E., so likes to raise money for medical research, as there is no known cure for the disease, at the moment." He explained briefly, before continuing, "Why don't you make your way home and I'll pick you up from there in, lets say, an hour?"

"If you don't mind, I'd be very grateful." the psychic signed, with relief.

"See you between twelve-thirty and one then." Lewis confirmed, and with that he closed the conversation.

12.35 pm Hemel Hempstead

Paul watched the Peugeot 405 roll up outside his house, as he crouched on the doorstep smoking a cigarette. Upon seeing Lewis, the psychic rose to his feet and wandered up the garden path to meet him.

Climbing out of the car, Lewis slouched across the grass. "Alright mate?" he grinned, as he looked down upon the consultant.

"Not bad." Paul flatly replied. "Sorry to drag you out at such short notice."

"That's what friends are for." Lewis stated in a gruff voice. "Come on then, let's get going." and with that, Paul backtracked to slam the front door shut, before he and Lewis ambled over to the Peugeot and got inside.

The two men soon found themselves travelling along the A4146, at high speed. Skilfully, Lewis negotiated the bends with ease, in a bid to return to his girlfriend. Neither talked much on the journey back to Slapton, for Lewis was too busy concentrating on the road conditions, whilst Paul's mind was consumed with the events of that morning.

In no time at all, Lewis was swinging his vehicle off the road and onto the wasteland, outside the house, just as Joanna arrived back from her parents.

"You're early." Lewis called across at his girlfriend, as he clambered out of his car. "I wasn't expecting you home for at least another half hour."

"It finished at twelve." she informed him with a smile, before averting her gaze to the consultant. "Hello Paul." she greeted him, "What are you doing here?"

Paul opened his mouth to explain, but was cut short by Lewis, "Paul's been given the elbow, by Faye. I didn't think you'd mind my asking him to come over this afternoon."

"No. Not at all." came the young woman's reply, as she smiled at the psychic. "So long as you don't mind playing with M.O.G.."

"Your spook is the least of my worries." Paul retorted, as the three of them made their way towards the front door.

Placing the key in the lock, Joanna half turned to Paul, and asked, "So why did Faye ask you to leave?"

"Because she reckons that M.O.G. has found a new home, in the shop cellar." He replied, as the three of them entered the house.

Joanna could not help laughing, as she lead the way through the kitchen and into the sitting room. "So what makes her so sure that the spook in her cellar is the notorious M.O.G.?"

"Because, up until today, the only person it seemed to affect was me. However, Ashley and his friend went down there this morning and got attacked. I've been trying to warn her about it for months now, but she's never listened to me. Anyway, she has convinced herself that I am responsible for taking it there, so I'm the one now out of a job."

Inviting Paul to make himself at home on the rocking chair, Joanna perched on the edge of the settee, next to Lewis. "So what are you going to do now?"

Paul sighed. "Expect I'll have to sign on social for a while, until I've found full-time

employment."

"What about your readings?" Lewis questioned him further; "Surely you're not going to give up that, are you?"

Paul gave them a weary smile. "My psychic abilities seem to be causing people nothing but grief. Maybe someone is telling me to get out of this game."

"Oh. Come off it." Joanna scolded him. "You are extremely gifted, Paul. To stop now would be such a waste. Neither Lewis, nor I hold you responsible for what has

been going on in this house. And as for Faye, how can she be so sure that we three are the cause for whatever it is in her cellar. After all, there is more than one evil spirit in this world." She then softened her tone. "Look Paul, you are not to blame for any of this. And the sooner you realise that, the better."

"Maybe not." he reluctantly agreed, as he flitted his sombre, brown eyes at her. "But, never-the-less, I do seem to be attracting evil spirits."

"Like moths to a light-bulb, eh?" Lewis grinned, as he leant back into the settee and stretched out his legs. "Or flies to a pile of horse ..."

"Thank you, Lewis." Joanna jokingly cut him short, as she hurled a cushion at him. "We're supposed to be cheering Paul up, here." She then turned her attention back to the consultant. "Tell you what, why don't you ask some questions for me to confirm, like we did the other Tuesday? Or, if you prefer, I can get you to ask the cards some questions and I'll divine the answers for you - I've got some Tarot cards kicking around here somewhere." And at a nod from Paul, Joanna jumped up and rummaged around her desk for her Tarot Of The Ages.

Returning to her seat, Joanna pulled out the cards from their box. She then handed the pack to Paul, whilst requesting that he shuffled the cards and cut them, with the question of his continuing with psychic work, firmly fixed in his mind.

Paul looked across to the young woman momentarily, with his doleful, almond shaped eyes, before he reached out and took the cards from her hand. Shuffling the cards, he thought of whether he should continue to be a professional psychic, before cutting the pack, with his left hand and placed them, face down, on the floor in front of him.

Joanna leant forward and spread the cards out, across the carpet, as she directed him further, "I would like you to pick a card from the pack to represent the key card for 'yes', then hand it to me." He did as she requested. "Now do the same for the key card for 'no'." He handed her a second card. Placing the 'yes' card on the carpet to her left and the 'no' card to her right, she continued, "I would now like you to pick four cards to go with the key card for 'yes', also handing them to me, and a further four cards to correspond with the 'no' card."

Once he had completed his task, Joanna turned over the five cards, representing the answer 'yes' to his question, followed by revealing the five cards, that represented the answer 'no'.

Scanning her eyes across the ten cards, she paused for a moment, before beginning her reading. "I will start with the five cards that represent 'no'." she informed the psychic, as she pondered over the cards. "The key card; The Moon, I see as representing deception or disillusionment. I feel that you will be deluding yourself if you are not careful. The reason I say this is because the next card, The Devil, lends itself to unexpected failure and self-destructing. You will also come across a lot of self-conflict, which could cause you to shut yourself off from all emotions. Imprisoning yourself with regret for what could have been." She informed him, as she played with the eight of swords. Then, moving on to the final two cards, the queen of clubs and The Star, she continued, "Narrow-mindedness will block you from all that you hold dear; faith, hope and inspiration. The proper balance of desire and work, hope and effort, love and expression must be allowed to enter your life, but with the set of 'no' cards, I feel that your shriving for these qualities will be in vain."

Joanna then turned her attention to the 'yes' set of cards. "However, these cards look much more favourable. Firstly, the key card; The Falling Tower, denotes that there will be complete and sudden change around you, with the abandonment of past relationships and unexpected events, to come. Sudden progress is definitely foretold," he stated, as she pointed to the eight and knight of clubs, "that will result in a journey into the unknown, to do with work." She then turned her attention to the three of clubs, "You have gained a lot of practical knowledge and understanding with what you do professionally and must use it to its best advantage.

This knowledge has been given to you with a purpose in mind - don't waste it."

Finally, she picked up the three of swords and, giving the psychic half a smile, she continued, "What you must learn to do, is remove yourself, emotionally, from those that scorn, or patronise you, for you hold within your heart a gift that is sacred and therefore, it must be cherished."

Placing the three of swords back on the carpet with the other cards, she asked, "Was the question about psyche, by some chance?"

Paul smiled. "Yes. I asked if I should continue to be a psychic. I guess, by your explanation, that the answer is yes, despite how I feel about things at the moment."

"We all get down about life at times, mate." Lewis interrupted. "I'm always pissed off with having to work in cow shit all day."

"I'm fed up of you coming home smelling of cow shit." Joanna jokingly retorted, as she flashed a cheeky grin at her boyfriend. She then turned back to Paul. "Why not advertise in the local papers; do psychic fairs; ask other new age shops if they have a

vacancy for readers? Don't give up just because some two-bit woman blames you for something that isn't you fault."

"Your right. I don't need Faye; I've built up a good clientele since working at the Oracle. All I need to is state that I now work from home, that's all."

"That's the spirit, mate." Lewis giggled, "Never let 'em grind yu down."

9.00 pm Slapton

The latter part of the afternoon, and early evening, had proved non-eventful, as far as M.O.G. was concerned. Paul, who entered the house that afternoon a nervous wreck, had found himself relaxing more and more as the day went on until finally, at nine o'clock, he felt confident enough to broach the subject of psyche.

Turning to Joanna, as a smile crept across his face, Paul asked, "Spoken to Edwardo lately?"

"Quite a bit, yes. He is a cheeky little sod." she indignantly replied.

"In what way?" Paul queried her comment, but before Joanna had chance to reply, Lewis blurted out, "He likes to pinch her bum."

"What?" Paul frowned. "That doesn't sound right. Jo, call Edwardo here, please?" But the bouncy, Latin entity entered the room without being summonsed.

Feeling the Mexican's vibrations, Paul began to speak to the spirit, in a stern manner, "Edwardo. Do you represent Christ's light?"

The Mexican began to reply, "Cei, oui ..." but Paul interrupted him and, with a raised voice, he reminded the guide, "In English, please."

"Please accept my apologies, amigo." Edwardo begged for forgiveness, as he placed his hand on his heart. "I am ... how you say ... very happy to speak the Mexicano, as I no speed the Englietre good."

Ignoring his remark, Paul scolded, "Just answer the question Edwardo. Do you represent Christ's light?"

"Cei. I am of the Christ's light."

Paul rose his voice a second time, "Then why do you get so familiar with Joanna? That sort of behaviour is not what I would expect from a guide."

Edwardo's voice then deepened slightly, as he excitedly retorted. "I am ... how you say ... liking Joanna. I liking to play."

"Not a good enough excuse, Edwardo. The Holy Spirit should never conduct themselves in such a way. You should never become too familiar with your charge. Understand me?"

"Cei." Edwardo replied, flatly. "I no do it again."

Paul then turned his attention to the bewildered couple sitting on the couch, and explained, "Edwardo is a young soul - by that I mean that he has not had many lives. If either of you are unhappy with his behaviour then ask him to leave your presence. If he does not do as you say, then order him out in the name of Jesus Christ."

"He is probably only letting me know that he is there." Joanna stuck up for the Mexican. "Maybe it is his way of keeping me cheerful at e moment."

"Do his actions make you feel uncomfortable?"

"A little, maybe."

"A young soul is susceptible to influence." Paul informed her. "Although he may represent Christ's light, he could still easily become too attached to you. Benjamin is a much older spirit and, therefore, far less likely to become over possessive. Any guide who becomes too fond of their charge will be told to leave. For Edwardo's sake, don't allow him to become to familiar with you, or he will find himself in a lot of trouble." The psychic then frowned, as Joe entered the room behind him, and Edwardo made his exit. "Edwardo's not your guide either, Jo." he announced, as he listened to his guides instructions. "He is Lewis' - so why he is spending so much time with you instead of his own charge, is a mystery to me."

"He's not doing any harm." Joanna pointed out.

"Maybe not now, but a jealous spirit can prove troublesome. He could even affect your relationship with Lewis, if his feelings for you get too strong."

At that point, Joe walked through Paul and stood before Joanna, his tall stance shadowing her dwindling frame. She looked up at the Egyptian and smiled, "Hi, Joe. What do you want?"

As the tall, aged man gave her a toothless grin from beneath his hat, she felt Benjamin's presence enter the room behind her. Then, before she knew what was happening, Joe placed his hands, one on her forehead and the other on her upper chest, whilst Benjamin placed both his hands on the back of her head.

Her head began to spin as the two spirits blessed her, making her aura expand and whiz around her body in a whirlwind of positive energy.

As Joe towered above her, she heard him speak; "You are weakening fast, child. You are a fraction of the woman I first saw. How much weight have you lost?"

Flummoxed, Joanna tried to think, as her head whirled like a spinning top. "I think, " she informed him in a slow and deliberate fashion, "I have lost a stone."

Although he neither saw nor heard Joe, Lewis looked across at his girlfriend as he heard her statement, an expression of shock on his face. "Have you lost more weight?"

"Yes." Joanna faintly replied. "Mum was worried about me today, as quite a lot of people commented on my losing weight, so I weighed myself to try and prove to her that my weight loss had stabilised, to find that I am down to eight and a half stone."

Interrupting her explanation to her boyfriend, Joe continued, "To fight, you must remain strong. I can only do so much to help, by blessing you, for I can only rejuvenate your aura. You must not lose any more weight, or you will become too weak."

"Sorry Dad." Joanna joked with the Egyptian, but he did not take kindly to her humour. "Listen to me, you must be strong, or you will not be able to fight your enemies." The two guides then withdrew, leaving Joanna feeling decidedly light headed, before sitting, one on each side of the young woman, giving her security that proved a most welcome change.

Paul's soft, soothing voice travelled across the room, "You alright Jo? You look a little pale."

Joanna gave a weary smile, as she tried to focus on the consultant's face. "I'll be fine in a minute, once the room stops spinning."

Lewis diverted his gaze across at the psychic. "What have they done to her?" he growled.

"Administering a blessing - healing Jo's spirit, if you like." He informed the dairy engineer, in a matter-of-fact fashion.

"Why?"

"Because she obviously needs it." Paul snapped, before turning his attention back to the young woman. "Do you feel calmer now?"

"Yes." Joanna then looked about her, "Where's Edwardo gone?" but, as she asked the question, she felt Benjamin dig her in the ribs. "You worry to much about those that are of no importance."

"I only asked, that's all." Joanna jumped at the Israelite, before clambering out of the settee cushions and knelt in front of the fireplace. She took a deep intake of breath at the irritation of the spirits in the room, then vexed by the whole affair, she found herself snarling, "I hate all these spooks around me. Why can't they all leave me alone."

"As you wish." came Joe's response to her request as he took off his hat, before both he and Benjamin rose to their feet and departed.

"Upset your guides, I would." Paul stated, sarcastically, but before Joanna had chance to respond, a rush of unrecognisable negative energy flew through the sitting-room door and began wrap itself around her, throwing the young woman to the ground.

"GET OUT OF ME." she shouted, as she felt the entity begin to enter her body, bringing with it a clammy, sweaty residue that soaked her skin and clothes. Panic-stricken, she crawled over to the settee and propped herself up against the seats, in the vain hope of escaping from its clutches.

"Say the Lords Prayer." Paul ordered, as he rose to his feet and marched over to her side.

Joanna tried to speak, but the words failed to flow from her mouth. "I can't." she replied, hysterically. "I don't know the words."

Suddenly, she felt Peter Two's hands on her psychic gate, and heard his soft voice, in her ear. "I am Peter and I represent God's light. Remember what I told you to say, Joanna. Acknowledge my presence."

Taking heed of his words, Joanna found herself blurting out, "The Holy Ghost is with me; your evil will not prevail." And as the words passed her lips, she felt the grip of the evil spirit slacken.

"The Holy Ghost is with me; your evil will not prevail." she acknowledged a second time, and immediately she spoke the words, she felt the presence of Joe and Benjamin re-enter and pull the entity from her, before dragging it to the far side of the room.

"Now repeat the Lords Prayer, after me." Paul commanded, and with that he said the prayer, line by line, allowing Joanna to recite the words, precisely and with conviction after him.

As the words of Lords Prayer were spoken, the spectre became weaker and weaker until it finally withdrew from the room and rushed back upstairs to lick its wounds.

Lewis jumped to his feet. "That is it. I have had enough of this." he growled as he glared about him. "M.O.G.; your days are numbered - do you hear me? Come hell or high water you are going to be exorcised."

M.O.G. suddenly appeared behind the stocky dairy engineer and stood there, scowling at the six foot four inch man. Feeling his hackles rise, Lewis placed a hand to the back of his head, smoothing down the raised hairs. "And don't think you can start fucking well messing around with me, either." Lewis bellowed as he turned around in

the vain hope of visualising the entity.

Joe and Benjamin moved forward, placing themselves either side of the ghost, but M.O.G. remained undisturbed by their guard. "It was not me, that time." he growled, as he looked past Lewis at Joanna. "I would never physically harm you. You have always accepted my presence without question, it is that cunt."

M.O.G. growled, as he pointed at Paul, "that has caused all this trouble, with his high ideals and talk of God."

"Where's your Bible?" Paul cut in.

Unable to take her eyes from the manifestation before her, Joanna replied evasively, "In the bedroom."

"Get it." the consultant ordered and, after a moment's hesitation, Joanna marched upstairs, to retrieve the Bible from under her pillow.

As she entered the bedroom, Joanna was struck by a wall of pure negativity, as the

thing tried to gain control over her a second time. Again, it encased her with its destructive intent, attacking her aura in the hope of finding a weak spot that could easily be cracked.

Feeling herself being pushed from her body, Joanna lost her balance and fell to the floor. Scrabbling along the side of the bed, she made a desperate bid for the Bible, but the entity clawed at her, preventing the woman from her quest.

Suddenly, Joanna's fear turned to anger at the evil revenant and, using all her new found power, she shouted at the top of her voice, "Fuck off, you wanker."

Immediately Lewis and Paul heard her cry, they left the sitting room and headed for the bedroom. Paul was the first to enter and immediately found himself being struck by the entity, as it turned its attack on him.

Taking advantage of its aversion to the consultant, Joanna grabbed at her pillow and pulled out the Bible from under it. She then threw the book across the room at Paul and, as he caught it, the entity backed off and stood in the shower unit, seething.

Paul fell to his knees, whilst still clutching the Bible, and began, "Lord, you said when two or three were gathered together, you would listen. I call upon the archangels Michael, Gabriel, Raphael and Auriel as protection against all that is evil here. Please hear our plea and keep your children from harm, which the evil that resides in this house is administering to them. Amen."

As he uttered the words, the darkened room suddenly became illuminated in the brightest yellow that radiated from the shining, burnished gold, of Michael's round battle shield. Secondly, the mother-of-pearl light of Gabriel cloaked the air, followed by the brilliance of pink and yellow from Raphael, that warmed the atmosphere. Finally, Auriel's spectrum hue, flashed with astral colours, emanated the room filling every orifice with the wrath of God.

Joanna looked first at Paul, then at the shower unit, but the entity had vanished, leaving the bedroom filled to the brim with positive energy.

The consultant then rose to his feet, handed Lewis his Bible and wandered back to the door. "I think you had better take me home." he muttered, "I am causing more trouble than it is worth by staying here."

They immediately left the house and drove off back to Hemel, in silence. It was only as they reached the outskirts of Adeyfield, that Paul spoke, in a soft, gentle manner. "When we reach my house, could you both come inside for a few moments? I've something I would like to get for you, as protection."

"Sure, no problem." Lewis bellowed, from behind the steering wheel.

Pulling up in front of the house, the three clambered out of the car and dragged themselves up to the front door. Paul then let them all inside and, inviting the couple to make themselves comfortable in the sitting room, he rushed upstairs.

Moments later he was down again and, as he walked past the two-seater that Joanna was perched on, he placed something about the size of an egg on the arm.

Joanna stared at the object, as it just sat there, and scratched her head. She then slowly stretched out a hand and, taking hold of it, she examined the article closer. "What is it?" she frowned, as she continued to stare at the odd shaped thing in her hand.

"It's a piece of rose quartz." Paul informed her, with a glint in his eye. "Its properties promote love, which is the ultimate protection against anything that is evil."

Joanna twisted the rough crystal in her hand, as she stared at it intently. "You know, I feel this stone is familiar to me."

"I got it from a market stall about five years ago. To be honest, I don't even know why I bought it. However, your need is greater than mine, so you are welcome to borrow it, until the house is sorted out." Paul informed her.

"It's beautiful." Joanna remarked, as she admired the stone.

Ignoring her comment, Paul continued, "I suggest that you carry it at all times, when in the house. It is of excellent quality and, therefore, will be a powerful weapon against anything evil. You might get a bit of a kick from it to start with though, rather like the feeling you had when Joe and Benjamin blessed you, but don't worry about that, for it is just boosting up your aura."

"Great. Thanks." Joanna expressed her gratitude. "To be honest, despite being a stubborn old sod by refusing to give in to el spooko, I am dreading going back home."

"Why worry. Your guides are here protect you, the Bible will protect you and now, you also have the rose quartz." he smiled across the room at her. "M.O.G. and company haven't got a chance against that lot."

Lewis, a prominent frown on his forehead, growled, "So, presuming that whatever it was in the bedroom was not M.O.G., what was it? Mandy?"

Paul shook his head. "No, it was not female in form."

"So it was M.O.G. then?" Lewis continued, trying to make since of the situation.

"It was not M.O.G., either." came Paul's reply.

"Then what the fuck was it then?" Lewis began to anger.

"I don't know." Paul's tone took on a sharper sound, as he responded to Lewis' increased agitation. "Somehow, something else has entered into the game."

"What are we living in, here." Joanna snapped, "A boarding house for evil spirits, or something?"

"I'm sorry, I don't know." Paul replied, sympathetically, as he looked from one to the other of his guests.

Lewis impatiently jumped to his feet. "This is ridiculous. It would appear that we've got more spooks in our house, than hell itself." The dairy engineer then turned to his girlfriend, "Come on, Jo. Time we were making tracks." and with that, he grabbed her hand and marched them both out of Paul's house and back to the Peugeot.

11.30 pm Slapton

Joanna lay quietly in bed, listening to the rhythmic sound of Lewis snoring. Placing a hand under her pillow she checked, for the umpteenth time, that both the stone and the Bible were safely tucked beneath her head, before taking a deep intake of breath and closed her eyes.

As she tried to relax enough to doze, she suddenly became aware of a pulsation coming into her head, from beneath the pillow.

Ignoring the sensation, she turned onto her side and wriggled around until she had found another comfortable spot. However, the electrical pulse continued, getting ever stronger as she tried, in vain, to sleep.

Irritated by the vibes that the stone bestowed, she grabbed the crystal and retrieved it from under the pillow, before venturing out of the bed and wandered off in the direction of the bathroom.

She held the stone tightly in her left hand as she creaked open the bathroom door and gingerly stepped inside. The rose quartz vigorously continued to thumped out its impulse, its energy forever increasing and strengthening with every step until, her legs felt so tingly that she had to rest on the side of the bath.

The rose quartz emanated an energy shield around her, and she could feel the power drawing up through the soles of her feet, through her legs and penetrating into her entire body. Her breathing quickened slightly as the experience continued, making her feel extremely light headed.

As she sat there, the knuckles of her left hand white from the strain of gripping the stone, she could almost hear the electrical pulses buzz and crackle around her. Then, suddenly, an excruciating pain erupted at the base of her spine and travelled up her back, like a zip being closed, to her shoulder blades. She cried out in agony, but Lewis did not hear her wail.

However, it woke the M.O.G. from his slumber and, entering the bathroom, he watched on with interest.

Her aura then started to contract, drawing into her heart centre until she felt as if her body were the outer shell. It condensed until it was in the very core of her soul, held firm for a few seconds, then violently exploded, sending streams of white and pink light out into the room, like a sparkler, completely obscuring the room from view.

Upon the impact of Joanna's aura, M.O.G. found himself being catapulted out, through the bathroom wall, and into the courtyard beyond. He then tried to return to his resting-place, but the power emanating from the young woman was too strong for him to re-enter. In a furious rage, he stomped around outside, blaspheming.

The antics also attracted the attention of the other, unknown entity, who joined him outside the house and proceeded to conger up a plan of action, for their revenge.

5.00 am Hemel Hempstead

Paul was sleeping soundly in his bed, when he was suddenly woken by Claire, frantically pushing and poking him.

"Go away, Claire." he moaned, as he rolled over to resume his slumber. But the girl, refusing to be ignored, jumped over the bed and continued to push and shove.

With sleepy eyes, Paul rose his head from the pillow. "What do you want, Claire?" But before she could answer, he felt a strong pair of hands wrapping themselves around his neck and squeezed tight.

Choking, Paul went to grab his attackers hands, but there was nothing there, only his own flesh. Reaching out in the darkness, he fumbled around for the bedside lamp.

As the light of the lamp chased away the night, Paul saw above him an unknown entity, his steel-blue eyes aflame with fury. He had a scare across a face that was obscured by tasselled, pepper-grey hair and wore a long, black cape, which draped over the bedclothes.

Paul struggled to free himself from the entity's clasp, but the wicked grin of the intruder showed no mercy. "Taketh thy breath for thouest thy last." It gave a deep growl, as the hands tightened around the consultant's neck.

Paul, gulping his final breath of air, caught just enough to splutter, "I order you out, in the name of the Father, the Son, and the Holy Ghost." And immediately he uttered the words, the spirit withdrew its clasp, enveloped itself in a black mist and was gone.

Coughing and spluttering, Paul slowly sat up in his bed, and rubbed his sore neck. He looked over at his clock, noted the time then, placing his hands together, he proceeded with the Lords Prayer and gave thanks that his life was spared.

CHAPTER TWENTY
15TH AUGUST 1993

11.30 am Slapton

Joanna and Lewis sat in the pews of the Holy Cross Church, listening intently as the Reverend Lawrence closed his sermon.

The rest of a handful of congregation rose from their seats and made their way to the church door, shaking hands with the Reverend as they left the cool, airy building.

Once the couple was sure that they would not be disturbed by anyone else, they too wandered over to the vicar who, by this time, was helping the warden's tidy up the hymnbooks.

The vicar paused from his work, as he saw them approach, and gave a warm, humble smile. "Hello, Joanna; Lewis." he greeted the couple as he guided them to a quiet corner of the Church, inviting them to sit next to him on one of the pews. "How are things?"

"Not good. Not good at all." Lewis informed the white-haired vicar. "Since we last spoke, Joanna has been attacked by the thing in the house a number of times - last night being both the most recent, and the most traumatic."

The vicar averted his melancholy eyes to the young woman. "You look stressed, definitely." he mentioned in passing, before continuing, "Are you still staying here?"

"Yes." Joanna confirmed, "I'll not let it drive me out."

The vicar then turned his attention back to Lewis. "I think at times like these, it is not necessarily the wisest thing to stay in a possessed house. I think, Lewis, that you should persuade Joanna to stay with family or friends, until the exorcism is administered."

"Believe me Reverend Lawrence, I tried to persuade her after she was attacked in the car, one and a half weeks ago." The dairy engineer informed the clergyman, "But she won't be told."

The vicar returned his melancholy eyes to the frail looking young woman. "So, how do you cope with the attacks?"

Taking a deep breath, Joanna proceeded to explain. "I sleep on the Bible and, if I feel threatened by it, or it tries to possess me, I say, 'The Holy Ghost is with me; your evil will not prevail', followed by the Lords Prayer." She then paused, fumbled around in her coat pocket and produced the rose quartz, before continuing, hesitantly, "Also, I was given this crystal yesterday as extra protection, which seems to be keeping the spook at bay, for the moment."

"May I have a closer look." the vicar requested, as he held out his hand and so, Joanna handed over the quartz for the vicar to inspect.

With interest, the Reverend Lawrence studied the rough, pink stone, before asking, "And what does this do?"

"Its electrical pulses promotes universal love, which is the ultimate weapon against evil." Joanna tried to explain, to the bemused vicar. "The crystal has healing properties, you see."

"How interesting." The vicar gave her a humble smile, as he handed the stone back to the young woman. "Well, if it works; use it." He then leant back in the pew seat. "I am glad that you both came here today, because, I'd rather talk to you face to face, about this matter - the telephone is so impersonal." His face then dropped, with an expression of despondency. "I contacted the Canon Fitzwilliams after we spoke on Wednesday but unfortunately," the reverend sighed, "he is in the mind that you do not require the services of the Church ..."

"Hang on one minute." Lewis' bellow echoed around the void of the stone building, causing the wardens to stop what they were doing and stare across the church at him, with distaste in their eyes. "Just look at her, she is wasting away." He growled as he pointed at his girlfriend, oblivious of the disruption he had caused. "This thing has become extremely dangerous and must be stopped, before it is too late."

The vicar smiled at him, sympathetically. "I can see how all this is effecting both of you. I have tried my best to change the Canon's mind, but unfortunately, he is not dealing with you first hand, unlike myself. If he was, then maybe he would realise the urgency."

Lewis lowered his voice. "I am sorry Reverend Lawrence, but that is no compensation. We turned to the Church because the Church deal with this sort of thing. What more proof does he need, eh? I don't know what else to do."

The Reverend leant forward, and tenderly touched his arm. "Do not distress yourself, my son. I shall give you the Canon's telephone number, so that you can speak to him directly, on this matter. The chances are, you would be more likely to convince him, than I. Telephone me at the vicarage tonight, about eight-thirty, and I will give you the Canon's number." The reverend then observed the expressions of relief on the couple's faces, as they rose from their seats, ready to leave the Church.

Lewis held out a hand and, as the Reverend rose, they shook. "Thank you for all your help, Reverend Lawrence." He gratefully bid the vicar farewell. "I apologise for taking out my frustration on you."

"I understand. God bless and protect you both." he smiled and with that, the vicar ushered them both out of the building.

8.30 pm

Sitting in the Peugeot on the grass verge just past the entrance to Horton Wharf Farm, Lewis dialled the Canon Fitzwilliams' number and waited patiently for a reply.

The telephone had hardly started ringing the other end, when a pompous sounding man on the other end answered it. "Vicarage." he stated, arrogantly.

"Canon Fitzwilliams, please." Lewis gruffly requested.

"Speaking." Came the sharp reply.

"My name is Lewis Chetfler and I have been given your number by the Reverend Lawrence, from Holy Cross Church, Slapton."

"Reverend Lawrence did inform me this afternoon, that you were going to telephone me, this evening." The Canon replied, in an imperious tone, "Your girlfriend has had further problems, I understand?"

"Yes, she has." Lewis confirmed.

"Is she there with you, at the moment?"

"She is sitting next to me."

"I would like to speak with her, if I may." The Canon's tone was full of self-importance, as he spoke to the earthy dairy engineer.

"I'll pass you over." Lewis informed the clergyman, relieved that he no longer had to deal with the man, before thrusting the mobile at his distraught girlfriend.

"Hello?" Joanna shakily spoke down the mouthpiece.

"Joanna, isn't it?" The Canon Fitzwilliams spoke to her, in his magisterial manner.

"Yes." she replied, serenely.

The Canon then took the lead of the conversation. "I understand from the Reverend Lawrence, that you wish for me to do an exorcism, at your house. Is that correct?"

"Yes." Joanna confirmed.

"And I also understand, from the Reverend Lawrence, that you indulge in occult activities, and you have books and other items of that nature, at your house. Is that correct?"

"Yes." Joanna's retort was slightly sharper, this time.

"Have you thrown away the books, yet?" the Canon asked, in a condescending manner.

"No, I haven't, because they have nothing to do with what is in my house." Resentment was prominent in Joanna's voice, as she replied to his question.

"Can you be certain that they don't? How can you expect me to help you, if you won't help yourself, Joanna."

"Look." Joanna began to explain the situation to the patronising clergyman on the other end of the line. "This spirit has been in my house ever since I first moved in, five years ago. There has been poltergeist activity there for as long as I can remember. Even my ex-husband experienced paranormal activity in the house years ago. The spook has not just arrived over the last couple of weeks, however, it has got dramatically worse during that time."

The Canon thought for a moment, then asked, "And what of that psychic fellow the Reverend Lawrence referred to. Does he still come around to your house?"

"Yes. Paul was there last night, when the latest attack happened." She graciously informed him.

"So, he instigated the assault then, yes?" came another supercilious question, from the Canon.

"No he did not. He merely witnessed it." Joanna found it increasingly difficult not to snap at the Canon.

"So why did it attack you, then?" The Canons voice had an air of superiority about it, as he asked the question.

"I don't know, just as I have no idea why it is in my house in the first place."

"So, what about this stone that you have got then. The Reverend Lawrence told me that you carry a stone about with you, for protection. Why is this?"

"The stone that the Reverend Lawrence referred to, is a rose quartz crystal and it protects me for it denotes love." She informed him, as she caught Lewis' eye.

"How might that work, then?" the Canon questioned the physics behind crystal healing.

"The crystal gives electrical impulses, similar to that of a watch battery, emanating energy. This particular crystal puts universal love into my aura, thus giving me protection from anything that is filled with hate, such as the evil spirit in my house."

The vicar pondered over her explanation for a moment, then retorted, "Well, I suggest that you destroy all the occult paraphernalia currently in your house, stop inviting Paul round, continue to carry your stone with you, and everything will settle down and go back to normal."

At that point, Joanna could cope no more and, unable to hold back her emotions and longer, she burst into tears.

Upon seeing his girlfriend in such a distressed state, Lewis snatched the phone from her grasp and, placing it his ear, he bellowed at the top of his voice; "Jo is at the end of her tether. She has lost over a stone in weight in the last two and a half weeks and is extremely distressed at the goings on, in our house. She can not sleep at night and I believe, is fast heading for a nervous breakdown. Now, what do YOU intend doing about it, Canon Fitzwilliams?"

The Canon thought for a moment, then, in a superior fashion, he replied, "I will tell you, what I just told Joanna. Until such time as she gets rid of everything that is connected with the occult, and continues to invite this Paul round, I can not see how I can possibly help."

"Are you suggesting that this is all in our minds?" Lewis bellowed down the phone at the Canon.

"Not at all. But, I do not feel that an exorcism is the answer." Canon Fitzwilliams reply showed no compassion.

"Look." Lewis growled. "You may think that you know the situation better than I, but you haven't even seen how all this is effecting my girlfriend. How can you judge the best course of action, without even meeting with us. What are you so afraid of?"

Suddenly, a break through. "Would you like for us to arrange a meeting, then?" Fitzwilliams asked.

"I certainly would, yes."

Lewis could then here paper being rustled, on the other end of the line before the Canon, after a moments pause, mumbled, "I am extremely busy all this week and most of next." he stated, coldly, "But I can fit you in on Friday, 27th August at five o'clock, here at the vicarage in Beaconsfield."

"That will be fine." Lewis confirmed.

"Right then, I'll write it down in my appointment book. Goodbye." and with that, the Canon slammed the hand set back on its hook, leaving Lewis listening to the dialling tone.

CHAPTER TWENTY-ONE
27TH AUGUST, 1993

5.00 pm Beaconsfield

Having parked the Peugoet in the car park, Lewis, Paul and Joanna ambled around the corner to the gated entrance of the vicarage.

The large, old house was tucked away to one side of St. Mary and All Saints Cathedral grounds, in the centre of Beaconsfield, surrounded by mature shrubs and Victorian plants.

Pausing at the entrance, Paul took a final drag from his cigarette as he stared up at the Canon's residence in adoration at its splendour, whist the other two continued to travel up the path, towards the oak front door. He then threw the butt to the ground and marched forward, to catch them up.

The vicarage door creaked ajar, to reveal an extremely tall and lanky, middle-aged man glaring at them fearsomely through the crack. "Joanna Waller and Lewis Chetfler?" he growled magisterially, from within.

"That's right." Lewis bellowed, in reply.

The door was then swung wide open and the two were begrudgingly invited to enter but, as the Canons glare fell on Paul, he snapped, "And who is this?"

Joanna stepped forward, "This is Paul Hitt. We brought him here with us today, as he has both witnessed and been attacked by, the spirit in the house."

"Well, you'd better come in as well, then." the Canon growled reluctantly, as he stood back to allow the consultant to enter his abode. "However," he continued, "I will have to ask you to sit in my study, whilst I discuss the matter with the other two. I will speak with you later, once I have finished with them." He then showed Paul into his office, opposite the front door.

As Paul entered, the Canon turned to him briefly and stated, "There are plenty of magazines here, for you to amuse yourself with, whilst I am gone."

Paul gazed about him, until his dark, almond shaped eyes fell upon a copy of the Bible. "Oh. This will do nicely." he gave the Canon half a smile, as he picked the book up.

Upon observing the psychic's response the Canon turned and, without uttering another word, the tall, lanky clergyman strutted out of the study and slammed the door tight shut behind him.

Composing himself, Canon Fitzwilliams forced a smile at the couple and, leading the way, he showed them into his meeting room, to introduce them to his assistant, Evangeline.

The room was large and rectangular in shape, with tatty, mis-matching furniture scattered around it, in a haphazard fashion. A large window overlooked a natural garden, with the Cathedral acting as a perfect backdrop to the scene.

Sitting with their backs to the window, Joanna and Lewis stared across the room at the Canon and his Colleague, who was dressed in a floating summer dress and cardigan.

Sitting down opposite the couple, the Canon leant back in his chair. "Now then, Joanna, tell me, in your own words, why you think you require us to exorcise your house." And so, the young woman told him all there was to tell.

When she had completed her tale, the Canon tapped the arm of his chair with his fingertips, before frowning, "And you think that this Paul person would strengthen your claim?"

"Certainly." Joanna nodded.

"I am not happy that you entertain such distasteful company, Joanna. I believe that Paul is the route of all your trouble." He then turned to his assistant. "Evangeline, what is your opinion on this matter?"

The woman flashed her eyes, first at the Canon, then at the couple huddled together in front of the window. "I think," she pondered over the best way to phrase her answer, "that there is certainly a problem here, which needs attention." The woman then leant towards Joanna, "And it is blatantly obvious, just by looking at you, that you have suffered much because of it. " She then reclined back into her chair, as she caught the Canon's eye, "However, I tend to agree with Mark that Paul is a bad influence on both of you."

"How so?" Joanna queried the woman's statement.

"I have a couple of quotes from the Bible, that I feel might help you to understand why we feel this is so."

Evangeline smiled at them, as she lifted a piece of paper from a coffee table to one side of her, before turning to the Canon, "If you don't mind, Mark."

"Not at all." he gave her an ingratiating smile.

And so, holding the paper up to her face, she began to read. "The first is the gospel of John 10;7 to 11 - 'Therefore Jesus said again, "I tell you the truth, I am the gate for the sheep. All who ever came before me were thieves and robbers, but the sheep did not listen to them. I am the gate; whoever enters through me will be saved. He will come in and go out, and find pasture. The thief comes only to steal and kill and destroy; I have come that they may have life and have it to the full'." She then explained, "Ministers of the Church are Disciples of Christ. Anyone who does not come in Christ's name is nothing more than a trickster and, therefore, their only intent are to confuse and destroy. From what the Reverend Peter Lawrence has told us, and your rendition of the events, it would appear that Paul is the instigator of all this, whether he is aware of that fact, or not."

"So why then has it proved so hard for me to get this far, with regard to help from the Church?"

At that point, the Canon cut in. "Because you refuse to believe that occult practices are born of Satan. Such rituals repulse God. You see, people such as Paul, think that

there are as many good spirits as evil ones - they claim to work with various spirits, that they confess are envoys of God. However, the truth of the matter is, there is only one spirit that is from God, and that is the Holy Spirit."

"Then what of angels?" Joanna enquired.

"They are not the same thing at all."

"And of the souls of those who have died and gone to heaven? What type of spirits are those?" She continued to question the Canon with an innocent air about her.

"The departed are in heaven and, therefore, can not be contacted by us on earth. Only tortured souls walk this earth, such as whoever it is in your house. Therefore, any contact with the dead, is communication with an unclean spirit."

Evangeline leant towards the young woman a second time, "Can you say, from your heart, that you trust Paul one hundred percent?"

"I trust him with my life." Joanna smartly replied.

"How interesting." Evangeline smiled, as she returned to her quotes on the page, "Maybe then, you will find the next quote of particular interest." And with that she began to read, "John 10;17 to 18 - Jesus said, 'The reason my Father loves me is that I lay down my life - only to take it up again. No one takes it from me, but I lay it down of my own accord, I have authority to lay it down and authority to take it up again. This command I received from my Father'. Surely, Joanna, you should trust Jesus with your life, not Paul."

"If I did not acknowledge Jesus Christ, nor God for that matter, then I would not have fought so hard to see you both, about an exorcism." She stated, coldly.

"However, Paul definitely has a better understanding of the supernatural than yourselves, for I have learnt much about Faith from him. Faith that has seen me through my darkest hours."

The Canon cut in a second time and, with an impatient air about him, he bellowed, "Then why not use the 'faith' that Paul apparently possesses, to rid yourselves of the thing, instead of bothering me?"

"Because he is not a trained exorcist, unlike yourself and therefore, his meddling could jeopardise mine, Lewis' and his own life. Could you have that on your conscience?" Canon Fitzwilliams shook his head in shame, as Joanna continued, "All I wish, is for someone to help me. I have done all the right things, in accordance with Church rules, to rid the house of this manifestation. I have approached two vicars concerning this matter, and now you; but all I find are obstructions blocking my path, every step of the way. First, I approached the deaconess from my mother's parish, but red tape forbid her to take any further action. I then met with the Reverend Lawrence and, despite his concern for mine and Lewis' welfare, you refused to listen to him, so the poor man found himself stuck in the middle and, to be honest with you, he is far too ill for all the hassle that we have put him through."

Seemingly allowing Joanna's comments to fly straight over his head, the Canon turned to Evangeline, "I am going to speak with Paul, then I will make my decision as to

whether or not we should pursue this matter, upon my return." And with that, he rose to his feet and arrogantly marched the room, leaving Evangeline smiling vacantly at the couple.

Paul had his nose buried deep in the Bible as the Canon entered the study. Upon hearing the clergyman enter, Paul looked up and closed the book.

"Right." Canon Fitzwilliams snapped, as he drew up a stool and sat, opposite the consultant. "I have heard Joanna's account of all that is going on, now I would like to hear yours."

"You think I'm evil, don't you." Paul enquired, in a soft, gentle voice.

"Your ethics are no concern of mine." The Canon retorted, sharply.

"Then why do you judge me?"

"I do not judge you at all." Canon Fitzwilliams scowled at the psychic.

"But you assume that I am the route of all this, don't you?"

"I believe that all occult activities invite trouble of this kind, yes."

"So you do hold me responsible." Paul confirmed the Canon's accusations.

"Occultist's do not walk with God, and that is why I am against you. Not you as Paul the person, but you as Paul the psychic."

Upon the clergyman's response, Paul thrust the Bible at him, stating, "Read Matthew 7:1 to 5."

Intrigued, the Canon opened the Bible and, taking a deep breath he read out loud for all to hear, "Do not judge, or you too will be judged. For in the same way as you judge others, you will be judged, and with the measure you use, it will be measured to you. Why do you look at the speck of sawdust in your brother's eye and pay no attention to the plank in your own eye? How can you say to your brother, 'let me take the speck out of your eye', when all the time there is a plank in your own eye? You hypocrite, first take the plank out of your own eye, and then you will see clearly to remove the speck from your brother's eye."

Upon completion of the quote, Paul requested, "Now read 1 John 4; 1 to 6."

Obligingly, the Canon turned to the relevant page, "Dear friends, do not believe every spirit, but test the spirits to see whether they are from God, because many false prophets have gone out into the world. This is how you can recognise the Spirit of God; Every spirit that acknowledges that Jesus Christ has come in the flesh is from God, but every spirit that does not acknowledge Jesus is not from God. This is the spirit of the anti-Christ, which you have heard is coming and even now is already in the world. You, dear children, are from God and have overcome them, because the one who is in you is greater that the one who is in the world. They are from the world and therefore speak from the viewpoint of the world, and the world listens to them. We are from God, and whoever knows God listens to us; but whoever is not from God does not listen to us. This is how we recognise the spirit of truth and the spirit of falsehood." The Canon looked up at Paul upon completion of the reading, and asked, "Do you hold Jesus Christ in your heart, is that what you are trying to tell me?"

Paul smiled, as he replied, "I acknowledge Jesus Christ as the Saviour and I recognise the Almighty Lord our God. I acknowledge the Holy Spirit and only converse with spirit that represent Christ's light."

"How can you be so sure?" The Canon growled.

"Because, as you have just read, I test the spirits, before indulging in any form of communication. If the spirit does not acknowledge Jesus Christ, then they are ordered to leave my presence. That is why I know that whatever is in Jo's house is not of God's light, because it neither acknowledges Jesus Christ, nor represents God."

The Canons expression turned to anger. "Well, I am sorry Paul, but although I do not believe that you realise it, you are walking the dark path of Satan; not God. Occultism is a safe haven for all that is evil and nothing you can say will change my views."

Unflustered by Canon Fitzwilliams' cutting remark, Paul continued, "Indulge me further; read Luke 6;20 to 26."

Sighing loudly, the Canon reluctantly flicked through the Bible for the quote, and read it out loud. "Looking at his disciples, Jesus said, 'Blessed are you who are poor, for yours is the kingdom of God. Blessed are you who hunger now, for you will be satisfied. Blessed are you who weep now, for you will laugh. Blessed are you when men hate you, when they exclude you and insult you and reject your name as evil, because of the Son of Man. Rejoice in that day and leap for joy, because great is your reward in heaven. For that is how their fathers treated the prophets. But woe to you who are rich, for you have already received your comfort. Woe to you who are well fed now, for you will go hungry. Woe to you who laugh now, for you will mourn and weep. Woe to you when all men speak well of you, for that is how their fathers treated the false prophets.'"

The Canon slammed the Bible shut. "I hope you are not insinuating that you are the reincarnation of Jesus?" he growled.

Paul laughed out loud. "Certainly not. I could never match up to a man like that. You insult Jesus by even suggesting such a thing. Besides, you insist that I am an evil psychic - certainly not the type of person that God would allow Jesus to be reincarnated into."

"Quite." Canon Fitzwilliams stated, in a sharp fashion, before softening his tone to enquire, "You appear to have a comprehensive understanding of the Bible. Have you done a Bible study course, at all?"

"No. In fact, I have never read it from cover to cover." Paul gave the Canon a warm smile, "I should really, there are a lot of excellent stories in it."

"Excuse me for asking but I am intrigued, if you have not studied the Bible, how then were you able to give me those quotes off the top of your head, like that?"

"I have a spirit with me, that is very hot on the Bible." But as Paul watched the Canon's eyebrows raise ready to fire the next question, he added, "And no, it isn't Jesus Christ."

"I never presumed it was." came the cutting reply, as the Canon rose to his feet and moved towards the door.

"So, are you going to help Jo?" Paul called across to him, as Canon Fitzwilliams reached the study door.

Turning, the tall and lanky man gave the consultant a false smile, "Come with me," he invited the young man, "and you will find out." And with that, the two men left the study and returned to the meeting room.

Evangeline, Joanna and Lewis all sat in silence, as Paul and the Canon entered, with a taught atmosphere that made all of them feel uneasy.

Inviting Paul to take a seat next to Lewis, Canon Fitzwilliams returned to his own chair and, making himself comfortable, he turned his attention to his assistant. "I recommend," he stated in a tone, too consciously dignified to be genuine, "that we visit Joanna and Lewis' house and do a requiem service. Do you agree, Evangeline?"

"Yes." came her response.

"Could you possibly get my appointment book for me then while I get a few details from Joanna - it's on the telephone table, in the hall." and with that, the woman obediently stepped from the room.

"Now Joanna." the Canon gave her a false smile, as he reached for a pen and note pad. "Do you have any history on this tormented soul?"

"Having spoken to a number of elderly villagers who knew those living at the house years ago, all I know is that his name is Jesse Healy and that he died about fifty years ago, or so." She softly advised him.

"So, you don't know of any family, or anyone who still lives in the village, that might be able to give you further information?"

"Like what?"

"Was he married, single, his age, that type of thing." The Canon waved his pen about, as he gave her some examples.

"I know that he never married. Apparently, his sister lived with him, until his death." She smiled at the clergyman, as she watched him jot down some notes.

At that point, Evangeline returned from the hallway, with appointment book in hand. Giving it to the Canon, she returned to her seat and sank into its cushions.

He then opened the book and, glancing over it's contents, he stated, "I think that the sooner we visit your house the better ... now, let me see ... Sunday afternoon alright with you?"

"That would be great." Joanna beamed with delight.

"Now, I will require the Reverend Lawrence to be there so, because he has an evening service at six-thirty, we'll have to make it five." He then scratched a note in the appointment book, before looking back to Joanna. "What is your full address?"

Giving him the information required, she then gave directions on how to get there. Gratefully, the Canon scribbled everything down before closing the book and placed it on the floor by his feet. He then turned his attention back to Paul. "What are you going to be on Sunday, bearing in mind that Jesse also attacks you?"

"I was thinking of being at the house as well, actually."

"I do not think that is a good idea." The Canon gave Paul a stern look, "I think it would be a far better idea if you were somewhere else. Do you know of a Church that might be open at five o'clock on Sunday?"

"St. Mary's in Hemel old town would be, yes."

"I suggest that you make sure you are there then, at that time." The Canon smirked.

Puzzled by Canon Fitzwilliams' request, Joanna asked "Why don't you want Paul with us? Surely it would be better if he were, otherwise it would just run off to find him, when you arrive at the house?"

"Because I don't think it is necessary for him to be there, that is why." came his sharp reply, before the Canon rose from his chair, stating, "Until Sunday, then?" and eagerly ushered the three out of the meeting room, to the front door.

Joanna was the first to step out into the daylight, having gratefully said her goodbyes, followed by Lewis who roughly shook the Canons hand.

However, as Paul went to follow them, Canon Fitzwilliams grabbed his arm, saying, "You live in Hemel I believe."

"I do, yes." Paul anxiously replied, wondering what was coming next.

"You know of the Church Of England Convent at Boxmoor?" Paul nodded. "I think you should take prayer groups there. If you are interest, I will telephone them, so that they will know to expect you."

"Thank you. I would be very interested, yes."

"I'll telephone them later this evening then." The Canon then held out his hand and shook Paul's. "God Bless you." And with that, Paul left the vicarage and jogged up the path to catch up with the others.

CHAPTER TWENTY-TWO
28TH AUGUST 1993

11.30 am Hemel Hempstead

Paul returned home, having spent the morning dragging himself aimlessly around the shopping centre. Wondering through to the kitchen, he opened the cupboard and grabbed a can of diet coke before ambling back through to the L-shaped sitting room and flopped onto the settee. He gave a deep sigh as he opened the can and lit a cigarette, before reclining into the cushions and allowed his mind to wander.

He immediately began to think of the meeting with the Canon and the way the clergyman had treated him, ridiculing the psychic for his work.

Paul pondered over Canon Fitzwilliams' accusations and, to his surprise, he began questioning the whole business of psyche, himself. Maybe the Canon was right after all, maybe he was evil.

His thoughts then drifted to the Oracle and Fay's allegation's about the thing in the shop cellar that had attacked her son, Ashley. Maybe, she was also right for, if he could incense the spirit at Joanna's house, then he was also capable of feeding whatever it was in her cellar with an equal amount of negativity, to make it more powerful.

Placing the diet coke on the table next to him, he took another drag from his cigarette, as he recalled the events in Joanna's house that first night when her sister, Debbie, was attacked. His mind then continued to the night he, Lewis and Joanna visited the Reverend Lawrence when something tried to possess the young woman in the car. There was also that Saturday, two weeks ago, when the thing tried to attacked both Joanna and him. Even

M.O.G. insisted that Paul was the cause of the trouble, and all because he was a psychic.

"Maybe everyone is right," he muttered to himself, "I cause nothing but anxiety to all concerned. What I have here is not a gift, it is a hindrance. I can not go on, I must close down and stop being psychic."

At that point, Paul felt a presence enter the room and, as he looked up, he saw his head guide, Peter, towering over him, the guides blue-grey eyes consumed with anger.

"Go away, Peter." Paul ordered, as he scowled at his guardian.

Ignoring Paul's command, Peter leant forward and grabbed the consultants collar.

"I order you out, in the name of Jesus Christ." Paul yelled, but Peter refused to leave.

Glaring up at his eccentric looking guide, Paul growled, "What do you want with me? I have had enough of the lot of you. I am fed up of being attacked, I am sick and tired of having insults thrown at me and am annoyed with spooks like yourself, ruling my life."

"So I understand." Peter sternly replied. "But there is no way you are going to back off now. I am not going to let you."

"Bollocks. If I decide to stop then I shall, and neither you nor anyone else can do anything about it."

Upon hearing Paul's words, Peter struck out at the coke can in temper, sending it flying across the room. The spirit then lifted the psychic to his feet. "Oh. Really?" the stockily built guide announced, "So you think it is your decision to make?"

"My life. My decision." Paul argued with the spirit.

Peter then shoved at the psychic, sending Paul staggering backwards. "Nothing is your decision. It is out of your hands."

Regaining his balance, Paul squared up to wiry haired guide. "You are sent to advise me not order me around, Peter." Paul reminded the spirit of his duties. "Therefore, if I feel it is best that I stop all this now, then so be it."

Peter aggressively pushed at Paul's shoulder, sending the young man off balance a second time. "And what of Joanna? What do you think will become of her if you decide to back out now, eh? And what of God, have you forgotten your oath to Him? Turning your back on psyche would be turning your back on God and that, my friend, is blasphemy."

"But my psychic abilities have caused nothing but grief. If I had not have been psychic, then I would never have gone to Jo's house in the first place. And if I had not have set foot in her house, then it would not have come to this. Canon Fitzwilliams was right, I am responsible."

Peter, infuriated that he could not get through to the man, grabbed Paul by his shirt and hurled the psychic across the room, sending him crashing into the wall. "And if you had not gone there, Joanna would have eventually persuaded someone else.

Imagine what would have happened if that had been the case, eh?" Peter growled, as he approached the crumpled psychic lying on the floor, "Someone else, probably with far less Faith in God than you, ignorantly stumbling into a psychic battlefield. That would definitely have destroyed both them and Joanna."

"But I can't do anything to help her." Paul stated coldly, as he glared up at the apparition towering over him.

Reaching down, Peter grabbed Paul's arm and, with the strength of a thousand men, he effortlessly lifted the psychic to his feet. "What then about Faith? Have you not ignited the flame in her heart, allowing her to see with her own eyes how all-powerful the Lord God is, eh?"

"God is just 'so merciful', isn't He?" Paul sarcastically growled. "I mean, He really has made it easy for us to convince His people to help us, hasn't He?"

"Never question God's motives." Peter scorned. "Question mine by all means, but not the Lord our God." The spirit then stepped back, away from the consultant. "You think your encounter with Joanna was a chance meeting, eh? How wrong you are, my friend.

It was your destiny to meet, as much as it is your destiny to use your gift of prophesy."

"Why then am I being tormented, by evil?"

"You will find out when the time is right. You are walking the pathway of learning – take deliberate steps to avoid the pits and hollows."

Feeling annoyance rise up from within, Paul straightened his stance, "But tomorrow it will all be over. Tell me, Peter, what have I learnt from this? What have any of us learnt from this?" The consultant then rose his voice, "I tell you what I have learnt, Peter. I have learnt that everyone has turned their backs on me. People of like-mind blame me, and the Church accuses me. I have no one to turn to, there is nothing left in me, my will has been crushed."

Peter grabbed Paul by the collar a second time; "You are so full of self-pity, aren't you? Just listen to yourself, you pathetic little man. Don't you realise that you are special? Can't you see that you are the only person who can rid Joanna of the evil that haunts her? Do not listen to the false prophets, for they speak with venom. Listen to your heart. Joanna and Lewis need you, that is why you must not turn your back on all that you believe in."

"But I have done my job. The Church have agreed to do an exorcism, so there is nothing further for me to do, now." Paul informed his guide, "Therefore, why are you so adamant that I must not give up being a practising psychic?"

"Because my dear, innocent lamb, the Canon Fitzwilliams is not conducting an exorcism at Joanna's house tomorrow, he is administering a Requiem. The

Canon has no intention of helping either you, Lewis or Joanna. The only reason he decided to go was to shut Lewis and Joanna up. The man is too afraid to be of assistance - he has too little faith."

Paul sank to his knees. "Then what will become of us? At this rate, it will destroy us all."

"You will know what to do, when the time is right." Peter mellowed his tone.

"Everything is fixed; it is all in place. Just be patient."

"When will it come to an end, Peter? Tell me, I order you." But the head guide just gave Paul a sad smile, before disappearing before his eyes and was gone.

CHAPTER TWENTY-THREE
29TH AUGUST, 1993

9.30 am Slapton

Lewis placed a frying pan on the hot hob ring and began warming up some fat, in preparation for his beloved fried breakfast. Then, leaving it to start sizzling, he poured some boiling water into a mug and carried the steaming hot coffee upstairs, to his girlfriend.

Entering the bedroom, he gave Joanna a warm smile, as she pulled up her black jeans. "Here you go, gi'l." he gave a hearty bellow as he placed the mug on the bedside table. "Thought this might set you up for the day." He then turned, and slouched out of the room, leaving her to finish getting dressed.

Lewis was outside, fumbling around in the back of his van, by the time Joanna ventured down the stairs. Totally unaware that he was cooking breakfast, she retrieved the duster, polish and hoover from under the stairs and wandered through to the sitting room to prepare the house for her guests.

Half an hour later, Lewis burst into the room, a bemused expression on his face. "Just look at this." he bellowed, as he held out his electric jigsaw.

Throwing the duster on the settee, Joanna wandered over to his side and took the tool from him. She turned the appliance over a couple of times, examining it closely, but could not see what all the fuss was about.

"Look at the plug." Lewis gave her a clue and, as she gave the tool a second look, she saw that the plug had somehow been forced through the handle.

"How on earth did that happen?" She gave Lewis a puzzled look.

"I don't know. I only used it yesterday; it was perfectly all right then. Somehow, when I wrapped the flex around it last night, the plug must have slipped through the gap."

Joanna tried to pull the plug back through, but the gap was considerably smaller than the plug. "Sorry Lewis, but I think that is impossible." She grinned as she tugged the flex.

"Oh. Well, better get the screwdriver then, and take the plug off ." and with that he turned and left.

Joanna was about to continue with her housework when she heard Lewis out in the kitchen, cussing, "What the fuck is going on, here?"

Rushing out to join him, Joanna's gaze fell upon her tall, earthy boyfriend as he scratched his head, whilst staring at the frying pan on the hob. "What ever is the matter?" she asked, in a concerned manner.

Looking up at her, Lewis bellowed, "Did you turn this hob down?"

Joanna shook her head, "No. I didn't even know it was on."

"I think your ghosts are playing games with me this morning. Admittedly, I forgot that I'd put this on for a fry-up, but look," he said, as he pointed to the knob, "it's been turned right down."

"Maybe you only put it on number one?" Joanna tried to rationalise the event, as she glanced at the knob.

"No, I definitely put it on three. I distinctly remember doing it."

"Just as well it was turned down then," she tried to make light of the situation. "Or the kitchen would probably be on fire, by now."

Lewis then turned his attention back to the jigsaw. "And as for this, the only way it could have got this way, is if someone had taken the plug off, put the flex through the handle, then put the plug back on again. However, since using it yesterday, it has been safely locked away in the back of the van, so nobody could have tampered with it."

"What does it matter?" Joanna tried to calm Lewis down. "Supernatural phenomena, or absent-mindedness, makes no difference." and with that, she returned to the sitting room, leaving Lewis mumbling away to himself, as he began unscrewing the plug of the jigsaw.

4.00 pm

With time fast approaching when the Canon was due to arrive, Joanna stood outside, soaking up some rays, as she nervously kept one eye on her watch. As she stood there, fussing Skimble on the fence, her next door neighbour, Harry, came whistling around the corner of his garages. "Hello, Jo. Enjoying the sun?" he called across to her, with that faint London accent of his.

"Thought I might get a tan, if I stand out here long enough."

Harry wandered over towards her, and leant against the fence. "Lewis told me you've got the Exorcist coming today."

"Yeah." Joanna gave him a nervous smile, as she ran her hand down Skimble's back.

"What time is he due to arrive?"

"About five." Joanna informed him.

"Well look, tell him to park in here, as there isn't much room on the waste land. Let me know when he comes and I'll open the gates for you."

"Thanks, Harry." Joanna beamed at her neighbour. "That is very kind of you."

"Not at all. What are neighbours for?" Harry smiled, before his attention was averted to Lewis, as the dairy engineer emerging from the house.

"Hello Harry, mate." Lewis bellowed, in a hearty fashion. "Thought you'd be busy washing your cars, with weather like this."

"Na, mate - the wife's got me cutting the lawn instead."

"Well, only an hour to go now, before the motley crew get here." Lewis jokingly informed all, as he glanced at his watch. "Do you believe in ghosts, Harry?"

"You hear of some very strange stories." Harry replied, diplomatically. "Daisy is really into that sort of thing."

"Well personally, I think it's all in the mind." Lewis gave a wicked grin, "An over-active imagination. Once you're dead, you're dead; pushing up daisies. It can't hurt you."

Horrified by his remark, Joanna turned to the dairy engineer. "How can you say that, after all that has happened?" and, with tears welling in her eyes, she pushed passed her unsympathetic partner and marched into the house.

Back in the sitting room, Joanna flopped down on the carpet in front of the fire and, sniffling, she began idly rearranging the candleholders on the hearth. As she played with the ornate brass ornaments, she suddenly became aware of another presence in the room, with her.

Turning towards the door, her eyes fell upon the misty figure of M.O.G., as he stood there, staring at her.

"And what do you want, Jesse? Come to gloat?" she shouted at the manifestation, hostility prominent in her voice. But to her surprise, the entity did not mock her, rather an expression of compassion crept across his face, as he gazed upon the young woman.

Getting up off the floor, Joanna stepped towards him. As she moved closer to the entity, she noticed a single tear roll down the spirits face, as he stood there silently, watching her.

"Worried about our fate, are we?" She attacked him, "Afraid of meeting with our maker?" But still, the entity showed no aggression towards the woman, just remained still and silent.

"Why Jesse?" Joanna found herself conversing with the spirit, "Why have you put me through all this? Just answer me that." But before Jesse could reply, Mandy entered the room, standing at his side.

Upon seeing the tall, slim woman, M.O.G.'s expression changed from one of compassion, to one of anger. Waving a clenched fist at Joanna, he growled, "I'll have your blood for this." before fading away from view. Turning to the female ghost, Joanna shouted, "Why don't you just leave me alone. I order you out, in the name of Jesus Christ." And with those words, Mandy disappeared too, leaving Joanna standing alone in a house she could no longer call her own.

4.45 pm Chipperfield

The Reverend Angela Butlers car rolled to a halt, outside Joanna's parent's house. Grabbing her Prayer book and a candle, the deaconess clambered out of the car, and wandered up to the front door.

Margaret, with a solemn expression, met Angela and invited the deaconess inside. "Thank you for agreeing to pray with us this afternoon, Angela." Margaret said, as she showed the woman into the sitting room.

"I am as concerned for your daughter, as you are, Margaret." The deaconess gave her a kind and gentle smile. "Prayer is a powerful thing and so, the more people that pray for Joanna's salvation, the better."

The deaconess, Margaret and Tony then took their places and, opening the prayer book at one of the marked pages, the deaconess lead the group, with prayers for protection.

4.55 pm Slapton

The Canon's rusty old vehicle rumbled off the road, onto the waste ground in front of the house. Moments later, he, Evangeline and the Reverend Lawrence had scrabbled out of it and were making their way up the path towards the front door.

Lewis greeted them, inviting the three into the cool kitchen, in an unusually quiet manner.

Joanna stood in the doorway to the sitting room as her guests arrived. "Please come through." she smiled at her guests and beckoned the three to follow her.

The Canon, carrying a large black case, was the first to enter and, giving the young woman a false smile, he stated, "I will need a small table, to use as an altar."

Obligingly, Joanna fetched a table suitable for the task and handed it to the Canon. He then proceeded to open his case and laid a purple cloth across it, before dressing the altar with a cross and candles.

As he worked on the altar, the Reverend Lawrence turned to Joanna and, with a humble smile and melancholy eyes, he asked, "Are you alright? You look a little stressed."

"I'm fine. But I will be glad when this is all over."

"Don't worry, Joanna. Canon Fitzwilliams knows what he is doing. You are in good hands now." The kindly Reverend comforted the distressed woman.

Having retrieved the Holy Water from its flask and poured the liquid into a golden cup, the Canon turned to Joanna and Lewis asking, "Have you both been confirmed?"

"No, neither of us have." Lewis replied. "Is that a problem?"

"Oh no." the Canon replied, pompously. "The only difference is that when we come to the communion, neither of you will be able to partake in the taking of the bread and wine. Instead, I will administer a blessing on you both." Canon Fitzwilliams then began to rummage through his case and withdrew some more items, required for the service.

Evangeline handed out some service sheets to the group, whilst they waited for the Canon. As she reached Joanna, she smiled and stated, "This will only take about half an hour or so, then it will all be over."

"I hope so." Joanna gave a nervous giggle.

"Right then." the Canon's voice filled the room. "Are we ready?" he asked as he gazed around the room for confirmations. "Reverend Lawrence? Evangeline? Joanna and Lewis? Then we shall begin."

As soon as he commenced with the service, the room became overwhelmingly oppressive, as the ghosts within the house, objected to the presence of God's men. Joanna found it increasingly difficult to breath as the Canon continued, oblivious to her distress, until she felt like she was about to faint. Then, as quickly as the room had been filled with anger and negativity, the sensation vanished, leaving the air smelling sweet and the ambience of the place free from evil.

5.00 pm Hemel Hempstead

Paul and his dad arrived at the large oak doors of St Mary's, just as the warden stepped outside and swung them closed behind him.

"May I sit inside?" Paul shakily enquired.

The warden looked the two men up and down, in a deliberated fashion, before coldly stating, "No you can not - the church closes at five."

"But I must. You see, an exorcisms being held today at a friends house, and the Canon who is conduction it, strongly advised me to find a safe haven."

"Well, you won't find it here." The weaselly little warden growled as he forcibly pushed the key in the lock, before turning it, to secured the church.

"Well, can't you let me and my dad sit in there for an hour?" Paul pleaded. "It's a matter of life and death."

"Don't be so dramatic, son. Besides, a warden has to be present at all times, if someone is in the Church, in case anything gets nicked. I have to get home, as my tea is waiting, so I can not hang around here any longer." and with that, he went to push past the consultant and his father.

Catching his arm, Paul suggested, "Well, why not lock us in the church? At least then, you can rest assured that nothing will get stolen."

"Don't be absurd." The warden growled, as he pushed Paul's hand from his arm, "I have never heard such a ridiculous suggestion, in all my life. Lock you in, indeed. Without supervision, there is no telling what you will both get up to." And with that,

the weaselly little man scurried off, leaving Paul and his father on the steps of the

church.

Paul's father turned to his son, and growled, "He must have a very warped mind, that one."

"Certainly no Christian." Paul sighed, in dismay. "Shame the other warden wasn't on duty this evening, he would have let me in."

"Well, what now then, Paul?" His fathers Devonshire accent filled the air.

"Guess we'll just have to sit in the church gardens and hope for the best." And with that, he made his way to one of the seats, with father in tow.

To pass the time, Paul's dad began to waffle on about football, in particular about Torquay Unit's promotion prospects. As Paul patiently listened, he suddenly became aware of a presence buzzing around him.

He looked over to his dad, who was staring into the distance as he rabbited on, but before the consultant could warn his companion, the entity attacked him, its hands wrapped firmly around the psychic's neck.

Paul began to crokingly utter the words to the Lords Prayer whilst his father, oblivious to his sons plight, continued with the one-sided conversation of Torquay united. However, the words of the prayer had little effect on the evil spirit, and it was able to sustain a strong grip, throughout.

Quickly thinking of another method, Paul gasped and whispered, "Your black magic and your black sorcery are powerless to injure me. I send thy curses, back to thee. Return, return by three times three. Return I say, so mote it be."

Immediately, the grip slackened and, leaving his father woffling to himself on the bench, Paul raced off across the lawn towards the church, the entity close at his heels.

Upon reaching the building, Paul placed both hands on its wall and said the Lords Prayer a second time, as the infuriated phantom kept a respectful distance, whilst Paul used the Church, for protection.

Bemused by Paul's behaviour, his father wandered over to join him. "What are you doing?" he questioned Paul's motives.

"Dad, I am being attacked by the thing from Jo's house. That is why I needed to get in the Church."

"Oh." His father replied, vaguely. "So, what do you think of Torquay's chances of promotion, then?"

"I don't know and I don't care." Paul snapped, "I've got more important things on my mind."

Suddenly, the weaselly little warden appeared with his brown and white whippet.

"Oi." he bellowed from the far side of the church, as he set eyes upon the two men,

"What do you think you are doing?" He then marched up to the consultant and his father, pulling Paul away from the church wall.

"Look." Paul glared at the little bureaucrat; "An exorcism is taking place, rght now, at a friends house. The evil spirit that they are supposed to be exorcising has decided to pay me a visit, because I was unable to get into the church. Therefore, the exorcism is now not going to work, because the said evil spirit is not in the house. Understand?"

"You expect me to believe a tall tale like that, sonny? The canon would have informed me, if you were telling the truth. Just keep away from my church. Go on, clear off."

Feeling a second assault from the entity coming on, Paul placed a hand on the Church wall, whilst turning to the weaselly little man, "The name of the exorcist is Canon Mark Fitzwilliams."

"Never heard of him." the little man replied then, pulling Paul away from the wall a second time, he continued, "Now get lost, you nutter, before I call the police."

Obligingly Paul moved away from the St Mary's, whilst continuing to mutter the Lords Prayer, to himself. His father then acknowledged the manner of the warden and reminded Paul of a similar incident years ago with a steward at Torquay's football ground, which had a similar attitude. However, Paul took no notice of his fathers comments, just continued to protect himself from the presence, until the warden had gone.

Once the warden had disappeared from view, Paul marched back to the church and, leaning against it, he began to absorb the protective energy of the building once more. He breathed a sigh of relief now he had found a way of stopping the entity from destroying him but, as soon as he began to feel more in control, the warden returned.

"Oi. Get out of my grounds; NOW." The weasel hollered, and with that he escorted Paul and his father to the garden parameters.

Once outside the church gardens, Paul's father turned to his son, and stated, "Well, it's useless hanging around here any longer. We might as well go home."

"I'll just sit on the wall for a bit." Paul wearily replied. "I think the church has given me enough energy to fight it off now, but I'd rather remain here, just in case."

"Are you still being attacked then?"

"It seems to have eased, but I don't want to take any risks."

"Alright then, Paul." His dad replied, as he glanced at his watch. "We'll stay here until six o'clock and then we'll go."

And so, the pair of them sat there in the sunshine, as Paul's dad continuing the one side conversation about Torquay United to pass the time.

5.20 pm

Debbie sat on her bed; a Bible clenched firmly in her hand. Both her boys sat either side of her as she prepared to read some Bible stories to her sons.

She was not a regular churchgoer, so she did the best she could by simply continuing to ask God to help her sister, in her hour of need. She was lost in concentration as her youngest, Tom, suddenly shouted out "What's this awful smell?"

"What smell?" she queried the boy's observation.

"Pigs." He replied, as he held his nose. "Horrible, smelly pigs."

"How do you know what pigs smell like?" she mocked him.

"I don't. That man in the doorway told me." Debbie's son informed her in a matter-of-fact fashion, as he pointed to the thin air, of the entrance of the bedroom.

Feeling fear creep into her, Debbie took Tom and Lee by the hand. "Now boys. I would like you both to help me pray for your Auntie Jo." She said softly, trying not to let the fear be heard in her tone.

"Why?" they grinned up at her.

"You remember when I told you about her ghost? Well, today she is having some vicar's around her house to help this ghost go to heaven, where he belongs. If we pray as well, it might help to persuade the ghost to go."

"Ok. then, mummy." and with that, Debbie began reciting the Lords Prayer to protect
her family, without letting on just how serious their encounter with the entity had been.

6.05 pm Slapton

The Canon, having blessed the final room in the house, returned to the sitting room. "That should do it." he flashed a false smile at Lewis and Joanna, as he began to tidy up his makeshift alter.

"Would you all like a cup of tea, or coffee?" Joanna glanced around the room, at her guests.

Reverend Lawrence was the first to reply. "I am afraid, Joanna, that I will have to make tracks to the church, to prepare for the service. It was most kind of you to offer,

though." He then turned to the canon. "Mark, is it alright if I leave now? There is
nothing further for me to do here, is there?"

The Canon looked up, from his task. "We have finished, Peter, you go on ahead. We'll see you later, at the church."

The reverend said his farewells to the Canon, Evangeline and Lewis, before turning to Joanna. "I apologise for deserting you, but I must go. Will you be coming to the service this evening?"

"Yes, we will."

"Wonderful. I look forward to seeing you all later, then." And with that, he made his way to the front door, and was gone.

Packing the final remnants into his case, the Canon gave a stretch and asked, in an ecclesiastic fashion, "Everything to your satisfaction, Joanna? Lewis? Has Jesse Healy gone?"

Joanna, absorbing the light, refreshing aura of the room, smiled, as she replied, "Yes. I think the requiem has done the trick. Thank you."

"Good." came a rather bold statement from the Canon, as he glanced, acrimoniously, at Evangeline. He then slammed the case shut and, locking its treasures away from the world, he continued, "Well, I think we had better make our way to the Church.

Shall we walk, or drive?"

"It's only a five minute walk, "Lewis informed the tall, lanky man. "It would be nice to go by foot, as it is such a sunny evening."

"That's settled then." The canon informed the rest of the group in a dictatorial manner, "I'll put my things in the car, then we can all walk to the church together. Come on, Evangeline." And suddenly, the canon, and his assistant were marching out of the house and off towards his car.

Turning to Lewis, Joanna smiled, "I'll just get a cardigan, then I'll catch you up." and with that, she ran upstairs to the bedroom, to retrieve the garment.

As she reached the top of the landing, she paused outside the bathroom door, which had been left ajar. She stared at it for a moment, then, curious of how the room would feel now that M.O.G. had gone; she swung open the door, and marched inside.

The room felt clear, the air sweet and the ambience free from negativity. Standing there, she felt peace come over her, as she allowed the positive feelings flow threw.

Smiling to herself, she turned to leave, but as she stepped towards the door, her hackles suddenly rose as a gush of negative energy rushed into the room, behind her. She stopped dead in her tracks. Could this be M.O.G.? Had he avoided being sent into the light? Surely the Canon had not failed in his task? "No." she tried to convince herself, otherwise. "It is all in my mind. Just an over-active imagination." And with that, she dashed out off the bathroom, grabbed her cardigan as quick as she could and rushed off, to join the others outside the house.

7.30 pm

Joanna and Lewis stepped out of the Church, with the Canon and Evangeline behind them. Joanna's parents had rushed over to Slapton, as soon as the Reverend Angela Butler had left their house, just in time for the six-thirty service and, were busy chatting to the Reverend Lawrence in front of the others.

Approaching the Reverend, Joanna held out a hand and shook his. "Thank you, Reverend. Both Lewis and I appreciate all you have done, for us."

"That is what we are here for." He gave her a humble smile. "However, although I hope this episode has now ended, should you have any further problems, please do not hesitate to contact me again." And with that, he moved on to the Canon and his assistant and began a conversing with them.

"Well?" Joanna's mother pumped her, "How did it go?"

"I'm not sure." Joanna replied, flatly. "It's probably just my imagination, but I thought I felt M.O.G.'s presence, just before we left to come to the service."

"Probably because your distraught at the moment." Her mother tried to convince the young woman. Margaret then changed the subject, "Your father and I thought we'd treat you and Lewis to a meal at the Carpenters Arms."

"Thanks. I haven't had chance to think of food, yet."

"I assumed that would be the case, so we thought you'd appreciate a treat. What time does the pub open?"

"Seven." Lewis piped in.

"We might as well go straight there then." Joanna's father suggested.

"The Canon Fitzwilliams' car is parked outside our house." Joanna informed them, "I think it only polite that we return with them to the house, first."

"Tell you what." Tony made a second suggestion. "Your mother and I will wonder down to the pub to get a table, whilst you return to the house with the Canon. Then you can join us, once he has gone."

And so, with that, Joanna and Lewis wandered back through the footpath towards Horton road with the Canon and Evangeline, whilst Joanna's parents ambled along Church road, to the pub.

Outside the house, the Canon firmly shook hands with the couple as he handed Joanna a prayer book, before he and his assistant clambered into his rusty old banger.

It was only once he had started up the engine and had slapped the vehicle into reverse, that Joanna suddenly became aware of blackness cloaking her.

As he began to roll backwards, she felt a hand grab at her neck. Instinctively, she started to say the Lords Prayer, but the entity refused to release his grip.

The Canon changed gears from reverse to first, and briefly looking over his shoulder, he slowly drove off the wasteland and onto the road.

Grabbing her boyfriend by the arm, she croaked, "Call him back." As she desperately tried to fight the entity off.

Lewis looked down at his girlfriend, bemusement written all over his face. "What's wrong?" he questioned her request.

"Just do it." she whispered, as she grabbed at her throat in the vain attempt to pull the phantoms hand from her neck.

Realising her distress, Lewis turned and shouted up the road at the Canons car, as its taillights disappeared around the corner. But the Canon did not hear the dairy engineer and soon had faded from view. As soon as the rattly old vehicle had gone, the entity released his grip from the young woman's throat and, with a heinous jeer, it departed, leaving Joanna and Lewis standing on the wasteland, alone.

Turning to his girlfriend, Lewis placed a comforting arm around her. "Come on, let's go to the Carpenters. We'll worry about this later." And so, they began to wonder along the road, towards the pub.

The couple joined Joanna's parents just as the landlady, Ann, wandered over with some menus. "Hello Jo; Lewis." She greeted them. "How are you today?"

Lewis made some small talk to the landlady, as Margaret looked upon her daughter, with dismay. Leaning over the table, she whispered, "Are you alright? You look terrible."

Fidgeting nervously on the chair, Joanna shakily replied, "It hasn't gone mum. In fact, it is worse now than it was before."

As Ann left her customers to mull over the menu, Margaret leant back and, catching Lewis' eye, she frowned, "Why didn't you inform the Canon?"

"Because he left in such a hurry that I didn't have time to call him back." Lewis replied, sternly.

"He should have made sure everything was alright, before leaving you like this." Her sharp remark carried around the pub. "Any fool could see that you are not alright. Mind you, I thought he was a terribly scruffy man - that always gives away a slovenly attitude towards one's work."

"Mum." Joanna tried to calm Margaret down. "He has gone, so that is that."

"Well, you can't go back the house now - not until it has been sorted out." Margaret continued, "Isn't there a hotel that you could go to?"

Lewis cut into the conversation between mother and daughter. "There's the motel down the road," he informed Joanna's mother. "I think we should stay there, tonight. Then I'll phone the Canon tomorrow, to tell him the worst."

"Good idea." Margaret agreed with him, but to her dismay, Joanna was not so keen on the idea. "Look. I have said this before and I am going to say it again - no spook is going to drive me out of my own home."

"Now you're being ludicrous. Just look at yourself, Joanna. Your father and I have had to watch, helplessly, at you wasting away over the last month. How much weight have you lost over that time, eh?"

"One and three quarter stone." Joanna mumbled. "I'm down to seven and three-quarter stone."

"Precisely. And there wasn't that much of you before then. Show some sense, girl, you can't go on like this. You'll end up killing yourself."

Feeling resentment well up inside, Joanna glared at her well-meaning mother and stated, "I refuse to let it get the better of me."

"Then you're a fool." Margaret growled back. "Did you know that Angela came round our house this afternoon, to pray with us?"

"No I didn't. That was very kind of her."

"Yes, it was. She is as worried about you as the rest of us are."

"Except for the Canon Fitzwilliams." Lewis piped in.

"Well, he is one on his own." Margaret agreed with Lewis, before turned back to her daughter, "Why don't you give yourself a break. The Lord God knows, you can do with it."

"No. I'll not let it win. Now, can we change the subject please?" And so, respecting her daughter's wishes Margaret began to chat about Holy Cross Church and the wonderful service that the Reverend Lawrence had conducted.

10.00 pm

Eventually, with the evening over, Joanna and Lewis said their goodbyes to Tony and Margaret outside the Carpenters arms, before venturing back to the house.

Lewis was the first up the pathway and, placing the key in the lock, he opened the door and wandered through to the kitchen.

Joanna timidly tiptoed through behind him but, as she stepped over the threshold of the kitchen, she felt a pair of hands grab at her throat. The entity then growled, in a deep, coerce tone, "Get thou oust of my house, whore."

"Not while there is still a breath of life in me." she screamed back at the manifestation, before pulling out the rose quartz from her jean pocket. "I send you the love of God. A love that is all powerful."

Upon sight of the crystal, the entity backed off and, with a blood-curdling snarl, it promised, "I wilst takest thy soul, before dawn." and with that, it evaporated into thin air.

Lewis marched back to his girlfriend's side. "I don't know what's going on, but for pity's sake, let's get out of here."

"No." she screamed and with a confident air about her, she marched up the stairs.

Lewis tailed along behind, as she reached the top of the stairs and to the bedroom door. But as she stepped into the room, a powerful surge of negative energy rushed at the young woman, sending her flying back out onto the landing.

Lewis watched on helplessly as his girlfriend, with grit and determination, regained her balance and marched straight back inside once more, singing out the Lords Prayer as she entered, with a confidence that he had never heard before. Upon hearing her convictions, the entity skulked through into the back bedroom, to escape from God's words.

Creeping into the bedroom behind her, Lewis saw Joanna retrieving the Bible from under her pillow. "What are you doing?" he tentatively enquired, as he saw the rage in her eyes.

"If it want's a fight," she informed her boyfriend, with vigour, "Then that is exactly what it is going to get." and with that, she proceeded to march off towards the bathroom.

"Where are you going?" He bellowed, as he grabbed at her arm.

"I am going to get ready for bed." and, pulling her appendage away from his grasp, she left the bedroom and strided into the bathroom.

Immediately she strutted inside, the manifestation grabbed her by the throat and physically pushed the young woman out of the room, pinning her against the wall opposite the door. Then it started to lift her up off the floor, using her neck as its handle.

Choking, Joanna lifted the quartz and placed it to her throat. Immediately, the entity let go, laughing venomously, as it did so.

Joanna then attempted a second entrance and found herself met by the welcoming committee again. This time, the entity stuck out at her, making the skin on her cheek tingle, where it made contact. It then thrust a blow to the stomach, causing her to double up. Winded, she leant against the wall, as she felt the negative aura of the manifestation wrap itself around her.

"Oh no you don't, matey." she growled, as she placed the Bible to her psychic gate. Immediately, the entity withdrew, then, after a moments pause to regain its strength, the manifestation grabbed her by her clothing and hurled her across the bathroom, sending the woman crashing into the vanity unit, whilst the Bible and the quartz fell to the floor, by the door.

Incensed, Joanna proceeded with the Lords Prayer a second time in a slow, deliberate fashion. "Our Father, who art in heaven," She recited, "hallowed be thy name; thy kingdom come; thy will be done; on earth as it is in heaven..." But as she spoke the words, the Spirit struck out at her, sending the young woman sprawling across the floor and losing her momentum.

Upon hearing the riot from the bathroom, Lewis appeared in the doorway, to see his girlfriend lying on the floor. "What the fuck is going on?" he bellowed. "You alright?" But before Joanna could reply, the entity grabbed at her neck, intent only on squeezing the life from her.

Struggling to fight the phantom off, she pointed at the Bible, lying on the floor in front of where her boyfriend stood.

Bending down, he picked up the book and threw it at her. Immediately she caught it, the entity released its grip and stood there, towering over her, laughing.

Propping herself up against the vanity unit, Joanna clasped the Bible to her chest and continued with the Lords Prayer. "... Give us this day our daily bread. And forgive us our trespasses, as we forgive those who trespass against us. And lead us not into temptation; but deliver us from evil..." As the words rang around the room, two angels appeared from no where, illuminating the entire area in bright, vibrant colour. Placing themselves either side of the negative spirit, they forcibly dragged it from the room, leaving Joanna gasping for breath, as she finished, "For thine is the kingdom, the power, and the glory, for ever and ever. Amen."

Realising that his petrified girlfriend was now out of immediate danger, Lewis escorted Joanna back to the bedroom. There was a slight clickiness in the atmosphere as they entered, but nothing compared to what had just been experienced.

Clambering into bed, the couple snuggled down under the duvet. However, there was to be no sleep for the young woman that night, for she only felt safe whilst reciting the Lords Prayer. It was going to prove a very long time, until dawn.

CHAPTER TWENTY-FOUR
30TH AUGUST, 1993

8.30 am Slapton

Lewis awoke from his slumber to find his girlfriend bolt upright in bed, staring into space.

"Awake at this hour, on a bank holiday?" he joked.

With dark rimmed eyes, Joanna turned to him and gave a weary smile, "I haven't had a wink all night."

"Well, it's your own fault, gi'l." he gave her an unsympathetic glare, before reaching over to his bedside table and picking up his glasses. "You should have spent the night at the Motel, like we all told you to do."

"Alright. Don't rub it in." She snapped. "Maybe I should just let it win. After all, I'm only living here - it's not as if it invited me to stay, or anything."

"Come on." His face lifted into a smile, as he reached over and gave her a reassuring cuddle. "I know why you made the decision to stay. It is just that I am worried about you, that's all." He then pulled back the covers and swung his legs over the side.

"Tell you what, I'll go and telephone the Canon Fitzwilliams, and get him to comeback and try again." And with that, he rose from the comfort of the bed and, struggling with his dressing gown, he wandered off downstairs.

As he ventured downstairs, he too began to feel a little uneasy. It was almost if something was watching him, but he could neither see, nor hear anything except for the padding of dog paws behind him and the distant sound of meows coming from the garden, as the family pets demanded breakfast.

He found his step quicken slightly, as he stepped through the kitchen, into the sitting room. The lounge seemed far from welcoming as he entered. He could not put his finger on the sensations that he felt, but the room was decidedly clicky and foreboding.

Reaching the telephone, he picked up the receiver and, fumbling around the desk for the Canon's number, he dialled.

The phone seemed to ring endlessly on the other end, giving him a feeling of abandonment. After about a minute he decided to give up so, removing the hand set from his ear, he reached down to replace it on the hook. Just as the hand set was about to make contact, he heard a faint voice stating, "Rectory."

Quickly placing the hand set back to his ear, Lewis bellowed, "Canon Fitzwilliams?"

"Speaking." came the magisterial reply.

"Hello, it's Lewis Chetfler here. " He gruffly informed the pompous Canon, "Sorry to disturb you at such an hour on a bank holiday." Canon Fitzwilliams did not respond so, not to prolong the embarrassing pause any longer, Lewis reminded him, "You came to mine and Joanna's house yesterday to conduct a Requiem."

"Oh yes." Canon Fitzwilliams replied, flatly. "Joanna better now?"

"No she is not." Lewis growled. "And neither is the house."

"Oh? How so?"

"The thing in this house has now resorted to throwing my girlfriend from one room to another. She did not have a wink of sleep last night, because of it." He bellowed at the Canon.

"Are you suggesting that the requiem did not work?" Sarcasm was prominent in the Canon's tone.

"I am not merely suggesting, Canon Fitzwilliams, I saw the whole thing with my own eyes." Lewis bellowed. "The thing is seven times stronger now, than it was this time yesterday."

"Listen to me, Lewis." The Canon informed him condescendingly, "These things generally settle down after a couple of days, then disappear completely. Just give it time."

"And, meanwhile, the thing in our house will probably either kill her, or possess her. I can't just stand by and watch her being destroyed. I think you should come back, immediately, to put a stop to our suffering."

"Oh come now, Lewis." The Canon's pompous tones travelled down the telephone. "Joanna is a very highly strung young lady and your friend, Paul, loves to be the centre of attention. It seems to me that neither of them are happy unless they can be dramatic about something or other. I thought you to be far more reasonable and level headed than either of those two. Don't let them convince you that Jesse Healy is out to destroy them. I have had a lot of experience with this type of thing and, believe me, it will settle down in a day or two. There is nothing to worry about."

"I am sorry to disagree with you, but even I have noticed the change of atmosphere in the house. You must come back." Lewis pleaded.

"You are letting your imagination run away with you - just like your girlfriend. Give it a few days then, if you still feel the same way after that, give me a ring and we'll discuss the matter then. Alright?"

"Why don't you believe me?" Lewis questioned the Canon's decision.

"Because you are hysterical." Canon Fitzwilliams explained. "That is the trouble with this type of thing, you see. People tend to wind themselves up about a ghost in the first place, then wind themselves up about a requiem, or an exorcism. The end result seems such an anti-climax after that and so, they go looking for things that simply are not there."

"So you are telling me that you are convinced that the requiem worked and Jesse Healy has gone from this house, and are certain that it was just Joanna's imagination that was throwing her around, kicking and punching her and tormenting her all night so that she was unable to sleep."

"More than likely, yes. And it is her involvement with the occult that has allowed her imagination to play such tricks on her. This is exactly the reason why the Church condemn such activities because the new age movement encourage their followers to converse with imaginary friends, that they believe are spirits sent by God, to help them. In fact, God would only send the Holy Ghost, or an angel, not any old spirit – and then, only at a specific time and place chosen by Him, not as and when we decide to converse with it. I believe that Joanna has constructed her own negative energy and it is that, that is attacking her; not Jesse Healy; not a demon; not anything other than her own creation."

"Well, it is nice to know that we can turn to the Church in our hour of need." Lewis growled, sarcastically. "I can not believe your unchristian attitude ..."

"Do not judge me, Lewis." The Canon's angry, authoritative voice came flooding though the telephone. "I have wasted enough time appeasing your notions and I do not like being made a fool of. Now, why don't you go and have a cup of tea, sit down and think this through logically. I am sure that once you have calmed down, you will arrive at the same conclusions as I; being that Joanna is just a silly little girl who yearns for some excitement in her life. Do not allow her to take you in, Lewis, keep your feet firmly on the ground."

"So that's it then, is it? You are refusing to help us any further." Lewis bellowed down the mouthpiece.

"I see no need to return to Slapton at this time, no. Maybe, should you still feel the same way by the end of the week then please, contact me again. But for the moment, I believe that there is nothing untoward going on." The canon paused for a moment, before continuing, "Maybe you should take Joanna to see her doctor. I suspect that he would be more able to help her, than I."

"Great. Well, thanks for all your help and advice, Canon Fitzwilliams." Lewis growled. "I will be sure to inform Joanna of your suggestions." And with that, he slammed the hand set back on its hook.

Dejected, Lewis slumped his shoulders and dragged himself out of the sitting room and back to the stairs. How could he possibly tell Joanna about the outcome of his conversation with the Canon? The clergyman's rejection could prove just enough to tip her over the edge.

As he reached the landing, he heard Joanna fumbling around in the bathroom. Knocking on the door, he gently pushed it open and loitered on the threshold, awaiting an invitation to enter.

Joanna met him in the doorway, gently patting her face with a towel, as she gave him a nervous smile.

"Well?" she pumped for an outcome, "Is he coming back?"

Lewis solemnly shook his head. "Sorry, Jo. He said it would calm down in a day or two."

"So this is it then?" The young woman held back her tears, as she gazed upon the condoling dairy engineer.

"Sorry Jo, I tried my best." He replied, sorrowfully, before turning to drag himself into the bedroom.

Pushing the door shut, Joanna sank to her knees and lowered her head, as the tears began to well in her eyes. "O Lord, why? Why do you not help me?" She whispered, but no answer came to her.

Wiping a trickling tear from her cheek, she looked upwards towards the Heavens. "God; I know that for most of my life I have rejected you. I never willingly stepped into a church to sing your praises, for I was too wrapped up in myself to allow you to enter into my life. Even now, I only pray for my own selfishness, I know that. But Lord, please hear me. I have approached your people, but they turned their backs on me. I took all the right steps, waiting patiently whilst the priests decided on my fate, but they show no mercy for me now."

She paused momentarily, as she fought off the flood of tears, before continuing, "Why do you look upon me with contempt? Have I been that detestable to you? Why, when I let you in, do you not lift up your hand and put a stop to all this? Look upon my suffering and deliver me, for I have not forgotten your Law. Defend my cause and redeem me; preserve my life. The wicked are waiting to destroy me, because I am yours. They wait patiently in the wings, until I am nothing more than dust. Then they will rejoice in the knowledge that I have been slain, whilst toasting the triumph by drinking from a cup full of foaming wine and spices. O merciful Lord, do not watch on, while they rape and murder me . Please, tell me what you want from me? Tell me, what must I do to be pleasing in your sight? All I ask for is an answer..."

Lewis turned on the radio in the bedroom, which momentarily broke Joanna's concentration as the music flooded the air. Rising to her feet, she recomposed herself before continuing. "I know I am not worthy of your deliverance, O Lord, but only you hold the answers in your hands. I implore you, Lord God Almighty, free me from the evil that dwells with me, before I perish in my affliction. Amen."

As she finished the prayer, Joanna caught the DJ's voice from the radio. "The time's now eight fifty, on this lazy bank holiday Monday - just in case any of you wonderful people out there are vaguely interested. The next record is a blast from the past – 1982 to be exact. Here it is, an all-time fav of mine, Duran Duran; Save A Prayer."

As the music started, she became aware of presence standing just behind her, to her left. Looking back over her shoulder, she saw the Israelite, his eyes full of compassion and his expression consumed with solace, as he gazed upon his charge. Reaching out a hand, he placed it on her shoulder in an effort to comfort the distraught woman. But, unable to hold back her sadness any longer, she clutched the towel to her face and wept, as Simon La Bon's dulcet tones cut deep into her emotions.

CHAPTER TWENTY-FIVE
30TH AUGUST, 1993

11.55 pm

Joanna did not remember drifting off to sleep, but it seemed that as suddenly as her head had hit the pillow, her imagination took her to the death-veiled land that she had visited so often in the past.

The bleak, dully lit landscape before her, still held no life; the ground was scorched; the trees bore no fruit; the sky thick with thunderous clouds.

Aimlessly gazing at the destruction around her, a sudden whisper of breeze caused her to turn round and there, sitting astride the blackest, most elegant Arab stallion she had ever seen, was the Israelite.

The shiny-coated equine pawed at the ground, impatiently waiting to be on its way, sending the dry dust spraying up under its belly. The stallion gave a single snort, as it pawed, expressing its impetuosity to full effect.

"Nice horse." Joanna beamed, as she examined the beast. "Knocks spots off that piebald monster, of mine."

Ignoring her flippant remark, the Israelite commanded, "Come now, child, we have not got much time." He then held out a hand toward the young woman, beckoning her to draw nearer.

"You're not expecting that poor animal to carry the pair of us, are you?" she questioned her guide, as she took his hand.

"Fear not. He has the strength of a thousand horses." And suddenly, she found herself being lifted off the ground and swung over the horses back, behind her guardian.

Immediately she made contact with the Arab, the Israelite dug his mount in the ribs. Half rearing, it lunged forward, sending Joanna off balance and almost falling to the ground. She grabbed out at the Israelites robes, pulling herself back onto the saddle, then clung on as tight as she was able, as the black stallion thundered off across the wasteland, in full flight.

The Arab covered the ground like a lightning flash. The horse moved so swiftly that it was difficult to catch the air in her lungs. On and on they went, galloping fast and furious towards the east where, on the horizon a speck of light could be seen, illuminating the skyline like a ray of hope amongst the desolation.

"Where are we going?" Joanna shouted at the Israelite, above the clamorous hooves and rasping gasps of breath from the mount beneath them.

"You will find out, when we get there."

"See you're as helpful as ever, Benjamin." She retorted, with a touch of irony, but the Israelite treated her comment with the contempt it deserved.

The flat, lifeless land slowly began to undulate, rising up either side of them, like great waves, until the travellers were galloping in the bed of a vast canyon. The walls on either side of the mile wide gorge became rugged, the rock face jutting out, revealing sharp, weapon-like stones that would surly skewer anyone who dared to scale their heights.

Strangely, this passageway to their destination reminded her of a previous dream only, in that vision the great rocks were replaced by grey, slimy bricks, and the mile wide bed of the canyon, was a mere eight foot wide alleyway. However, the escape routes appeared the same; either ahead, into uncharted waters or back to the dismal, lifeless land.

"You're not taking me to meet any clergymen, by some chance, are you Benjamin?" She queried, as she recalled the previous dream.

"I am taking you where there is help at hand. Just as you requested."

As the two rode like the wind, the canyon suddenly seemed to burst open, to reveal the most glorious sight; Joanna had ever had the pleasure to witness. Before them, nestled amongst a ring of mountains was a vast, circular shaped valley, which must have had the radius of about three thousand miles. In the centre of the dale was a most radiant and beautiful city, its brilliance shining across the world, like a precious jewel.

As they rode into the outskirts of the valley, the Israelite abruptly pulled the Arab to a halt, sending Joanna crashing into her guide. "What you do that for?" She snapped.

"It is obvious that you were so much in ore of what was eight and a half thousand stadia away, that you did not bother to notice what is a mere 35 cubits before you."

Following his direction, Joanna looked down to the ground and, to her horror; less than fifty feet away from them was a vast crevasse, completely surrounding the fortified city.

Joanna scanned the length and breath of the chasm, but there was no way of crossing the vast abyss and their quest now seemed hopeless. "What do we do now?" She questioned her guardian as she stared into the hole.

"We wait." he replied, softly.

"For what? A miracle?"

The Israelite half turned in the saddle and gave her a rhy smile. "If that is what you wish to call it then yes; a miracle."

Sitting there patiently on the handsome stallion, Joanna found her mind wondering off the conundrum of how to enter the valley and away to the vibrant city beyond. Tugging at the Israelites robes, she asked, "So, what is that place?"

"It is the city called Yerushalaym Shel Sahav." He informed her softly, his eyes sparkling, as he gazed at its splendour.

Non the wiser, she replied with a simple, "Oh."

"Do not concern yourself, we will be there in no time."

"Now that would be a miracle." Joanna growled under her breath.

Suddenly, movement in the distance, from the direction of Yerushalaym Shel Sahav, caught both their attentions. Moving swiftly towards Joanna and the Israelite rode a fearsome rider, with eyes like blazing fire and robes that dripped with blood. He wore many crowns upon his head, for he was the King of kings, and he had a name written on him that no one knew but he himself.

"Looks like trouble." Joanna delivered a cold statement, as she watched the rider and his powerful white horse draw closer to them. But the Israelite, looking back over his shoulder towards the young woman corrected, "No, not trouble. Your miracle."

As the rider reached the far side of the crevasse, he halted his mount and drew his sword. "I am called Faithful and True. I tread the winepress of the fury of the wrath of God Almighty. No one enters here that is not of the light. Identify yourselves, strangers, or be cast into the pit of despair." And with those words, he sliced the air with his sword, instigating an eruption of malt and lather from the abyss, obscuring him from the two riders on the far side.

"I am the Israelite of the twelfth gate." Benjamin cried out, as his stallion reared up in fright, at the spectacle before them. "I am of God's light."

As suddenly as it had erupted, the fury from the pit died down. As the smoke cleared, Joanna and her guide were able to set their gaze upon the rider and his horse once more, as the animal fearsomely twisted and turned beneath him.

"Israelite. I know of you. You are permitted to enter." The rider then pointed to the young woman, timidly hiding behind the man in black robes. "But I know not of this woman. She is mortal, is she not?"

"Yes. She is the one to whom I have been assigned to."

"But her time is not yet written in the Book of Life. I can not let a spirit which is still housed within the vessel of an earthly body, pass over. Only the dead can enter."

"You rule over the nations with an iron sceptre, Faithful and True, and with justice you judge and make war. But I have authority from higher than your supremacy, to allow this mortal to enter."

"Then enter you shall Israelite." and with that, the rider on the white horse pointed his sword towards the crevasse, this time making the ground shake under the horses feet, sending the equines into panic stricken rears a second time.

The earth tremored from within the void. The rolling, thunderous sounds below ground bellowing out of the chasm as a vast, stone bridge made its steady way up from the depths of the pit, until it was flush with the ground on either side.

As soon as the bridge stopped rising from the depths, the rider on the white horse called across the crevasse, "Cross and fear not." And Benjamin confidently spurred the Arab on, as it hesitantly stepped onto the newly formed overpass.

Joanna closed her eyes tight, as the animal crossed the stone bridge. She dared not look, too full of fear at the realisation of the infinite drop below her.

As soon as they reached the far side, the Israelite patted her arm. "It's alright now." he stated, in a soft voice, "You can open your eyes. We are on the far side."

Joanna looked back over her shoulder momentarily, to convince herself that they were, in fact, now out of danger. She then looked across at the rider on the white horse, who was sitting astride his muscular equine, with a power and majesty that she had never seen before.

The King of Kings pointed in the direction of the great city and, as his mount twisted and turned beneath him, he called to them, "Ride like the wind fellow-servant, for there is not much time. God be with you." and with that he vanished in a dense, white mist leaving Joanna and her guardian alone once more.

The Israelite lost no time and spurred his handsome animal on, in full flight, across the land before them. Each galloping stride of the horse seemed to cover fifty miles, bringing Yerushalaym Shel Sahav closer and closer, until they were almost upon it.

The city was a fabulous sight as it stood, like a jewel, in the centre of the valley. It had a great, high wall surrounding it, made from bloodstone, which was laid out like a square. The wall hosted twelve gates; three on the eastern wall, three on the north, three facing to the south and three on the west, with each gate constructed from a single pearl.

The foundations of the city wall were decorated with twelve precious stones. The first was jasper, which gave a sense of balance to the spirit; the second, sapphire, aided a strong connection with the higher self, giving clarity and inspiration; third was the 'gatherer', fluorite, and forth was emerald, the unconditional love stone of deepest green. Fifth was rose quartz, emanating forgiveness and compassion; the sixth, carnelian, which brought joy and warmth to the soul, whilst seventh was celestite, the stone of heaven. Eighth was beryl, a hard mineral of many colours; the ninth was topaz, which radiated peace and tranquillity; tenth was the joy stone, chryosprase, whilst eleventh was jade, which poured out divine love, courage, justice, modesty and wisdom. Finally, the twelfth stone was amethyst, which cut through all illusion, bringing the lower natures to a higher consciousness.

As Joanna and the Israelite arrived at the twelfth gate to the east, he pulled up his mount and stood there quietly, waiting for an invitation to enter. Joanna stared in awe at the splendour within the city walls, for inside was a great street made from pure gold, like transparent glass, lined by marbled pillars.

Suddenly, two figures obscured her view. Looking down from the stallion, Joanna saw an angel wearing a white tunic, with his wings held out high behind him. He carried with him a platinum staff, entwined with serpents made from emerald, and wore a golden laurel upon his head, whilst on his feet were winged sandals. Around the angel a lithe, writhing figure made of pale blue mist, glided around his master. The tenuous and indefinite form continually changing shape, as it moved.

"Lord Raphael." The Israelites voice broke her analysis of the two beings, "Keeper of the Book of Truth; ruler of the east; guardian of the air; protector and healer to the souls that pass into the spirit world; I call upon you and your elemental servant, King Paralda, to take this woman that accompanies me into the great city and place her before Imanu'el."

Standing tall and majestic, the angel held out his left hand, welcoming Joanna into his presence. The Israelite then helped the young woman to the ground and encouraged her to move forward, by administering a gentle nudge to the back of her shoulder. But Joanna was reluctant to go to the winged man and his servant and refused to step towards them.

"What is the matter now?" The Israelite growled in her ear. "Do I have to hold your hand all the time?"

"But these beings intimidate me. Come in with me, Benjamin." she pleaded with her guide.

"Certainly not." came his rasping reply. "I have travelled far enough. Go. They will not harm you." But Joanna still refused to enter into the great city with the two escorts that guarded the gates.

Then, from behind the angel and his servant, came the familiar flamboyancy of Zaphenath-Paneah, with his gold chain around his neck and that bishop-like hat of his. "I will escort the child in, brother." He announced, as he approached her and, with that, Joanna willingly took the Egyptian's hand and was led inside the city.

No sooner had she passed through the twelfth gate, than found herself in a moderately sized L-shaped room, completely constructed from white marble, with many pillars supporting the ceiling high above her. It was completely void of furniture, although a large plinth, where a bed once graced, stood to her left opposite the window.

She looked about her for Zaphenath-Paneah, but he was no where to be seen. However, to the far side of the room, standing by a large, open window draped with fine netting, stood a man peacefully staring out onto the city beyond.

The netting floated gracefully in the breeze around the man as he gazed into space, seemingly totally unaware of her presence in the room. He was not tall, only about five feet six inches in height, and was of slight build. He had a round, boyish face, which supported a tawny coloured beard and shoulder length hair that was straight and without lustre at the roots, but from the level of the ears, it was curly and glossy. The ends of the hair had been sun-kissed and were far blonder than the reddish-brown roots, which was parted down the centre.

Hesitantly she stepped forward, towards the man, but still he did not acknowledge her. She continued to approach him, until she was at his side. Looking at him, she saw that the man was crying, as he stared into space, the tears trickling down his unblemished face.

Reaching out a hand, she placed it upon his shoulder to comfort him. It was then that he acknowledged her and, turning to face the woman, his kind but sad face lifted into a gentle smile.

"I am glad that you have come." The man greeted her, as he placed a beautiful, straight hand upon her cheek.

"Why do you cry so?" Joanna found herself asking, as she lost herself in his brilliant blue eyes that seemed so deep, that they touched his very soul.

"I weep for the blameless." came his soft, kind reply. "I pity their suffering."

"Are you Imanu'el, the person I am supposed to meet?"

"I am he." He smiled. "You have been brought here to see with your own eyes what will be given to you, if you let me into your heart." He then swept his hand about the room, allowing her to see the emptiness that it held. "This is all that I can offer, as my token of love for you."

"How can you say that this is all that you can offer, when you give me the gift of love? Surely, your love for me is far richer than any material thing."

"You speak with wisdom, child, but temptation is waiting to sway your thinking; to take away the simplicity that my love brings. Soon you will be taken from this place to a world full of false riches. This is your test, to see how pure your love for me is. A test to see where your heart really lies."

"Why do I need testing?" she frowned.

"It is not a case of 'why', rather a case of 'how'. There are two ways to rid yourself of the evils that haunt you - the hard way, and the easy way. The hard way is to fight Satan; the easy way, to join him. To walk with me will cause you much suffering and persecution; to enter into the house of the Prince of Darkness rewards you with many wonderful riches, for your allegiance to him. You have the choice and it is now time for you to choose." He then leant forward and kissed her tenderly on the forehead. "You must follow your heart, hear what it is telling you and go with it. Either way, I am not your judge and will continue to love and weep for you, whichever path you choose."

"But surely I have already chosen. After all, I have been fighting against evil, not been in allegiance with it."

"And now you will be tempted to join them, with many false promises and worthless splendours. You see, child, you are special in your own right. You are both a powerful ally and a mighty enemy. They fear you and respect you. If you were to fight with them, instead of against them, your soul would prove a most valuable asset."

He then turned his attention back to the window and began staring out of it, once more. "Now go child, decide your fate."

Leaning forward, Joanna kissed Imanu'el on the cheek, before turning away and headed back towards the doorway of the room. Reaching it, she grabbed the golden handle and swung the door wide open. Beyond was the radiance of the beautiful city, the light emanating from its very core, but as she stepped over the threshold, she suddenly found herself entering a gloomy, two storey ballroom; the walls decorated with red wallpaper, embossed with black motifs, and a carpet of beer-stained red. Black ash pillars and handrails adorned the place, cutting the vast space into many intimate areas, with dim lighting that concealing their true identities.

Looking around her, Joanna saw a deserted dance floor in the centre of the room, its wooden boards slightly raised from the carpeted surround. There was a black banister along one side of the square stage-like construction, which cut her off from it. At regular intervals, chard supports rose from the banisters, to the ceiling above, obscuring her view.

The ceiling to the ground floor ran around the edge of the dance floor, creating a balcony above from which the dancers could be observed. An open, black ash staircase wound its way upward, from where she had entered.

Only a handful of people were scattered around the ball room, drearily staring into their empty glasses. A disc-jockey stood to the far side of the dance floor, mumbling into the microphone, as he placed another record onto the turntable.

Joanna began to amble around the room, observing the partygoers as she went. In the corner sat a lonesome, raggedy man, supporting his head on one hand, whilst flicking the ash of his roll-up onto the carpet, with the other. He seemed completely oblivious of what was going on around him, too full of himself to worry about anyone else.

Hanging over the balcony banister, were two women with their arms entwined. They were adorned with tawdry jewellery, skimpily dressed and wore thick, aggressive make-up. Leering at the people below, they broke their taunting momentarily to amorously kiss, before continuing to vulgarly ogle at their audience.

Below the lesbians were two young bikers sitting with their backs to the dance floor. Dressed in leathers and denim, their concentration was firmly fixed on two white lines trailing across their table. Taking a fifty pound note, the first rolled the paper, placed one end to his nose, whilst the other to one of the lines. He then snorted, allowing the substance to travel up the tube, into his nostril. The second then took the fifty pound note from the other and did the same using the second line. The two then leant back in their black ash chairs and rolled their eyes at the ecstasy of the experience.

Sitting on the opposite side of the dance floor to the bikers, were a man and a woman, groping each other with animal passion. They were then joined by another couple, aroused by the exploitation, forming a promiscuous sexual party, full of frenzied indulgence. The orgy showed no restraint, nor did the four concern themselves about

morality, for they were too feverish from carnal depravity.

A fight suddenly broke out by the stairs, as two spivs frantically jabbed flick knifes at each other. An elegant woman, dressed in red satin, ran round them in the vain hope of trying to break up the skirmish, attracting the attention of each man in turn.

They hollered at each other, as they fought. Each squaring up to the other, trying to avoid a full frontal attack. One was holding a large wedge of money in his grubby little hand, which the other was trying to grab. The woman pulled at the jacket of the man with the money, trying to convince him to part with it, but the mean-faced gangster responded by forcibly pushing her away, sending the woman flying into the stair rails.

With fevered outrage the other man lunged at the one with the wedge, the knife piercing deep into his stomach. Clutching his wound, the expression on the mean-face turned, firstly to one of utter surprise, then of shear agony. The grip on the hand holding the money slackened, and the notes came tumbling out in a cascade of paper. Without loosing a moment, the second man pushed the wounded one across the carpet and, with malice and greed, he began gathering up the money from the floor.

Screaming hysterically, the elegant woman ran over to the loser, as the notes were forcibly pushed into the second spiv's trouser and jacket pockets. The conqueror then turned once more to his opponent, whose gaping wounds was being tended by the woman in red satin. Stooping down, he grabbed the wounded mans hair and, pulling back his head, the winner placed the knife to the neck, and sliced the blade across it, creating a cavernous hole oozing with bright red blood.

The loser's body then became lithe and flaccid, as the life was extracted from it. The winner stood over the mean-faced man momentarily, a broad victorious smirk on his face, before turning to walk away, without any sign of conscience for what he had just done.

As Joanna looked on in horror at the sight before her, she suddenly became aware of someone standing at her side. Looking over her shoulder, she saw a man in his mid forty's, of slim physique and pale complexion, with neatly cut hair that was shaped around his ears, but slightly longer on top, allowing the loose curls to give it volume.

His left eye was brown, his right blue, with a slight hook to his nose and thin, mean lips that turned downwards at the edges. He wore a mottled, light grey suit, comprising of loose fitting trousers and a blazer that framed a white, stiff-collared, shirt supporting a garish, multi-coloured tie, which brought the whole ensemble to life. He was indeed a vain man, for time had been spent on his looking so clean, crisp and irresistible.

"Come and dance with me." he requested in a soft, slightly feminine tone, seemingly unaware of the violence and depravity around him. His face then lifted into a smile that showed dimpled cheeks, as he held out a hand and grabbed hers. Then, without waiting for her reply, he guided Joanna to the dance floor and held her close.

Struggling, she freed herself from his grip and pulled away. But, as she went to walk off the dance floor, he grabbed her hand a second time, refusing to allow the young woman to leave his presence, and said. "Leave me and you will live to regret it."

"No I won't, because you are too in love with yourself, for my liking." She then shook herself free from his grasp a second time and, as she backed away from the man, she continued, "I do not belong here and I don't belong to you."

The man, unflustered by her resistance to his charms, gave a knowing smile "Oh. But you do so belong." he smirked, as he held out a hand towards her. "Come with me and I will show you." And with that, he began to take slow, deliberate steps towards the young woman.

Insisting that she would have none of it, Joanna turned to march off the wooden boards, but as she stepped towards the edge of the dance floor, the ground beneath her began to shake, making her lose her balance.

The man reached out and caught her as she fell, his arms firmly coiling themselves around the young woman's waist. "Do not resist." he softly whispered in her ear. "There is no escape for you now."

As soon as he spoke the words, the dance floor began to sink through the foundations of the ballroom. Joanna looked across at the DJ, in the hope that he might save her from her plight, but the disc jockey was too busy rummaging through his collection of records to notice her plight.

As the floor beneath her descended into the depths, great walls of soil and rock built up around her like a prison cell. High above, the rotating mirrored sphere reflected the disco lights, sending an array of dotted technicoloured beams around the room above. But the dance floor prison was cold and dark, and becoming gloomier by the second as it continued to travel downwards. Only Joanna and her warden seemed to exist now.

The floor seemed to continue to descend for ever, the journey never seemingly to end, until finally, to her right Joanna saw a speck of reddish, orange light creep through a crack between the wall and the wooden boards.

The speck then began to grow and expand, as it spread across the floor, until it reveal a cavern beyond lit by flaming torches and iron cradles full of lighted coals. Then, as the boards became flush with the floor of the grotto, it jolted to a halt, revealing a hoard of anxious faces. The man then grabbed Joanna by the arm and forcibly dragged her from the prison, to the awaiting crowd, beyond.

The first to approach Joanna and her escort was a tall, imposing figure. He had cruel, yet strangely handsome features; short jet-black hair and burgundy wings that stretched out behind him, with tinges of orange, yellow and smoky grey dappled amongst the feathers. His robes were of the blackest velvet, with a breastplate, which had engraved upon it, the mark of the Beast.

"You have done well, Keeper." He praised the man in the light grey suit, before turning to the young woman. "Welcome to my kingdom. Would you care for some refreshment, after your journey?"

Joanna shook her head, "I want nothing from you." she snarled at the dark angel.

"Oh come now." the winged man gave her a lordly smile, "I only show you hospitality. You are an honoured guest here, Joanna." He then clapped his hands together, enticing a soot-covered slave to dash forward, with a silver tray holding two goblets, filled with foaming wine and spices. Gracefully reaching out a claw-like hand, the dark angel took one of the goblets and handed to at the young woman, as he continued, "To refuse my conviviality would be, after all, the height of bad manners for any guest, would it not?"

Marching forward, straight past the angel, Joanna gazed upon the sight before her, and coldly stated, "But I am not you guest - I am a captive here."

Giving a deep laugh at her comment, the winged man turned and joined her, whilst she gazed. "Do you have the faintest idea of who you are talking to?" He enquired, in a slow, deliberate fashion.

"Surprise me." she replied, sarcastically.

"Anger me not, or you will find I can be the most ..." He paused momentarily, trying to find the best noun, before continuing, "... unsympathetic of enemies."

"Really." She replied, her tone showing no fear. "So do tell me, what is the reason behind my being brought here?"

"I want to make a bargain with you." The dark angel gave her a hard, callous smile as he handed her the goblet a second time. "But first, let me introduce you to some of my most favoured amongst the Underworld." And with that, he grabbed her arm and pulled her round, to meet the higher ranking of his anointed.

She recognised the first immediately, for he was the scar-faced man, with long tatty grey hair and drooped eye, that had led the army of dark forces against her, in previous dreams. His forehead still boasted the reversed pentagon, which strangely seemed far more prominent at this time than on past occasions, and the expression on his face seemed to ooze evil self-satisfaction, as he stared down at her with a steely blue eye.

Upon seeing her reaction to the sorcerer, the dark angel gave a rye smile and said, "Of cause, you two have met before. How absent minded of me to have forgotten such an event. He is such a handsome fellow, don't you think?"

"That is the ugliest thing I have ever seen." Joanna disagreed with the dark angel's appraisal of the sorcerer. "Your own creation, I take it?"

"Certainly." He gave a self-satisfying smile. "My archangel of despair. Turned out rather well, hasn't he - even if I do say so myself."

Raising her eyebrows at his questionable ideals, Joanna suddenly caught sight of movement behind the black cloak of the sorcerer. Taking a closer look, she observed the little creature, as it scurried about, in the shadows.

"That," the dark angel informed her, "is one example of my vast collection of demons. Cute, don't you think?" He then beckoned the tiny creature to come forward, for a better inspection, and dutifully it hopped out from the cover of darkness.

The demon was about three-foot tall, with scaly, black skin and a long, thick tail. Its body was shaped rather like a two-legged dinosaur, but the head was more likened to a bat, in form. With beady black eyes, set to the front, and a snubby little nose that sunk into its round, wrinkled face, it snarled at the young woman, with a large mouth full of razor sharp teeth. Set either side of its bald head, were two large, gnome like ears and its hands and feet were like vulture claws.

The dark angel then stepped forward and, swinging a foot in the demons direction, he sent it leaping into the shadows once more. He gave Joanna an evil smirk, as he chased it off, before continuing with his introductions. "You have already met the keeper of the gates." He stated as he pointed at the man in the light-grey suit, "And the deliciously ravishing full-figured woman to his right," he continued, as he drew her attention to an utterly hideous and vulgar hag, standing next to the keeper, "is the Whore of Babylon."

Joanna looked across at the mother of prostitutes, dressed in purple and scarlet, who was glittering with gold, precious stones and pearls. She too held a goblet, filled with the filth of her adulteries, which had excessively intoxicated her.

Turning back to the dark angel, Joanna growled, "And what makes you think that I would ever wish to associate with you and the evil that dwells here with you? The Archangel of Despair fought against me. Taliesim came forth from the light to send him back from whence he came. Why now do you change tack?"

"My dear," the dark angel took the goblet from her grasp and held it to her lips, "Drink the sweet, refreshing wine and concern yourself no more. Yahweh created me, just as He created you. We are of the same light. He moulded me first, then He moulded you. We all come from heaven." He then tried to force the liquid down her

throat.

With a swift action, Joanna swiped out her arm, sending the goblet, and its contents, flying across the room. "And there was war in heaven." She began to recite Revelation, reminding the winged man of who he really was. "Archangel Michael and his angels fought against the serpent, and the serpent and his angels fought back. But the serpent was not strong enough, and they lost their place in heaven. The great serpent was hurled down. He was hurled to the earth, and his angels with him."

The slightest touch of anger slipping through his controlled tones, the dark angel replied, "I am the first of the Archangels. I stood at Yahweh's right hand. I was as powerful as Him, because I was of Him. He betrayed me; not I, Him. I was double-crossed and exiled, without true judgement. Do you think that action was just?"

"It is not for me to judge God's actions, nor to judge yours. But I know where my heart lies, and it is not here, with you."

The winged man threw his head back and laughed, loudly. Then, dragging the young woman over to a large chest, he flung back its lid, revealing gold and jewels of every colour imaginable, inside.

Turning to her, he grinned, "And would the one to whom your heart lies, reward you with riches such as these? I think not. A soul gets nothing in return for walking with Yahweh, except a misty promise of a paradise that simply does not exist." He then grabbed at the treasures and held them out in front of her. "These are real - touch them. These are not idle fantasies. Look at how vibrant they are; how precious; how pure."

"Not as pure as the foundations laid at Yerushalaym Shel Sahav." She retorted. "These are dull and lifeless in comparison. They hold no properties; they have not qualities; they are of no value to me."

The fury rose within the dark angel at her words and, with a bellowing roar, he hurled

the jewels across the floor of the cavern. Then, recomposing himself, he turned back to Joanna and said with venom, "But your name is not written in the Book of Life, therefore you would never be allowed to reside at the city of gold. Nothing impure will ever enter it; the cowardly, the unbelieving, the vile, the murderers, the sexually immoral, those who practise magic arts, the idolater and all liars - their place is with me. Your place is with me."

"My heart holds love - love that is more precious than gold. Love is the one thing that you are abject to, and appalled by. You despise love and loathe it. You condemn sentiment. But Imanu'el resides in my heart, as does the Lord my God. Nothing that you offer me can ever take that away, because that is all I need. Not one living soul is flawless, because you walk with the living and continually tempt them with charm and falsities. But I will never be coaxed into the Underworld by your luscious words and syrupy wine."

The dark angel smiled down at Joanna's words, before beginning to attempt to allure her to his kingdom, using another tact, "Walk with me a while, won't you? Allow me to show you around - no strings." And with that he gently took her arm and led her towards a stone wall, to the centre of the cavern.

As they reached the wall, Joanna leant over the top, to see a large pit below, full of chained and manacled zombie-like souls lifting stones into crude barrows. None of them acknowledged either her, nor the dark angel, as they toiled - just continued mining.

In the centre of the pit was an obese slave driver, holding a cat-o'-nine-tails in his thick, powerful hands. He wore only a leather mask, loincloth and sandals, whose straps criss-crossed over his shins. At regular intervals the tormentor struck out at a subservient villein, with an evil snigger, sending the poor soul cowering to the ground in terror.

"You see before you, the borrowed souls." The dark angel informed her, as he allowed her to view the horrors within the pit. "These souls do not belong to me - in the true sense of the word - they are merely spending a short time here, before returning incarnate to the earthly dimension. The names of these spirits were not written in the Book of Life and so, the rider on the white horse sent them into the pit to reside here, with me."

Joanna gazed upon the pitiful souls, with dismay. "What crimes deserve such ill-fate?" She questioned the Lord of the flies. "I thought people either walked with God or with Satan. Explain to me what this grey area means?"

Wrapping his arm around her shoulders, he placed his lips close to her ear, and whispered, "I will be delighted to explain this to you. Look into the mine and pick a soul."

Staring at the multitude of sad figures, her eyes fell upon a cardinal, partially obscured by the shadows. "What about him?" she pointed at the high-ranking Roman Catholic clergyman. "Why is a member of the Cloth condemned to such torture?"

"Ah." The winged man replied, as a dashing smile slowly crept across his face. "I am glad you picked that one."

His arm then tenderly trickled down Joanna's back, to her waist, as he began to seduce the young woman. "I am very proud of this catch. This man died thirty-four years ago, at the age of sixty-seven. He first joined the Roman Catholic Church when he was twenty-four and quickly moved up the ranks, until he reached the principal status of Archbishop, in your time, nineteen hundred and forty. He taught the virtues of the most important moral qualities; justice, prudence, temperance and fortitude.

However, he did not practice what he preached, for he had a fetish for young boys, and would often entertain himself with the innocent little lambs. He also indulged himself with generous helpings of consecrated wine and stole Church funds by using donations from the congregation to line his own pocket, whilst his flock lived in abject poverty around him. He was arrogant in attitude, hard in judgement and full of self-importance. He used his position for his own gain, not for honourable spiritual guidance. He had a heart of stone. His activities were never uncovered whilst he lived, but all were recorded by his attending angels and put before Faithful and True upon his death. That is why he is down there now, and will remain there until it is his time to be reborn, to learn his lesson."

"But Catholic's constantly confess their sins, for redemption. Did he not repent on his death bed?"

"Oh yes." the dark angel gave an evil grin, "Confessed he did - multitudes and multitudes of sinful disclosures. But this practice is a man-made superstition – wrongdoings judged by men; penance's administered by men. Yahweh judges a soul on the whole of its life; from birth to death, not just from the last confessional."

"So then he is an evil man, yes?"

The dark angel shook his head. "No, he is not. You see, like you, he was brought to this room, to see if he would honour and serve me, the Prince of Darkness. But he refused. He is now paying for his crimes, because he still wishes to return to Yahweh, the fool. He now knows that he lived a sinful life and understands that karma will decide his fate in the next, for he must suffer himself for the suffering that he had inflicted on others. However, if he had chosen to join me, instead of continuing on the pathway to Yahweh, his slate would have been wiped clean, and therefore, therewould be no karma to repay, come his next life."

"So, how long will he be in the pit?" Joanna enquired, as she pitifully looked down upon the cardinal.

"He has another sixteen years to go, before his sentence is complete. However, you must understand that, as a soul needs neither sleep nor food, there is never any rest for the wicked. Therefore, fifty years in the pit will seem to the soul more like one hundred and fifty."

The dark angel then pulled her closer to him, and sighed, "This brings me onto the fate of your soul, dear Joanna." before guiding her away from the walls of the prison and escorted the young woman across the cavern towards two great, heavy doors, framed with sooty rocks. Either side of the doors there hung flaming torches, the light that they emanated, danced about them like that of moonbeams, breaking through a canopy of trees.

"What of my soul?" Joanna snarled back at the winged man. "You know where my loyalties lie and that I have not lead a wicked life. Besides, I need not remind you that I am not dead at this time. So then, how do you probably bargain for a soul that is not available."

"A soul is always available to me - living or dead." He grinned. "And as for wickedness, you should read that precious bible of yours, more often. Does it not state that adultery is a sin? You are married to Jon, therefore you are adulterous to him, by living with Lewis."

"I have divorced Jon. Therefore no forbidden practice has been done." She corrected him.

"On the contrary." The dark angel continued, "Yahweh said, 'A wife must not separate from her husband. But if she does, she must remain unmarried or else be reconciled to her husband.'"

"But," Joanna explained his quotation, "God did not intend for me to become a slave of men. Surly, it is better for me to have one partner, as my equal, than to burn with passion. God gave me a body that could not be satisfied, because of a cruel and unloving husband. I know that my body was not given for sexual immorality, for it is sanctified. The body is a temple for the Holy Spirit, received from God. My body is not my own, but bought at a price, by God. Therefore I honour my body, as I honour God. I have not sinned."

"Then what of soothsaying?" He taunted her further, "This is undoubtedly a wickedness, in the eyes of Yahweh."

"Only if it is used for personal gain; such as material wealth, harming others or ego." Joanna replied, calmly. "Jesus Christ prophesied many events. For example, he predicted when and how he way going to die - including who was going to betray him and who was going to deny him. Noah prophesied the great rains and, despite ridicule from those around him, he built a huge ark - because of soothsaying. Moses led the Israelites out of Egypt, because of prophecy and Joseph was able to tell of future events, through the interpretation of dreams. How can all these people be detestable in the eyes of the Lord, when they are God's people?"

"But, my dear, you are not one of them. Do not fool yourself into thinking that you are. You are of no importance to Yahweh - none at all."

"Then why am I here?" She snapped. "If I am of no importance to Him, then why am I so important to you?"

The dark angel threw back his head and gave a loud, roaring laugh. "You are nothing to me. The only reason you have been brought here, is for your own personal gain."

"How generous of you." she retorted, sarcastically.

Glaring back at her, he growled, "Don't take that tone with me, not if you want my help." Joanna went to speak, but he held up a hand, commanding her silence. "The attacks from the Archangel of Despair can be halted. I only need give the command and he will return here and bother you no more. All I ask in return is your oath, and your life will become plentiful."

At that point, they reached the great doors and, with a majestical signal from the dark angel, they creaked open, revealing a large ornate hall, beyond.

As they stepped over the threshold, the winged man, continued, "Look about you now, Joanna. My palace holds many wonders, does it not?"

Joanna gazed about her and absorbed the sight. The walls were finely decorated with jewels and precious metals. Hematite pillars rose high above her, that supported a ceiling of garish spender. The floor was highly polished within the pillared surround and checked in pattern, like a chessboard, incorporating some sixty-four squares, with each one measuring about fifteen feet across.

High above her, mounted on the walls, were long spikes; their sharp points ready to impale anything that came into contact with them. However, their reason for being there seemed obscure, for nothing could enter the room, except from the great doors.

To the far side of the hall, sat two thrones made from obsidian, their black velvet textures shone out for all to admire. Keeping the young woman close to his side, the dark angel guided her across the chessboard floor, to the ceremonial chairs. He then broke his grasp of the woman and eased himself into the larger of the two, leaning back boastfully, as he laid his hands on the arm rests. "Befitting, don't you think?" He flashed an awesome smirk across to the young woman, before surveying his estate.

"Suits you perfectly." Joanna gave an innocent smile, in return.

"I think so." He agreed, before leaning forward, towards her, "And you can sit at my right hand. Swear allegiance to me, and you can be my queen."

"No thanks." she replied. "The colour doesn't suit me."

In a fit of outrage, the dark angel reached forward and, tightly grabbing her arm, he pulled the young woman close to him. "Insolence is not something that I entertain around here." He scowled, before letting go of her arm, and pushed her away again.

"Just think for a moment of your options."

"Options?" Joanna enquired with interest.

With a softer tone, the winged man began to explain the facts. "Join me and I will give you peace of mind; respect from your peers; knowledge so vast that all will look upon you in ore. You will be all powerful and, with my protection, untouchable by your enemies."

"And what do I have to give you in return?"

"I will take you as my bride and you will be faithful only unto me. All I want from you is your loyalty, so that the fruits from your womb will walk the earth with my blood and my blood alone."

"But I could never love you." she retorted, "For I despise all that you stand for."

The dark angel became slightly angered once more. "What has love got to do with the deal, eh? Love is not important. You loved Jon, but he certainly did not love you. Never the less, you still married him, did you not? All this talk of love - you sound like a stupid little teenager." He then leant back on his throne once more andlightened his tone. "Think about the advantages. Do not dismiss such a bountiful offer, just for the sake of love."

"And what if I do not agree to this deal?"

The dark angel gave a smirk, as his cruel eyes flitted about him. "Then I shall not command the withdrawal of the Archangel of Despair, and he will destroy you - and by the looks, it will only take about another five to six weeks, before you die."

"But death is not important, for then I will go to Yerushalaym Shel Sahav."

"Oh please." he retorted sarcastically. "Have you learnt nothing of your visit here? You will be taken to the pit to repay your penance, like everyone else."

"Penance for what, exactly?"

"For not being a regular church goer, for one." The dark angel gave a broad, satisfying grin. "You only turn to Yahweh to save your own skin - never a thought for Him, whilst everything was going in your favour. How selfish of you."

"God is merciful, even to the likes of me." She confidently replied, although a nagging spark of uncertainty began to flicker in her mind, as she spoke the words.

Sensing that he had finally found a crack, the dark angel jumped on the moment, "How can you be so sure? Has He told you Himself? I think not. Yahweh has far too many important things to do, looking after those who have always showed their loyalties to Him, to worry about a skinny little runt, like you. Why risk the salvation of thousands, for one measly soul of no importance? That is exactly what He will be saying to himself, right now."

"Then I will take that risk. Should I die and be flung into the pit, then at least I will know in my heart that I suffer for God and not rejoice with you."

"And is that your final word?"

"Yes."

"Then I will tempt you no more." The dark angel closed the conversation, before rising to his feet and added in a casual manner, "But there is the small matter of your leaving."

"Matter of my leaving?" Joanna repeated, perplexed as to why he should make such a statement.

"Yes." He smirked. "You see, nothing can leave here until they have paid a toll. The souls in the pit pay with hard labour; my angels pay with their loyalty. But how might you pay?"

"Just open the gates and let me walk out."

"But I can't do that." The dark angel informed her, with an air of supremacy. "The rules state that everyone who enters must pay, before they leave. I made the rule myself. Excellent, don't you think? Anyway, I can not bend the rules for one insignificant mortal, or everyone who enters here will expect me to do the same for them. You must appreciate my predicament, it can be very tiresome being the ruler sometimes because, no matter how much you want to help, others wait for an opportunity to criticise your leadership skills."

"My heart bleeds for you."

"Oh come now." he gave her a knowing smile, "Don't be like that. Now let me think, how can you pay ..." The dark angel then began pacing the floor, pondering over a way to capture his pray once and for all. Suddenly, he stopped dead in his tracks and, raising a finger to the skies, he shouted, "Ah ha. Got it. You like playing chess, do you not?"

"Yes, when the mood takes me."

"How then about this idea?" He grinned, as he clasped his hands together. "You play chess against me. If you win, then you may go free. But, if I win, I will decide your fate."

"Where's the catch?"

"No catch, only a couple of itsy-bitsy conditions."

"Which are?" Joanna continued to pump.

Taking a deep breath, the dark angel began to explain the tedious details. "One; no more than twenty five moves per player, to get the opponent into check-mate. Two; if the game is not complete by the end of the designated moves, I am declared the winner. Three; an hourglass will determine the maximum amount of time that the game may be played. Four; naturally, I will play with the black pieces."

"Fine. Then I will play."

With delight, the dark angel clapped his hands together, in a deliberate fashion and immediately the chequered floor in the centre of the room became filled with black and white holograms, scrabbling about like living beings.

The white pieces consisted of eight angels, which represented the pawns; two church spires, being the rooks; two angels, their wings outstretched, riding white horses denoting the knights; two bishops as bishops; the Madonna representing the queen and God as king. However, the black pieces took a far more sinister appearance. The eight pawns were winged demons, similar to the one she had seen in the cavern; the rooks were represented by a ring of witches around a blazing fire; two writhing serpents with seven heads, hosting ten horns on each head, denoted the knights; a warlock took the place of each bishop; in the place of the queen stood the whore of Babylon and finally, the king of the black pieces was the goat of Mendips, himself.

Taking his place on the far side of the chessboard, next to a golden table supporting the hourglass, the dark angel called out for an assistant. Immediately, the great doors flung open and in marched Edwardo, taking off his sombrero and bowing to the winged man, as he entered.

Surprised to see the familiar little Mexican, Joanna called out to him, "What are you doing here? Go back, before it is too late." But before Edwardo could reply, the dark angel stated in a callous fashion, "This man that stands before you is an intermediately. He will count the number of moves, nothing more. He is impartial here - to be sure that neither of us cheat."

Then, with a gesture from the dark angel, Edwardo took his place by an abacus, consisting of twenty-five large spheres held within its frame.

"Ready to begin, my darling?" the winged man called across the board at Joanna the same time as turning the hourglass over, sending trickles of sand seeping from the upper dome, into the lower transparent section. "Then let us play."

Joanna looked across the life-sized board at the fidgeting pieces before her, all waiting anxiously for the battle to begin. Each square had a mark upon it, identifying it from the rest, consisting of one letter and one number. She then began to ponder over the best possible way of tackling the game, for her opponent was sure to be an excellent player.

After a moments deliberation, Joanna called out, "Pawn; B1 to D1." The white angel immediately obliged and elegantly flew forward, as Edwardo moved the first square across the abacus.

Laughing out loud, the dark angel began to taunt her. "How innocent you are, Joanna." His face then dropped, as he bellowed, "Pawn; G4 to F4." ordering the demon to scurry forward, to take its new position on the board.

Joanna immediately knew her opponent was going to administer a full frontal attack. It was typically arrogant of him to be so blatant about his intentions. However, she knew that the only way to truly triumph, would be the element of surprise, so she decided to play it cool and, in a soft voice, she said, "Knight; A7 to C6." The angel on the magnificent animal, jumped over the angels before him, landing on the dark square. The horse then showed its supremacy by rearing up and cutting the air, with its forelegs, whilst its rider pointed a sword towards the heavens.

As Edwardo slid the second sphere across the abacus, the dark angel gazed upon his opponent's move, with relish. He delighted at her lack of momentum in the game, for she showed no plan in her efforts. This was going to be all too easy for him. What a wonderful way to claim a soul. Smiling to himself, he growled, "Queen;H5 to F3", before looking across at the young woman with desire in his eyes.

The Whore of Babylon moved diagonally across the board two squares and stood there, tempting the enemy with her adulteries.

Using a second decoy, Joanna requested the pawn on the square marked B5 to move forward one place, which it dutifully did as Edwardo counted three on the abacus. She could easily have moved it forward two places to put an instant stop on her opponents plans, but did not wish for the dark angel to change tact just yet. Better to seem vulnerable now, than to be vulnerable later in the game.

The dark angel threw back his head and roared with laughter at her stupidity. Now confident that he could easily triumph over the young woman, he bellowed, "Bishop; H3 to E6", sending the warlock marching diagonally across the board, to his new post.

Smiling to herself, Joanna requested the angel on the white horse to move from C6 to D4, challenging both the Whore of Babylon and the warlock.

The dark angel mumbled to himself, as Edwardo moved the forth sphere across the abacus, for he could no longer continue with his attack and had managed to jeopardise one of two pieces, in the process. He drummed his fingers on the table next to him, as he thought of another strategy. He knew that he had no option but to move his queen, for this was his strongest piece. After a moments deliberation, he roared, "Queen: F3 to G4", and scowled at his opponent, as the Whore of Babylon moved diagonally back, one square to cover the warlock.

Gazing upon the board, Joanna could see that her king was still vulnerable. She would have to construct a defence mechanism, using her angels, to stop an attack from the winged man, to the right hand side of the board. Sighing, she said, "Pawn: B6 to D6." sending the angel gracefully flying forward, two squares.

Determined to make his opponent retreat, so that he could make way for the Whore to move, the dark angel immediately ordered the gruesome little demon, scratching about on square G3, to scurry forward to its new permission on E3, threatening Joanna's knight. Edwardo gave a snigger as he swept the fifth sphere across the abacus, for he could see the rage begin to bubble up from within the winged man.

Joanna scratched her head as she scanned the board, for the next move. She could not take her opponent's warlock, because the queen covered it, nor could she leave her the angel on the white horse where it was, for her knights were her strongest pieces. Determined not to retreat, Joanna swiftly decided on her move, and shouting, "Knight D4 to E2", she watched as the angel and his mount jumped over to its new permission, with the horse rearing up once it had reached the dark square.

Despite Joanna's knight being on the diagonal to his queen, the dark angel could not destroy her piece, for the white rider was covered by one of her angels. He neither liked being made a fool of, nor did he like having to retreat. As Edwardo moved the sixth sphere across the abacus, the dark angel bellowed, "Queen: G4 to F5" and sneered across the board at Joanna, as the Whore of Babylon seductively advanced to her new square.

Joanna immediately realised what he was attempting to do, for her opponent could still get her in checkmate in four moves. As Edwardo prepared himself to move the seventh sphere across the abacus, Joanna shouted, "Knight A2 to C1" and watched on as the second angel, with outstretched wings, spurred on his magnificent mount to its new square.

Oblivious that Joanna had realised his intentions, the dark angel continued with the second attack and, with a gruff bellow, he ordered, "Queen F5 to D5", sending the monstrous woman forward.

Joanna knew that the dark angel did not like retreating once he had advanced. She also realised that his queen was going to have to be taken, should she have any chance of winning the game. The only way that she could take the Whore of Babylon, would be to entice her opponent into a false sense of security, whilst covering her own pieces at the same time. After a moments deliberation, she called out, "Pawn: B2 to C2" and dutifully the angel glided forward, to cover the pawn on the D1 square.

As Edwardo counted the eighth move, the dark angel looked over the board in dismay. His queen was fast becoming weaker and the only option now, would be to allow more of his pieced to advance. He also had to rid the board of his opponent's knights, for he knew that she used them to their full potential and so, they must not be allowed to advance. Scowling, he snarled, "Pawn: G1 - F1" and glared at the little demon, as it scurried forward one square, challenging the white rider.

Immediately, Joanna requested the retreat of the angel on the white horse, back to the C3 square, as Edwardo slid the ninth sphere across the abacus.

The dark angel was not pleased with her move, for now the knight was ripe for taking his queen a second time. He had two options, either the Whore retreats, or she moves across the board to the only safe square available. His ego did not allow a retreat so, with an evil roar, he ordered the Whore to move across the board to the D2 square.

Joanna smiled to herself, as she observed his move. The dark angel was beginning to lose his temper and it showed in his play. Without pausing, she softly requested, "Knight C3 to E4", challenging his queen, yet again.

The dark angel's eyes began to take a harder expression, as he took a deep intake of breath. He could either take the queen back to D5, or move it diagonally back, one square, to E1. However, the Whore of Babylon would be of no use to him back at D5 so, reluctantly he growled, "Queen: D2:E1" and watched on, with flaming eyes as the Whore retreated.

Immediately her opponents move was complete, Joanna confidently continued, "Knight: C1 to D3", as Edwardo moved the eleventh sphere across the abacus.

The situation seemed hopeless for the dark angels Whore now, for she could move no where without being taking by a white piece. But the winged man was shrewd and knew that Joanna would not risk losing one of her most favoured pieces, not even for his queen. Turning the tables on a seemingly hopeless situation, he glared across at the young woman with an evil grin, as he roared, "Knight H2 to F3". The writhing serpent, with seven heads, slithered across the squares to its new post, covering the Whore of Babylon. The dark angel then gave a deep, gravely laugh, as he stated, "I know exactly how you play, my darling. You would never risk losing one of your most powerful pieces, not even for such a prize as my queen. It would be foolish of you to sacrifice a knight for the sake of pride, don't you think? We will declare this insignificant battle a stalemate."

Smiling sweetly across the board at her opponent, Joanna calmly stated, "Knight: D3 to E1" and immediately the angel and its mount flew triumphantly through the air and struck down the Whore of Babylon.

The grotesque woman gave a hideous scream as the angel's sword pierced through her before she was flung through the air and impaled on one of the spikes high above them, on the walls.

The Whore was dead and the white rider triumphant. But his victory was short lived for, as the Mexican moved the twelfth sphere across the abacus, the dark angel roared in outrage, "Knight: F3 to E1", ordering the serpent to advance on the angels square and devour both it and its mount with ease. The winged man then stood there, inflamed in fury, as he glared across the board at the young woman. "You think you are clever, don't you?" he growled, as he crashed his clenched fist down onto the table at his side. "But now I fight to the death."

Ignoring his taunting, Joanna gazed across the board, contemplating her next move. With the Whore of Babylon out of the game, she could now work on her attack. Then, with a confident air about her, she said, "Pawn B4 to C4", as Edwardo recorded the thirteenth move, challenging the dark angels serpent with her queen.

"Pawn: G8 to E8" he bellowed, without giving his move much thought, and obediently the little demon scurried forward two squares, giving the rook behind it access to join in the game.

Edwardo's hand hovered over the fourteenth sphere, as Joanna pondered over her strategy of attack. Then, after a pause, she called out, "Queen: A5 to E1".

The Madonna glided diagonally across the board to the writhing serpent. As she met the beast, it hissed at the gentle virgin, whilst striking out at its enemy. But her power was too great for the beast and slaughtered, it crashed to the ground, before evaporating into thin air.

"Check." Joanna grinned across the board, to her opponent, as the Madonna took siege of the square.

Incensed, the dark angel scowled at the board, before growling, "King:H4 to H5" and seethed, as the Goat of Mendips moved to its new square.

Unable to resist a knowing smile, Joanna then requested her knight to move to the G3 square, and with relish, she stated triumphantly, "Check again.", as Edwardo moved the fifteenth sphere across the abacus.

The dark angel began to growl under his breath, as he observed her attack on his king. He had no choice, but to move the Goat of Mendips diagonally forward one space, giving his opponent the gift of his rook. With a sulky growl, he ordered, "King: H5 to G4", before acknowledging Joanna with a daggered glare.

"Not quite so powerful now, are you Mephistopheles." She mocked him, before continuing with, "Knight: G3 to H1. Knight takes rook.", as Edwardo counted the sixteenth move.

The angel and his magnificent mount boldly rode into the burning flames at the centre of the coven. The fire extinguished itself the moment he reached the square and the witches scattered. As he struck out at the powerless hags, they too were flung through the air, joining the Whore of Babylon on the spikes. His horse then reared up triumphantly at conquering the enemy, as the angel held his sword up high in the air.

The dark angel glared across the board, with menacing eyes. He had lost three important pieces and could not afford to forego any more. Also, all the major pieces were clumped together in one corner of the board and that situation had to be rectified. Composing himself, he worked out a strategy plan to regain control of the board and stated in a quite, confident manner, "Knight: H7 to F6." Upon his command the second writhing serpent slithered around the array of demons blocking the way, and placed itself at its new post.

Joanna knew that a few pawns would need to be sacrificed to make way for her bishop to enter into the game. However, her white rider was of no use to her in the corner of the board so, deciding to move that first, she requested, "Knight: H1 to G3." With fighting vigour, the angel and his mount moved next to the Goat of Mendips, their splendour showing magnificently, as they landed on the white square next to the black king.

The dark angel was not amused. He sensed that he was in gave danger of losing to the young women and that the only way to allude her for the designated moves, would be to get the Goat of Mendips away from the scene as soon as possible. Because of Joanna's move, the knight now covered the diagonal square to his left. The king could retreat to the square behind him, but should his opponent move the knight again, he would be back in check. He could retreat diagonally, to the H3 square, but feared that would cause him to be blocked in, without any effective cover. So, after contemplation over all the options, he decided to move the Goat of Mendips diagonally forward, to F3.

Joanna looked across at the dark angel and, catching his eye, she gave him a sweet, innocent smile. She then gazed upon the hourglass, as the sand continued to trickle from the upper dome, to the lower transparent section. To her surprise most of the sand had fallen through the narrow channel, so . there was no time to waste, with an estimated ten minutes to go.

Turning her attention back to the game, she called out, "Pawn C4 to D4", as Edwardo moved another sphere across the abacus, recording the eighteenth move.

"Like a lamb to slaughter." the dark angel jibbed at her decision, as he threw back his head and filled the room with a wicked laugh. Then, recomposing himself, his face took a stern, foreboding expression, as he bellowed pompously, "Pawn: E3 to D4."

The demon scurried diagonally forward and wrestled with the angel, before the hideous little monster lifted the defeated angel above its head and threw it into the air, impaling the pawn onto one of the spikes. "Demon takes angel." The dark angel informed all, with glee. "I do so love it when a wretched little feather-brain gets run-through by a spike, don't you my dear?"

"Pawn: C2 to D2" Joanna continued with the game, without giving the winged man the benefit of showing any emotion.

As Edwardo moved the nineteenth sphere across the abacus, the dark angel wandered around from the far side of the board and joined Joanna's side. "One question, my dear." he grinned down at her, mockingly, "Why did you not take my demon, with another of your angels?"

"Because I do not see the point of taking a life, for the sake of it."

"But now, I could take another of your cute little angels, with my demon. You have jeopardised the life of one of your precious feathered friends for the sake of morality. Why is that?"

"Make your move Mephistopheles, and stop wasting time."

"Certainly, my darling." He charmed her, before turning his attention back to the board and fearsomely roared, "Knight: F6 to D5", before returning to his opponent and continued, "See, my dear, I am not an unreasonable soul, either. It is such a shame that you can not see it."

Ignoring his remark, Joanna continued with her next move, "Pawn D2 to E2 - check."

"I think you are losing your grip, dearest Joanna." He gave a broad grin as he flitted his eyes from the young woman to the pieces, then back to Joanna again. Taking a deep breath, he opened his mouth wide and roared triumphantly, "Pawn: F1 to E2, takes pawn and no longer in check.", as his demon scuttled forward and threw the angel to the spikes.

Joanna could not help but smile, as she gazed at the defeated opponent for, in only two moves time, he would be in checkmate, and she would be free.

She scoured the board at the clump of black pieces, with the scattering of white around them. Then, looking directly into the dark angel's cold eyes, she said in a soft and calming manner, "Bishop: A6 to E2."

The bishop raced across the board, as Edwardo recorded the twenty-first move on the abacus, and struck out at the demon, resting on the square, with his sceptre. The clergyman then hooked the end around the disgusting little creature's neck and hurled it high in the air, to meet with its fate on the spikes.

"I think you will find you are now in check, again."

Joanna smiled sweetly at the dark angel, at the sight of the bishop on the E2 square.

Finding that he only had one square to run to, the winged man reluctantly groaned, "King: F3 to E3", and watched on defiantly, as the Goat of Mendips stepped forward, to its new position.

Joanna flitted her eyes across to the hourglass, momentarily, as the final few minutes worth of sand tumbled through the narrow channel, into the lower dome, before turning back to the board and, with a victorious tone, she said, "Bishop: A3 to C1" and as her second bishop moved into position, she proclaimed, "Checkmate."

The dark angel glared upon the board with choleric disgust. How could he possibly have been beaten by such trickery? In outrage, he swiftly turned his attention to the hourglass, but the last few grains of sand were still making their way to the lower section. He then turned to Edwardo, and scowled at the abacus, showing the twenty-two moves that had taken place.

"I think," Joanna called across to her opponent, catching his attention, "that I have beaten you fair and square. Now, you must keep your part of the bargain and let me go free."

The hard, enraged face of the dark angel stared back at her, with furious contempt. "Bargain? What bargain?" he growled. "You tricked me and that makes the game null and void."

"Tricked you? How?"

"By leading me to believe that I need not take your angel with my demon on the nineteenth move." He retorted, with gritted teeth, "If I had not have listened to your righteousness, then I would have had my demon destroy your angel without any hesitation."

"Then it is your own fault for listening to me, instead of your own intuition. Can I be blamed for your being tempted by the idea of integrity?"

"Well, now I am changing the rules." He bellowed across the room at the young woman. "Win or lose, you are not leaving this place - now or ever. I have had a stomach full of bargaining."

Turning to the Mexican, Joanna called, "Edwardo. Help me get out of here." But as she spoke the words, the dark angel threw back his head and gave a blood-curdling laugh. "Edwardo now walks with me. Your welfare is no longer his concern."

"If you are unwilling to stand by your half of the bargain, then I will have no choice but to declare war." Joanna yelled at her captor then, with no other option open to her, she clasped her hands together and began to cry out the Lords Prayer with all her might.

Within moments, the heavy doors into the great hall burst open, and in flooded a hoard of angelic warriors. Leading the army were the Israelite, on his handsome black stallion, and Faithful and True, astride his white charger.

Close at the heals of the invaders, were the demonic armies of the underworld, but the dark angel reluctantly raised up his arm and called for a halt to the battle, as Faithful and True guided his mount to the dark angels side and pointed his sword at the black breastplate engraved with the mark of the Beast.

The Israelite cantered across the chessboard, to his charge and, grabbing her arm, he hoisted her up onto the horses back.

With an evil glare, the dark angel composed himself and instructed his army. "Let them go, the girl is not worthy of the effort. There will be other times and other places when we will be better prepared to conquer." And with that, Joanna and the Israelite cantered back through the multitude of angels and demons, to the safety of the light.

CHAPTER TWENTY-SIX
31ST AUGUST, 1993

9:30 am Slapton

After such a troubled night, Joanna decided to take a day off work in order to try and pursued the Cannon to return to her home, one more time.

Since Lewis' phone call to him the previous morning, Joanna had learned of her sister's experiences during the Requiem and felt this new information might be enough to pursued Rev Fitzwilliams that the problem had, indeed, not gone away.

Taking plenty of change out of her purse, and the Canon's card, she wandered round the corner to the village public telephone box so she could talk to the Canon without interference. Piling the coins on the shelf at the side of the phone, she held up the card with one hand, whilst nervously dialling the Rectory number with the other.

The phone had hardly rung when she heard the familiar voice of the Canon, stating "Rectory."

"Hello Canon Fitzwilliams; Joanna Waller here." She introduced herself.

"How can I help?" he replied, flatly.

"Sorry to trouble you again, but since Lewis phoned you yesterday, I've found out some worrying news."

"Go on?" The Canon invited her to continue.

"I had a phone call from my sister yesterday. She said that whilst the Requiem was taking place Jesse appeared at her house, frightening her and her two children half to death."

"Tell me what happened, exactly." he indulged her further. And so, Joanna explained how her sister made a point of reading Bible stories to her two sons at the appointed time of the Requiem and how the spirit had spoken to Tom.

"I've not heard of that before." The canon replied, a slight irritation showing in his voice.

Undeterred, Joanna continued, "And, since Sunday I can not enter any room in the house without being attacked. The only way I can enter, is if I say the Lords Prayer as I step over the threshold. If I don't, the thing in my house tries to consume me. What is more, as soon as I move from that room to the next, it attacks again, so I have to repeat the process all over again. It is wearing me down. I don't know how much longer I can fight it …"

"Joanna." The canon interrupted her, his irritation turning to anger. "As I said to Lewis yesterday, I believe what you are experiencing is nothing more than psychosomatic. As such, your imagination is manifesting itself into physical feelings because you don't want to believe that a Requiem is sufficient to lay Jesse Healy to rest. As I said to Lewis, give it a few days and things will calm down. I will ring you next week to see how you are getting on but, for now, I simply do not think what you are telling me are sufficient grounds to return to your house. Goodbye." And with that, the Canon slammed down the receiver, leaving Joanna listening to the dialling tone.

5.30 pm Hemel Hempstead

Lewis gave two loud knocks at Paul's front door, as Joanna stood behind him. Moments later, Paul creaked open the door and peered outside into the hazy sunshine.

"Watch yu, Paul." Lewis bellowed, as he gave a hearty chuckle. "Thought we'd pop round to fill you in on the latest, if you don't mind."

"No, not at all." Paul softly replied before opening the door wide and inviting his two guests inside.

Scattered around the room, the three stared at one another, all anxious about starting to tell of their tale. Paul was the first to break the silence; "It did not work Sunday, did it?" He said in a flat tone.

"No." Lewis bellowed, "And what is more, when I phoned the Canon Fitzwilliams the next day, as well as Jo phoning him again this morning, he still refuses to believe that we have a problem."

"So he is not coming back to the house, then?" Paul tried to clarify the situation.

"No. Well at least not in the foreseeable future." Lewis continued, "He believes that things will settle down in a day or two."

Paul turned to Joanna. "What are your thoughts on the matter?" He gave her a gentle smile.

"It is far worse now, than it ever was before." The young woman replied, flatly. "Somehow, we must convince the Canon to return, but how, I do not know."

"I don't think that the Canon can help you, because the thing just left your house and joined me outside St Mary's whilst the requiem was taking place. If I had have been present, the outcome might have been different, but Fitzwilliams would never allow this to happen. He is too afraid of me."

"What other options have we got then?" Lewis bellowed across the room, as Paul lit a cigarette.

"Later on Sunday evening I visited the Spiritual Church in Apsley." Paul informed them with a serious tone, as he took a drag from his Superking. "I got a message that seems to make sense."

"Something that will help us?" Joanna enquired, as she watched Paul rise to his feet and, wondering over to the incense burned on the side, he proceeded to organise burning some Sandalwood pure essential oil.

"Triangles." He stated flatly, as he placed a few drops of the oil into the bowl of the burner.

"Is that it, triangles?" Lewis bellowed, "Not very helpful, is it?"

"Think about it." Paul corrected him, as he returned to his seat and took another drag, "There are a lot of triangles inter-linked here. Firstly, there is you, Jo and I. Then there is the Reverend Angela Butler, the Reverend Lawrence and the Canon Fitzwilliams; the M.O.G., Mandy and Emma, not to mention Faye, Jo and me. Even at St Mary's on Sunday there was my dad the warden and me. In each case, there is a break in the triangle. For example, take us three; Fitzwilliams made sure that I could not be present on Sunday, therefore breaking a triangle. Between the three clergymen; two were willing to help, but one was not - breaking a triangle." Paul paused momentarily to inhaled on his cigarette, before continuing, "Emma, Mandy and M.O.G. - one shows ill intent towards us, the other two do not - breaking a triangle. With The Oracle; Faye told me to leave because of Jo - another breakdown concerning three people. Even on Sunday as my dad and I were trying to seek sanctuary in the Church, the warden refused to let us inside and finally, he even ordered us out of the grounds. Triangles can protect but, if there is a weak link, they cause the adverse effect."

"So, what are you driving at?" Lewis frowned, as he tried to make sense of Paul's theories.

"The only people that can get rid of M.O.G. are us three, united."

Joanna cut in, "You mean do the exorcism ourselves? Are you mad? That is absurd. None of us have the first idea of what we are doing. It is too dangerous. I vote we continue to harass the Canon until he gets so fed up with us bugging him all the time, that he returns to the house to finish what he started."

"But he would refuse my being there and that breaks a triangle." Paul insisted.

"Wait just a moment." Lewis bellowed, as he turned to Paul and scowled. "You can't risk all our lives because of some flimsy message. You haven't got the first idea of how to go about an exorcism."

"Maybe not, but I do have complete faith in my guides and trust them with my life. With their help, I know we will succeed."

Joanna and Lewis looked across at each other in utter disbelief. How could the psychic even suggest such a thing? He may have complete trust in his guides, but that was not enough for them. After a moment's deliberation, Joanna turned to the young man and asked, "But faith and trust can only stretch so far, Paul. To put your life, and ours, on the line for a whim and a prayer is not a good enough reason. Let those who have trained to deal with this type of thing do the job. It is just not worth taking the risk."

Suddenly Joe entered the room and stood, tall and proud, to Paul's side. Looking past the psychics shoulder, Joanna joked, "Your wearing your hat, Joe, must be official business." Smiling briefly across at her, the spirit then stepped into Paul's body and stood there, protecting his charge.

Immediately this had happened Edwardo appeared, along with the Israelite, shortly followed by M.O.G. and Mandy. As they entered the room, a gust of wind blew out the night light and the burner began to vibrate violently on the side, creeping forward towards the edge, until it finally tipped over, sending the Sandalwood scented water spilling onto the floor.

In a trance state, Paul stared across at Joanna and asked, "Tell, me, whom can you trust in this room?"

Unaware that she was answering Joe and not Paul, she replied, "Both you and Lewis."

"What of Benjamin? Do you trust him?" He continued to question her.

"With my very soul." Came her perplexed reply, for she knew not where this questioning was leading to.

"And God? Do you trust Him?" Paul's voice deepened, as he allowed Joe to take control.

"Certainly." She replied.

"And what of Edwardo? Do you trust him?" Joe questioned her further, through his charge.

"I am not sure."

"Then ask him if he represents God's light." Joe instructed her.

Turning to the bouncy little Mexican, Joanna did as she was requested. "Edwardo, do you represent God's light?"

"Cei." came Edwardo's uncharacteristically flat reply.

"Well, tell us all what he said." Joe pumped her to repeat Edwardo's response.

"Cei." Joanna repeated Edwardo's answer; "He said 'cei'"

"Now get him to answer the question properly." Joe commanded, in an authoritative manner.

Again Joanna asked Edwardo the question, but still he only replied with the one word, "Cei."

"Then Joanna, he no longer represents God, therefore must be treated as an envoy of Set ." Joe instructed her. "For Edwardo has been tempted by the dark forces that surround us all."

Immediately Joe spoke the words, through Paul, the little Mexican flared up in anger and flew at the psychic, locking himself inside the young mans body along with the Holy Spirit.

Undeterred by the event, Joe continued, "Then hear me, when I tell you that I speak on God's behalf, for I represent God's light. You prayed for help and now your prayer has been answered. Paul has been instructed and will, in turn, instruct you when the time is right." His attention then turned to M.O.G. and Mandy. "I say to you, try and take this mans soul, if you dare, for the time is now ripe for justice to be done. This day is the final battle for Taliesim. This is the day when he will triumph over your evil. Come, enter the House of David only if your might is stronger than the Lords."

In response to Joe's words, both entities rushed forward and entered Paul's body, sending his face and stance into continuous changes as each entity tried to take the psychic over, in turn. His aura blackened and his features twisted and turned, as the faces of Edwardo, M.O.G., Mandy and Joe showed through, one by one. A large, white bubble then appeared around the young mans body, locking all four spirits inside, ensuring that none of them could escape.

"What is going on?" Joanna called out. "Stop this. You're going to kill him."

"It is too late to turn back now." Joe stated, in a calm, soothing voice. "It has been decided by higher than you. This is the only way to rid yourselves of the evil that dwells with you. Have faith, for faith has no bounds."

Paul then spoke, "You had better be right on this one, Joe, for this stretches my faith to the limit." The psychic then jumped up and began gathering some items in preparation for the exorcism. Firstly, he grabbed the Bible, followed by a purse filled with amethyst quartz runes, then a white candle and finally, the oil burner and the bottle of Sandalwood. He then placed the contents in a plastic bag and, grabbing his leather jacket, he marched towards the door. "Come on, we haven't much time." he stated and with that Lewis and Joanna, having no other choice, submissively followed the consultant out of the house and up to the car.

As they got into the Peugeot 405, Lewis took the driving seat, Paul sat next to him in the front, whilst Joanna climbed into the back with the dog. The psychic then turned to the dairy engineer, as Lewis turned the key, and coldly informed him, "We also need some still mineral water. The garage up the road sells bottled water. Stop there and buy some."

Without questioning Paul's statement, Lewis sped up the road to the garage, to purchase the mineral water, as instructed.

Once the water had been obtained, they found themselves back on the road, racing towards the A4146. As they reached the Leighton Buzzard road, Paul turned to Lewis a second time and stated, "We will have to bless the water. Drive to the Amaravati Buddhist Monastery at Great Gaddesden." Again, Lewis followed the instructions given to him and headed for the Monastery without uttering a word.

They arrived at Amaravati about ten minutes later and, as Lewis swung his red saloon off the road and through the gateway of the Monastery, the peace of the place wrapped itself around them, unconditionally welcoming them into its presence. The driveway was lined with fruit trees, which lead away to a cluster of timber-framed buildings of the Monastery beyond. A handful of the Amaravati Sangha wandered around the grounds with their shaven heads and traditional robes, seemingly unaware of the three in the car. The Sangha did not concern themselves about strangers, for all visitors were welcomed by the monks and nuns of the Theravada tradition, no matter what their beliefs, or reason for being there.

Half way up the drive, Lewis swung the Peugeot off the tarmac drive and onto the grass parking spaces, to the side. Grinding to a halt, he turned off the engine and glared at Paul. "What now?"

"We walk into the gardens and find a bench." Came the psychics slurred reply, as he clutched the bottle of mineral water.

The three then clambered out of the vehicle and began to wonder across the grass, towards the Monastery gardens beyond. Paul found it increasingly difficult to walk, and staggered about like a drunkard, for all but one of the entities inside him were determined to show their anger at being forced to enter the sanctified grounds.

Finding a shady bench under an oak tree Paul eased himself into the seat, with a taught expression on his blackened face, and placed the bottle at his side. He paused for a moment to gather his thoughts, then said in a soft, inoffensive tone; "You will have to bless the water, Jo, because I am unable to do so. This is the only way to guarantee that the water is then Holy."

"Me? How?" Joanna asked, baffled as to why he thought she was capable of such an act.

Smiling, Paul allowed Joe to speak through him, although not without difficulty, and instructed Joanna on the procedure for the blessing, which she administered, step by step, as he commanded.

Once the water had been made Holy Paul was no longer able to hold the bottle, for the powerful divine liquid inside now scolded his palms causing them to blister. This miracle surprised Joanna for she had never before witnessed such a thing as, to her; the water bottle felt cool and refreshing to the touch.

The three then made their way back to the car and for Paul, they could not depart from
the Monastery of the Theravada tradition quickly enough, for the positive energy that radiated from Amaravati infuriated the negativity within him.

Back on the A4146, Lewis placed his foot hard on the accelerator, and sped off towards Slapton. He turned on the radio-cassette, in an attempt to ease the tension that was building inside the vehicle. Filling the car came Enya's haunting tones, as she sang, 'Cursum Perficio', which had been inspired by the inscription on Marilyn Monroe's last home - My Journey Ends Here.

"This song doesn't exactly give rise to confidence." Joanna stated coldly, from the back seat. "Can't you put something else on?" And so obligingly, Lewis changed the cassette, which began to play Ultravox's Hymn. "Oh. For goodness sake - just turn it off." Joanna growled. "Your choice of music is giving me the willies."

"Keep your hair on." Lewis shouted over his shoulder as he ejected the second choice of music. Then, turning to Paul, he continued, "Women. Can't live with 'em; can't live without 'em."

Ignoring her boyfriend's sexist remark, Joanna turned to Paul. "So what's happening once we get to the house?"

"It would be best if Lewis went inside first, to prepare the house, before we enter." He informed her over his shoulder, before turning to the dairy engineer, "If that's alright with you, Lewis?"

"Fine. What do you want me to do?"

"First, the runes must be placed in a circle, in the centre of the sitting-room floor, then you must light the incense burner and put three drops of Sandalwood and the Holy water into the bowl of the burner, which will act as extra protection for both you and Jo. Finally, place the candle to the west corner of the room, but do not light it until after I have entered the circle."

"What will you be doing, while I'm in the house? Waiting outside in the car?"

Joanna then piped in, "I've got to go and check on Zephyr. Paul can come round the farm with me, if you like."

"Good idea." Lewis grinned back over his shoulder at his girlfriend. "Then you can keep an eye on him. I'll drop you both off outside the pub, then go on ahead. If you finish before I do, wait outside until I give you the ok to enter. Alright?"

"Thanks Lewis." Joanna reached over the driver's seat and placed her hand on his shoulder, expressing her gratitude.

It was not long before Lewis was swinging his car off the A4146 and heading for Slapton. At great speed, he flew down the winding lane lined with neat hedging, until they reached the outskirts of the village and proceeded to drive down Church road towards the T-junction.

At the end of the road Lewis swung the Peugeot left, in front of the Carpenters Arms, and screeched the car to a halt to the far side of the car park entrance. The anxious looking psychic and the young woman then climbed out of the vehicle and, slamming the doors shut behind them, they watched helplessly as Lewis put his foot hard on the accelerator and sped off, towards the cottage.

Without uttering a word Joanna led Paul across the road, to the entrance of Bury Farm. Then, she wandered up the driveway towards the farm buildings beyond the house, with the young psychic in tow.

Turning the corner at the end of the drive, the two ambled across a grass lawn at the front of the farm house, and headed for the field gate, which boasted an orchard of apple trees, beyond.

As they reached the gate, they heard the distinctive call of Fred, as the ginger tom came trotting across the yard towards them. Turning, Joanna beckoned the aged cat to approach, but he needed no encouragement and was soon rubbing around her legs.

Paul then bent down to fuss the tatty tom cat, but as he reached out a hand to stroke the animal, Fred backed off and, with his ears flat against his head, the cat began to snarl and hiss at the possessed psychic.

"Fred. What's up with you?" She tried to comfort the distressed animal, as he threatened the man with the black aura.

"Animals have a very strong sixth sense." Paul explained, as he winced. "Fred obviously knows that there is a war inside of me."

The old tom then placed himself firmly between Joanna and the consultant, refusing to budge whilst the man remained a threat to his human friend.

At that point, a thunder of hooves broke their attention from the feline and, looking across at the gate, they watched on as Zephyr approached them at high speed. The piebald then slid to a halt, just short of the gate and snorted loudly.

Leaving Fred to keep guard, Joanna wandered over to the gate and entered the field to examine her cob for any injuries that he may have obtained during the day. With a welcoming whinny, Zephyr stepped forward and nuzzled her hand, in anticipation of a tip-bit.

"You silly old sod." Joanna greeted the piebald, as she gave him an affectionate scratch behind the ear, "Thinking of your stomach again, I see. Piglet."

In reply, Zephyr roughly pushed his head into her torso and began vigorously rubbing his face against her, showing his pleasure at her arrival. "Yes. I know you love me, Zeph." Joanna giggled, as she tried to push the piebald's head away from her. "But you are still not getting any carrots from me, no matter how cute you act."

Disgusted that his efforts had been thwarted, the piebald gave a discontented snort, before turned away from her to try his luck with his owner's companion. But as soon as he set eyes on Paul, Zephyr flattened his ears, raised his head high in the air and began rolling his eyes in a menacing manner.

"Zephyr." Joanna scolded the equine. "Stop pulling faces." But the cob was not going to tolerate the presence of the man, and began kicking out at the gate in protest.

"I think we'd better leave." Joanna called across to the psychic, as she came back out of the field. "You are upsetting the animals too much."

"That's the best idea you've had all day." Paul replied, with a vagueness and hesitance that was not in character with his normal behaviour.

"Come on then, we'll wonder back to the house and wait outside until Lewis gives us the nod. I'll pop back later, after you've finished what you've come here to do." She smiled across at him and, with a protective ginger cat in tow, the two proceeded to wonder back along the driveway to the road.

Having made their way back up the road, the two stood outside the house, with Paul leaning against the Peugeot for support.

"What does my aura look like?" Paul shakily enquired, as he swayed about, under the strain of the spirits within.

"Jet black." Joanna gave a sympathetic smile, before adding, "Except for a single beam of the purest white coming down from above, penetrating into the crown of your head."

"I feel terrible." Paul continued, as he rubbed his face with his hands. "My body feels so heavy. So cold."

To try and take his mind of his predicament, Joanna enquired in a soft voice, "So what is the plan of action, once we are inside?"

Giving her a distant smile, Paul stated, "Firstly, I must enter the circle of runes. No one else must enter - only me. Whatever happens to me inside the ring, you must promise that you will not, on any account, cross over inside the enclosure. Promise?"

"I promise." Joanna frowned.

Paul then continued, "Firstly, we will all say the Lords Prayer." He then proceeded to quote her four readings from the Bible, instructing her to read them in the order to which they had been given. "You must say these line by line, then wait for me to repeat what you have read. Should I say, or if you think I might have said, any part of these incorrectly, then you must make me recite the words again. No matter how many attempts it takes, I must say the words correctly, if we are to succeed. The rest can wait until we have completed that stage." His eyes then became clouded and his mind drifted off to daydreams of days gone by, leaving Joanna with the burden of trying to remember all that had been told her, with no margin for error.

Lewis then barged through the front door, allowing Nell and a flood of cats to escape from the kitchen. "The house is ready and three of the cats have been fed. I'll put Nell in the car - out of harms way - then we'll all go inside."

Once the dog was safely placed back inside the Peugeot, the three wandered up the garden path, without uttering a word. Lewis entered the house first, but as Paul reached the threshold he grabbed Joanna's arm and, opening his mouth, Joe spoke through the consultant. "Do not be alarmed by the atmosphere in the house, child. Benjamin is close at your side. You are safe."

As the three entered the kitchen, Joanna felt the oppresiveness bear down on her, like a lead weight. The air was so thick, that she could hardly catch her breath and, with the fear of suffocating, she began to panic. The Israelite placed a comforting hand on her shoulder as she turned to her peers, stating, "Sorry folks, but I am going to have to open a window." and with that, she dragged herself to the kitchen sink and opened the pane wide, allowing a gush of fresh air to enter the sultry, stale atmosphere within.

As the three entered the sitting room, their lungs became filled with the scent of Sandalwood as it, and the Holy water, evaporated into the air of the room.

Paul became increasingly agitated but, without hesitation, he instinctively stepped into the ring of runes. He then knelt down in its centre, facing west towards the candle in the far corner of the room, and quietly ordered, "Light the candle now."

Lewis did as instructed, whilst Joanna sat on the arm chair, facing east, and opened the Bible at the first quote given to her. Lewis then took his place at her side and crouching down on the floor, he crossed his legs.

"We will commence with the Lords Prayer." Joanna informed all without any emotion and, with an intake of breath, they began. But, as they spoke the first few lines, Paul began to choke on the words, unable to continue.

Jumping up, Lewis ran out into the kitchen and got a glass of water. He then returned and went to hand it to the psychic. "Stop." Paul choked, through his gasps for breath.

"Put some Holy water in the glass." Lewis did as he was instructed. "Now place it on the carpet just outside the circle. I will take it, if I need it." The psychic then turned his attention to Joanna. "I can not manage to say the Lords Prayer without help. You will have to say it, line by line, for me to repeat."

And so, they started again, with Joanna taking the lead and both Paul and Lewis repeating the words, as they were told.

Paul began to sweat under the strain as the evil locked inside him, venomously protesting at the divine words. He felt sick and faint, almost unable to control the writhing, malicious souls within. But he was not afraid, for he also felt the strong, positive presence of his trusted guide, Joe, as the Holy Spirit comforted him in his hour of need.

Unable to bear seeing Paul's suffering, Joanna turned to the Bible and began with the first set of readings, "The Lord is my shepherd, I shall not be in want

... " she proceeded and listened as Paul whispered the words after her, whilst trying to catch his breath.

She then continued with the following few lines and, as the psychic repeated them, there seemed to be some ease to his suffering. However, the fourth line was the first real indication of what they were dealing with. With a soft, controlled tone she read, "Even though I walk through the valley of the shadow of death, I will fear no evil ..." Paul repeated the words with slow deliberation, but as he reached the last part, he stated, "... I will fear evil ..."

"I will fear NO evil." Joanna repeated the words. "Repeat after me; Even though I walk through the valley of the shadow of death, I will fear NO evil..."

Paul recited the words a second time, "Even though I walk through ..." but he lost his train of thought half way through the psalm and a vague expression crept across his face.

"The valley of the shadow of death ..." Joanna prompted him and, with a hoarse voice, he continued, "Even though I walk through the valley of the shadow of death ..."

"I will fear NO evil ..."

"I - will - fear - no - evil." His face showed sheer agony, as he recited the words.

Joanna then continued to read, giving him only a few words at a time, in an effort to help him all she could. With difficulty, he just managed to find enough strength to say the psalm for protection, despite the continual attacks from the evil within.

Once the psalm of David had been read, Joanna turned to the next quote and, with an air of authority about her, she continued with the readings. This reading was all about praising and acceptance of God. It talked of the law of the Lord as being perfect, the statutes of the Lord as being trustworthy, and the precepts of the Lord as being right. The second reading also asked for forgiveness of all hidden faults and to keep the three from wilful sins. Finally, Joanna finished the reading, saying, "May the words of my mouth and the meditation of my heat be pleasing in your sight, O Lord, my Rock and my Redeemer."

Paul repeated the words with a vagueness, which showed all the signs that he was being tested to the limited. His face was pale, as he huddled on the floor. The only thing that kept him going was the belief that this was the only way to rid all of them from the stench of evil that he had captured.

However, as Joanna commenced with the quote concerning judgement, the evil took a stronger hold of Paul, in a desperate bid to destroy him, before he destroyed them.

In a quiet, controlled manner, Joanna read out loud. "You say, 'I choose the appointed time; it is I who judge uprightly'..."

Paul opened his mouth to repeat the words but suddenly, with a curdling scream, he wrapped his arms about him, an expression of sheer agony on his face.

"You must fight through the barriers of pain." Joanna instructed him. "Repeat the words, after me - You say,..."

Taking a deep breath, Paul winced as he mumbled, "You say, ..."

" ... 'I choose the appointed time; ...'"

Clutching his body, Paul continued with slow, rhythmic deliverance, "... 'I - choose - the - a-ppoint-ed time ; ...'"

"... it is I who judge uprightly ..." The young woman continued, as calmly as she could.

" ...it is I who j ..." Paul paused, gave a hard swallow, then carried on, " ... it is I who j - judge up-right-ly ... " The excruciating pain shot right through his body, like a thousand swords, sending him crumpling onto the carpet.

"... To the arrogant I say 'Boast no more' ..." Joanna continued, trying not to allow the fear to show in her voice.

With conviction, Paul repeated her words, " ... To - the - arr-og-ant - I - say, - 'Boast - no - more ...'" as he lifted himself upright again.

" ... and to the wicked, 'Do not lift up your horns' ..." and as she spoke the word, she lifted up her hands and began to send him healing.

Feeling the white light penetrating into the ring of runes, he found himself able to repeat the words, with better control. The words flowed from his mouth with crisp, confident sounds.

Joanna continued. " ... In the hand of the Lord is a cup full of foaming wine mixed with spices; ..."

Paul, now beginning to feel as if he were in the conquering position, delivered the words with conviction, the control over the wicked within showing, as the words flowed from his mouth.

" ... he pours it out, and all the wicked of the earth drink it down to its very dregs ..." Joanna sang, but as Paul opened his mouth to repeat the words, he suddenly collapsed inside the ring of runes. Moments later his spirit rose from the puckered body on the floor and stepped over the circle of runes and stood next to the young woman. Stopping in her tracks, Joanna looked first at Paul's body, then across at Lewis.

"What's happened?" Lewis bellowed, as he heaved himself to his feet and dashed across the room, towards the psychic.

"NO." Joanna shouted. "Do not enter the circle."

"Then what do you suggest I do? eh?" Lewis growled. "I think he's dead."

"Hand me the holy water." Joanna commanded and, as she took hold of the bottle from her boyfriend's grasp, she tipped the cool, refreshing liquid out on her palm.

With all her might, she then threw the water over the psychic inside the ring of runes. Paul's spirit then left her side and, with a second cupped hand of water thrown at the young man, the consultant's soul returned to its home of flesh, and his body stirred.

Lewis gave a loud sigh and, turning to Paul, he stated, "What a relief. For a moment there I thought we had a corpse on our hands."

With sad eyes, full of tiredness and pain, Paul looked up, across to the young woman, "Please repeat that last line, for me." Without hesitation, Joanna did as requested, before allowing the consultant the repeat the words as before.

Then, a revelation. As she spoke the final verse she suddenly became aware of two dark spirits leaving the House of David. The first was Edwardo, holding his sombrero in his hand. As he stepped out of Paul's body a beam of brightest light flooded the ring of runes and he ascended to heaven.

The second to leave was Jesse Healy but, as he departed from the earthly body he turned briefly to Joanna and held out his hands towards her, begging for forgiveness.

Then, he too, stepped into the light and was gone, leaving Mandy to battle it out alone.

Flicking through the Bible for the last quote that was given, Joanna proceeded with the first line, " God, the nations have invaded your inheritance; they have defiled your holy temple ...""

Paul suddenly sat bolt upright and recited the words, with renewed vigour and enthusiasm.

She then continued, " ... Pour out your wrath on the nations that do no acknowledge you, on the kingdoms that do not call on your name ..."

As Paul repeated the words, his aura suddenly became much stronger, almost vibrant, as the evil that dwelled within, began losing its grip on the young mans body.

" ... may your mercy come quickly to meet us, for we are in desperate need ..." she called out, then paused for Paul to repeat the words before continuing, "Before our eyes, make known among the nations that you avenge the outpoured blood of your servants ..." As Paul began to say the words, the room suddenly became filled with power and light.

At the same moment, Mandy stood up out of Paul's body and turned to face him. The woman's tall, elegant figure towered above him, as her dark eyes bore down, full of fury at her thwarted plans.

The consultant gazed up at her with bemusement, for he could not understand why it was Mandy who had put up such a fight. However, his question was soon answered for, before his very eyes, the tall slim woman began to twist and turn before him, distorting her looks; forever changing appearance to confuse and frustrate.

Not allowing her attention to be distracted by the dark woman, Joanna buried her head in the Bible once more and continued, with Paul repeating after her, word for word.

By the end of the forth quote, it became apparent to Joanna exactly who the true identity of Mandy was. For there, towering over the psychic in his long dark robes and tatty, pepper-grey hair, stood the scar-faced Archangel of Despair.

The archangel stood proud; his long cloak wrapped about him; the black shield firmly hooked over his left arm; the steel sword held boastfully aloft in his right hand. "Behold my might." he roared, "Thou doest fighteth thy final fight." and with that he crashed the sword downwards through the psychic, cracking Paul's aura in two.

Paul screamed with pain as the sword was run through him. He clasped his hands to his head, and the pain blinded him. Then, with every effort that he could muster, Paul turned towards the flickering candle in the western corner of the room, just as the sun was about to set, and shouted, "Sun god of life, power, mystery and wisdom. Sun god of life, power, mystery and wisdom. Sun god of life, power, mystery and wisdom. Release this house from the evil within it."

Upon the words, a flash of light stuck Mephistopheles' envoy, causing him to falter just as he was about to administer another attack on the consultant. However, this did not deter him for long, and in moments the scar-faced man had regained his composure and was rising the weapon high above his head, ready for a second blow.

Again Paul shouted out the Egyptian prayer to Amen, "Sun god of life, power, mystery and wisdom. Sun god of life, power, mystery and wisdom. Sun god of life, power, mystery and wisdom. Release this house from the evil within it."

The archangel of despair sliced the sword through the air, at the consultant but, as the sword was about to strike the young man, a second bolt of light collided with the blade, sending the weapon spinning off into oblivion.

With Mephistopheles' most favoured now disarmed, Paul sang out the request for deliverance a final time, in the knowledge that the dark forces were almost defeated.

As the words passed his lips, a multitude of gold's, blues and greens rained down upon the iniquitous being. The scar-faced man held the shield above his head, trying to shelter from the abundance of light that poured down from the heavens above, but the situation now seemed hopeless.

Upon seeing the archangels of despair's predicament, Joanna reached for the holy water and proceeded to throw the contents of the bottle at the weakened entity. The evil man screamed in agony, as the liquid struck him, burning every part that was dowsed with the divine solution. The ground then opened up beneath him allowing charred hands to reach up from the depths of the earth, for the slaves of the underworld had to strive to save the wretched manifestation.

Empty handed, the scar-faced man descended into the hole, to meet his fate at the hands of the Prince of Darkness. As the hands dragged him down, the gaping orifice closed above him, delivering the house from his depravity.

Dazed, Paul sat in the ring of runes, as Joe stepped out of his charge and placed his hand on the young mans head. "You have done well." the Egyptian smiled down at the consultant, as he administered the healing, "You showed great courage, in the face of evil. Now. Bless the House Of David and all those who dwell in it. Then you're job here will be done. Praise be to the Lord God Almighty."

"Thank you Joe, for your assistance." Paul whispered, as he rose to his feet to in order to complete his task.

After the house had been blessed, the three returned to the sitting room and sat in stunned silence for a while; each consumed with their own private prayers of thanks. It was only when a loud thud was heard coming from the kitchen that their minds came back to the moment.

Jumping back to reality they froze in terror and just stared at each other, not daring to move for fear of what might have materialised in the kitchen beyond.

Lewis was the first to speak. "What the fuck was that?" He growled as he glared, first at Joanna, then at Paul.

"Do you want me to take a look?" Paul gave a nervous smile.

"No. I'll go." Lewis replied bravely and with that, he jumped to his feet and marched out of the sitting room.

Moments later he returned, a broad grin on his face.

"What?" Joanna screeched at her boyfriend, the look of dread prominent on her face.

But Lewis just pointed towards his feet revealing one very hungry Fred, as the aged cat rubbed around the dairy engineers legs whilst vocally expressing his desire for his tea. "He jumped in through the window." Lewis then gave a hearty bellow, before stooping down and gave the cat a tickle under the chin.

"Well I never." Joanna stated, then rose from her seat and wandered over to her feline friend. "For the first time ever, Fred has come inside the house."

The cat then trotted over to Paul and, with a loud purr, he began rubbing around the psychic to show that there was no longer any malice between them.

"There's your proof." Paul gave both Joanna and Lewis a broad grin as he ran his hand down the ginger tom's back. "The house must be rid of evil, or Fred would never have entered it."

"A psychic cat, eh?" Joanna grinned and, turning, she wandered out into the kitchen whilst shouting over her shoulder, "Come on Frederick Von

Kattenhausen - feed time." And with that, the tatty old tomcat trotted out after her to receive his well-earned tea.

Two days later ...

Joanna sat there watching the television whilst Lewis prepared supper. Things had been refreshingly peaceful around the place since the exorcism. She gave a quiet satisfied sigh, as she picked up her mug and sipped at her coffee. The steam curling around her face, carrying with it the aroma of roasted beans, which comforted her.

It was only as she went to place the mug back on the mat that she became aware of two entities entering the room to her left. Feeling her heart pick up a beat, she turned to see who had entered uninvited.

Staring intently at the wall, she saw two nuns wearing starched wimple's standing there. Then, as she watched on, one nun turned to her left whilst the other, to her right, then they parted the way with demure air. As they parted company, Joanna became aware of a third figure standing behind them. She instantly recognised this entity; for it was none other than Jesse Healy himself.

Horror-struck, she opened her mouth to scream out but, her throat was so dry from fear, her screams remained silent.

Then Jesse passively stepped forward into the room and stood a few feet away from the wall in silence, his hands clasped together in front of his stomach.

"What do you want?" Joanna rasped. But Jesse just smiled gently back at her.

Terrified that he had returned to attack her, Joanna then shouted out "Get away from me. Leave me alone." Instantly, Jesse and the two nuns removed themselves from the room.

Upon hearing the commotion, Lewis marched into the sittingroom. "What's wrong? Why are you shouting?"

"It's Jesse." Joanna replied, fear prominent in her voice. "He's returned."

"What did he do to you?"

"Nothing. He just stood there, looking at me." She then went on to explain exactly what had happened and how the nuns had led him into the room.

Upon hearing this, Lewis took his partners hands and, with a gentle smile, he said, "Maybe ... maybe he just wanted to let you know he is alright now? Maybe you should give him a chance to tell you what needs to be told?"

"I'm too afraid." Joanna growled.

Lewis moved away from his partner momentarily to retrieve the Bible and rose quartz from the table, before returning to her side once more. "I understand why you feel like that but I think you should ask him to return." he smiled, as he handed her the book and stone. But, before she had chance to request the spirits presence, Jesse reappeared; this time without his habit-clad escorts.

"What do you want, Jesse?" she asked him again, this time with a much softer tone.

Jesse bowed his head, a shimmering tear trickling down his face. "I have two things I must convey" he replied in a melancholy fashion. "Firstly; I apologise for my actions and what I put you through. I am repentant and seek forgiveness although I do not deserve it. Secondly; I thank you with all my heart and soul for releasing me from my hell-on-earth and returning me to God. I am of Gods light now and I am finally at peace. This is what I want to convey to you and I will trouble you no more after this day." Smiling softly back at him, Joanna gave the spirit an acknowledging nod.

Upon her acceptance of Jesse's words, Benjamin entered the room. "Joanna." he firmly stated. "It is God's Will that Jesse becomes one of your circle."

"I'm not sure about that, Benjamin." Joanna replied, a little surprised that her enemy of the morning is now to become her confederate by evening. Then, turning to Jesse, she asked "What do you think about this, Jesse? Do you want to be one of my guides?"

Jesse smiled. "When I took ordinance with God upon my Judgement day, I requested the position as token of my gratitude to you for setting me free. God agreed and I have His blessing. I would be honoured to stand beside you and watch over you until it is my time to return to earth in physical form."

"But it was Paul who released you, Jesse, not I." Joanna questioned the spirit. "Why do you not want to stand at his side instead?"

Benjamin could be seen giving a knowing smile, as Jesse clarified his reasoning "It is you who spoke the words of God. It is you who released me from the clutches of evil. It is you who shows me mercy now. Not Paul."

Joanna scratched her head and thought for a moment. In her mind it was Paul who risked everything the rid them of the evil residing in the house, not her. It was Paul who had instructed her each step of the way, for she had no knowledge of such things. It was Paul who had true faith in his heart, not her. In her mind, she was not at one with God, unlike Paul, for she had carried doubt in her heart during the exorcism. In her mind, she was not worthy of God's blessing. After a moments pause, she replied softly, "I'll have to give this serious thought, Jesse. And if I do decide to accept you as a guide, I will keeping testing you until I am sure I can truly trust you."

Jesse nodded. "Very wise. Give it serious thought and test me all you want, I will not do anything to harm you again, for I now represent God's light." And with that both Jesse and Benjamin disappeared, leaving Joanna and Lewis alone in the sitting room once more, to ponder over the latest revelation.

* * * * *

Matthew 12:24-28

But when the Pharisees heard this, they said, "It is only by Beelzebub, the prince of demons, that this fellow drives out demons."

Jesus knew their thoughts and said to them, "Every kingdom divided against itself will be ruined, and every city or household divided against itself will not stand. If Satan drives out Satan, he is divided against himself. How then can his kingdom stand? And if I drive out demons by Beelzebub, by whom do your people drive them out? So then, they will be your judges. But if I drive out demons by the Spirit of God, then the kingdom of God has come upon you."

* * * * *

POSTSCRIPT

PAUL HITT
In 1995, Paul went on to present a 40 minute VHS video produced by Quantum Leap, entitled
Tarot: A beginners Guide to reading the cards. ASIN: B00004WI6Z
In 2006, it was re-released as a DVD. ASIN: B000FAOB1Y. Both formats are available to purchase at Amazon and other retailers.

JONATHAN
Jon remarried and is currently an Associate Director at an architectural design company based in Horsham. He went on to make a full recovery, after his ordeal at the cottage.

LEWIS
Lewis became a director of his own pyrotechnics company in 2005 and currently lives with his partner, Rosemary, in Chesham.

GERALDINE
Geraldine is still based in High Wycombe working as a psychic , clairvoyant and medium, as well as exhibiting her psychic art.

JOANNA
Joanna met her current partner, Martin, in 1996 and continued to live at the cottage in Slapton for a further 8 years, without demonic paranormal incident. Sadly they were forced to sell the cottage after Martin was paralysed in a serious motorcycle accident in December 2003.

CANON MARK FITZWILLIAMS

On 19th March 1994 it was announced that the Rev Mark Fitzwilliams (Team Rector, Beaconsfield Team Ministry) was to be appointed Priest-in-charge, Hambleden Valley group ministry (Oxford).

Sadly, Mark passed away on 30th December 2003 aged 67. May he rest in peace, with God.

THE CHRISTMAS DECORATIONS ...

These mysteriously reappeared, in 2004, when Joanna and Martin were moving home. They were found inside a plastic bag, under the chimney flu's in the loft, along with a whole host of other decorations. Neither Joanna, Martin, Lewis or John had brought the majority of them into the cottage, nor were those decorations, or the bag they were in, left there by the previous occupants. Weird!

ROSE QUARTZ

Prior to the final exorcism, this quartz was without blemish. However, upon retrieving the stone from her pocket post final exorcism in Chapter 26, Joanna noted that, what looked like a small, dark brown mark, had appeared just under the surface layer of stone. This was circular in shape, approximately 3mm in diameter and looked solid in structure.

This mark remained within the quartz for 17 years. The stone itself was tied to, and became a part of, a Native American prayer stick which Joanna often used for meditation, prayer and healing purposes. Then, on 31st August 2010, the stone fell from its bindings during a meditation session and, as Joanna caught the quartz, the dark brown 'blob' released itself from the stone and landed on the settee beside her. Joanna picked up the object and, placing it in the palm of her hand, she began to study it. Curiously, it appeared to be moving.

Intrigued, Joanna decided to give the object a closer inspection under a magnifying glass. But, despite this, she was still unable to make it out in detail. However, she did notice that, instead of being circular, it had straightened out, to approximately 5mm in length and, when she poked it with her finger, it wriggled, writhed and jumped around in her palm as if it were alive. It felt rubbery in texture and seemed to be made up of lots of smaller inter-linked components, to make one larger mass.

Once she had completed her inspection, and none the wiser for having done so, Joanna then promptly threw the 'blob' in the dustbin.

As for the rose quartz itself, this was totally undamaged and no small fragments of stone were ever found in or around the area from which it had fallen from its bindings. In short, there was no logical explanation as to how the 'blob' could have escaped out from beneath the surface of the stone.

AN INTERESTING STORY INVOLVING ANOTHER TRINITY

Circa 1994-95, three Church of England Dioceses embarked on a mass exorcism. The Diocese of Oxford, St Albans and Peterborough collectively held a service at each location at the same time, following a marked increase in supernatural phenomena. The Church blamed the rise of interest in witchcraft and occult practices for this occurrence.

Three Cathedrals were used, being *Christchurch Cathedral in Oxford, Cathedral Church of St Peter, St Paul and St Andrew in Peterborough* and *The Cathedral and Abbey Church of St Albans*. The idea being that Milton Keynes and the surrounding area be targeted, as this was where the increase in exorcisms were most prominent.

Slapton is located pretty much in the centre of the triangle formed by the three Cathedrals. On the day of the Exorcism, Joanna was sitting at her desk in the sitting-room, facing towards the window. As she worked, she suddenly became aware of the cottage being filled with light, followed by a large, marble stairway emerging from thin air behind her. The stairs ran from the centre of the sitting-room floor, up though the ceiling and beyond into obscurity. This staircase remained there for approximately half to three quarters of an hour, during which time many hundreds people were observed ascending it. Most of these spirits did not acknowledge her presence except for one particular elderly gentleman, who was with his golden Labrador. As he started to ascend the stairs, he turned, smiled and waved at her, as if to show his relief at being 'set free'.

After half an hour or so, the stairway and the divine light dispersed, returning the cottage back to normal. It was only a few weeks later, that Joanna learned of the Church Of England's mass exorcism. Seems it worked rather well.

God Bless

7417762R0

Made in the USA
Charleston, SC
01 March 2011